Joe Lavers was a leading player in the City of London Reinsurance Market for over twenty years where a three piece suit and Parachute Regiment tie were his visible trademarks. He travelled extensively on business, circumnavigating the globe on a number of occasions. Since retiring from full time employment, his knowledge of both the business and markets is repeatedly called upon by others.

His services have been sought by companies from as far afield as Bermuda, America, Scandinavia, the Middle East and, of course, London as an expert or arbitrator to assist in disputes between insurers. In a recent arbitration the panel described him as 'a somewhat larger than life character'.

THE
MONEY-GO-ROUND

Joseph R Lavers

The
Money-Go-Round

Vanguard Press

A CIP catalogue record for this title is
available from the British Library
ISBN 1 903489 90 3

Vanguard Press is an imprint of
Pegasus Elliot MacKenzie Publishers Ltd.
www.pegasuspublishers.com

First Published in 2002

Vanguard Press
Sheraton House Castle Park
Cambridge England

Printed & Bound in Great Britain

Chapter 1

It was simply a coincidence. One of those strange quirks of fate where the consequences cannot be foreseen, but are of a dimension that could not be assimilated at the time.

Andrew Barton was fighting a losing battle with his eyelids as the limousine glided through the outskirts of Miami. It was his first overseas trip for the company. The claims people normally flogged away in the office, metaphorically hewing the wood and carrying the water, whilst the brokers and producers travelled the world in style. As the Cadillac flowed along the freeway his mind wandered back to the meeting with the Chairman.

Allan Jennings had been something of a mentor for Barton. When the companies had merged ten years previously everyone had been surprised that Jennings had been appointed as Chairman and Cameron Carter dispatched into the wilderness.

Barton's first direct dealings with Jennings was in 1978 when he was an Associate Director of the company. He had been volunteered to host an evening out for three clients from the Middle East. Unfortunately nobody had warned him of their penchant for live entertainment.

The dinner in the Savoy Grill had gone well. His guests had displayed a taste for an extremely expensive claret and very old Armagnac.

He was about to leave them after dinner when they insisted he join them at a club off Regent Street. They arrived at the More Than a Penny for 'em Club giving the appearance of being in the mood for a long night.

Barton, as host, had by now completely lost control of events. Before he knew it they were seated, each accompanied by a topless hostess. Champagne appeared on the table and disappeared down throats faster than a cheetah pursuing its prey. By the time he managed to extricate himself from the situation he had a bill for over a thousand pounds.

The following day he had, with much trepidation, told his Director of his plight. The Director had sympathised with him but said that a bill of such size would need counter-signature from the Chairman. That afternoon he was called to the Chairman's office.

Allan Jennings was a big man, and not just in size alone. Whilst he stood just over six feet tall, his personality made him appear larger. He had what could only be described as an aura of self-confidence, which seemed to fill the room. Barton had heard stories of the younger Jennings but knew not the truth of them. Whether or not he had been a top cadet at Sandhurst and subsequently served with the Gurkha regiment and the Special Air Service was beyond Barton's knowledge. The more esoteric tales of time served in Colchester military prison were whispered and not to be repeated. Even now, many years later when a friendship had developed between the two, Barton still felt an illogical hesitancy about the familiarity of addressing Jennings by his Christian name.

"We all get into situations like this," Jennings began, a twinkle showing in his eye, "and most of the time we have to grin and bear it." The churning inside Barton's stomach subsided slightly. "Those three you took out last night are worth over a quarter of a million in brokerage to us," the Chairman continued. "If you have to pander to their basic needs then so be it." He signed the expense request and passed it back to Barton who clutched the document, and its mortgage-saving signature, with relief.

"Oh, by the way," Jennings added as an aside. The agitation returned to Barton's intestine.

"If you do get caught in that situation again please don't use that particular club."

Barton, whose heart was beginning to subside from his mouth, nodded effusively and muttered about the prices charged.

"It's not the prices, all those types of clubs are much the same," Jennings continued, a smile touching the corners of his mouth. "It just happens that the woman who owns that club tried to kill me some time ago. I'd rather the company didn't support her, that's all."

Since that time Barton's career had progressed in leaps and bounds. The previous year he had been appointed to the main board of the company and made responsible for all claims operations within the group. He had been sent to Miami to ensure that future dealings with the newly formed Insurance Exchange of the Americas would be set up on an effective basis.

He wasn't really looking as the car turned into a wide, tree-lined road. The sign was just there. It said Barton Boulevard. The cogs inside his head started to whirr.

Six months earlier he had been glancing through the mountain of post that usually covered his desk. One report caught his eye. It came from a loss adjuster in Miami and gave details of a fire in a truck rental yard. The claim itself was insignificant. The total damage was only $1,500,000 and the cause an electrical fault. He saw scores of similar notices every day.

It was the address that had caught his eye. His birthday was 18th December and the location of the claim was 1812 Barton Boulevard. He had read the report from start to finish simply because of the coincidence.

On impulse he tapped the glass partition that separated the driver and asked him to stop at number 1812. Two hundred yards later they eased to a stop in front of a large ranch-style house. The post box proclaimed it to be 1812 Barton Boulevard. It was also clear that this residence had been there for considerably longer than six months.

Barton asked the driver to wait and burrowed in the valise for his camera. He got out and took several photographs and then told the driver to continue the journey.

The hotel room was sumptuous. It had a huge balcony, which overlooked the manicured gardens. There was a six-foot-round jacuzzi and two sun loungers at one end, a table and four chairs at the other. A large notice on the jacuzzi declared it to be dangerous for one person alone to use it. In America it is compulsory to warn everyone about any danger, real or imagined, to avoid being sued if something untoward occurs.

He phoned room service and ordered a burger and fries. He

resisted the temptation to request a companion to share the jacuzzi to guarantee his safety. The irony would probably have been beyond the humour of the intense young man on reception.

An ice-cold Amstel came from the mini bar. The clock/radio in the room told him it was 10pm. His body was yelling at him that it was 3am. He decided to ignore the dire warning and filled the jacuzzi. Two more beers were placed adjacent and he sat and let the foaming water pummel away his tension.

It was six in the morning when he gave up the attempt to make his body work to American time. A cold shower revitalised him. He ordered breakfast and read through the notes for the day's meetings. The mystery of the house on Barton Boulevard that should have been a truck yard nagged at the back of his mind.

"Mr Barton's office," chirped his secretary's voice.

"Debra, it's Andrew."

"Oh hello, how was your flight?" she trilled back.

They exchanged pleasantries. He had inherited Debra Hanson as his secretary at his last promotion. She could be best described as highly efficient in a scatterbrained sort of way.

"Do you remember a few months ago we got a claim advice for a rental yard on Barton Boulevard?" he asked.

"I remember, you told me the number was your birthday."

Barton was relieved that she confirmed his recollection. "Can you dig out the file and let me know the address of the loss adjusters." She promised to find the information as soon as she could and with a cheery, "Byeee," she clicked off. An hour later Debra telephoned with the answer.

His first appointment was not until lunchtime so he decided to pay a visit to the adjuster.

He wandered out into the oppressive humidity and waved a taxi down. He gave the address to the driver and relaxed back in the seat. It was only five minutes before the car stopped outside a bar called Henry's Tapas. Barton checked the address and, sure enough, the bar and the adjusters had the same location.

He looked around for another entrance but none appeared to exist. Inside there was a long bar with tall stools for the customers. Tables were set out along the other wall with bright cheque tablecloths. He sat on one of the stools and ordered an Amstel.

"Do you know a company called Merriman Adjusting Inc? I've been given this address but it must be wrong," he asked the barman.

"The only Merriman I know is Paul who comes in occasionally," the man replied. "Why do you want to know?"

"I'm over from London on business and one of the people I want to see is this Merriman Adjusting. I've been given this address but there's no offices here."

"Paul's got his fingers in a lot of pies so it could be him. If I see him do you want me to ask?"

Barton accepted the bartender's offer and gave him his business card. "If it is him, I'm stopping at the Coral Reef." He finished the beer and hailed a taxi back to the hotel. He was now even more confused.

He picked up the pocket Dictaphone and said, "Check on 1812 Barton Boulevard claim. Address is a private property not a rental yard. The loss adjuster may also be fictitious." He clicked the switch to off and returned it to his briefcase.

He arrived at the Insurance Exchange of the Americas just before twelve. The theory behind the exchange was to create a market in one location for insurance business. It was basically supposed to be a, sort of, copy of Lloyds of London.

Americans are a wonderfully inventive race and have developed many magnificent conceptions. They are not very good, however, at copying the ideas of others. Compared to Lloyds the exchange was a minnow to a whale. One or two brokers wandered about looking sheepish. They were not used to this trading face to face and it showed. The only thing that Barton found impressive about the whole place was the security guard at the entrance who looked as though he could easily go ten rounds with Muhammed Ali.

He was pointed in the direction of his lunch date. Carlos Pedrosa was diminutive in stature. In his stockinged feet he probably weighed no more than 120 pounds. Barton estimated that this would be increased by another ten pounds when the total weight of the gold accoutrements that adorned his wrists and neck was added. He had a dark swarthy complexion and jet black wavy hair. He greeted Barton enthusiastically, too enthusiastically for Barton's liking.

Over lunch Pedrosa went to great lengths to stress his wealth and influence. The capital that financed his syndicate was predominantly South American. What was clear to Barton was that Pedrosa wanted something and it was likely that, whatever it was, other people would not want to give it. It was soon obvious that Pedrosa knew little about insurance and looked upon the business as a means of generating cash. What the cash was used for was something Barton did not want to know.

By the time coffee had arrived Barton had decided that he would recommend to the board that the company terminate any connections with Pedrosa. In the insurance business trust is implicit in every deal. The concept of *uberrima fides* or utmost good faith is the cornerstone on which insurance transactions should stand. Barton had the feeling that Pedrosa worked not to the notion of *uberrima fides*, but 'you bury me if I die'.

Barton fought a valiant rearguard action in keeping the conversation general. Pedrosa certainly had some deal in mind and Barton studiously evaded the subject. In desperation he raised the topic of 1812 Barton Boulevard. He told Pedrosa of the non-existent rental yard and disappearing loss adjuster. Pedrosa listened with what appeared to be little interest. When the story was told Pedrosa looked at his Rolex and said, "Gee is that the time. I have to rush." He shook hands with Barton, wished him a cursory farewell and left.

Barton was thoroughly bemused. One second he was being pushed into some dubious deal and the next Pedrosa was gone. He finished his coffee and made his way back to the exchange.

The next two meetings were equally unsatisfactory. Both wanted to set up special arrangements which whilst not illegal certainly fringed on it. The exchange was relatively young and some of the investment came from what is best described as less than transparent sources.

Jet lag was beginning to take its toll as he made his way back to the hotel. He took little notice of the two men who were window-shopping. Suddenly they stepped in front of him and he felt a smashing blow to his abdomen. All the breath was driven from his body and he doubled up in agony. He gasped for breath as he staggered into the hotel. A woman looked at him and screamed.

Chapter 2

Allan Jennings was being assaulted by his five-year-old son when the shrill ring of the telephone interrupted their battle.

"Allan, it's Freddie." The voice insinuated trouble. Freddie Jarvis was one of only two former directors of Manning Steele to survive following the merger with Jennings' company.

"What's the problem, Freddie?" Jennings asked.

"I've just had Carlos Pedrosa on the phone. Andrew Barton has been shot in what looks like a mugging."

At first Jennings did not absorb the information he was being given. "But Andrew's in Miami," he muttered.

"He was mugged outside his hotel earlier on today. He apparently was shot twice in the stomach and is now in intensive care. There is a high chance he won't pull through," Jarvis continued.

"What about Mandy, has someone spoken to her?" Jennings asked, concern for Barton's wife in his voice.

"Carol is with her. I've organised a flight for her early tomorrow morning but I think someone should go with her."

"Are you offering?" Jennings enquired.

"I think it would be preferable if Carol went. She would be better at the comforting bit than me." Carol Jarvis was a plump jovial lady with a heart of gold. If Barton's wife needed a shoulder to cry on she was the obvious choice.

"Ok, sort it out. Is there anything else I can do?" Jennings was angry at his inability to help.

"No, I'll organise it all. I'll give you all the detail in the office tomorrow." The line clicked dead.

"What's happened?" Pansie asked, knowing something was amiss.

"It's Andrew Barton," Jennings replied, "he's been shot."

"What?" Pansie asked, incredulous.

"He's in Miami on business. It seems he was mugged outside his hotel. He was shot twice. He may not pull through," was the reply.

Pansie noticed that her son was now taking a considerable interest in their conversation and decided that it was not a topic for a five-year-old at bedtime.

"Come on, Charlie, it's time to climb the wooden hill." Pansie Jennings took the boy in her arms. As she tucked him into his bed she thought that one day he would be breaking numerous hearts. He had his father's build and strong features but his partly oriental jet black hair and hazel eyes came from her.

Jennings was in his study when she returned.

"How the bloody hell do you know about it, George?" she heard him say. He looked up as she came in and said, "Hang on a minute," to the telephone.

"It's Uncle George." He indicated the telephone. George Pinter had been one of Jennings' father's dearest friends. He was also the Daily Record's best known journalist. He had been the Record's expert in security matters since the early 1950s. After serving for most of the war in the Balkans organising the resistance he had tried commerce, industry and the civil service before falling into journalism by accident. He was looked on in awe by many in Fleet Street.

Jennings returned to the handset. "Go on, George."

"My editor has just rung. It has just come through on the wire and he knows I know you," George Pinter explained. "He saw that the guy was a Director of Corby Manning and wanted to know if I could get any more information."

"Fucking newspapers," Jennings spat. "The bugger's not even dead and you are hovering around like a pack of vultures."

Pinter had total empathy with Jennings' views, but a story was a story and had to be followed up. "I'm sorry, but the story will be printed and it's better that it is right rather than wrong," Pinter said quietly.

Jennings knew his reaction to an old friend was unreasonable. "I know, George," he said placatingly, "I've only just heard myself. All I know was that he was shot outside his

16

hotel. It sounds like a mugging."

Pansie could still not believe the news. The Bartons were not just business colleagues but friends. They lived but a few miles away. She knew that Mandy Barton would be devastated. As Jennings replaced the receiver she poured two large Glenfiddichs and passed one to him. Jennings stared into the amber spirit.

"Is someone with Mandy?" Pansie asked.

Jennings nodded in affirmation. "Carol Jarvis is there. They are flying out to Miami first thing tomorrow."

Jennings tossed back the whisky. His mind was dragged back to the desolation he felt ten years previously when Pansie had been stabbed and her very being hung by a thread. "Why does it always happen to the good guys?" he groaned. He took his wife in his arms and sobbed.

The next morning Mandy Barton arrived at the hospital two hours after her husband had succumbed to his injuries.

The funeral was two weeks later. Mandy wanted a small family interment with just a few close friends. She had fought the tears that wanted to flow since seeing her husband's insensate body but finally lost the battle as Jennings read the soliloquy.

"And the dead who are in Christ shall rise first. Then we who are alive who are left, shall be caught up with them in the clouds to meet Christ in the air, and so we shall always be with the Lord. Comfort one another with these words."

The words from the First Epistle of St Paul to the Thessalonians burst the dam she had built to hold the flood back. The tears soothed her pain like balm on an open sore.

At the house Mandy valiantly evaded the well-meaning who wanted to offer her solace. She did not want her pain alleviated, it would be part of her for life. She would manage her grief and be stronger.

As Jennings was leaving she gave him Barton's briefcase. "I don't know what is in this. If there is anything I should have, send it to me." He kissed her softly on the cheek but his constricted throat would not allow words to come.

That night Jennings held Pansie as though he would never

17

let go. Once he had nearly lost her and the terror of loneliness gripped him like a vice. They did not make love, they did not need to.

***

"Check on 1812 Barton Boulevard claim. Address is a private property not a rental yard. The loss adjuster may also be fictitious." Barton's tinny voice spoke from the machine on Jennings' desk. He pressed the rewind and listened again.

"Debra Hanson speaking," her voice chirped into Jennings' ear.

"It's Allan Jennings here, Debra. Do you know anything about 1812 Barton Boulevard?" he asked.

She thought for a moment and replied, "That's the file Andrew telephoned me about before he was killed." Her voice choked a little as she spoke. "I have it here if you would like to see it, Mr Jennings."

The file was yet another uninteresting report of a fire loss. The adjusters seemed to have dealt with the matter with absolute efficiency. The fire had started in the showrooms, probably caused by an electrical fault. It had spread rapidly and destroyed the showroom, offices and much of the equipment that was stored. The cost was $1,248,000 which had been agreed by the three Lloyds underwriters.

The loss itself was run of the mill. Nothing in it would normally attract the specific attention of the Claims Director of the group. Jennings guessed that the only reason Barton would have studied the report was the coincidence of names, but what led him to speak that note into the dictaphone?

He turned to the placing file and saw that the business had been produced by a broker in Jacksonville called Hart Davies. Freddie Jarvis had dealt with the placing of the reinsurance. The rental yard was insured by a company on the Insurance Exchange in Miami and the whole reinsured into Lloyds. The exchange company received a premium of $67,500 and had paid Lloyds $62,500 to take all of the risk.

It also showed that any claim above $10,000 was again reinsured from Lloyds into Comet Property and Surety Inc of

Grand Cayman. He studied the reinsurance and it seemed that the Lloyds underwriters had paid a premium of $50,000.

He jotted the numbers down. By his calculations the Exchange company was guarantied a profit of $5,000. The next in line was Lloyds who were certain to profit by at least $2,500. The whole structure made no commercial sense.

That lunchtime Jennings and Jarvis were having a snack lunch in the upstairs bar of the Marine Club. Jennings related the information he had obtained. "This is one of your accounts, Freddie, have you got any ideas?"

"I can only guess that Andrew must have got it wrong," he responded. "We get quite a lot of one-off risks from Hart Davies. Paul Merriman adjusts all their losses in Florida and he certainly exists. I've met him several times. I'm out in the States next week so just to be sure I'll check it all out."

Jennings noticed that Jarvis' body language was defensive and wondered why. Before he could continue he was interrupted.

"What's all this?" the voice came from behind them. "If you can't find another underwriter to buy lunch for you can buy me one." Larry Payne was a leading light in Lloyds. He underwrote for two Syndicates one being the third largest in Lloyds; the other, his baby, was limited to names who were personal friends of his, and undoubtedly received only the best of the business offered.

His looks belied his character. He was average in height, build and looks. His facial features resembled every photo-fit that had ever been produced. In fifteen years he had developed from being an entry boy on one of the smaller Syndicates to Chairman of the Non-Marine Association and one of the richest men in Lloyds.

"What are you two plotting?" he asked as a pink gin was placed in front of him. "Oh, by the way, I'm terribly sorry about Andrew. Will there be a memorial service?" Jennings nodded to indicate that an excuse to over-indulge would be provided. The market celebrated both joy and calamity with identical vigour.

"We were just talking about a piece of business you wrote," Jarvis interjected. "A truck rental yard from Ted Hart."

"Old Ted! Bloody good business that is. He has this chute in the Caymans with money pouring out of its ears. The risks come in my front door and I push them straight out again and keep a lump of the premium for no liability. As a name you'll be pleased to know I always feed the baby a piece of each." Payne saw nothing unusual in the practice of arbitraging rather than underwriting. If he could dump the risk on some other idiot and still make a profit it was eminantly more favourable than keeping the risk himself and possibly making a loss. He certainly was not the only underwriter to take advantage of innocent foreigners. The term chute had become part of the market jargon. It was used to describe a contract into which the underwriter could pour all his dirty laundry, or bad business as it was better known, and still come out with a profit.

"You know him well, do you?" Jennings asked.

"About five years," Payne answered. "Always produced good business or bad business with a good chute and what's more he is a member at Sawgrass so I get to play golf there whenever I'm in Jacksonville."

Jennings thought no more of the elusive rental yard until a note from Jarvis appeared on his desk two weeks later.

Re: 1812 Barton Boulevard

I investigated the situation we discussed relating to the above claim. It seems that there have been a chapter of incidents which coincided to give Andrew the wrong impression.

Paul Merriman, the adjuster, used to have a small office at the rear of a bar called Henry's Tapas. He was located at this address when he adjusted the claim. Three months ago he had to move to larger premises due to expansion of his business. He is now located in Jacksonville.

I discussed the claim with Paul who expressed surprise that the address was given as above. The property above is the private residence of the owner of the rental company and it appears that this has been used instead of that of the yard which is located on the other side of Miami. The policy gives the owner's address as he controls several such places across Miami.

I have advised Larry Payne that the incorrect address was shown on the report and he has noted this on his files.

Jennings read the note and attached it to the file. The explanation seemed totally plausible.

***

"If you are happy with the itinerary I'll start to make the reservations." Mary Cantor sat opposite Jennings, her notebook on her lap. A good secretary should be the wife in the office without the sex. Mary was exactly this. Jennings had inherited her when he became Chairman following the death of Charlie Corby.

"This looks all right," Jennings started. He was flying directly to Miami and then on to Atlanta, Kansas City, Chicago, Philadelphia, New York and Bermuda. The name Sawgrass popped from the recesses of his brain to the frontal lobe. Jacksonville was only a relatively short hop from Miami. If he could find a reasonably sound justification it would be nice to play both Sawgrass and the Tournament Players Club. It would certainly enhance the American part of the trip.

"Give Freddie Jarvis a ring," he continued. "It might be worth visiting Hart Davies in Jacksonville."

Two days before he was to leave for the USA, Jennings was glancing through the post before it was distributed. He very seldom took more than a cursory glance but found it valuable to note the odd item and subsequently throw a question at the Director concerned to keep him on his toes. Sandhurst had taught him the need to keep subordinate officers on the ball.

The claims post filled seven binders. He began to flick briefly through the mass of advices and requests for money. As he moved binder one from the 'to be seen' side of his desk to the 'have seen' he noticed Merriman Adjusting Inc's letterhead. Simple curiosity made him read the report.

It gave details of a fire at a plant hire operation in Ponte Vedra near Jacksonville. The blaze had started in an earthmover which had exploded. As a result the offices and storage depot had been destroyed. The resultant damage was estimated at $3,000,000. He made a photocopy of the report and returned the original to the mountain of post.

***

The temperature was in the nineties and the air hung heavy with the humidity. Sweat poured off Jennings as he unloaded his cases from the hire car. The three days he had spent in Miami had been both hectic and tiring for Pansie and him. They had been wined, dined and entertained to the point of exhaustion. A few days at Sawgrass with just Ted Hart to see would make a pleasant change, although neither would pick Hart as ideal company.

As he entered the condominium the blast of cold from the air conditioning struck him like a wind from the Siberian plains.

Ted Hart had arranged for Jennings to use one of his condos on the Sawgrass complex. The lounge area was large enough to play a game of mini rugby. Two bedrooms were to the right of the hallway. The first had a king-size bed. The American version of such is at least eight feet wide. These beds were designed for sleeping not sex. By the time one party had scrambled the distance across this vast divide to reach the other, any desire would probably have been sapped away.

"We'll need a megaphone to say goodnight to each other," Pansie laughed as she unzipped her suitcase.

"I'll meet you in the middle," he responded taking her in his arms. They had been married for nine years, yet just touching his beautiful Chinese enchantress started a stirring in his loins. Pansie's body reciprocated and the unpacking was left to its own devices.

***

The strident trilling of the telephone broke their sleep. Jennings' eyes searched for the location of the noisy interruption to his dreams. Pansie found the antagonising instrument first and answered its insistent call. She passed him the handset saying, "It's Ted Hart."

"You found the place OK," the voice said. Hart had an accent that had started in the Bronx but had softened a little through exposure to the southern drawl. "I'll pick you up for dinner at eight if that's all right." Jennings affirmed. The Rolex on his wrist told him it was four thirty. He returned the phone to its resting place and took her in his arms.

Ted Hart was brash in a way that only a New Yorker can be. He was wealthy and had a partiality to showing it, particularly to waiters. He suffered from a predilection to finger-flicking whenever anything was needed or when he wished to demonstrate his own importance. To Jennings he was a parody of a Humphrey Bogart gangster only much shorter. He and Pansie had only met him once before and disliked him immediately. He began to wonder if a game of golf at Sawgrass was worth the aggravation.

The restaurant, however, was excellent. The waiters scurried about pandering to the ego of the short noisy customer in the knowledge that demonstrable subservience would bring a large tip. The lobster was simple. Grilled in butter with just a hint of garlic, enough to add to the flavour but not to overpower it. A dish of melted butter sat by each of them to supplement the gentle flavour of the meat from the claws.

"Are you happy with the way our business together is going or do you think it could be improved?" Hart wiped away the liquid butter that ran down his chin.

"At the moment we are both making money so it seems to work," Jennings replied without committing himself.

"I am not so sure that the Comet Property and Surety can be too happy," Pansie interjected.

"Pansie used to be a leading underwriter with the Swiss," Jennings commented in reply to Hart's quizzical look. "I often pick her brains. The only way to get the help of a consultant for free is to marry them." He chuckled. Pansie slapped him playfully on the arm.

"I shouldn't worry about them, they get a lot of very good business as well. They have just been unlucky on the Florida rental programme." Hart dabbed away at his glistening chin. "They are involved in several other programmes through other brokers in London."

Jennings took this last comment to be a warning to mind his own business. He knew in commerce one had to deal with both friend and foe and treat each with equal civility, but Hart had kindled an instant animosity in him at their first meeting, a view shared vehemently by Pansie.

"I wouldn't trust that man even if God endorsed him," Pansie said later that night as she slipped into the huge bed.

***

The next morning Hart arrived sporting the most outrageous outfit. Golfing dress is permitted to be flamboyant but salmon pink trousers with a turquoise shirt is extreme.

They arrived at the golf club. The car was taken to be parked and two other helpers took their clubs to the first tee. The professional's shop was jammed full of clothing and equipment. The walls displayed various trophies from the PGA tour. The changing rooms were resplendent with armchairs to ease the aching bones of tired golfers. If an item of clothing were left it would be pressed, polished or both by the time the owner returned.

The Tournament Players Club is the home of the US PGA Tournament Players Championship. It is the most prestigious tournament outside of the four majors. The course was designed for the purpose of hosting that event. Jennings was a six handicap player but the course was designed for the very best of the professional players. There is no rough to be found. If fairways are missed the next shot will be played from sand, palm trees or the ball extracted from the water hazard where it had come to rest. To Jennings there seemed to be more water than grass on the course. The saving was that Hart found even more trouble than Jennings.

By the seventeenth Jennings led by two holes even though his score was six worse than his handicap.

The seventeenth is not a long par three, a mere 130 yards, but the green sits in splendid isolation in the middle of a lake. Jennings struck a gentle eight iron, which flew to the heart of the green. Hart struck a seven and the ball sailed over the green to a watery grave. He reloaded and withdrew his eight. This dived into the lake at the front. He rammed the club in the bag vowing to buy a seven and a half iron and conceded the match. Jennings' day was made as his birdie putt ran straight and true into the hole.

Over lunch, a club salad large enough to feed a family of four, Hart talked about a new account that he had to offer. Jennings had tried unsuccessfully to change the subject, but Hart was like a ferret with a rabbit in its sights.

***

Pansie lay by the pool, the sun beating down on her. The night before had disturbed her. She did not know why but Hart made her feel wary. She knew her husband's company dealt with him but wished they did not. She had no grounds for any suspicion, but suspicion she felt. Though she had never told Jennings, she had felt the same about Stuart Rittle ten years before. She closed her eyes and could see the pudgy little man aiming the Walther at Jennings.

Eventually the churning in her head forced her into some action. She dressed and went to the car. She toured about with no particular objective in mind. As she drove along the coast road she spotted the blackened remains of what had been a group of several buildings. She stopped and looked. Beside the burnt out buildings were the twisted remains of a heavy machine.

Jennings' briefcase was on the rear seat. She remembered him showing her a loss report for a machinery yard in Ponte Vedra. The report was on the top when she opened the case. As she thumbed through the report she realised that this had to be the site of the claim. Report in hand, she went across to the crippled earthmover and surveyed the site. In the past she had worked with loss adjusters and knew where to look and what for. The fire had certainly started in the machine. The spread was consistent with the description in the report.

An hour later she had satisfied herself that the report was genuine and that the fire had occurred the way it was reported. Why did she still feel this unease? A Dodge flat-back turned off the road and onto the site. The young man approached her cheerily.

"Can I help you?" he smiled.

"No, I'm just being nosy," she replied.

He looked at the paper she was holding. "You're from South

East Property and Casualty," he exclaimed. "I thank you. I thought that it would take months before you paid out." Pansie did not reply. "You are from my insurers, aren't you? That's their report in your hand."

"Actually no, I'm from London but part of the claim was reinsured there. I was just passing and, being nosey, I stopped to look." She hoped that this would satisfy him.

"Well ma'am, if you have any connection with the cheque I got for $800,000, as the owner, I thank you." He smiled and offered his hand. She took it and acknowledged his appreciation.

She sat in the car re-reading the report. Neither South East Property and Casualty nor a settlement of $800,000 appeared.

***

Jennings was not in the happiest mood when he returned. Whilst he had enjoyed the golf course, his pleasure was greatly tarnished being accompanied by Hart. It was a part of the business to have to deal with others you disliked, but Jennings' feelings went beyond that to distrust. The proposal made at lunch seemed too good to be true. It seemed to guarantee both substantial turnover of premium and a healthy profit. Why did he feel uneasy? He had decided to review the whole connection with Hart when he returned to London.

He went through the patio doors and his mood changed immediately. She cut through the water hardly making a ripple. Her movements were, in his eyes, more graceful than a dolphin. She saw him and pulled herself from the pool. The tiny bikini showed her body, slim and smooth. Her long, exquisitely formed limbs glistened. Her deep hazel eyes smiled at him. He took her in his arms and carried her to the bedroom.

"What else have you done today apart from swimming and making love," he whispered.

"I've been to see one of your claims." She pouted as she spoke. "You remember you showed me that plant hire fire, I've been to see the site."

"Why on earth did you do that?" he asked.

"I went out for a ride and just came across it. I also met the good looking young man who owns it."

Jennings feigned jealousy and said, "So?"

"He told me he was very grateful to his insurers for paying him $800,000 so quickly." Jennings' eyebrows rose quizzically, Merriman adjusting had valued the claim at $3,000,000.

"He also told me the insurers he was grateful to were SouthEast Property and Casualty not Sea Shores," she continued.

"But the insurers were the Sea Shores Syndicate on the Miami Exchange," Jennings interjected. "Where do South East come into it?"

Pansie shook her head. "You tell me. The young man saw the report from Merriman and recognised it. But he recognised it as the adjuster employed by SouthEast not Sea Shores. I think you have a conundrum that needs looking into."

***

By the time the American Airlines flight landed in Bermuda Jennings was a little tetchy. He understood that the Federal Aviation Authority had designated all internal flights as non-smoking but Bermuda was British and the arrogant bastards had classified it as an internal flight. His first JPS had disappeared before reaching immigration.

The drive from the airport to Hamilton crosses the island. The twenty mile an hour speed limit ensures that the visitor can absorb the wonders that nature has bestowed on this tiny paradise.

Bermuda is an emerald set in a turquoise crystal sea. The land is lush and bountiful. Every hue of green is on show. This is the background to a plethora of colour from the flowers and trees, which adorn the bantam utopia. Pretty houses, all painted in pastel colours, nestle in rich colourful gardens. At night the still air is serenaded by a soft, tinkling that sounds like miniature bells resounding in unison. It is, actually, the tiny tree frogs, no bigger that a thumb-nail, singing to the moon from their haven in the palm trees.

They arrived at the Princess Hotel in Hamilton and were shown to their suite on the executive floor. The balcony overlooked the pool and the small jetty where guests could take a ferry to the sister hotel in Southampton. A warm breeze carried the aroma of a multitude of blooms and blossoms as it brushed the skin.

Jennings only had three companies to see on the island but had decided to have a few days holiday before returning to the realities of the City of London.

They were in the bar when Eric Randall arrived. Randall ran the company owned by Corby Manning on the island. The business was somewhat diverse ranging from broking insurance to managing captive insurance companies for multi-national corporations. Many major companies had found that it was beneficial to set up their own insurance company and self-insure part of their own business. Bermuda had the advantages of being tax-free and a beautiful place for the Chief Eexecutive to visit. The combination of the two is a pairing that most Chief Executives found irresistible, which accounted for the numerous brass plates outside accounting firms declaring them to be the registered offices of this or that captive insurance company. And the plethora of Chief Executives of multi-national companies to be found on the numerous, golf courses on the island.

Jennings' mood was totally relaxed. In his hand was a pint of English beer and next to him was the woman he loved. After three weeks of lunching and dining, often with boring and/or obnoxious clients, and drinking fizzy frozen beer, he intended to savour the next few days and pamper his exquisite wife.

Eric Randall greeted them over-effusively and ordered another round of drinks. He was just under six feet and his skin the deep brown that only a combination of wind and sun could give. He was an enthusiastic sailor and had his own small yacht moored in the marina.

After dinner at the Yacht Club Randall suggested that they should go to The Club. It was a short walk. The night was clear and warm and the miniature frogs were serenading the stars. The Club was the collecting place of the insurance community. On such a small island everyone knew each other. Those who were in insurance socialised with their own as did those in other industries.

Several greetings were offered in their direction as they entered. Their eyes were not accustomed to the dim lighting and the welcomes were returned cordially prior to actual identification of their source. The music was, as ever, intrusive. This was the type of place to take someone with whom you have little in common as conversation was virtually impossible. Drinks were ordered and consumed and the process repeated. After three repeats Jennings and Pansie pleaded travel weariness and they escaped.

They sat in the quiet of the hotel bar nursing a nightcap.

"You must be pissed off with him by now. It's about time you found yourself a real man." Both recognised the voice that bellowed at them from across the bar. The only thing that had changed about Peter Huber in the last ten years was his job. He was now one of three General Managers in the Zurich Head office of his company. He had responsibility for all their non-European operations.

Huber was both taller and wider than Jennings. As a young man he had spent several years working in Sydney. His character was a mix of Australian brashness combined with the composed logic of a Swiss banker.

They both greeted him with genuine pleasure. Whilst he had been Pansie's boss in Hong Kong he was also a friend. Apart from that, without his timely intervention, she could have been a widow within minutes of becoming a bride.

Huber had arrived that evening from Zurich. He had obviously travelled well as the Australian side of his personality was dominating the Swiss. The older Huber grew, the more his sojourn in Australia influenced his personality.

"I see you are still getting the company to pay for you to come to the sunshine and bonk," he bellowed as he slapped Jennings on the back. "Bloody brokers are all the same. Warts on the arse of commerce."

Jennings ignored the expected jibe at the role of the intermediary. "What are you here for?" he asked.

"I'm supposed to be visiting a few captive insurance companies. They like it when a General Manager as important as me visits them, good for their ego," he chuckled. "Mind you, half of them have the same bloody address. They are probably just brass plaques on the wall with poxy accountants doing the paperwork."

"You have to do things like that when you become as

magisterial as you are now, Peter," Jennings laughed.

"Bollocks. The real reason I'm here is to play golf. The bloody accountants are an excuse."

"I didn't know you were a golfer," Jennings commented.

"I wasn't until a year ago. But if you want to see the Chief Executives of any companies at conferences the only place you can find them is on the bloody golf course. I decided that if I couldn't beat them I'd have to join them. I started playing and now I'm hooked." Huber delivered the statement with a broad grin.

They talked over times past as the rounds of drinks flowed at Huber's usual rate. A game of golf was arranged for two days hence much to Pansie's delight. She would now be able to explore all the shops along Front Street without Jennings puffing behind her muttering darkly about shopping. It was an impossible task to enjoy shopping whilst being followed by a short-tempered husband constantly enquiring about what you want to buy. The pleasure in a real shopping expedition is that the shopper does not know what is wanted until it is found and when it is found it is exactly what was wanted.

The next morning Jennings, his tongue slightly furry and his head fragile, made his way along Front Street towards the offices of Corby Manning. Randall produced black coffee immediately the name of Peter Huber was mentioned. Huber had a reputation world wide as a fearsome socialiser.

Their first appointment was with a company that dealt with the captive business of an American textile company. In the last year it had also started to underwrite business that was unconnected with their owners. The Internal Revenue Service had recently started to question the activities of captive companies in tax havens. Many companies had begun to accept non-captive business to muddy the waters as seen by the IRS.

The President's office was sumptuous in a brash manner. All the seats were white leather and the furniture ebony. The paintings on the walls could have been described as impressionist. The impressionist paints how he feels and Jennings was of the firm opinion that, whoever this one was, he felt sick.

Jennings' visit was more for public relations than to actually try to obtain business. Bermuda was the responsibility of Freddie Jarvis. The conversation, as a consequence, was polite and general.

"It looks as though the Illinios rental business with Freddie could be quite beneficial to us both," commented the President.

Jennings looked quizzical and said, "I'm sorry, I can't remember Freddie briefing me on this. What rental business would this be?"

"Of course, you've been travelling," the President replied. "Freddie was here a couple of weeks ago. It's an agent in Illinios who has programmes for truck and heavy plant rentals. Freddie has a company in London who is interested in writing the business but is not licensed in Illinios. I've agreed that we would issue the paper and the London company would reinsure us 100%. Ted Hart in Jacksonville owns the agent and he seems happy with the arrangement. We get 10% of the premium for issuing the paper and you get brokerage on the business coming to us and on the reinsurance to London. Seems good for both of us."

Jennings said nothing, he simply made affirmative noises. He was dubious about the way the deal was structured and more than a little anxious about further involvement with Hart.

The rest of the day could, at best, be described as uneventful. They had lunch with the President of a Chartered Accountants who, to ensure that the lunch was an experience to remember, was accompanied by his actuary. The latter was living proof of the story that says people become actuaries because they find accountancy much too exciting.

The afternoon was even worse. The company they saw was the captive of a glass manufacturer. The intricacies of glass making would have been the General Manager's specialist subject if he were to contest *Mastermind*. He was firmly of the opinion that, as a glass plant was constantly on fire, the chance of unexpected damage was non-existent.

Jennings arrived back at the hotel late in the afternoon. His brain was numb with the methodology of glass making and the nagging anxiety of the company's growing connections with Hart.

Through the glass shower door he saw her body swaying as

the cascade of water washed away the dust of the streets. Her body was as beautiful as the first time they had made love, over ten years ago in the Mandarin Hotel in Hong Kong. Her breasts were firm and her legs long and supple. Her movements were graceful and erotic. She seemed to be performing a sensuous dance as the rivulets of water ran down her soft skin.

"I thought I was going to wash away before you would join me," she whispered as Jennings stepped into the shower.

***

The taxi dropped Jennings and Huber at Riddles Bay Golf Club just before twelve. The sun shone in a cloudless sky and the tips of the palms danced in the light breeze. The course was not long but perfectly manicured.

Huber, who was still a novice, had mastered the art of hitting the ball enormous distances but still had problems with the direction.

The course runs by the sea with one hole where the drive is played over an inlet in the ocean. The water was clear and sparkled in the bright sun. The ocean floor was littered with hundreds of balls, including three of Huber's. As his fourth drive plunged to join the others in the clear blue lagoon anyone within a square mile would have heard Huber questioning the marital state of the parents of golf's inventor.

By the time the second drink arrived Huber was becoming calm. The expletives were now being delivered every other sentence rather than every other word. The arrival of the third drink nudged his memory from his bad to his good shots.

"I was looking forward to the golf, particularly after yesterday," he complained.

"What happened then?" asked Jennings.

"I spent the whole bloody afternoon with Derek Harman. Not only that, he had this actuary in tow who could bore for Switzerland."

"Don't you complain," Jennings retorted, "I had the bastards for lunch. That actuary couldn't talk about anything other than numbers, averages and means. He will probably drown crossing a river that is, on average, two feet deep." The joke was old but both men laughed.

"The thing that surprises me," said Huber, his tone becoming serious, "is that all these captive companies have huge capital sitting here and all they do on non-captive reinsurance is fronting. They have the licences and let unlicensed companies use their paper for a fee."

"What do you mean, Peter?"

"Half the companies I have seen do accept unrelated business. But it is then reinsured 100% to London or somewhere else. In most of the cases the reinsurer then gives away most of the account to another company in the Caymans, the Turks and Caicos or back here in Bermuda."

Jennings thought for a moment. "I suppose that by just fronting up the business they get a percentage of the premium and no risk."

"The re-insurances that London buys virtually guarantee them a profit as well. The last reinsurer in line gets about sixty percent of the premium and ninety-nine percent of the bloody risk," retorted Huber. "It makes no sense."

"How do you know all this?"

"They wanted to find out if our company in London would be interested," Huber responded. "I told them to fuck off, we are risk carriers not book keepers. Apart from that the list of brokers in the States to deal with was not exactly the top drawer."

"Was Hart Davies one of them?" Jennings' interest was blossoming.

"Ted the pickpocket was one of them," Huber nodded in affirmation. "Why do you ask?"

"I can't tell you now but please don't lose your trip notes. I may want to talk about this again." Jennings' tone intimated that the subject was closed, at least for the present.

The conversation returned to golf. After two more drinks each had developed total recall on every good shot played by themselves, all bad shots played by the other and complete amnesia on the remainder of the round.

Chapter 3

The week after his return to London was chaotic. A dispute had developed between Jennings' biggest client and one of their re-reinsurers. Both sides were preparing to put on the boxing gloves and sue each other. It took all his skill as a diplomat and negotiator to get the parties to speak to each other. When he had greeted the two in reception they had the demeanour of feuding adolescents. Once they had sat down and talked it became apparent that most of the dispute arose out of a misunderstanding. During the second meeting, over lunch, they agreed on a satisfactory compromise. Both departed after lunch swearing their undying friendship, which had been sealed with several bottles of Moët & Chandon paid for by Jennings.

It was Friday before he had time to read through his trip notes which had been transcribed by the thoroughly efficient Mary Cantor. Attached to the notes was a claim file with the annotation, "I presume from your jottings you wish to see this file. M.C.."

He opened the dossier, which related to a fire at Commodore Plant Hire in Ponte Vedra, and read. The claim had been finally adjusted and settled for $2,565,000. Comet Property and Surety had paid $2,555,000 and Lloyds $10,000. The total amount had been paid to the SeaShores Syndicate in Miami. There was not a mention of SouthEast Property and Casualty who according to the owner had paid $800,000.

The intercom bleeped telling Mary that she was needed. Jennings asked her to copy the file and gave her the trip notes for circulation among the Directors. In the back of his mind he hoped his notes on the claim would flush out further information.

The computer terminal was humming away on the side of his desk. He entered his password and was greeted by the menu.

Screen Enquiries were summoned and the parameters of the report he required set. Three seconds later it appeared on the screen.

Hart Davies – Jacksonville USA
Year 1982

Reinsured	*Sea Shores Syndicate*
Gross Premium	*$668,000*
Reinsurance Premium	*$601,200*
Retained Premium	*$66,800*
Gross Claims	*$11,950,000*
Reinsurance Recoveries	*$11,950,000*
Retained Claims	*$0.00*
Retained Profit/Loss	*$66,800*

He pressed *Screen Print* and the printer began chattering. The instruction *Page Down* brought up the second page of the report.

Reinsured	*Lloyds*
Gross Premium	*$601,200*
Reinsurance Premium	*$526,200*
Retained Premium	*$75,000*
Gross Claims	*$11,950,000*
Reinsurance Recoveries	*$11,930,000*
Retained Claims	*$20,000*
Retained Profit/Loss	*$55,000*

Again he instructed the machine to print and then turn to the last page.

Reinsured	*Comet Property and Surety*
Gross Premium	*$526,200*
Reinsurance Premium	*$0.00*
Retained Premium	*$526,200*
Gross Claims	*$11,900,000*
Reinsurance Recoveries	*$0.00*
Retained Claims	*$11,900,000*
Retained Profit/Loss	*($11,373,800)*

He repeated the instruction to print the page.

He sat for a while looking at the three pages he had taken from the printer. In the previous year on this scheme Hart Davies had produced a premium of $668,000 which had resulted in claims amounting to $11,950,000 and yet both SeaShores and Lloyds had made a profit. The results for the Comet were an unmitigated disaster. He wondered how long they would be in business.

He picked up the telephone and dialled the number of the Financial Director.

"Collins speaking," a cheery voice answered.

"Geoff, it's Allan, have you any financial information on Comet Property and Surety in the Caymans."

"Actually I had their balance sheet in last week." Geoff Collins was a Chartered Accountant with the personality to match. "I am just sending out a circular on them. They had a bad year last year, in fact they had a loss of eighty million dollars. Their free capital was down to seventy million until last week when a further one hundred and forty million was put into the company."

"Who owns them?" Jennings was intrigued why anyone should invest further money in a ship that was obviously attempting to impersonate the *Titanic*.

"Christ knows," Collins responded, "it's some sort of consortium but we don't know who. A Cayman company is not exactly subjected to the same scrutiny as over here. As long as the money is there the local controller seems happy."

"Will you prepare a full report on them for me with everything we know about the company?" Jennings gave the instruction. "There is no panic as I'm in the Far East for the next couple of weeks, but I'd like it for when I return." He did not bother to await a reply knowing that Collins would not offer one.

Collins replaced the receiver with a sigh. He looked at his desk which was neat with everything in its logical place. The request from Jennings was only a minor irritation but in his organised world he found most of the requests of the producers exasperating. His carefully ordered schedule would have to be rearranged simply because the Chairman had got a bee in his bonnet. He had the firmly held opinion that all the producers in the company were totally incapable of forethought. They would suddenly have whims and, as a result, the administrative staff would have to produce page upon page of information that was never actually needed, or indeed ever used.

***

A week later Jennings was watching the tower blocks skim past the wing tips as the Boeing 747 glided along its final decent into Hong Kong.

The Mercedes was cool. Thankfully he was the only passenger on the flight stopping at the Mandarin Hotel and he did not have to share the courtesy car.

He sat by the coffee table sipping the green tea as the valet unpacked his case. The room had a comfortable familiarity and many happy memories. He always requested the same room when staying at the Mandarin. It was here that he had first made love to Pansie ten years previously. He wished she were here now.

He thought of her. Tomorrow she would take their son, Charlie, to his first day at school. He could remember little of his first day other than his mother trying not to cry, and failing. The memory of the welcome by a thin-faced nun leapt into his mind. He had been told that Kindergarten would be fun but the woman in black reminded him of a vulture about to pounce on its prey. His stomach had knotted with fear and he wet himself.

The jangling of the telephone interrupted his musing.

"Good, you were on time." Sutcliffe's voice was jaunty. "Is seven in the bar too early for this evening?" Jennings confirmed that seven was certainly not too early and replaced the receiver.

Richard Sutcliffe was sitting on one of the stools at the bar. Since their first meeting some ten years before, Jennings had always arranged for them to meet whenever he was in Hong Kong. In that time Sutcliffe Investigations Inc had grown to an international company of some stature. There were now branches in USA, UK, Europe, and several other Far Eastern locations. The fifteen years that had elapsed since he left the Metropolitan Police to go to Hong Kong had been extremely fruitful.

Sutcliffe had also grown. He was still only five feet eight but the good living had made him portly. He waved at Jennings and pushed a beer towards him. "Let's drink to that nice healthy bonus you've just had," he smiled.

"How do you know about that? It won't be public until the next report and accounts are published."

"If you have a phone line into your computer system I can talk to it," Sutcliffe replied. "All this new technology is wonderful for my business. Everybody is getting on-line computer systems using one computer to feed all their sites. That means that we nosy buggers can hack in and have a look."

"Is that legal?" queried Jennings.

"A lot of our work has to tiptoe along the precipice of legality. We have to bend a few rules occasionally. You know that." He stressed the last three words. Whilst he had never been told the full story of Jennings' clash with Cobra, he knew that some of his actions went beyond the rule of law.

Jennings accepted the pointed barb and nodded. "You have a point," he commented.

"The real reason I mentioned your bonus," Sutcliffe continued, "is to show you how vulnerable your information is and, of course, to sell you on our services."

"Sell me what?" Jennings interjected.

"I have people who can hack into most computer systems, including yours. If we can do it so can others who might be acting for your competitors. The information you store is the heart of your company and it is virtually unprotected. What we can do is to design a defensive system for you to stop outsiders gaining entry."

"We already have security. There are bloody passwords all over the place. I have to change mine every month. How do you get past that?"

Sutcliffe looked at Jennings' giving the impression of a patronising schoolteacher. "When we access your machine the first thing we look for is your security system. Your security system then tells us everybody's password, the terminal they accessed from and the data requested. Last week you requested data on a firm of brokers called Hart Davies, am I right?"

Jennings nodded.

"What you need is to protect yourself from the sort of expertise I have available. If you want to stop a burglar get another one to tell you how to do it."

Jennings mused for a moment. What was being put to him was both logical and, apparently, needed. "How would you stop it then?"

"Sorry, Allan, secrets of the business. I can have the defences installed but I won't tell you how to do it. This is a new field and presently we have an edge. I won't give that away."

Jennings smiled. Over the years he had seen the change in Sutcliffe from straightforward private dick into a full-blown wheeler dealer. "OK will you give me a quote?"

Sutcliffe grinned. He had used the ploy of hacking into systems and feeding confidential information back to the Chief Executive many times since setting up his computer security service company. Once they knew what could happen they were all eager to buy his services.

"Now the selling is over," Jennings said, "if I wanted to obtain confidential data about another company could you get it for me?"

"The simple answer is yes I could. Whether I would is another matter."

"Dependant on how big the fee, I suppose," Jennings laughed.

"Not entirely. It would also depend on what information you wanted and why."

Jennings decided to leave the subject at that point. He could have uses for Sutcliffe's services but was unsure why or when. At the present he was satisfied to know what could be done.

They had dinner at the Jockey Club. The Cobi beef, which melted in the mouth, was supplemented by a light mustard sauce and vegetables cooked to the point where the flavour peaked. Sutcliffe consumed a bottle of Fleury followed by several Armagnacs. Ten years previously he had been recuperating from hepatitis and could only drink water. Since then he had manfully made up for the year-long sabbatical from alcohol.

As Sutcliffe became more jovial, Jennings gently, pumped him for information on whose data could be accessed. It seemed that all major commercial companies had or were investing in the latest technology. His own company was moving to a full database system where the raw information was held and could be accessed and analysed from terminals. More and more terminals were being replaced by personal computers allowing the user to write his own sub-routines to analyse the information held in the main system.

Technology was racing forward. The microchip had revolutionised the hardware that was available. New machines, like the IBM 38, brought the analysis of information to the desk of the user.

Sutcliffe was in full flow about the technology revolution when Jennings threw in a question.

"Is it possible to get into a bank's computer?" he asked. Sutcliffe affirmed it was. "How about insurance commissioners and controllers?"

Sutcliffe looked surprised at the question. "There you are talking about government bodies. The thing about them is that anything related to defence or their own political fiddles is as secure as a virgin in a chastity belt, but trade departments, such as insurance, are not viewed to be targets. I would say they were fairly easy to break into. Do you want to then?" he asked.

Jennings laughed. "Not at this moment, I was just interested."

Over a nightcap in the Clipper Lounge at the hotel they arranged to have a preliminary meeting in London. Jennings hoped that Sutcliffe would be able to decipher the alcoholic scrawl in his diary, but decided to confirm the meeting in writing on his return to London just in case. Sutcliffe waved a convivial farewell as he left.

The next morning Jennings arrived at the offices of Pansie's former employers. The office was a reflection of the company. It looked extremely efficient and also very Swiss. A huge aerial photograph of the company's headquarters in Zurich dominated the reception area. A notice board welcomed Mr Allan Jennings to the company and the receptionist, who he had never met, welcomed him by name as he entered. The charade was to give the impression of efficiency combined with the personal touch. Jennings often wondered how often a casual, unannounced, visitor was offered regal treatment by mistake.

Heinrich Schmidlin's office was more homely. A photograph of his wife and children stood proudly on the corner of his desk. Schmidlin was Austrian by birth and had the easy-going attitude of a Viennese.

The ritual of offering coffee or green tea was completed by the delivery of coffee in a dainty Minton coffee jug. The porcelain cup tinkled on the saucer as the secretary passed it to Jennings.

"How is your business?" Schmidlin asked, not really needing an answer. Jennings knew that Schmidlin's company only dealt with brokers on an occasional basis. For his part he only visited them as a matter of courtesy arising from his friendship with Huber. The consideration extended to him was because he was a friend of the General Manager rather than Chairman of an insurance broker.

The conversation was always stilted to begin with. Both knew that there was little chance of entering a business relationship with each other. It was usual, after the initial polite enquiries, to revert to the topic of football, which was Schmidlin's passion. This time was different.

"I have this offer from one of your competitors in London and wondered if I could ask your opinion." Schmidlin had little knowledge of the etiquette of dealing with brokers. To show one broker's business to another would be viewed as a mortal sin in London. He passed Jennings a copy of a letter.

"As you see we are being asked to front for some business out of Thailand. A new company is being formed and wish to buy reinsurance. A company called Armitage Reinsurance in Bermuda has agreed terms but the Thais want to contract with a company in this area. The business comes to us and we reinsure it into Lloyds. That is then reinsured to Armitage. I have the balance sheet of Armitage." He passed the glossy document to Jennings.

Jennings opened the folder at the balance sheet. The company had a capital of $100,000,000. He turned to the profit and loss account which showed a premium for the last year of $40,000,000 and a profit of $36,000,000. He whistled as he reached the profit. "I don't know what business they do but I wish I had some," he muttered. He turned back to the Chairman's statement at the front of the report.

"Since the formation of the company three years ago the demand for financial reinsurance has grown substantially. Our expertise in this field is unrivalled in the world market. It is our constant objective to continue to develop financial vehicles which meet the needs of our clients and offer us continued profitability."

"What sort of business is being offered by the Thais?" Jennings asked. Schmidlin passed him a broker's slip, which he read.

The risks insured were financial guarantees given to developers in Thailand for performance of contracts, which were undertaken by companies who were not resident in Thailand. Companies would enter into construction contracts in Thailand. Part of the agreement required stated completion dates. If these were not met they would be subject to heavy financial penalties. They were required to purchase insurance for the value of these penalties from a Thai company.

Schmidlin waited for Jennings to read the document. "This is not the sort of business we would normally be interested in. But in this case we are asked only to front. We end up with no risk as we are reinsured 100% and we keep 10% of the premium for doing nothing other than let our name be used in the reinsurance agreement. I don't like turning down $1,000,000 of profit. My only worry is about the Armitage. How do I know they are sound and will pay, because if they don't we will have to."

"What about Lloyds?" Jennings asked. "They are reinsuring you, not Armitage. Your contract will be with Lloyds. If Armitage fail they might not get paid but they still have to pay you."

"I agree that would be normal," Schmidlin answered. "In this case, however, there is a condition that states that Lloyds only have to pay when they have been reimbursed by Armitage. If Armitage default, Lloyds don't pay us, they simply transfer to us all their legal rights against Armitage."

"The other thing is that Lloyds cannot accept credit or surety risks under their rules. They have no authorisation to take such business." Jennings wondered how the rules were to be bent.

"Apparently they intend to call it a political or contingent risk to get round that small problem." Schmidlin shrugged. "Some Lloyds men can be very inventive if there is a large enough profit to be had."

"It's a strange one indeed," Jennings muttered as he leafed through the balance sheet again. "So Lloyds actually takes no risk at all. All they get is a commission for processing the risks through their books."

"It seems that way," Schmidlin replied. "I queried this with Wilkes and he told me that was the way his client insisted that the programme was placed. I can only guess that they deem it to be good publicity to show that Lloyds are supporting the operation."

"Expensive bit of advertising," Jennings said under his breath.

He continued reading the report, stopping at the notes. Note 1 listed the trading activities of the company as all forms of financial reinsurance. The second note stated that, in addition to the capital, the company had an evergreen guarantee for $200,000,000 from the Benefit and Asset Bank of Miami.

"What about this guarantee, " he asked. "If the guarantee is evergreen it's the same as an open ended bank guarantee and it can't disappear without you knowing. It's almost as good as cash in the bank. That should give you comfort."

"It should," replied Schmidlin. "That bank has assets of over two billion dollars, but the whole deal seems too good to be true. If I accept, all I do is sign two reinsurance agreements and then get ten percent of the premium for nothing."

Jennings looked at his Rolex. Normally he would have left long before his next appointment but today had intrigued him. He wondered why one of the largest reinsurers in the world had been approached with such an offer. He knew Jimmy Wilkes. He had been one of Carter's stalwarts at the time of the merger. Jennings distrusted the man and had encouraged him to leave. Wilkes joined Bannister Ellis only months after Carter's demise.

"I am afraid I have to go Heinrich," Jennings said. "I'd love to know what you decide to do." They shook hands and Schmidlin promised to tell Jennings the outcome.

The rest of his trip was uneventful. The meetings in Singapore, Perth and Adelaide were all successful to some degree. He spent the weekend in South Australia, on Kangaroo Island, scuba diving and relaxing. Pansie had told him, in their numerous telephone conversations, that Charlie was enjoying school and not to worry.

He arrived at the Sheraton in Sydney late on Wednesday evening. As usual an envelope awaited him. Mary Cantor ensured that his personal mail followed him around the world. The cost of paying couriers to deliver papers to each hotel prior to his arrival was astronomical but Mary insisted he must be kept up to date.

He showered and poured himself a beer before sitting down to read numerous inconsequential internal memos. They included such interesting matters as new menus for the boardroom and a reminder to change his password on the computer. He was becoming befuddled with the amount of non-essential information that passes around a major company when he saw a memo from Jarvis.

To   *Allan Jennings*

From   *F. Jarvis*

Subject: Commodore Plant Hire – Ponte Vedra

I noted the matters you raised in your trip notes following your visit to the States and have made enquiries relating to the above.

Following the fire at the insured's premises claims arose for the following:

1   *Damage to buildings.*
2   *Damage to contents.*
3   *Damage to stock and equipment stored outside.*
4   *Damage to equipment held in trust.*

Following the fire the buildings and all the stock and equipment were destroyed. Two insurers were involved in the claim i.e. SeaShores Syndicate and SouthEast Property and Casualty. SeaShores insured the Buildings, contents and stock and equipment owned by the insured. SouthEast insured equipment held in trust by the insured.

In addition to hiring plant Commodore also offered storage facilities for heavy equipment to other companies. As a result they incurred warehouseman's liability for that equipment while held in trust. This liability was insured with SouthEast.

In view of the size of the fire both insurers agreed that they would appoint the same loss adjuster viz. Merriman Adjusting.

The claim paid by SouthEast was just over $800,000 which would explain the comment made by the owner to you.

Should you need any more information please advise me.

Jennings re-read the note. The explanation seemed plausible so why did he feel uneasy? The only cause for any doubt would be how the claim for goods in trust could be agreed so quickly. All the original owners of equipment would have to be contacted and a value agreed before settlement could be made. It also raised the question of to whom the payment was made. In usual circumstances the insurers would pay the owners not the trustee. He put the note away and poured another drink.

Had there been no connection between the claim in Barton Boulevard and Commodore Plant Hire the explanations could have been accepted without question. Unfortunately there was a connection. Both claims had the same insurers, reinsurers and loss adjuster. They were also both Freddie Jarvis' accounts. Jennings resolved that he would make his own enquiries on his return.

Chapter 4

NEW YORK

The limousine glided along Fifth Avenue and stopped outside the Sheraton Tower. The bellhop opened the door and Carter alighted, proffering a five-dollar bill. He crossed the huge reception area towards the lifts, which serviced the Tower. The elevator whisked him to the thirty-fifth floor.

The suite overlooked Fifth Avenue. On the pavement below ant-like figures scurried to and fro, each oblivious of the existence of the others. New York was a city apparently totally devoid of the courtesies, which separate the human from the other inhabitants of the planet. Below two ants were coming to blows over which spotted a vacant taxi first.

He went to the bathroom and splashed his face with cold water. In the mirror he saw what he had become. His blond hair was both receding and surrendering to the invasion of their grey compatriots. His eyes were hard with deep lines extending from their corners like a delta. Six years in the penitentiary had taken their toll.

He poured a Jack Daniels and swallowed it in one mouthful. Another followed. He took the third to the coffee table. Sitting beside it he opened his attaché case and pulled out the letter. It had arrived that morning before he had left Hilton Head.

Dear Cameron,

I think you should know that Allan Jennings has asked some questions about two of the claims on the special schemes. Both have been reported on by Paul Merriman who may be getting a little lax.

I enclose copies of my notes on the claims, which I believe should satisfy Jennings, for your information.

I suggest that for the present we do not expand the connection with Corby Manning until I am satisfied that the situation has calmed.

Yours sincerely

Freddie

Carter examined the letter and the notes, anger raging in his gut. It was ten years since he had nearly grasped real power. When he had stood over the prostrate body of James Dowie his feeling of elation outstripped any orgasm he had ever had. The news of the explosion at Gatefield Manor then the merger with Corby Lannin had crushed the dreams he had nurtured for the previous five years. Jennings' words cut into him like a scimitar.

"I know of your involvement with Cobra. You have twenty-four hours to resign and leave. If I ever hear of you operating in the London market again I will make all the information I have public. As you know, the penalty for treason is still hanging."

He had left for New York the next day.

Even there the spectre of Jennings haunted him. He had tried to return to the reinsurance business but the bastard blocked every opportunity. The only route was the disreputable end of the market. That was why he had become involved with Joe Scorsi.

The cocktail party had been organised by Denning Drury to coincide with the annual general meeting of the Reinsurance Association of America. The Association was the lobbying organisation for the American reinsurers and occasionally used Denning Drury. They were attorneys for several influential congressmen and specialised in the financial markets. They also had a number of extremely rich clients whose sources of income could best be described as murky.

Carter had accepted the invitation in the hope of making contacts to help him back into the business. Instead he was introduced to Scorsi by Hank Drury.

"Let me introduce you to Joe Scorsi." Drury took him by the elbow and propelled him across the room. "Joe, this is Cameron

Carter." Scorsi was swarthy with black greasy hair. He reminded Carter of a Mafia hit man in a 1950s 'B' movie.

"A former Deputy Chairman of Lloyds of London, I'm honoured," Scorsi said a little over-effusively. Carter responded politely. He did not really want to meet this man as he was searching for a bigger fish who had not yet been got at by Jennings.

"I am actually setting up an insurance organisation myself," Scorsi continued. "You have knowledge of the international markets far above anyone else here and I would appreciate the benefit of your expertise, for a fee, of course."

Carter's ears pricked up. To date all his contacts had been polite but evasive. He would arrive at a party, receive courteous greetings and then find himself in the centre of a huge void as the other doyens of the industry studiously avoided contact. Here was someone who wanted to use his erudition and pay him for it. "I would be happy to talk to you, Mr Scorsi," he replied.

"Call me Joe." Scorsi reached in his pocket and pulled out a gold case containing his business cards. He proffered one to Carter. "Ring me tomorrow and we can fix an appointment."

The office was on the eighty-ninth floor of the World Trade Centre. The furnishings were somewhere between elegant and ostentatious. The carpets were deep and lush which left Carter wondering whether they needed to be vacuumed or mown. The receptionist could have been on the centrefold of Playboy instead of behind a desk.

Scorsi rose from behind a six-foot ebony desk to greet him and motioned him to sit at the coffee table. Once he was seated the receptionist leaned forward to ask how he would take his coffee. The neckline of her silk blouse surrendered to gravity and Carter was looking directly at the most beautifully formed breasts he had ever seen. A pleasant pain invaded his groin as he requested milk but no sugar. She saw the direction of his eyes and lingered before standing.

"Did you ever see tits like that?" Scorsi interrupted his erotic thoughts as his eyes followed her swaying hips through the door. "And she can type. Karen is a real asset."

"Now, Cameron, I have this little company in South Carolina," Scorsi continued. "I want to develop it in the international market. There's too much competition in the domestic. What I need is a figurehead who knows the world markets. You fit exactly what is needed and I am prepared to make a very substantial offer."

Before Carter could answer the coffee arrived and he found himself studying the magnificent cleavage. Again she tarried as she set out the cups. She leaned across him to serve Scorsi, her breast almost brushing his face. Chanel Number 5 wafted over his nostrils.

"I could be interested but would have to know much more." Equilibrium was beginning to return to Carter's mind.

"Of course." Scorsi took a large file from his desk. "I have all the information here."

It took three hours to study all the information. The company was called Pilot Insurance and was located on Hilton Head Island. It appeared to be owned by a Mexican land company and backed by substantial investments in the Caribbean. Another part of the group was a reinsurance company in El Salvador who would offer reinsurance facilities for the international business. Pilot had a capital of $25,000,000 and currently accepted some homeowners business in the Carolinas. The capital was under-used leaving plenty available to develop an international account. The concept was to develop a network of agents in the international markets to produce the business.

When it came to personal terms Scorsi suggested that Carter should have a basic salary of $200,000 plus two per cent of the premium generated by the company. "I think the best way of dealing with the percentage is for the agents to pay it out of their commission. That way you can have the money paid off shore," Scorsi proposed.

"I would like some time to think about this," Carter commented when they finished studying the papers.

"Of course," Scorsi replied. "You take the papers away and we'll have dinner tomorrow night to see if you have any problems. A car will pick you up at seven."

That night Carter burnt the midnight oil assessing the possibilities. He analysed the potential numbers assuming good and bad results. He concluded that, with the reinsurance from the company in El Salvador, the worst that could happen would be the company becoming insolvent in three years. In that time he would have received a salary of $600,000 and premium processed would have been $150,000,000. This would give him $3,000,000 sitting somewhere hidden and tax-free. His reservation was that Scorsi was thought to have connections with organised crime. He decided to raise this the next night.

It was just before seven when the doorbell chimed in his apartment.

She was dressed in a pale blue chiffon dress with a neckline that plunged to the waist. A long shapely leg showed through the split skirt.

"Mr Scorsi is bringing his lady friend with him so I am to be your escort for dinner," she pouted.

Carter forced his eyes away from her cleavage and smiled. "The pleasure will be all mine," he said politely.

She poured him a martini from the bar in the limousine. As they drove through Manhattan she leaned across him to point out the sights. Her hand rested gently on the inside of his thigh. Her touch was soft yet firm.

Over dinner they talked generally about the proposal. Carter did not raise Scorsi's alleged dubious connections as he would prefer to do this privately.

"There are a couple of small things I forgot," Scorsi said as the waiter served American-sized steaks. "First the company has a condominium for the President. It's on the Shipyard plantation and backs onto the golf course. Second you have some staff but you will need a personal assistant. If you are happy I would suggest Karen. She's much too good for the little she has to do in my office and I know she would be an asset to you."

Carter felt her hand gently squeeze his arm. "I love South Carolina," she whispered.

The air was warm when they left the restaurant. Carter promised an answer to Scorsi within a couple of days. The next few hours would have a major influence on that decision.

"Would you like to have a coffee at my place?" she asked as the limousine slid away from the restaurant.

"I would love to have anything at your place," he replied, hoping she would pick up the innuendo.

"Well you could be my boss so I have to do as I'm told." Her hand moved from his thigh and she softly caressed his swollen flies.

The car stopped outside an apartment block on Battery Park. "We won't need you any more tonight, Jimmy," she told the driver as she alighted.

Her apartment was spacious with an enormous picture window overlooking the park. "Help yourself to a drink. I'm going to change into something more comfortable." She went through a doorway, presumably to the bedroom.

Carter threw his jacket and tie onto a chair and poured himself a scotch. He turned and she was silhouetted in the doorway. Her negligee was translucent rather than transparent. The white silk clung to her breasts, her reddish-brown nipples standing out like small beacons. Below her flat stomach he could faintly see the dark triangle of pubic hair against her white skin.

She came towards him and pressed her nipples into his chest. She undid his flies and began to explore his distended penis. Her hands were cool and his erection throbbed. She knelt down and loosened his belt. Her warm soft tongue massaged his genitals. Her lips were like a whirlpool drawing his erection into an abyss of ecstasy.

The following morning Carter accepted the post of President of Pilot Insurance. Two days later he and his very personal assistant were on a flight to Charleston.

The condominium abutted the tree-lined second fairway of the championship course. The pool was kidney shaped and filled with clear blue water. The jacuzzi stood beside the pool, inviting them to partake. Karen produced a bottle of champagne and two glasses, which she placed beside the inviting lagoon. Her dress slipped to the floor and he watched as her lissom body sank into the foaming water. He joined her and they made love.

The first three months with Pilot were frenzied. In order to produce the volume of premium he needed Carter had to set up a network of agents in all the major markets. He visited London, Paris and Brussels looking for the right partners. He knew that within five years the company would go bust and he would have little future prospects of working. He would have to ensure that, during that time, abundant funds had found their way into his personal domain. He needed people with apparent integrity and a rapacious nature. It was not difficult to find what he needed.

The agencies were set up in each centre. They were not licensed by the local authorities as they would only accept business subject to confirmation from Pilot. The fact that the confirmation would be automatic appeared not to worry the local controllers for insurance. Each agent would own forty per cent of the agency. Each agency was paid a commission of ten per cent of all premium that they processed. Consequently each agent received four per cent of all premium. This was paid into an off shore account. The rest of the commission, after Carter's rake off, was fed into companies owned by Scorsi and his associates.

Carter decided to further feather his own nest by setting up an agency in Grand Cayman, which he owned. All business from the other agents was channelled through Grand Cayman and a further ten per cent of the premium disappeared, half to Carter and half to a company in the Turks and Caicos Islands owned by Scorsi. Each of his agents operated similar schemes. Business from London would be passed through Paris and Brussels before reaching Grand Cayman. By the time the premium reached Pilot over forty per cent had already disappeared into avaricious pockets.

Large parts of the business were reinsured into the company in El Salvador. This, of course, travelled via Grand Cayman and another ten per cent vanished.

Carter sat back and watched as the money accumulated. His bank accounts in Bermuda and Switzerland grew. He attended the office only occasionally as the delights available to a resident of the island were too tempting to ignore. He sailed, played golf and made love. Karen was the goddess of lovemaking. Each time they coupled it was different. She transported him to the top of the mountain of gratification.

In the first report and accounts he wrote off most of the value of the condominium in the assets of the company. Having set the book value at $10,000 he arranged for Karen to purchase it.

It was three years before the demands of those needing

payment exceeded the pillaged funds that arrived at Pilot. During that time over $300,000,000 of premium had started its journey towards Pilot. Only $150,000,000 had arrived.

Carter had expected the edifice to implode and it came as no surprise when the Carolina Insurance Commissioner intervened. As the investigation proceeded it became apparent that not only had the premium been pillaged but the capital of the company had been raped. The reinsurer in El Salvador disappeared and Pilot was left owing $1 billion and no funds to pay them.

Carter was unconcerned as he had over $20,000,000 in bank accounts that could never be traced. He had a pin-prick of concern when the FBI joined in the investigation of the company but perceived them to be a nuisance rather than a threat. It came as a bolt from the blue when he was arrested and indicted on twenty counts of fraud and racketeering.

Scorsi produced both his bail and an attorney. During his first meeting with the attorney it was made clear to him that if he stayed quiet about the involvement of Scorsi he would be looked after. To the contrary if he did not, he would also be looked after, but in a very different fashion. He chose to plead guilty and made a deal with the prosecutor. The court case was short and Carter was sentenced to ten to twenty years. He knew he would be paroled in six.

As long as you have the right connections and enough money the State Penitentiary is not such a sinister place. America is the epitome of the market economy and virtually anything can be bought. After a few months occasional weekend releases could be bought. These were spent with Karen who delighted in liberating his pent up carnality.

He became part of the prison's elite. Several of Scorsi's former associates were inmates and he was drawn into their clan. The tentacles of the organisation, of which Scorsi was a part, spread far and wide.

After six years he was paroled into the community having been, according to the corrupt governor, a model prisoner who was fully rehabilitated and ready for life in the outside world. His bank accounts had diminished by just over one million dollars, which had been the cost of making his incarceration acceptable.

His first week of freedom was spent at Shipyard with Karen. They hardly left the condominium. They only put clothes on to enjoy the lascivious sensation of the other removing them. They indulged, rapaciously, in gratifying their sexual impulses. Scorsi's arrival was an unwanted interruption.

"Now that you've had a week to fuck the penal system out of your memory, it's time to talk about the future." Scorsi's accent was somewhere between the Bronx and Corsica. "Me and my associates have a proposal for you."

Scorsi outlined the requirements of his associates. They needed money to be moved across international borders without attracting attention and the amounts would be substantial. It was obvious to Carter that it was dirty cash that needed laundering.

"We think that the insurance business offers opportunities," Scorsi continued. "The little scam with Pilot started with $25,000,000 in Carolina and finished with over $100,000,000 in pretty little tax havens."

"I'm afraid it's unlikely that you will be able to repeat that." Carter sighed at Scorsi's lack of perception. "The report by the Carolina Commissioner on Pilot has been seen all over the world. A lot of similar operations have been shut down. Insurance controllers, unfortunately, now know what could be done and are looking out to stop it."

"You're supposed to be the fucking expert. There must be other ways," Scorsi retorted.

"There are, but they will cost."

"How much?" snapped Scorsi.

"I would have to set up a network with legitimate operators and feed through them. I would guess about twenty per cent of the money processed would go in costs." Carter was already sketching out a plan in his mind. "I could formulate some ideas for you if you wanted. I will want a fee of $250,000, in advance, to come up with a proposal."

"You've picked up some real greedy habits in the slammer," Scorsi muttered. "How do you want the money?"

Carter had embarked on a new career.

The jangling of the telephone interrupted Carter's musing.

"I'll see you in the Irish bar in ten minutes." Scorsi, like many Americans, thought that at least one of his ancestors had to have come from the Emerald Isle.

The bar was on Fifth Avenue about two minutes' walk from the Sheraton. It appeared small from the outside but made up for its lack of width by depth. The counter was some twenty yards long with high barstools running its length.

Scorsi sat at the far end of the bar, already half-way through his first Guinness. "Do you want one of these?" he asked as Carter approached. Carter declined and ordered a Bass ale.

"How are things running?" Scorsi enquired.

"They're fine except for that one-off you wanted. I had to arrange the whole thing too quickly and one of the operatives was sloppy. There's a bastard in London asking the wrong questions." Carter's guts churned with bitterness as he thought of Jennings.

"Is there anything I can help with? My associates have a multiplicity of skills."

Carter knew exactly what Scorsi was implying. "You could help," he replied. "There is an adjuster in Jacksonville who needs to retire."

"Give me the details and I'll sort it for you," Scorsi spoke quietly. "What about the bastard in London, do you need any help there?"

Carter shook his head. "If I need to I have a surprise reunion for him." If Jennings was to be dealt with he would retain that satisfaction for himself. He gave Scorsi a sheet of paper containing Merriman's name and address.

Scorsi slipped the paper into his breast pocket. "Consider it done," he said. "Now, down to current business. I have got a new source and, over the next year or two, we will have to more than double the amount we are moving."

Carter whistled through his teeth. "That's over a billion dollars. I will have to cast a lot wider than we are at present. I have started looking at other markets but it's very early days for them."

"Don't give me the salesman's bullshit," Scorsi smiled. "My new sources are prepared to offer twenty-five per cent rather than the present twenty, on one condition. They want a detailed plan of how the transfers are achieved in writing."

"Forget it," spat Carter. "If I put anything in writing I'm in the shit if someone fucks up and the whole thing blows up. One stretch in the can is more than enough."

"You take the document to them and sit with them while they read it," Scorsi replied. "They then give it back and you take it away with you. Also I think I can squeeze another five per cent out of them."

"I'll think about it," Carter responded. They finished their drinks. As they left the bar Scorsi patted his breast pocket. "This problem's gone," he said. "Just make sure you sort out the London end."

A week later the remains of Paul Merriman's speedboat were washed ashore at Ponte Vedra. His body appeared two miles down the beach a day later.

The inquest recorded a verdict of accidental death following an explosion caused by a faulty fuel line. Carter read the brief newspaper report in the Concorde lounge at Kennedy Airport.

Chapter 5

It was just after eleven and the bar of the More than a Penny for 'em Club was beginning to fill. The patrons had been to the theatre or dinner and chose to top off their evening at the club.

The waitresses, clad only in fish-net tights, thigh-length boots and tiny skirts, flitted among the customers. They were paid a commission of two pounds for every drink they served. Their trays were carried high above their heads enabling them to brush ogling clients with their firm naked breasts.

By twelve o'clock customers would be gravitating to the downstairs salon. The small dance floor was surrounded by low tables, each of which were encircled with plush two-seater settees. Each customer would be required to share his dais with a hostess for company. An acceptable fizzy Spanish wine would be served under the guise of champagne. Of the hundred pounds charged for each bottle the hostess would receive twenty-five.

After 1am the hostesses were allowed to negotiate further services with the client provided that at least two bottles had been paid for. The cost of the ministration would depend on what was required and the duration. The amount would be added to the bill prior to the going of the couple and the club received a fee of fifty pound for each departure.

Many of the hostesses departed and returned before the club closed at 4am. Often their job was made easier by the client. Alcohol has both a plus and minus effect on the male of the species. It stimulates the part of the brain that produces the sexual imagination. To the contrary it disconnects the brain from the remainder of the body leaving the organ needed to carry out the act totally traumatised. Often the hostess would return early, having failed to awaken the dormant genitalia of the drunken owner of a credit card.

Penny Hacker sat at the end of the bar surveying her domain. She was the only female in the bar who was not topless. Her figure was trim and her legs long and shapely. The neckline of her dress was cut low enough to encourage observation. The split in her skirt ran the length of her thigh. In the early days she had been a hostess herself until realising that she would be better off simply taking a commission on the favours offered by her employees. Occasionally she would give high spenders the benefit of her undoubted sexual prowess for free. This was always with the proviso that she also found them attractive.

She looked along the bar and noted the numerous company credit cards standing to attention at the back of the counter waiting to be pillaged. The throng was growing. Her expert eye was cast over the melee. In one corner was a group of young brokers. She knew that they were limited to remaining upstairs. Their company cards were not up to the costs that could be incurred downstairs.

She watched as two men, who looked late fortyish, pushed through, accompanied by two in Arab dress. They did not stop but made immediately for the downstairs salon. She followed them to ensure that they were given the best hostesses. The Arabs were offered her two finest girls. One was being fondled, clumsily, even before she sat. She winked at the girl, knowing that the bill at the table would probably exceed a thousand pounds before the evening was out. The girl smiled and brushed her hand along his thigh, thinking that five hundred would be a reasonable fee for the after hours work.

Back upstairs Penny resumed her seat and continued to study the clientele. She recognised his face but could not remember from where. His stature was distinguished and his blond hair was flecked with grey. His eyes showed a hardness with dark lines meandering from their corners. He smiled at her.

"It's Penny Hacker is it not?" he asked.

She nodded. "I am sorry, I know you but I can't remember from where," she replied.

"I would think not," he said. "We only met the once when I happened to be in the same little pub as you and Leonard King."

The mention of King's name tore at her heart. She closed her eyes and could still feel his gentle hands exploring her body. She dragged her mind back and smiled. "I still don't remember."

"I apologise," he said. "My name is Cameron Carter. Leonard and I used to meet regularly at Gatefield Manor. We met when I stopped for a drink at that little hotel in Caversham. I believe you and Leonard were stopping there."

The memory came flooding back. Carter had been on the council of Cobra. She and King had arranged to spend the night in Caversham and they had been in the bar when Carter arrived. He had stopped for two hours and all the time her loins had been wanting King inside her. "I remember now," her voice panted slightly. "Nice to see you again."

"Nicer than last time, I think," he rejoined. "I recall you may have had other things on your mind then."

"Was it that obvious?" she laughed.

Carter's drink arrived. He sipped it, thinking of the best way to broach the subject of Jennings.

"It was not until I read about your trial that I put two and two together and realised that Leonard's top agent was a woman," he started. "Do you still have a sideline or have you retired?"

She smiled, remembering the skills she had learned and how they had been used. "When Leonard died there was little further use. I still regret the failure." She visualised the needlepoint driving toward Jennings' back and could feel Huber's vice-like grip as it stopped her. "I still do the odd special assignment now, for special people." She smiled.

"Perhaps you would consider me to be special," Carter smiled. "Mr Jennings is still causing problems, and I may need to have him out of the way."

Anger swelled in the pit of her stomach like a balloon inflating. The gaping void in her life left by King's death was like a festering sore. Jennings had caused that emptiness. Even after ten years, fury gnawed at her insides.

"How?" she asked simply.

"An accident would be nice but it does not really matter," said Carter.

"And how much?"

"It could be worth $50,000 to have him out of my hair," Carter responded.

"Half in advance." She wrote a number and gave it to him. "That account number at the Union Bank in Zurich."

"If I need you I will make the payment. If you get the money the job's on." Carter finished his drink and left.

***

The telephone on Jennings desk trilled.

"Hello, Allan." Sutcliffe's voice sounded cheery. "I presume lunch is still on for today."

Jennings' confirmed it was and they arranged to meet in the Marine Club.

He picked up Collins' memo and read it again.

To: Allan Jennings
From: Geoff Collins
Comet Property and Surety Inc
The company was registered in Grand Cayman in 1981. At that time the capital was $10,000,000 with a further $90,000,000 of contributed surplus giving it an available asset of $100,000,000. This asset and all subsequent injections of capital are in the form of Letters of Credit drawn against the Benefit and Asset Bank of Miami rather than cash.

In the first year of operation it showed an overall loss of $48,000,000. Following this the shareholders contributed a further $98,000,000 taking the free assets to $150,000,000.

We have received the last financial year's results which show a further loss of $80,000,000. Again the shareholders have reacted by contributing additional funds to the surplus. The latest input amounted to $130,000,000 taking the assets to $200,000,000.

On the basis of the capital and free reserves the security of the company seems first class. My first concern is that if the losses suffered by the company continue to escalate the shareholders may no longer choose to support the company. If the contributed surplus of $190,000,000 is withdrawn the security of Comet becomes very questionable.

My other area of doubt is the identity of the actual shareholders. The only fact we know is that the investors are a consortium under the trusteeship of The Benefit and Asset Bank of Miami. This bank has been subjected to at least two investigations by the Federal authorities. Whilst it has emerged with a clean bill of health, the rumours still abound that the bank is closely connected with organised crime.

Jennings folded the note and placed it in his pocket.

***

The Marine Club bar was half full when Jennings arrived. The main topic of conversation was the scandal that was emerging from Lloyds. The rumours were that certain underwriters had been paying substantial reinsurance premiums to off shore companies owned by themselves and their cohorts. One of the parties said to be involved was the Chairman of a insurance broker.

Sutcliffe arrived as Jennings was finishing his first drink. They ordered a round and took the drinks to a table in the corner.

"I hear all your dirty washing is coming out," Sutcliffe said. "Off shore companies and money disappearing, that's not like the City."

"It's only rumours," Jennings commented.

"No smoke without fire," retorted Sutcliffe. "My people have had a little dig and I think you will find that there is more to come. Just wait for the story of a big broker, a leading underwriter and a little bank in Liechtenstein."

"What are you on about?" Jennings was now intrigued.

"My people have been doing a little investigative work in other people's computers. There is going to be the motherfucker of a scandal. By the way, your company seems clean. We had a look." Sutcliffe grinned. He knew he now had Jennings' attention and would easily sell him a security system.

"I've passed your report to our systems people and asked for their comments." Jennings had no intention of being pushed into non-essential costs.

"They are going to tell you that your system is secure. If they don't they'll be admitting that they've fucked up." Sutcliffe passed a computer printout to Jennings. "You manage four

Syndicates in Lloyds. That is a list of all their reinsurances. That came from your system."

"All right, I believe you but I still have to go through the procedures." Jennings put the paper in his pocket.

"There is something I would like your help with." He took Collins' memo from his pocket. "There is a company in the Caymans owned by a consortium with a bank as trustees. I would like to know exactly who owns the company." He passed the paper to Sutcliffe.

Sutcliffe whistled as he read the final paragraph. "Benefit and Asset are said to have some very dubious connections," he commented. "I'll get my people on to this."

"It's private work, Richard. I want you to send the report to my home not the office."

A week later the scandal started to break. Several directors of a major brokers and a leading Lloyds underwriter appeared to be implicated. As more and more information leaked into the public domain the press had a field day. The story even made front page news in the tabloids, much to the delight of the latest politician to be discovered with his trousers down, who only made the inside pages. Jennings instituted a full investigation of his own company's operation and found, to his relief, that Sutcliffe had been correct.

***

HILTON HEAD ISLAND

"Fuck it," snapped Carter, throwing the newspaper on the floor.

"What's the matter, honey?" Karen sat up on the sun lounger.

"Some bastards in Lloyds have been on the bloody fiddle. The shit has hit the fan and the world and its mother is sticking their noses in."

Karen slipped on her robe and walked into the house. "Is that a problem then?" she asked.

"I've got to come up with a scheme to double the amount we are dealing with. I had quite a lot targeted into Lloyds and now that could be fucked. I am going to have to juggle all the bloody numbers again before next week."

She poured a Jack Daniels and took it to him. "I can help you if you like." She let her robe slip open revealing a firm breast covered in soft white skin.

"That's not the sort of help I need," he replied, fondling the warm orb. "In two days I have to be in New York with a written plan for Scorsi's new client."

"You need to relax," she said, unbuttoning his shirt, "You think better then."

He surrendered to the inevitable and carried her to the bedroom.

***

NEW YORK

The conference room at the Vista was large enough to accommodate the Security Council of the United Nations. He sat across the huge table when Carter entered. He was built like a heavyweight boxer. His hair was ginger and cropped to no more that an eighth of an inch. He towered over Carter when he rose to be introduced.

"Cameron, let me introduce you," Scorsi started.

"No names," the big man interjected. "Just call me Tom Smith."

Carter's proffered hand was enveloped and subjected to a violent shaking. Smith resumed his seat and opened his briefcase."Well, Mr Carter, tell me what you can do and how."

"I understand that we are talking about substantial sums of money," Carter began. "Because of the size of the operation I will have to operate in a number of different markets and channel through several centres. The process will need very tight control and I do need to know where the money is coming from and where it is going to."

"That is not decided, yet," the big man answered. "For the moment let's say it is to be moved from Africa, the Middle East and South America to Europe. Is that enough?"

Carter nodded, muttering "What about fucking Asia?" under his breath. He smiled and continued, "Thats fine. This is the outline." He passed a folder to Tom. "I think it is best that you read it and then ask any questions."

Smith read the document through several times, making notes as he read. He closed the folder. "How long will it take to set this up?"

"The quickest it could be done would be six months. The companies in Cayman and the Turks and Caicos can be organised fairly quickly, but Bermuda may take a little longer. With all this crap that has come out of Lloyds in London, the locals are being a bit more wary than they used to be."

"That fits my timescale," Smith commented. "Keep Scorsi abreast of how things are going and when you want the capital." He passed the folder back to Carter. "Thank you, gentlemen." He shook their hands and turned to leave. He stopped and said, "Just one thing, Cameron, I will want all letters of credit drawn on a bank in Switzerland, not here." With that he left.

"What the hell was all that about?" Carter snapped at Scorsi.

"He wants it done, so get to it," Scorsi replied.

"You want me to start setting up companies on the basis of a half hour meeting with someone who's name I don't even know."

"Just trust me," Scorsi said placating, "this guy is one hundred per cent."

"You can fuck off. I am expected to shell out thousands of dollars setting up this operation."

Scorsi placed his hand on Carter's arm. "If you check with your bank in Basle, you will find that $500,000 has been deposited. That's to cover your expenses."

Two days later Carter flew to Bermuda.

Chapter 6

The taxi pulled into the drive of his house in Woldingham. It had been one of those days. Meeting followed meeting, each raising new problems to solve.

As he entered the house he was assailed by his son. Five-year-olds possess boundless energy and expect their parents to be endowed with the same. Jennings picked the boy up and carried him into the lounge.

"Put your father down, Charlie," chided Pansie. "You are not staying up late tonight." The boy looked a little crestfallen. His plan to get in first with his father had screwed up.

She shooed the boy upstairs saying, "Get into bed and I will come and read you a story." She took Jennings in her arms and kissed him. His arms encircled her.

"Go and sit down, I'll get you a beer," she whispered.

She returned with a glass in one hand and an envelope in the other. "You have a letter from Richard Sutcliffe," she said, passing it to him. "I'll go and tuck Charlie in."

Dear Allan,

Comet Property and Surety Inc.

Following our talk I have made some enquiries about the backing of the above company. There are four companies who invest in Comet under the trusteeship of Benefit and Asset Bank.

The companies investing are the following:

1) Timberland Investment Inc – San Francisco

2) Kerrigan Realty – Miami

3) Torrance Fund Management – New York

4) Capital Investment Inc – Chicago

Each company owns twenty-five per cent of the capital of the company. The interesting part comes when looking at the contributed surplus. When the company was formed a surplus of

$90,000,000 was contributed with each of the investors putting in a quarter. In the second year a further infusion of $98,000,000 was made. This was paid as follows:

Timberland Investment Inc	40%
Kerrigan Realty	30%
Torrance Fund Management	15%
Capital Investment Inc	15%

The next infusion was $130,000,000 and again the contribution was not equal. This amount was split as follows:

Timberland Investment Inc	35%
Kerrigan Realty	25%
Torrance Fund Management	25%
Capital Investment Inc	15%

All the capital put into the company has been in the form of letters of credit rather than cash. The total amount contributed by each shown below.

Timberland Investment Inc	$109,700,000
Kerrigan Realty	$ 86,900,000
Torrance Fund Management	$ 72,200,000
Capital Investment Inc	$ 59,200,000

These total $328,000,000 of contribution and from this a total of $128,000,000 had been withdrawn at the last year end. There have been further drawings on the facilities since but I have not obtained the details.

I do not know if you know the four investors, but should you not I set some further detail.

Timberland Investment Inc

This is a privately owned investment company whose source of funds is somewhat of a mystery. The investors appear to be numerous private individuals but there is a deeply held suspicion that the company is a front for the gambling, protection and other rackets of the Umbari family.

Kerrigan Realty

You will be most interested to know that this appears to be the only realty company in the US which is not involved in property. The rumour is that it fronts the rackets for the Cirrolla family.

Torrance Fund Management & Capital Investment
If my sources are correct these are both fronts for the Carpessa
family.
I do find it somewhat strange that the leading three families in
organised crime are investing in an off-shore insurance
company that consistently loses money. I can only let you
surmise at the reasons.
Should you need me to do any further work, please let me know.

Yours sincerely
Richard

Pansie returned as he finished the letter.

"What's the matter, Allen?" she asked. "You look as though you have just lost your major account."

He gave her the letter, saying, "Read that and tell me what you think."

Pansie read the document and then placed it on the table.

"Do you do any business with them?" she enquired.

"Freddie places some reinsurances of Lloyds with them. As far as I can see they are all reinsurances where Pedrosa in Miami acts as a front. Lloyds keep a tiny part and punt the rest off to Comet. The results on the total account are crap but Pedrosa and Lloyds make money."

"What made you ask Richard to make these enquiries?" she asked.

"It all started with Andrew being killed. Then you came across that young man who had been paid by the wrong people. Both were Freddie's accounts and came from Pedrosa and through Lloyds. I wondered about the coincidence and asked Richard to have a burrow. I wish now I hadn't."

"Now you know," she smiled, "what are you going to do?"

"I think I am going to tell Freddie that we don't use these buggers any more. I am certainly not intending to get involved with Comet. I'm too old to start mixing it with their owners. The best thing is to let sleeping dogs lie and forget I ever heard of them."

"I'm glad to see that you are getting sensible in your old age," Pansie laughed.

He took her in his arms. "I am not too bloody old for some things."

***

Freddie Jarvis bustled into Jennings' office.

"You wanted to see me, Allan?" He sat down and crossed both his legs and arms. The thought flashed through Jennings' mind that Jarvis' body language was invariably in the defensive mode. He always sat with both arms and legs presenting a palisade.

"I want to have a chat about Comet Property and Carlos Pedrosa," Jennings started.

"Bloody good business," Jarvis blustered. "We must have pulled in over $100,000 in brokerage over the last year."

"That's all very well," Jennings continued. "The problem is that I have now got some information on the antecedents of Comet and I don't like what I hear."

"What are you talking about?" Jarvis' voice took on a slightly nervous edge. "They have a huge capital and are owned by a bloody great bank in Miami."

"I'm afraid you are wrong there." Jennings saw that Jarvis' bodily defences had tightened. "The Benefit Bank are only trustees. The actual owners are a little more sinister. My information is that the actual owners are the three leading families in organised crime."

"Absolute rubbish," Jarvis said. He had decided that attack was the best form of defence. He uncrossed his legs, disentangled his arms and leaned forward aggressively. "I have been dealing with them for three years. They have always paid their claims and new capital has been put in every year. They are the sort of reinsurer we pray for."

"Why do we only use them for business that comes from Pedrosa? If they are that good we would show them our whole account," Jennings retorted.

"I have tried, but they have declined all our other offers." Jarvis sat back in the chair and re-folded his arms. His charge from the trenches seemed to have worked.

"Don't you find that a bit strange? They only accept crap and

69

refuse the good accounts."

Jarvis shrugged his shoulders. "I've been in this business a long time and have given up on trying to apply logic to the actions of underwriters. Whatever you say, we earn bloody good commission and they always pay their claims. I wish all our reinsurers were like them."

"I am sorry. Freddie, that is by the by. The owners of Comet are not people that I want this company to deal with. As I am the Chairman and own fifteen percent of the company I am afraid that means that we will not use them any more." Jennings did not want the discussion to continue into acerbity. "I will issue instructions to Geoff Collins to put Comet on our blacklist. I am also going to make any further dealings with Pedrosa subject to my specific approval."

"You're the fucking Chairman, do what you want." Jarvis stormed from the room, slamming the door.

Jennings sat, bemused by the Jarvis' reaction. In the past decisions had been made to stop using other companies. All had been accepted in apparent good grace. This time the veneer that hid Jarvis' true feelings had not just slipped, it had disintegrated. Why should he be so incensed over Comet?

Jennings shook his head. He pressed the button on the intercom and asked Mary to take some dictation. The memo blacklisting Comet was circulated that afternoon.

"I have Larry Payne for you," Mary's voice chirped in Jennings ear.

"Larry, how are you?" Jennings' voice was the breezy, cheerful one used for major clients.

"I'm not happy." There was an edge in Payne's tone. "I think we ought to have lunch as there's a problem we should discuss."

Lunch was arranged for the next Monday.

***

They were in the jacuzzi when the postman delivered his wares. Breakfast had been eaten on the terrace, by the pool. Karen had worn only a silk negligee and Coco Chanel. He saw the darkness of her nipples showing proudly from the soft white skin that surrounded them. Over breakfast their hands had touched and both wanted the other. The champagne bottle stood, unopened, by the foaming bath. They had satisfied their desires and now lay, letting the spume wash over their bodies.

Carter, reluctantly, climbed from the water. He wrapped a robe around him, wishing his powers of recuperation were better. He rubbed the towelling to dry himself and wandered into the house. He saw through the window that the postal service had delivered. The small red lever, that said I have a letter, stood proudly to attention on the post box. He donned his slippers and retrieved the mail.

Karen had lain awhile in the jacuzzi. Her orgasm had been drawn from the depths and her body still shook with its intensity. Carter had always been an exceptional lover, occasionally her body was taken beyond her imagination of the greatest lovers. Her eyes were closed, her mind reliving the explosion of an orgy of sensuality, when his voice, anger boiling, penetrated her dream.

"That bastard is going to haunt me until I fucking die." His voice revealed both anger and fear.

She slipped from the bubbles and donned a towelling robe. Her body still was alive with the desire for him. "What bastard?" she asked.

He threw a letter across the table at her.

"That bastard Jennings. Read that."

She had never seen him so ferocious. He slammed the door as he left the room, cracking the glass. She picked the envelope from the table and extracted the contents.

Dear Cameron,

I have just left a meeting with Allan Jennings.

He has been investigating some of the reinsurances we place for Carlos Pedrosa. I do not know where he got the information, but he seems to know about the financial backing behind Comet. I do not believe he knows any more than general details of the ownership, but he has decided that we should no longer deal with them. He has also set a requirement that any business from Carlos must be approved by him. This means that any further business will have to be constructed using different markets, or I am unable to place them. The alternative is that I resign from

Manning Corby and move all my business to another broker. I would like you to let me have your views.

Yours sincerely
Freddie Jarvis

Carter returned, now fully dressed, and slammed the door again. "I'm going to get that bastard off my back if it's the last thing I do." His voice croaked with rage.

"Don't worry, honey." Her voice was mollifying. "We have other fronts to use and several reinsurers. It's only a matter of changing the players and Freddie Jarvis carries on as normal. He was due for a career change anyway."

"You don't know Jennings. He's like a beaver. Once he has one twig, he won't stop until he has built a fucking dam. There is only one way to stop him."

She stayed quiet. He had told her how ten years before Jennings had destroyed Cobra and, along with it, Carter's dream of real power. She knew that Carter's manifest hatred was hiding an undeniable fear of Jennings.

Carter looked at his watch, picked up the telephone and dialled an overseas number.

"I would like to transfer $25,000 to an account at the Union Bank in Zurich." He gave details of his own account and that to which the money should be transferred.

***

PICADILLY, LONDON

Penny Hacker sat in her usual place, the mistress of her own private kingdom. A fresh battalion of credit cards stood, in close rank order, along the back of the bar. The downstairs salon was already half full. Tonight would be very lucrative, but it was not this that lightened her heart. In her Chanel handbag was a letter from her bank in Zurich. It simply told her that she had received a payment of $25,000 from a bank in Liechtenstein. Only she knew who it came from or what it was for. The payment was her signal to exorcise the spectre of her failure to eliminate Jennings ten years previously. Every time she thought of making love with King, that chimera haunted her. Had she not failed, King would still be alive to satisfy her orgiastic needs. Now she would cauterise the open wound of her failure.

"Penny Hacker, is it?"

Her thoughts were dragged back to the present. For a moment she thought he was King. He was tall and there were still signs of the deep brown hair among the grey that had overrun his dome. His square jaw was topped by high cheekbones. The pale blue eyes had laughter lines dancing from their corners. She smiled her confirmation that she was indeed Penny Hacker.

"My name is Freddie Jarvis. I'm a friend of Cameron Carter." He saw her eyes light up and assumed that Carter and this handsome woman were more than just friends. He did not know that her eyes reflected excitement at the coming exorcism of her nightmares.

She smiled. "Nice to meet you, Mr Jarvis. How can I be of assistance?"

"I think it is I who may assist you. I understand that you have a little job to do for Cameron and he has asked me to assist you in any way. I am a Director of Manning Corby. As you probably know, Allan Jennings is my Chairman."

"I see," she replied, "perhaps we should go somewhere a little quieter." She called the barman. "I'll be in my private quarters. Don't disturb me unless it's important."

The barman nodded. He knew that when the boss went to her private rooms with a customer it was, almost certainly, to give him the benefit of her undoubted sexual expertise.

The sitting room was decorated in shades of apricot with the furniture and curtains in a matching cloth. In one corner stood an enormous Sony television. On the other side two video screens sat, resplendent on a large oak desk. One screen showed the upper bar and the other the salon. Downstairs some customers were already trying to paw the mammary glands of their designated hostess. The hostesses were offering both encouragement and discouragement in equal measures, knowing that proximity with just a little contact would increase desire and consequent fees for after hours coupling.

Penny opened a bottle of real champagne, not the rubbish reserved for the customers, and poured two glasses.

"Sit and make yourself comfortable," she smiled. His vague physical similarity to King had already decided her on how the evening would conclude. Already her loins felt warm with anticipation.

He took the glass she offered, raised it and said, "Bonne chance." Her body language told him that business would definitely be followed by pleasure.

"I'll just get out of my working clothes and then we can talk."

Jarvis removed his jacket and placed it on a chair. The heat of growing desire was raising his temperature.

She returned in a few minutes. The negligee was full length and made from shimmering silk. The collar and lapel were silver fox fur. She walked across the room towards him. The negligee swung with the movement of her hips. It was tied loosely enough to give him a teasing glance of pubic hair as it oscillated from side to side. She poured more Bollinger and sat beside him. He started to loosen his tie and she stopped him.

"Business first, and then that is my job." Her hand rested on his thigh, her fingers teasingly close to his, now distending, erection.

"Tell me about Jennings' office."

He had to force his mind away from the delights to come. As he described the layout his eyes remained locked on the firm round breast that peeped from underneath the fur.

"Why does he have two telephones on his desk?" she interrupted.

"One is linked to his secretary and the other his private line." He tore his eyes away from the soft globe.

"He has his own private line?" she queried.

"All of the main Board Ddirectors do. Sometimes we want to talk without any chance of someone listening."

"What about the security in your office? Could I get in and out without being noticed?"

"If you are with a Director, you can. The reception is manned permanently and all visitors have to enter their name in a book and collect a badge. If, however, you are with me there is a private entrance to the building and only the Directors have keys. We can use it between eight in the morning to eight at night."

"That's all I need to know," she whispered. "Perhaps I can loosen your tie now." She stood, took his hand and led him into the bedroom.

Her body caressed his as she removed his tie and then shirt. She knelt and slowly slid his zip. She could feel his hardness. Her tongue stroked his penis and her hands caressed his scrotum. She stood and turned her back to him saying, "I feel a little overdressed."

The robe slipped from her shoulders and fell to the floor. He cupped her breasts, one in each hand, teasing her nipples between his forefinger and thumb. She reached behind and started to massage his swollen member. He slid one hand across her firm flat stomach and through the soft hair that guarded her genitalia. She was warm and moist to the touch.

He lifted her and lay her on the bed. Her body was exquisite. He explored her body with his eyes, his hands and his lips. She pushed him, gently, on to his back and mounted him. He lay there fondling her breasts as she pressed him deep inside her. She was a master at the art of lovemaking. She repeatedly bought him to the edge of orgasm and then let him subside. Finally the beautiful pain within her could no longer be controlled. Her vagina enveloped him and drew his orgasm from the depths of his being. Hers erupted from a bottomless pit and engulfed her soul. As they lay in each other's arms she did not think of King.

***

CITY OF LONDON

Larry Payne was already at the bar in Wheelers when Jennings arrived. He was in deep conversation with two other underwriters. All three greeted Jennings as he approached.

"I've asked Kieron and Jack to join us," Payne stated. "They could be interested in my problem." The statement had a hint of threat.

Kieron O'Sullivan towered over Jennings. He had played second row for the Irish as a young man. He still turned out occasionally for the Lloyds Rugby Club. He was underwriter for three large marine syndicates and Chairman of the Lloyds Marine Excess Committee.

Jack Green was short with a face that had an amazing resemblance to a stoat. He was Deputy Chairman of the Aviation Committee and had two syndicates under his wing.

The conversation over lunch revolved around any subject other than reinsurance. Jennings began to wonder at the purpose of the meeting. The coffee arrived with a bottle of Payne's special Taylor's vintage port. The bottle, as tradition requires, was passed around the table in a clockwise direction. Jennings passed and ordered another beer.

"You probably wonder what all this is about, Allan," Payne started. "I thought that it would be better to get the food out of the way before we had to get serious."

Jennings said nothing.

"I understand that you refuse to do any more business with Comet in the Caymans. What I would like to know is why?"

Jennings had foreseen that this was the likely reason for the lunch and had prepared himself.

"I have heard certain stories about the actual owners of the company which I do not like. If they are true, and I believe them to be so, it is a company that no one would deal with."

"That is all very well, but what are these stories?" O'Sullivan interrupted.

"My information is that the real finance behind the company is three organised crime syndicates in the States. They are people neither I nor my company are prepared to do business with."

"I have never heard anything so preposterous in my life," Green interjected. "I visited them last year in Grand Cayman. Brian Alexander, who runs the company, is an excellent chap. He was Vice President of a company in South Carolina. If you are trying to tell me he is tied up with the Mafia, you must have gone stark staring mad."

"I'm not mad." Anger crept in the edge of Jennings' voice. "I have irrefutable information that the investors behind the trustees are Timberland Investment, Kerrigan Realty, Torrance

Fund Management and Capital Investment."

"And who the fuck are they supposed to be?" Payne broke in.

"I am told that they are financial fronts for the Umbari, Cirrolla and Carpessa families. Based on that I don't want any dealings with them."

"I understand your concerns." Payne sounded placatory. "What you have to remember is that these are only suspicions. We have a lot of business with Comet and would find it extremely difficult if we did not use them."

Jennings tried not to show his growing annoyance. "The business you do with them is to give them shit. The original business is crap but you keep part of the premium and fuck all of the claims and pour the rest down their chute. Over the past three years that company has lost $130,000,000."

"I don't think that how we manage our business is anything to do with you," Green snapped.

Jennings looked at him. He facial demeanour reminded him of Ratty when hearing of Mr Toad's latest escapade in his car. The aggression of his response was totally unexpected.

"If you consider it your duty to criticise my underwriting," Green carried on, "I do not wish to have anything further to do with you or your company."

Jennings was taken aback at the vehemence displayed by Green. In the back of his mind he knew that the financial implications of losing all of Green's business were relatively small but also knew that Lloyds was a leader market. If Green pursued this line, and it became generally known, other more valuable lemmings could follow him. He decided to oil the waters, at least for the time being.

"Look, Jack." He forced his tone onto a friendly paternal mode. "All I am saying is what I have been told. In the light of the information I have, at present, I had to make the decision I made. If it comes out that the information I have is faulty I will reverse that decision and apologise unreservedly to Comet and anyone else who feels slighted. I can't say fairer than that."

"I will make sure I am there when you grovel," Green muttered. He looked at his watch and said, "I have an appointment." He perfunctorily shook hands and left.

"I did not realise he had such a tie in with Comet," Jennings muttered as he watched Green depart.

"They are quite important to several people," Payne responded. "Over the last two years my results would have been $3,000,000 worse without them."

"Bollocks," Jennings replied. "If their chute had not been behind the business you would not have accepted it."

"That may be so, but whatever you say I have made a nice profit when they are involved. I do not want to lose that profit. If I were you I would think long and hard about any decision you make."

Within those words, Jennings knew that the implied threat was to remove all business from his company. He found the reaction both surprising and excessive.

He left the office early that evening. He could not concentrate. The machinations from the lunch scrolled around his mind. As Jennings waved his usual goodnight to the commissionaire at the main entrance, Jarvis was bringing a visitor in through the Directors' private entrance at the rear.

"Oh, goodnight, Freddie." As the lift door opened Geoff Collins was surprised to see Jarvis with an attractive woman. Normally, if Jarvis had a beauty to show off, he would bring her in the front door. Jarvis muttered a greeting and scrambled along the corridor. "I will never understand brokers," sighed Collins.

Jarvis opened his cocktail cabinet and poured a vodka for Penny and a large scotch for himself.

"I thought you told me that nobody would see me," Penny half scolded.

"Don't worry about him," Jarvis replied. "He's the Finance Director. He can only remember balance sheets and profit and loss accounts."

By seven the Directors' floor was empty, apart from Jarvis and Penny. They walked to Jennings' office. The mahogany desk stood with its back to the window. The plush chair was pushed neatly into the kneehole of the desk. Side by side stood the telephones. The first had a multiplicity of buttons to connect the user to differing parts of the Manning Corby empire. The second was plain cream with a simple push button dail.

Jarvis waited by the door. He knew no one would come but

felt better checking. Penny skilfully removed the base and squeezed the package into the space. Her deft fingers connected the device and she replaced the plate to the bottom of the set. She nodded to Jarvis and they left.

"I want you to stop with me tonight," she whispered in the taxi from the City. "I have waited over ten years for tomorrow to come. I want you in bed with me when the newsflash comes. Then I will make love to you as you have never known it."

***

Pansie was surprised to see Jennings so early. Usually he would leave the office around six and have a couple of pints in the Ship to relax. He was seldom home much before eight.

"Are you trying to catch me out?" she laughed as he held her. "Your dinner is still cold."

"I just got fed up. I had a very strange lunch today," he replied.

He went to the fridge and got out a beer. "Would you like something?" he asked.

"No thanks," she responded. "Sit down and tell me about your lunch."

They sat at the kitchen table. All their serious conversations took place around its heavy pine top. His father had been the same. All his life-changing decisions had been made there.

Jennings told her of the lunch and the unexpected reaction of Payne and Green.

"I can understand Jack Green," Pansie commented. "If there was a gold medal given for being pompous he would win it every year. Larry Payne is different. He can't be worried about the few thousand he makes out of Comet. All he does is arbitrage the business and keep some spare change as it passes him by."

"I know," rejoined Jennings. "But he was quite serious about moving his whole account from us."

"There has to be more to it than we know," Pansie mused. "There has to be something on the side between them and Comet. But what?"

"I don't know but I'll do my best to find out." Jennings

79

antagonism was beginning to rise. The implied threat from Payne had irked him.

"Why not have a word with George and Jim?" Pansie suggested. "Someone outside the business might throw a different light on it."

"Good idea," Jennings responded. "What would I do without you?" he laughed.

***

"Pinter speaking," George Pinter snapped. His mind was rehearsing the abuse, should the caller be selling double-glazing. "Oh, it's you, Allan, how are you?" He was slightly disappointed that it was Jennings. His mood was not the best and a disembodied voice to insult would have made him feel better. He had spent the last four months on a rather juicy story and today it had collapsed around his ears.

"You sound a bit cantankerous," Jennings laughed.

"So would you be if you had just seen four months' work go phut."

"How about I buy you lunch?" Jennings asked. "It might cheer you up. I have a problem and I would like to pick your brains."

"If you want to pick my brains," Pinter responded, "it'll cost you. How about I see you in El Vinos about twelve tomorrow? I rather fancy another dose of their Montrachet followed by the hundred-year-old Courviosier."

"That's fine," confirmed Jennings. "I am going to ask Jim Cross along as well."

"I am honoured," Pinter remarked. "The head of MI5 and the great white hope of the City, both sharing bread with me."

"Bollocks!" was the expected and received retort.

Jennings then rang Cross and made the same arrangements. Thirteen years before, Jim Cross had been planted as a minder in Colchester Prison by the SAS following Jennings' court martial. Had it not been for him it was likely Jennings would not have survived his period of incarceration.

The pall of gloom had lifted slightly from Jennings' mind. He took Pansie in his arms. "I might have a lie-in tomorrow, Mrs

Jennings, if you have nothing else to do. Then you can come and have lunch with us."

She smiled. "That sounds nice to me. It's ages since I saw George or Jim. I'll give Gwen a ring and meet her in Harrods after lunch."

***

CORBY MANNING'S OFFICE

It was seven in the morning. The sweat stood out on Katerina's brow. Every Tuesday she had to complete three hours' work in two. This then left time to phone her parents in Budapest. She had come to Britain three years earlier to make her fortune. She had discovered that the streets of London were not veneered with gold. What she had found was that her Hungarian qualifications were useless. Now she studied during the afternoon. In the early mornings and late evenings she worked as a cleaner. She went from her early morning cleaning to sell copy designer cloths in Petticoat Lane.

Though her life seemed a constant drudge she always had Tuesday morning to look forward to. She had heard all the stories of cleaners being sacked for making telephone calls but knew they were the stupid ones. All the calls were logged on a computer but nobody would ever check the Chairman's private line. On Tuesdays she would drink the Chairman's vodka, smoke his JPS and telephone her parents to tell them how well she was doing.

The vodka bottle tinkled on the rim of the Stewart crystal glass. She sat at the desk, opened the cigarette box and lit the JPS with the silver table lighter. She leaned back in the seat and closed her eyes. For a moment she was the Chairman.

The vodka finished, she reached for the telephone. The handset purred in her ear as she reached forward to punch the familiar number on the keypad.

She was no longer alive when her body crashed through the toughened glass window and spiralled to the pavement twelve floors below.

***

"We are just receiving news of an explosion in the City of London." the clipped voice of the BBC newscaster resonated from the radio. "It is believed that one person has been killed."

The champagne cork burst from captivity followed by a spume of the frothing liquid. Penny poured two glasses and passed one to Jarvis who lay beside her in the bed. "To success." she almost shouted the words, and threw the empty glass over her shoulder, not caring where it landed. Jarvis repeated her words and action.

"Now, Freddie Jarvis," she said, taking his hand and placing it between her thighs, "We are going to fuck like no one has ever fucked before."

***

Even the Chairmen of multinational companies have to revert to children occasionally. This morning Jennings was playing truant. He had phoned his secretary at home and told her to cancel the morning. The pleasure of doing the simple things is a joy often denied to the high flyer. Jennings had cooked breakfast, taken his son to school and made love to his voluptuous wife that morning. Thoughts of the office had been banished to the back of his mind. The telephone had rung and he had delighted in ignoring it. This morning he was not available.

The eleven o'clock train had been practically empty. There was no conflict with other passengers for the right to a seat. To travel out of the rush hour was an unadulterated pleasure for the regular commuter.

The taxi delivered them outside El Vinos in Fleet Street just after twelve. Pinter was at his usual table but seemed agitated.

"Thank Christ you are all right." Pinter's eyes showed relief.

"Of course I am, why shouldn't I be?" Jennings asked innocently.

"You don't know about the explosion."

"What explosion?" Jennings wondered whether Pinter was losing his mind.

"Someone planted a bloody great bomb in your offices. It

went off about half past seven this morning. Someone was killed and I've been trying all morning to find out who."

"It was one of the cleaners." None of them had heard Cross arrive. As head of MI5 he had been contacted within minutes of the explosion. "The bomb was wired into your telephone, Allan."

It took Jennings an age to assimilate what he was being told. "Are you saying that my office was booby-trapped?" he asked.

Cross nodded. "A device was planted in the base of the telephone for your private line. Fortunately for you, one of your cleaners was saving some money by using your phone for her private calls. According to your company's computer she has been ringing her parents in Hungary every week from your office. The question is, who would want to blow you away, Allan? It's obvious the cleaner wasn't the target."

Jennings shook his head. He looked at Pansie. Her pallor was that of a ghost.

"What's happening?" Her voice was a whisper.

"I don't know, but let's sit down and think it through," Jennings replied.

They waited for the drinks to arrive. Jennings' mind was in turmoil. He wanted to believe that the business with Comet had nothing to do with the morning's events but his logic insisted that there had to be a connection.

"Let's look at the obvious first," Cross opened the discussion. "Planting of bombs is usually connected with terrorists. The most obvious in this country are the Provisionals. Apart from being in the SAS fifteen years ago, can you think of any other reason why you should be a target?"

Jennings shook his head.

"When you were in Northern Ireland were you responsible for putting anyone away who might have been released and is now looking for revenge?"

Jennings racked his brain trying to remember anyone who could identify him. The SAS may have taken the terrorists but were never identified. They were never called to offer evidence in court, nor were they part of the interrogation team. If they became known they were withdrawn from the Province.

"I can't think of anyone," Jennings responded. "If we were

recognised we either took the bandit out or we left Northern Ireland. That was standard procedure."

Cross passed a list of names to Jennings. "These are the Provisionals that have been released in the last six months. Do you recognise any of them?"

Jennings studied the names. "The only one is Conan O'Doyle. We took him in Armagh. He was coming from Dundalk with a cache of Armalites in the boot of his car. But we just took him, tied him up and left him for the RUC. I can't see how he could have recognised anyone, we all wore balaclavas."

"OK." Cross decided to widen the possibilities. "Is there anyone else who might have a reason for wanting you out of the way?"

"How about the Mafia?" Jennings mouthed the suspicions he did not want to contemplate.

"What the hell are you into?" interjected Pinter.

"I'm not into anything, George. I have been doing a little digging and I'm not sure whether I like what I've found out."

He related the tale to them from the mugging of Andrew Barton to Sutcliffe's letter. He did not mention the odd reactions of Payne and Green. This could be saved for later.

"Are you telling us that some insurance company belonging to the Umbaris, Cirollas and Carpessas has lost $130,000,000 and their people still have kneecaps?" Pinter commented.

Jennings nodded.

"I've heard of bad underwriting but that takes the bloody biscuit." Pinter shook his head in disbelief.

"Who is the insured that gets all this dosh?" Cross asked.

"Comet do not pay the insured, they are reinsurers. On the business we have they pay the claims to Lloyds who then pay it to Pedrosa's syndicate and then he pays the insured."

"Who does Pedrosa pay it to?" Cross had an inkling that he knew the name Pedrosa, but did not recall from where.

"To his insureds, whoever they are," Jennings shrugged. "All the syndicates are audited each year so the claims should be kosher."

"That shows an outrageous misplaced trust in auditors," Cross laughed. "You should see some of the companies we have doing little deals for us. From what you tell me I would bet that

Comet is actually a laundry. If you look at it simply, the families invest in an off shore company which loses money. The money is paid to various insureds who all may be the same person. The cash has travelled across several borders in an apparently quite legal fashion. It's a nice simple way to move money about without attracting attention"

"Your trouble, Jim, is that you have been too long in the espionage business. We are talking about covers that are being transacted through Lloyds and the international markets. The people you are talking about are some of the doyens of the industry. Why should they get involved in this sort of chicanery?"

"Why did Jack Profumo fuck Christine Keeler?" Cross commented. "Avarice and lust can be a highly intoxicating cocktail. Anybody will go for the main chance if the price is right."

"What do we do now?" asked Jennings.

"First you start being a lot more careful. Whoever it is that's after you may have another try. The same applies to you too, Pansie. If Allan is a target so could you be." Pinter rubbed his moustache, a sure indication of his deep concern. Even as a child Jennings knew that Uncle George's moustache was the real indicator of his mood. He had grown it immediately on his return from the Balkans at the end of the war. "Only the British wax their moustaches," he had told anyone who would listen. "I've spent four years looking like a bloody Slav and I intend to look British from now on." His treatment of the facial embellishment always revealed what was in his mind. The violent friction, which spoiled its symmetrical shape, showed both anxiety and anger.

"Both Jim and I have quite a few connections," Pinter continued, "and we'll have to burrow around to see if we can dig up any facts. In the meantime you keep your head down and out of sight."

"What about Richard Sutcliffe?" Pansie interpolated. "Can he delve into Pedrosa's operation to see where the money actually goes?"

"Of course," Jennings muttered. "How come I can never see the obvious and you can?"

"That's one of the mysteries of the Orient," Pansie chuckled, "and the fact that the male of the species is totally incapable of seeing the blindingly apparent."

The exchange lightened the mood of the group for a moment. Both Pinter and Cross knew that whilst Jennings and Pansie reciprocally adored each other, this was mostly revealed by gentle teasing of the other.

***

Pansie had disappeared in the direction of Harrods when the lunch finished. Her mind was in a turmoil from what she had been told. She had wanted to telephone Gwen to cancel the planned shopping expedition, but both her husband and Cross had dissuaded her from doing so. That afternoon Harrods was not the exercise in indulgence that it was intended to be, but an interminable time to be spent fearing the worst and praying for the best.

Jennings decided to return to the office. The building was still sealed off by the security services whilst the bomb squad combed for other devices. Jennings had guessed that certain of his compatriots would have made for a friendly bar. The Marine Club had been barren of Manning Corby staff and the Lime Club was his next port of call.

The bar was buzzing with all manner of staff from the company. When Jennings entered apprehension showed on the faces of the more junior members of staff. It was not the thing to be caught drinking at four in the afternoon by the Chairman.

Geoff Collins stood by the bar. He waved at Jennings. "A pint is it, Allan?" he garbled. Collins was not a drinker in the mould of the producers, but when he had the taste he joined in with enthusiasm. "Lucky you had the morning off or you could have been blown out of the window," he slurred.

Jennings smiled an acknowledgement and surveyed the bar. Jarvis was at a corner table with Larry Payne. They looked across and nodded a greeting. Jennings noted that the table had sat three for lunch and wondered who the other was. The question was answered when Green tapped his shoulder.

"Allan, I am sorry that I was a little abrupt yesterday. Larry has been lecturing me all lunch about it." Green was slightly unsteady, undoubtedly caused by the attentions of the house claret. "That company are a very useful chute for me and I would hate to lose them. That's all I was implying."

"Don't worry, it's all forgotten," Jennings replied amiably. "Let me get you a drink?"

Green declined, saying that he should rejoin his party, and lumbered rather than walked to where Jarvis and Payne sat. Payne whispered something to Green and nodded at the reply.

Within half an hour the throng began to disappear. The call of the early train and the Brownie points to be earned from the spouse for arriving early encouraged many to leave.

"You must have really upset a client for them to plant a bomb in your office." Jennings turned and was looking straight into the eyes of Jimmy Wilkes. He had taken an immediate dislike to this weasel-faced man when the two companies had merged. When Wilkes had resigned to join Bannister Ellis Jennings had been delighted.

"Why do you say that, Jimmy?" Jennings asked non-committally.

"It was your office that was bombed, wasn't it?"

"Maybe it was just because it had Chairman on the door. I'll wait and see what the police have to say." Jennings tried to keep the edge of annoyance out of his voice.

Wilkes took his drink from the bar and wandered across to join the three in the corner.

"Old Freddie looked like he was on a good thing last night." Collins' voice penetrated Jennings thoughts. He raised his eyes quizzically.

"He was bringing in this really classy lady through the back entrance. Probably had a bit of nookie in the office," he rambled. "Blond hair, green eyes and legs a mile long."

Jennings took little notice of Collins' burbling. He finished his drink and made off in the direction of London Bridge.

That evening he telephoned Sutcliffe and asked him to do a little more illegal interrogation of someone's computer.

Chapter 7

The next two weeks were frantic. The executive floor was closed for repair and refurbishing leaving the Directors housed in temporary offices. Files were stored in whatever was available and preparing for the Reinsurance Congress in Monte Carlo became a nightmare.

It was seven on Thursday evening before Jennings had all his papers ready for the congress. Fortunately he knew that Pansie would be better organised than him as they were leaving the following morning. Most people travelled on the Saturday except those who had been invited to a Dutch Insurance company's golf day. They would be on the tee at Mount Angel when the others were leaving for UK airports.

The sun was warm as they alighted from the aircraft at Nice and made their way towards immigration control. Baggage collection was its usual chaos. It is an immutable anathema that three cases which are given to an airline together will be always separated by twenty minutes when arriving in the baggage hall of the destination.

Eventually the cases and golf clubs were gathered together and transported to the taxi rank. This was to be a good week for the taxi drivers of Nice and even more for those in the principality. The big Mercedes flew over La Grande Corniche and down into Monte Carlo. It turned into Leouws Hotel and stopped.

Pansie and Jennings checked in whilst the taxi was unloaded. Arriving the day before the bulk of the delegates had certain advantages. Reception was not filled with fractious underwriters and brokers demanding to be served as each was, in his own mind, more important than the others. The second benefit was that the tip required to secure a room with an ocean view was somewhat less than it would be the following day.

The room, on the fourth floor, was spacious with a six-foot bed as the centrepiece. Jennings telephoned room service and ordered club sandwiches. From the mini-bar he produced champagne and some beer and took it out to the balcony. He remembered not to close the door. The portal to the balcony can only be opened from the inside. In years past many wives or sometimes 'nieces' of dignitaries in reinsurance have trapped themselves on the balcony, not realising this vagary of the designer. After sending the partner off for his day's business they decided to take a little sun. The air conditioning only works when the door is closed, so they closed it. It was only later they comprehended that they were trapped, developing serious sunburn and suffering from a swollen bladder, until the return of their spouse.

Two years previously much merriment was had when one lady, bladder distended and body colour moving from pink to red, managed to attract the attention of the occupant in the room adjoining. The potential rescuer went on to her own balcony, to find out how she could assist, and closed her door, leaving both ensnared.

Pansie joined Jennings. The champagne was perfectly chilled. The sea was dark blue and white horses danced on the wave tops. The warm afternoon sun caressed them. Here was the calm before the ensuing chaos of the coming week. The tranquillity was rudely interrupted by the shrill of the telephone.

"I'll see you and Pansie in the piano bar at seven," Huber's voice roared. "I've booked a table at Rumpoldis. The last one drunk can pay the bill."

***

Carter and Scorsi had arrived an hour earlier on the Air France flight. They were sharing a suite at the Hermitage. Over a late lunch Carter had given Scorsi some detail of the people he would meet.

"I will stay in the background. With my history at Pilot it is better that I am not seen with you. All we need is one fatuous rumour and we could fuck up the whole thing." Carter knew that the City rumour factory had temporarily transferred to Monte

Carlo and anyone seen to be consorting with him would automatically be classified as a crook and outwardly castigated.

***

There were a few people from the market in the bar when Pansie and Jennings arrived. Huber had taken up residence on a table near the piano. Most people would avoid this table as the piano drowned out most conversation. Huber, however, spoke at a level of decibels that could match an orchestra let alone a mere piano. The pianist normally took a break when confronted by the big Swiss' voice.

A glass of champagne and a Stella Artois sat at the table awaiting the arrival of Pansie and Jennings. Huber crushed Pansie in a bear hug and then clutched Jennings' hand and shook it violently. Some people in the bar looked around in disbelief at the commotion.

They sat and Huber started to wave energetically at the waitress to replenish the drinks. The evening was to be a long one.

"Before we start, Peter," said Jennings, trying to instil authority into his voice, "I am playing golf tomorrow at seven and I want at least four hours' sleep."

"Don't worry," Huber replied patronisingly, "I'm playing in the same competition. We can have dinner and then a few beers in the Tip Top bar. I promise to have you in bed before three. That should give you time for a quick fumble and three hours' sleep."

Both Pansie and Jennings smiled at the last remark. Huber's sojourn in Australia had left an indelible mark on his character and humour.

As the next round of drinks arrived Jennings noticed a group sitting across the bar. He initially recognised Jarvis and Wilkes. There were three others at the table. Two of them were former Directors of Manning Steele who had left when the merger with Corby Lannin was announced. The other had jet black oleaginous hair and looked as though he was auditioning for a part in *The Godfather*.

"Do you know the Italian-looking bloke with Freddie

90

Jarvis?" he asked Huber.

Huber, to whom subtlety was an anathema, stood up and peered across the room. "Never seen him before in my life. Do you want me to find out?" Huber was about to set off in the direction of the other table.

"No, it's not important." Jennings put his hand on Huber's shoulder to encourage him to assume the sitting position. Huber subsided and flapped his arms in the direction of the bar to indicate more drinks were required.

Jennings watched the group across the room, intrigued at their demeanour. Everyone else in the bar was chattering and drinking happily. The real business did not begin until Saturday and the early arrivals tended to use the Friday as purely a social exercise. Jarvis' group was huddled around the table in deep discussion. Their demeanour appeared almost conspiratorial.

Eventually Jennings' curiosity became too much. He went to the gents and returned passing Jarvis' table.

"Hello, Freddie, how was the drive down?" Jarvis had elected to drive to the conference. For someone with a fringe benefit car the mileage that can be used up travelling to Monte Carlo was a very valuable resource to present to the tax gatherers.

"Fine," replied Jarvis, "I found a fantastic hotel to stop just outside Lyon."

Jennings nodded a greeting to the three others he knew and looked at the swarthy man. "I am sorry, I don't believe we know each other. I'm Allan Jennings."

He rose and extended he hand. "Joe Scorsi, nice to meet you."

"Joe owns several managing agents in the States," Wilkes interjected.

Jennings muttered a polite response to Scorsi. "Enjoy your evening," he said and returned to his own group.

"So who is he, you nosey sod?" asked Huber, for once his voice at a level that could be heard by only half of the bar.

"His name is Joe Scorsi," Jennings responded. "He is supposed to own some managing agents in the States."

Pansie touched his arm, "I've seen that name somewhere before. I think it was in the scandal sheet."

Jennings smiled at the reference to scandal sheet. His company subscribed to a monthly newsletter which seemed to have ears in all places. Each month the latest rumours would be aired and new information on old ones fed to the waiting public. The proprietor was a little eccentric but his sources seemed excellent. Several luminaries had stated their intention to sue for libel but had quietly disappeared when the factual evidence of their misdeeds was presented to them. Pansie, who still sometimes yearned for an active involvement in the business, often read the various periodicals that Jennings brought home.

"Can you remember where you saw it?" Jennings asked.

"It must have been several years ago. It was some scam in Florida."

"That's enough business." Huber picked up their glasses and placed them in their hands. "Drink up, it's time to go and play."

They left Leouws and climbed the hill towards Rumpoldis.

***

Two orange juices and three coffees had failed to remove the fur from Jennings' tongue. The golf clubs seemed to weigh a ton as he dragged them from the boot of the taxi. The cloud was descending and laying a thick damp fog over the golf course. Golf on Saturday morning had seemed a good idea in London. The reality was now less attractive. Jennings felt pangs of jealousy for Prince Rainier and his minders who were the only people allowed to ride around the course in a buggy.

The changing room was full of tired eyes and thick heads. The only person showing signs of life was Huber. He was still slapping people on the back and assaulting their eardrums. They had left him in the Tip Top bar at three that morning and, judging from his comportment, he had come straight from there to the golf club.

The golf did little to change Jennings' mood. By the time he reached the long climb to the sixteenth he was wishing that he had taken up bowls. He had seen three balls disappear off the side of the mountain into the oblivion below and amassed a meagre twenty points. Huber had started the process of sobering up after six holes without scoring. They stood on the sixteenth tee both agreeing that what they needed was a drink. Fortunately for both, the last three holes are relatively flat and the potential for cardiac arrest diminished in their minds.

"Five hundred francs a hole on the last three," Huber instructed and proceeded to hit a huge hook. The ball hit the high banking, which ran the length of the hole and leaped back into the centre of the fairway. Fortunately for Jennings the tee is raised. His drive was only inches above the ground until it left the tee, then it was fifty feet high. The ball gambolled up the fairway in what is best described as a long nobble. From there his play deteriorated.

Huber was ensuring that everyone in the bar had a drink *and* was aware that it was being paid for out of the one and a half thousand francs that he had won from Jennings. He had poured down two Ferna Brancas for his hangover and was now in full flow again.

"Did you have a good evening?" Jennings turned and saw Freddie Jarvis behind him.

"Too good," he replied. "You know what Peter is like when he gets the taste. How about you?"

Jarvis smiled. "A few drinks with some old mates. Mind you I've never met Joe Scorsi before. I don't think I would want to deal with him, he is sharp as a razor."

Jennings nodded, wondering why Jarvis had bothered to specially mention Scorsi by name.

By Saturday evening the congress was beginning to flow. Most of the delegates had arrived that day and the bars were overflowing with bonhomie. Once a year acquaintances were renewed with the vigour of long-lost friends. Gaps in appointment schedules were filled and lunches and dinners confirmed.

Jennings always reserved the Saturday night for dinner alone with Pansie. For the rest of the week they would either be guests or hosts, sometimes together sometimes separately. Saturday night was theirs. He had booked a table at Chèvre d'Or in Eze. The restaurant, quite rightly, had a reputation worldwide for its cuisine. For the rendezvous week it was necessary to book many months in advance and confirm several times. Even so some have arrived to find that their existence is denied and their table usurped.

The meal had been a gastronomic extravaganza. Jennings had ordered the *soufflé framboise* for sweet and glanced around the restaurant as Pansie drooled over the phenomenal selection of cheese that was offered. Scorsi caught his attention. He gave the impression of being the host. There were five guests at the table, three of them known to Jennings. They were General Managers of Australian companies in Perth, Adelaide and Melbourne. To the observer it looked as though a deal had been struck. Glasses were being raised and toasts made.

He motioned to Pansie. "What are they doing with a US managing agent? They don't accept direct business from the States."

Pansie glanced discreetly over the array of cheese. "That's a peculiar group," she commented. "Three Australians, a Filipino and an Indonesian. I wonder what their connection is?"

"You know all of them?" he asked.

She nodded and told him that the other two were Chief Executives of their companies.

Jennings' unease grew. He had met Scorsi the previous night and been told he was a simple American agent. Now his connections stretched to Australasia. He wondered where he would appear next.

The answer came on Wednesday. All the companies from Bermuda combined to host a party at the La Mona restaurant near the Sporting Club. The party starts at 11.30 in the morning and carries on until the guests run out of steam. The hosts are easily recognised by the uniform of Bermuda shorts.

Jennings and Pansie arrived just after twelve. They manoeuvred the greeting line and pressed through the throng towards the bar. As the drinks arrived Jennings noticed Scorsi esconced in the far corner with three of the hosts. They were deep in conversation.

A week in Monte Carlo with all expenses paid would be many people's dream. The reality is that, by the Friday, most of the delegates are tired and short-tempered. A combination of too much rich food and drink combined with too little sleep eventually takes its toll.

Their hosts had looked quite relieved when Jennings and

Pansie wished them goodnight after dinner. It was only just after eleven but both felt as though they could sleep for twenty-four hours. They walked along the seafront from the Beach Plaza towards Leouws. The bright moon smiled down from a clear sky. They were both feeling relaxed. The business had been completed and now they would only need to raise one more head of convivial steam when the ritual farewells were wished in the bar at Nice airport.

They went into the casino to have a night cap and a flutter on the tables. Greetings were given and received as they pressed through the throng surrounding the bar. Huber was holding court at one end and waved at them to join them. Drinks arrived and both were slapped lustily on the back.

"Your little greasy friend." Huber's voice was almost a whisper. "I rang our people in New York to see if they knew him. They tell me he used to be tied in with an old friend of yours and may still be."

Jennings said nothing. He knew that Huber would extrapolate the information he had into a much finer story than the original.

"Your erstwhile colleague Cameron Carter and Mr Scorsi were supposed to be very close. The story is that Scorsi was the bankroll behind Pilot and made more money out of the fiasco than even Carter, and he didn't have to go to jail."

"How do you know this, Peter?" Jennings asked.

"There was a lot of information that was not published in the Insurance Commissioner's report. It seems that the Commissioner deemed it unnecessary to detail all his findings. Coincidentally he ended up with a million-dollar condo on a golf course in South Carolina. According to my people Scorsi was a sleeping partner in all of the agencies given out by Pilot. About eighty per cent of the disappearing money was reckoned to go to him."

"I thought Carter had worked the whole deal," Jennings interjected.

"He was the front man. The actual money was put up by a consortium through a bank as nominees. The rumour was that the consortium was actually Scorsi under several pseudonyms."

The reference to consortiums and banks had an uneasy

familiarity for Jennings. "Do you know which bank was involved?" He queried.

"I think it was called Benefit and Asset or something like that."

The more Jennings heard, the less he liked what was being related. "When are you next in London, Peter?" He asked.

Huber told him that it would be at the beginning of November.

"I would like to know more about this. Why don't you come down to my place for the weekend at the end of your trip and we can talk."

Huber nodded in affirmation. "I will get my secretary to organise the details with yours."

Chapter 8

Saturday was only the second night that Carter had been out of the suite for dinner. All week he had been briefing Scorsi on the people he was to meet. Carter was well known to too many of the delegates and, following the Pilot enterprise, had a reputation for skulduggery. If he had attended the meetings with Scorsi rumours would have abounded, some true, some specious, but each a fine story to be related in a hostelry. Any such stories could interfere with their plans.

The suite was comfortable and the room service menu extensive but after three days he began to feel he was back in the penitentiary. By the Wednesday his claustrophobia was becoming manic. He had escaped to Nice where he had the blessed relief of being among people who did not know him.

"Steady up," said Scorsi as Carter ordered their second bottle of Chardonnay. "The guests haven't even arrived."

"Fuck off, Joe," retorted Carter. "I've been stuck in that bloody room for a week. Apart from that, they are not guests, they are partners."

The new bottle arrived at the same time as Jarvis and Wilkes. These two were the lynchpins of the programme that needed to be assembled. The whole concept had been developed in Carter's mind during his time as a guest of the State but to make it work he needed people in the sort of positions that these two occupied. There were other smaller players but his two former colleagues pulled the real strings.

Greetings were exchanged, drinks poured and the social niceties offered and reciprocated. Scorsi would never understand the English. Their constant outward show of civility, even to people they hated, was abhorrent to him. If he disliked someone he felt it to be his bounden duty to ensure that they were made aware of it.

"What went wrong on the Jennings front, Freddie?" Carter asked amicably.

"I'm sorry about that. It was a little unfortunate," replied Jarvis. "Had everything planned but forgot to allow for the bloody cleaner who was fiddling phone calls. We'll make sure next time."

"It may not be such a good idea," commented Carter. "This new deal will extend our resources enough and I don't want too many waves."

"You had better tell Penny that yourself when you see her tomorrow. She wants the bastard and wants him badly." Jarvis' voice revealed both laughter and anxiety.

More wine arrived, eventually followed by food. The four sat in the half-empty restaurant until two the next morning, drinking to their future prosperity and current inebriation.

***

LA MANGA CLUB, SPAIN

Carter's villa on the La Manga Club overlooked the eighth green of the South course. It was set in half an acre of ground. The pool at the back was kidney shaped and one of the few heated pools on the complex. The villa was sumptuously furnished in traditional Spanish style. Each of the four bedrooms had a bathroom en suite with the two largest boasting the addition of a jacuzzi.

Penny Hacker had arrived on the morning flight from Gatwick to Murcia and was unpacking her case when she heard crunching up the gravel driveway. Footsteps went around the side of the house. Looking out of the window she saw a blonde with a figure that many women would kill for. She studied her with a professional eye, thinking that she could charge a rich Arab well over a thousand pounds for a night with this one. Blonde hair and blue eyes were worth an extra five hundred pounds to oil-laden purses.

She watched as the woman walked around the pool. Her hips swayed gracefully from side to side in unison with strawberry blond locks. She tapped on the verandah door. The

98

woman turned, saw Penny and a smile illuminated her face. Penny's valuation doubled when the smile lit the woman's perfectly sculptured features. Penny wondered how a beauty such as this could be satisfied with Cameron Carter.

The tap on the window startled Karen. Whenever she arrived at the villa her first inclination was to survey the grounds to see what the agents had and had not done. She was used to the total efficiency of the American resort managers and the attitude of mañana, which is tradition in Spain, invariably annoyed her. She had decided to get all the rows with the resort managers out of the way before Carter and the other guests arrived. She had forgotten that Penny was arriving that day.

Penny was not what she had been expecting. Karen knew of Penny's past exploits and was expecting someone more butch with craggy features and gnarled hands. Through the glass she saw a woman who exuded confidence. Despite being ten years older than Karen her figure had retained its youthful contours and her eyes sparkled with an enthusiasm for life that was often lost after the teen years.

Penny slid the door open and strolled towards the pool side where Karen stood.

"You must be Karen, I'm Penny." She proffered her hand and Karen reciprocated.

Initially both were in a defensive mode. When two attractive women, who have heard of the attributes of the other from third parties, first meet there is always a natural caution. These two were no exception. By the time they had unpacked and then shared a bottle of *Jumilla Rosada* by the pool the wall between them was beginning to crumble, and a reciprocal liking was developing.

Karen insisted that it was a tradition in the *Villa Carter* to consume Kir Royale whilst changing for the evening.

Penny sat in the jacuzzi letting the warm bubbles re-invigorate her soft white skin. She closed her eyes and imagined sharing the warm waters with Jarvis. Six months previously it would have been King her body craved for. She still felt a passionate rage at King being taken away from her, and despised Jennings for being the person who destroyed him, but this was now tempered by the thought of being in Jarvis' arms.

The room became suddenly silent as the timer switched off the foaming jets that massaged her. She drained the last remnants of the Kir and, reluctantly, decided it was time to return to the real world.

Karen was sitting by the pool taking the last of the day's sun. She wore a tangerine sleeveless silk top which complimented her rich golden tan.

Penny poured herself another Kir. Both were now feeling light-headed and giggly.

"I think that we should eat at the Bistro tonight," Karen said. As it was Penny's first visit to the La Manga Club she agreed.

The evening breeze was warm and the sky glowed orange from the recently departed sun. They strolled up the hill towards the square at Bellaluz. The square was encircled by several restaurants and boutiques. At the end was the Bistro. Several tables were already occupied.

The Bistro exuded holiday relaxation and ambience. Miguel, the owner, sat at the bar surveying his domain. The walls around the bar were a cavalcade of photographs of Miguel with the numerous celebrities who graced this paradise. Stars of stage, screen and sport smiled out from all the walls, each accompanied by the diminutive figure of their host.

"Karen, it is wonderful to see you again. Is Cameron with you?" Miguel recognised Karen as a long-valued customer.

"He is arriving tomorrow," Karen replied. "This is my friend Penny."

Miguel took her hand and flamboyantly kissed it. His eyes showed a hint of recognition although he did not know why this lady's face seemed familiar. Penny retrieved her hand and smiled graciously.

Miguel had bought the restaurant soon after the development of La Manga had started. Before that he had lived for many years in England. He had owned a restaurant in Limpsfied in Surrey. The restaurant had a fine history, having been graced on many occasions by the Churchill family.

Penny and Karen sat at an outside table. The air was warm and water from the fountain danced in the moonlight. They both ordered the speciality of the house, which was a pork fillet with apple and sultanas. A bottle of the house Rosada was produced, poured and drunk. By the end of the meal both were overflowing with good cheer.

"You're not at all what I expected," Karen giggled as the fiery potato liquor arrived with coffee. "Cameron has told me about your exploits and I was expecting someone butch with coarse hands and thick legs."

"I'm sorry to disappoint you," smiled Penny. "I do wear gloves when I'm playing with plastic explosive. Anyway, from what I've heard about you I expected a gangster's moll with thick make-up and a capacious arse." They both chortled with delight.

"Tell me," Karen continued. "What is the story behind this asshole Alan Jennings?"

The drink had the usual effect on Karen. It took away her inhibitions and raised her voice several decibels. Miguel, who was talking to the customers on the next table, pricked up his ears.

As a young man he had played football in the Spanish League. When he went to Surrey he was coming towards the end of his playing days but was still skilful enough to hold his own in intermediate football. He had played, for several years, in the Limpsfield Blues team. The two full backs in the team had been lifelong friends. Allan Jennings and Tony Hacker had been those defenders.

He looked more closely at the cool-looking woman with Karen and slowly recognition dawned. She was Penny Hacker. As a waiter he had learned to listen to different conversations with each ear. Whilst giving his apparent attention to the other table he listened for Penny's reply.

"I intend to get that bastard if it is the last thing I do," she whispered. "Ten years ago I would have been in the top echelons of society and with the man I adored. Jennings shattered all those dreams." Her eyes shone as she fought back the tears that for so long she had suppressed.

Miguel smiled as he passed their table and asked if the meal had been good. He went behind the bar, took out his diary and flicked through the pages. He had last seen Jennings in June that year and remembered asking for his address.

***

The men arrived just after lunch the next day. Karen was opening the second bottle of *Jumilla* when she heard their car pulverising up the gravel drive.

The four disgorged and started unloading cases and golf clubs. Greetings were offered, introductions made, more chairs moved to the poolside and several more corks were removed from bottles.

"So you are the famous Penny Hacker," said Scorsi, his eyes removing her bikini in his mind. "How does someone with your skills come in such great packaging?" The warm sun and cold wine were having their effect on him.

Penny smiled indifferently at him. She was well used to the lack of subtlety in the New Yorker's approach to the opposite sex. In her club the English customers were looking for 'company' whilst the Americans wanted a 'bit of tail'.

Scorsi noted her insouciant response and continued, "It's a pity you fucked up on the Jennings job."

Jarvis stood to interject on Penny's behalf. She held up her hand to stop him.

"I won't fuck up again, I assure you." Her voice was quiet.

Wilkes looked quizzically at Jarvis. He had not known about Jennings' inquiries and was puzzled to hear his name mentioned. He started to speak. Jarvis held his finger to his lips so he stopped.

"Bloody cleaner on the fiddle, no one would have expected that." Scorsi commented. Even through his mild alcohol-induced haze, he realised that Penny was annoyed and not a lady to be tarried with.

Wilkes stood and went into the villa. The talk about a cleaner had brought the realisation of what had happened. This scheme was a nice money earner but violence was not part of his agenda. His logic had allowed him to assess an at worst situation of a couple of years in an open prison for minor financial skulduggery with a huge pot of money in a bank in the Cayman Islands awaiting his release. That scenario had now become life inside as an accessory to murder. He poured three fingers of Scotch and drank it in one gulp.

"Are you alright, Jimmy?" It was Carter's voice behind him.

"What the fuck is going on, Cameron?" he asked. "Did you have anything to do with that bloody explosion in Allan Jennings' office?"

"He was getting too bloody nosey. It was necessary," came the simple reply.

"I don't want any more to do with this. A little bit of money shifting is one thing but murder and I'm out."

"You don't realise who you are dealing with, Jimmy. No one gets out unless it is in a box." The chill in Carter's voice brought a knot of terror into Wilkes' gut.

"You had better come back and put on a holiday face." Carter turned abruptly and left.

***

WOLDINGHAM, SURREY

Charlie Jennings was the Lone Ranger fighting evil with his trusty sidekick when Cross' voice interrupted his fantasy.

"Your mum and dad are home, Charlie," the voice shouted from the window.

He ran around the house to be confronted with the predicament faced by all five-year-olds when their parents return from a trip: who to greet first.

Jennings saw the boy and remembered being faced with the same dilemma as a child. He went to the back of the taxi and busied himself unloading the cases. Charlie, the decision now taken out of his hands, ran to Pansie and hugged her.

"How was Monte Carlo?" Cross asked, as he helped Jennings bring in the cases. Cross was shorter that Jennings, but heavy across the chest and shoulders. He picked up two of the cases as though they were empty.

"You know, Jim, too much food, too much drink and too little sleep," Jennings replied.

Charlie struggled into the house hauling his mother's carry-on case knowing that this bag was most likely to contain the surprise for him.

Jane Cross brought in a tray of coffee while the gifts were being distributed by the returned prodigals. Charlie grabbed the electric racing car and rushed out to the back to become Jim Clarke or Graham Hill.

"I presume that you are both desperate for good English food," Cross said, "and, of course, beer."

"You've booked a table at the Haycutter tonight, I presume," Jennings laughed. "I must be getting old if I'm that predictable."

"You are," Cross smiled. "George and Gwen are coming down as well."

Coffee finished, Pansie went upstairs to unpack, and Jennings to the study to open his post. There was the usual pile of junk mail exhorting him to buy, invest or donate. The rest were bills, other than a letter with a Hong Kong postmark. He turned the envelope over to open it. The back proclaimed 'Sutcliffe Investigations.'

Dear Allan,

Carlos Pedrosa/Sea Shores

As you instructed I have carried out some further investigations into payments to and from the above.

We started by tracing the two payments into SeaShores for which you gave me details. Within a week of their receipt payments approximating the amounts received were made to separate accounts in different names. The payments were made by bank transfers rather than cheques. The accounts were not in the names you advised.

In view of this we investigated the accounts to which the monies were transferred. Both accounts appeared to have a fixed transfer arrangement for all monies over $100 to be transferred to an account at the Banco Centrale in Panama City. The account at Banco Centrale is in the name of a Colombian company named Barrancabermeja Investments.

Based simply on a hunch I instituted a check on all payments made by SeaShores by transfer rather than cheque. I traced 175 accounts to which monies had been transferred. Of those 175 accounts a majority (164) had automatic transfers to Barrancabermeja Investments. The total transferred into this account over the last twelve months is in excess of $40,000,000.

I can only hypothesise that, either Barrancabermeja is a major client of SeaShores, or the payments do not represent insurance claims.

Should you want me to carry out any further studies please advise me.

I enclose my invoice for your attention.

Yours sincerely
Richard Sutcliffe

Jennings re-read the letter several times not really wanting to accept what it was saying. He put the letter in his pocket.

George and Gwen Pinter arrived just after six that evening. They were immediately arrested by young Charlie and taken out to the racetrack he had built that afternoon on the patio. Pinter joined in with the enthusiasm of a seven-year-old whilst Gwen watched. She was of the old school when boys were boys and girls were girls. Motor racing, even in miniature, was not the sport for ladies. Seven laps and twelve crashes later they extricated themselves.

The baby-sitter arrived in Jack Martin's people carrier. She sat regularly for Jennings and Pansie. She wished them a nice evening as she shooed them out of the door and watched as the six clambered into the Espace.

"Haycutter, I presume, Allan," Martin said cheerily.

The ladies had settled at a table in a corner of the bar of the Haycutter while the men attended to the important business of obtaining beverages. The bar was particularly busy that night and service a little slow.

Jennings gave Cross and Pinter the letter to read while he tried to attract the attention of the barmaid. Eventually the drinks arrived and were passed among the gathering.

"What do you think?" Jennings asked.

"Cocaine," Cross answered simply.

"It must be," Pinter interjected. "Mafia money starts in an insurance company in Grand Cayman and ends up in a Colombian investment company. What else could it be?"

Jennings nodded in affirmation. When he read Sutcliffe's letter he had known this was the answer but wanted not to believe it. The thought of his own company being used to launder money for this contemptible trade made him sick in the stomach.

"What do I do now?" It was as much a cry for help as a genuine inquiry.

"Give me and Jim a copy of that letter," Pinter replied. "We both have connections and will see what we can find out. Leave it at that for now and let's go and see the ladies and talk about pleasant things." The subject was closed for the rest of the evening.

Jennings lay that night with his voluptuous wife in his arms. She felt the tension in him and asked why. The story spilled from his lips. Dealing in the powder of death was repugnant to Jennings.

Three years before, one of his young brokers had been found dead in a gutter in East London. He had been a hard worker with a big future. He had first tried cocaine at a party thinking that one sniff could not harm him. Within a year he was injecting the filth into his veins. First he lost his dignity followed by his pride, his wife and family and eventually his life.

Pansie listened in horror as the tale emerged. She herself had seen the abomination of addiction in the Far East.

"What are you going to do?" she whispered.

"I've got to stop it somehow," he replied. "But it isn't just us that are being used. Richard says that $40,000,000 has gone through Pedrosa. Only $11,000,000 of that is through us."

She held him close. "Don't take any risks. I love you and don't want to lose you." Her eyes filled with tears.

***

LA MANGA, SPAIN

The big American arrived on an Iberia flight at Alicante on the Wednesday.

Wilkes was returning to London. Carter had delivered him to Murcia Airport and then driven on to Alicante. There had been little conversation on the hour's drive back to La Manga. The American had simply confirmed to Carter that he was to introduce him as Tom Smith.

He recognised Penny as soon as they were introduced. Four years ago there had been a problem with one of the attachés at the embassy in London. When he drank he talked too much and he drank more than he should. She had been given the contract and performed it beyond their expectations. Somehow she had arranged that the attaché was found drowned in his own vomit after a night's drinking. The finding of accidental death was both pleasing and unexpected.

Only Smith noticed the hint of recognition in her eyes.

The party dined that evening at La Finca. Carter picked the restaurant knowing that their plank steak would be large enough to assuage an American's need for huge amounts of red meat.

Smith seemed uncomfortable in the crowded restaurant. He didn't like being in or being seen with crowds.

"Don't worry, Tom," Carter spoke placatingly. "Nobody notices anything here. They even ignore Sevy Ballesteros." The last statement was a little stretching of the facts. The Ballesteros brothers were often seen on the complex. Whilst they undoubtedly attracted the attention of the other visitors it was invariably from a respectful distance. The comment, however, had the desired effect of relaxing Smith.

By the time the peaches in cognac were served Smith had consumed seven dry martinis and was joining in the revelry. He smiled at Penny. "Do you still have the club?" he asked. She nodded.

"Did you know each other before today?" Jarvis asked, a little puzzled.

"We've done a little business together in the past," Penny answered demurely. Jarvis decided to change the topic.

She stood, naked, before the full-length mirror. Her body belied her near forty years. The breasts were still firm and pointed, the stomach smooth and flat. Her thighs had grown fuller with the years but this was an improvement. At school one of her nicknames had been ostrich because of her long but less than shapely legs.

He came behind her, his erection already becoming distended. His arms enclosed her and he cupped her breasts in his hands. "I know there were others before me," he whispered. "But I hate to meet them."

She turned and slid her hands inside his thighs. "My business with Tom was not sex," she smiled and slowly dropped to her knees. Her tongue meandered across and down his chest and naval. He felt his member being encompassed by her soft lips and her tongue caressing him.

She lay on the bed as his lips explored her body, her nipples, her naval and then her womanhood nestling among its triangle of soft pubic hair. She felt her orgasm rising and squeezed his scrotum. They joined together and pleasure and pain interfused in a rising surge of passion. Her fingers dug deep into his back as the fountain of her ardour flooded its rapture through her body.

"I'm jealous of anyone who's been with you," he sighed, holding her tightly in his arms.

She stroked his hair and whispered, "You're the only one I want now."

"What about Smith?"

"That wasn't sex, he was with the CIA and needed a little cleaning up done." She playfully slapped his buttocks.

Jarvis stiffened. "He was with who!" he exclaimed. "What's his connection with Carter and Scorsi?"

"I don't know, my darling, but I think you should find out."

***

"Is there some sort of shit that you are not telling me about?" Smith slapped the table.

Penny and Karen had driven to Los Belones to do some shopping and the other four sat around the table by the pool.

"There is no shit," replied Scorsi. "What's your problem?"

"Penny Hacker, that's the problem. Who are you having hit and why?"

"That's private and nothing to do with our deal," Carter snapped.

"It had fucking better be," snarled Smith. "I need total security on this and any lapse won't be alive very long."

"Don't worry." Scorsi wanted to smooth out the discord. "The deal is virtually in place. All we need is the numbers and where you want it put. Our operation is ready to run."

"I want to test it first before we get into real hard-ball." Smith's doubts still nagged at him. "I want to shift $10,000,000 from South Africa to France. How do I do it?"

Carter looked at Jarvis. "Any ideas?"

"South Africa to Europe is too direct," Jarvis mused. "Israel, West Bank," he exclaimed. "Agency in South Africa underwriting for an Israeli company. Reinsure it into London, Brussels or even Bermuda and then on to France or a French captive."

"But the claims would be going the wrong way," Carter commented.

"Who said anything about claims. We set up a book of Export Credit Guarantees or other suretyships. They pay huge premiums and don't have many claims. We move the money in underwriting profits not losses. That way everybody's happy. People only scrutinise the unprofitable. If you make money they kiss your arse."

"That seems fine but who the fuck wants shekels?" Smith broke in.

"You don't know the business," Carter replied contemptuously. "Nobody uses the shekel, it's too unstable. All the business out of Israel is transacted in dollars. We convert the rands to dollars before it leaves South Africa and then run the whole process in dollars until the end user puts it into francs or whatever currency takes their fancy."

Smith realised that he would have to trust these people sometime. Grudgingly he said, "Well, you had better set it up and report to me when you can start moving."

"The front is easy but I have to have an end user in France. It's up to you to tell us who."

Smith and Scorsi left on the Friday.

The four remaining were dining in Los Belones that night.

"Don't worry about Allan Jennings," Penny said to Carter, "I will make sure that he ceases to be a problem soon."

"I think we should let that ride for a while," Carter replied. "He seems to have gone quiet and I don't want any waves until this deal is up and running." Penny looked disappointed.

"Don't worry," Carter smiled. "He's yours but just wait."

***

The postmark on the letter was Los Belones. Jennings guessed it was from La Quinta Club at La Manga. He had bought four weeks' membership at the club when it was being developed. For twenty thousand and an annual fee he had his own villa for four weeks a year and as a sweetener he had founder membership of the golf club. He opened the envelope and retrieved its contents. It was not from La Quinta. The heading on the paper was La Bistro.

Dear Allan,

I am writing to you as you could be interested in a conversation I heard in the restaurant last week.

One of my regulars is called Cameron Carter who owns a villa near the south course. Last week his girl friend Karen was in with an old friend of ours. At first I did not recognise her but when your name was brought up I realised it was Penny Hacker.

When your name was mentioned she told Karen that she intended to get that bastard if it was the last thing she did. I presumed that the bastard was you as it is an apt description.

I remembered reading about the problem at your wedding in the newspaper reports of her trial, and thought you should know that she still appears to carry considerable malice against you.

I hope you don't think I am being too morbid but I hope you will be careful. You're a good customer and my waiters would hate to lose your tips.

I look forward to seeing you and Pansie when you are next down here.

Sincerely yours
Miguel

Jennings passed the letter to Pansie.
"What is going on?" she asked.
"I don't know, but I am going to find out."

***

CORBY MANNING'S OFFICE

It was near the end of the Friday Directors coffee meeting when a nearly forgotten comment suddenly had a meaning. The business had finished and the usual banter was being exchanged whilst the dregs of the coffee were consumed.

"Womaniser," said Collins. "If that was an Olympic sport Freddie Jarvis would be odds on for the gold medal."

Collins' comments in the Lime Club the day of the bomb sprang into Jennings' brain. "He was bringing in this really classy lady through the back entrance. Probably had a bit of nookie in the office. Blond hair, green eyes and legs a mile long."

Jennings asked Collins to stay when the meeting finished.

"This conversation is strictly between you and I," Jennings began. "Do you remember telling me about a woman with Freddie the night before the explosion?"

"I remember her," he replied. "Bloody gorgeous piece. I'd kill to get her into the sack. Why do you ask?"

"I can't tell you at the moment, but could you recognise her again?"

Collins nodded. "What is all this about Allan? Has she got anything to do with the bomb?"

"I don't know. It's maybe just a wild supposition on my part. Leave it for now but this is strictly between the pair of us."

Collins left the room even more convinced that all producers were barking mad.

Jennings was signing the late post when a booming voice reverberated around his outer office. "Is the tall ugly one in?"

Mary Cantor smiled graciously. "He is expecting you Mr Huber. Go straight in."

Huber bounced into Jennings' office, grasped his hand and shook it vigorously. "Come on, sign the rest of the bloody post and you can buy me a drink on the way home."

Jennings resigned himself to the fact that he and Pansie were in for a boisterous weekend. The post was signed and returned to Mary. They exited stage left from the office in the direction of the Ship Inn. Thirty minutes and three pints of Theakston's best bitter later, they headed across London Bridge in the direction of a train. At the station Huber made straight for the off licence and demanded a six-pack of Hurliman and the same of Bass.

Jennings' usual travelling companions welcomed the addition of Huber to their number and the journey became a party.

Pansie heard Huber expressing his grateful thanks to the taxi driver as he alighted. She opened the door and was engulfed in a bear hug.

"You must be fed up with him by now. Run away with me."

Pansie extricated herself and Huber turned his attention to Charlie. He had been waiting, excitedly, since returning from school that afternoon. Whenever Uncle Peter arrived he was always accompanied by several goodies for the young Jennings.

"Young Charlie," cried Huber lifting him in one arm and carrying him into the lounge. "Let's see if there is something in my bag for you."

The boy's eyes lit up as he looked at the bright red car pictured on the box.

"Now that is a real car," Huber whispered as Charlie opened the box. "Tomorrow we can have a race."

The boy extricated the remote control, placed the model Ferrari on the carpet and set it in motion. The McLaren his parents had bought from Monte Carlo was now at the back of his grid.

Huber produced Chanel perfume and Frigor chocolates for Pansie and a box of John Player Specials for Jennings. The formalities now over, beer was produced and consumed.

Pansie, having worked for Huber for several years, was aware of his colossal appetites and had planned accordingly. Dinner was traditional English steak and kidney pudding with mashed potatoes, followed by treacle tart with rivers of custard. The babysitter arrived just before the taxi to transport them to the Haycutter.

Several of the locals greeted Huber as he breezed into the bar. He was genuinely liked and had a delightful habit of buying numerous rounds of drinks. To add to those attributes he was also a pathetic player of both darts and shove halfpenny *and* insisted on playing for money. By ten that evening the whole bar was swinging with Huber leading the orchestra.

At seven the following morning Jennings was drinking steaming black coffee in a vain attempt to remove the coating from his tongue. Cross and his wife Jane were due to arrive before eight and a tee time had been booked for the three men at nine.

Huber bounced into the kitchen. He had been awake for over an hour. Charlie followed him into the kitchen, his face bright with triumph.

"He's too good for me," laughed Huber. "I had the Ferrari and he beat me in the McLaren then I had the McLaren and he beat me with the Ferrari. You've got a budding Fangio on your hands here, Allan." He poured a coffee and sat opposite Jennings.

"You have a problem you want to talk about?" he enquired.

Jennings nodded. "Wait until Jim arrives, he may have some more information. We can have a chat after I've taken money off you at the golf club."

Cross arrived just before eight. He had first met Huber at Jennings' wedding and had never forgotten his dumbfounded look as he took the syringe from Penny Hacker's hand.

Huber clapped him on the back, knocking half the wind from his lungs, and engulfed Jane in a convivial greeting.

The clubs were loaded into Cross' Daimler Sovereign and the three men left for the golf club.

The course was a picture that no artist could capture. The trees that lined the fairways were every hue from mahogany to golden. The plethora of autumn colours danced gently as the breeze massaged the limbs of the trees. Huber seemed transfixed by the spectacle. His first drive was perfectly positioned among the trees to enable him to take a closer look.

All three were naturally competitive and the £100 a corner wager was well worth fighting for. They stood on the eighteenth, still with all to play for. Huber reduced the four hundred and twenty yard hole to a drive, a nine iron and a putt. Neither Cross nor Jennings could match him.

At Huber's insistence the bet was not settled until they were in the bar. "I want an audience when I collect your money," he said roaring with glee.

Once he had satisfied himself that all the members in the bar knew whose money was paying for the round, Huber brought the drinks across to the table. Cross and Jennings were trying to appear inconspicuous with little success.

"What is this little problem you have?" Huber asked.

"I suspect, and Jim agrees with me, that my company is being used to launder drugs money," Jennings replied sombrely. "I also think that we are not the only ones involved."

Jennings related the tale of Comet and his suspicions about the ownership. He showed Huber the letter from Sutcliffe.

"And, possibly, right in the middle of the whole shooting match is Cameron Carter and that greasy bastard Scorsi," Jennings concluded.

Huber was silent for a moment. "How can I help?"

"When you were in Bermuda you told me of several captive companies that were only interested in fronting arrangements which were being shot into London. Can you tell me who they were?"

Huber nodded. "I have them in my briefcase. Do you think that they are involved?"

Jennings shrugged his shoulders. "You tell me. I'm beginning to get paranoid about everything. There was an offer from Jimmy Wilkes that Heinrich showed me in Hong Kong. Again it was a fronting deal with business coming out of Thailand and ending up in Bermuda. The deal looked kosher but was it?"

"Armitage?" Huber asked. Jennings nodded.

"Heinrich sent that to me. I told him to accept it. Now you are beginning to worry me."

"What I would like, Peter, is for you to let me have the details of the Bermuda companies and anything else you have on fronting deals that you've done or had offered."

Chapter 9

Collins studied the photographs. "She's younger in these and not as suave, but that's the woman. How do you know her?"

Jennings said nothing. The photographs he had shown were old pictures of Tony and Penny Hacker. He had hoped that the woman with Jarvis was not Penny but now he knew she was. He had always looked upon Jarvis as a friend. Was he actually an enemy?

"She was married to an old friend of mine," he answered. "I am going to need your help, Geoff and it will have to be in strictest confidence between us."

Collins looked quizzically at him. "You are beginning to sound like James Bond."

"The situation is," Jennings continued. "I have my suspicions that some of the business that Freddie produces may not be what it seems. What I need is details of all Freddie's accounts where there is a front for Lloyds or a company and where it is then reinsured on to an overseas market. I want everything for the last three years."

"That's a tall order. I'll get one of the girls to start as soon as possible." Collins was used to getting odd requests from Jennings and the other producers. He had given up asking why figures were needed as usually the reason, to his mind, was incongruous.

"I'm sorry Geoff, I want you to do it. I don't want anyone else in the company to know they are being produced." Jennings' tone left no room for argument.

"How soon do you need this?"

"I'll be in the States for the next ten days. Could you have it ready for when I return?" Collins realised it was an order not a request.

***

The air conditioning in the limousine came as a blessed relief. He had arrived in Miami just after lunchtime and the humidity cohered to him like damp cling-film. The driver met him in the arrivals lobby and escorted him to the car. As they left the cooled building the hot damp air had engulfed him. He poured himself an ice-cold beer from the cocktail cabinet and settled back in the soft leather seat. His first stop on the way to the hotel, would be 1812 Barton Boulevard.

Before leaving London he had looked through the claims files for the SeaShores rental yard account. He had noted the five largest and intended to look at each one. Barton Boulevard was to be the first.

The car glided to a halt in front of a western-design house set back from the road. Jennings alighted and was again saturated by the humidity. The doorbell chimed and an elderly distinguished man answered.

"Good afternoon," Jennings said politely. "I am sorry to trouble you but I understand that you are the owner of Phoenix Trailer Rentals."

"I'm afraid you have the wrong person," replied the stranger. "I have never heard of Phoenix Trailer Rentals."

"I'm sorry." Jennings pointedly studied the file of paper in his hand. "Are you Mr Colin Michaelson?"

"Afraid not, young man," was the affable reply.

"Could he have lived here before you, sir?"

"I had this place built twenty-five years ago. Only me and my family have lived here." An edge of annoyance crept into the man's voice.

Jennings closed the file. "I am terribly sorry to have troubled you. Someone in my office has given me the wrong information." Jennings used his best English accent and the affability returned to the stranger's face.

"Don't worry, young man, happens to all of us." Saying that he closed the door.

Jennings sat in the hotel room, the file open on his lap. He read Jarvis' memo.

I discussed the claim with Paul who expressed surprise that the address was given as above. The property above is the

116

private residence of the owner of the rental company and it appears that this has been used instead of that of the yard which is located on the other side of Miami.

The bald statement was a lie. The owner knew nothing of Phoenix Trailer Rentals. Neither the telephone directory or the telephone company could shed any light on the existence of the company. It seemed that it had never existed.

The following morning Jennings took a taxi to the other side of the city. The address turned out to be a truck rental yard.

A receptionist with long legs and a short skirt greeted him as he entered the office. He asked to see the proprietor in his best British Broadcasting Corporation accent and was shown into an office.

"I am sorry to trouble you, Mr Ellery," he started. "I am instructed by Lloyds of London relating to the fire at these premises last year."

"What have Lloyds of London got to do with it?" Ellery retorted. "I was insured with South East Property and Casualty."

Jennings was a little taken aback by this revelation. He regained his composure and continued. "I know that sir, but Lloyds reinsured part of the risk. I have simply been asked to confirm the actual settlement value of your claim."

"South East paid me just over $700,000. Is that what you want to know?"

Jennings smiled, thanked Ellery graciously and left.

He opened the file in the taxi. Merriman Adjusting had confirmed the claim at $1,800,000 and Lloyds and Comet had settled on that basis to SeaShores. "The plot thickens," mused Jennings. Two nights later he flew to Jacksonville.

The buildings at Ponte Vedra were spruce and new. The plant was neatly laid out at the back of the premises in soldierly rows. The office was bright and communicated an air of quiet efficiency. The owner, as Pansie had described him, was young and handsome. He greeted Jennings slightly defensively. Jennings explained he was from London and simply confirming some details of the claim.

"I have to say that I was delighted with the way the South East acted," the young man said, appearing relieved. "I had a

117

cheque for $800,000 within three weeks and the balance of $125,000 a month later. There was practically no interruption to my business."

"Were there any payments to the others who stored equipment here?" Jennings asked.

"Don't do it," came the reply. "I've only enough room for my own plant."

Jennings sat in the taxi, the document open in front of him. The report showed the insurer to be SeaShores and the claim paid was $2,800,000. Both Lloyds and Comet had settled.

"Here we are, Mac."Tthe taxi driver's voice interrupted his thoughts. "920 Parkinson."

The taxi was stopped outside a roadside diner. The billboard proclaimed, 'Sam's Diner.'

"Are you sure this is 920?" Jennings queried.

"Of course I am." The driver's voice hinted at an element of pique. "I've been coming here since I was a boy."

"Do you know if there is a truck rental yard on this road?"

"Never seen one," came the reply.

Jennings asked him to return to the hotel.

The following day Jennings hired a car and drove to Orlando. The address that should have been a rental yard was a rather elderly supermarket.

***

The giant jet engines droned in his ears. The stewardesses scurried up and down replenishing drinks. The flight was unusually full for midweek.

Jennings thumbed through his notes. The bare figures stared at him from the pad in front of him. SeaShores had received over $9,000,000 for five claims. Three of the locations did not even exist and the other two were not insured by SeaShores. All had full loss reports from Merriman Adjusting and appeared to be valid claims. None were. He closed the file and returned it to his briefcase, not really knowing what his next step should be.

***

Carter paced the room, annoyed by the lateness of his appointment. Smith had arranged to meet at three and the time was now nearly four. He picked up the telephone and was about to dial when there was a rapping at the door.

Smith strode in, offering no apology. He sat, opened his attaché case and proffered a sheet of paper. "There is your end user," he said. "Have you set up the rest of the deal?"

Carter nodded confirmation and took the paper. "Can we use their captive company?" He asked.

"As long as the money gets to where it should, do what the fuck you like." Smith did not like Carter or his associates, but needs must. He disliked like using ex-cons and Mafioso but had been forced into the situation. This first transaction would test how good their system was and if it went wrong the shit would hit another fan rather than his.

"Is there anything else?" Carter asked.

"You have all the details. All I want now is for $10,000,000 to be in those assholes' hands within six months." Smith closed his case and left.

Carter looked at his watch. It was now gone nine in the evening in London. He dialled Jarvis' home number. The line buzzed three times before Carol Jarvis answered.

"I am sorry, Cameron, he is out in London tonight. He's stopping at the company's flat, but won't be there until late. I think it is one of those charity boxing dinners."

Carter thanked her, hung up and cursed. The deal was almost complete. An agent was set up in Cape town and the deal signed with Sharom in the West Bank occupied territories. The re-insurances in London were in place but subject to further reinsurance being set up for them. He now had the means to put that in place and Freddie was out on the piss.

He telephoned the More than a Penny for 'em club and asked for Penny.

"Is Freddie coming round for a rumble tonight?" He asked.

"If you mean is Freddie visiting me tonight, the answer is yes," she replied with a chuckle.

"Will you ask him to ring me." He gave the telephone

number of the Hotel.

"I'll make sure he rings when you are rumbling with Karen."

Carter replaced the receiver smiling. His mind's eye could see Karen's lissome body, and he wished he had not left her in Hilton Head. He poured himself a drink and flicked on the television.

***

Jarvis and his guests were a little the worse for wear when they arrived at Penny's club. The boxing evening at the Press Centre had been its usual success.

The concept of these evenings is to set dining tables around a boxing ring. These would then be populated by overly rich business men from the city resplendent in dinner jackets and multi-coloured bow ties. They would be supplied with food and excessive alcohol prior to the commencement of the boxing. Once the booze has taken effect raffle tickets would be sold at inordinately expensive prices and various items would be auctioned for five times their value.

The boxing would usually be a match between juniors who would put heart and soul into their endeavours. The watching throng will place substantial bets among themselves on the result of each fight. This resulted in the audience vociferously baying for the blood of the young boxer who did not carry their money.

Though the behaviour was somewhat divergent from the original thoughts of the Marquis of Queensbury, a substantial amount of money was invariably raised for a worthy cause.

Jarvis' party disappeared downstairs to further deplete the assets of their host. Jarvis told one of his minions to look after the guests and joined Penny at the bar. She smiled at him and her body shivered knowing that later its desires would be assuaged.

"Cameron wants you to ring him," she said, passing him the number. He kissed her and whispered, "I'll only be a minute. Can I use your flat?"

"The company is Mutuelle Avionique in Amiens," Carter read from Smith's note. "They have a captive in Jersey who you can use. The man to speak to is Thierry Mersonne."

Jarvis jotted the names down. "When can the South Africans

start to send premium?"

"As soon as you set it up. Just do it as quickly as possible and let me know." The line went dead.

He saw her reflection in the mirror. He had not heard her open the door. The silk negligee clung to her breasts and her dark brown nipples pouted through the diaphanous material. Her hands were soft as they slipped the clothes from his body. The silk slid from her shoulders. Her body was a golden tan except the delicate white of her breast and loins, which the bikini had protected from the rays of the Spanish sun.

***

The file was marked, 'Private and Confidential for addressee only'. Jennings recognised Collins' writing.

The report listed over twenty facilities that had been placed by Jarvis. Jennings scanned through the list noting the names that recurred among the reinsurers and original producers. Hart Davies figured prominently as did SeaShores, Comet, Larry Payne, Kieron O'Sullivan and Jack Green. The name Armitage Reinsurance appeared three times. There was an obvious pattern but only to someone who knew the model.

Other companies appeared more than once. There were two in the Turks and Caicos Islands and three in Bermuda. It was, however, the last entry that intrigued Jennings. All the other contracts originated in the USA and connected through London to a tax haven in the sun. The last seemed to emanate from Israel to a French-owned company in Jersey. The interest reinsured was suretyship, which meant that Lloyds did not appear, as they were unable to accept such business. The account was being processed through Corporate Credit and Surety who were a small specialist company. Jennings wondered whether this was a genuine deal. None of the others had any involvement in either Israel or the tiny island in the English Channel.

He put the folder in his briefcase and pressed the buzzer on his intercom.

"Yes, Mr Jennings," Mary answered jovially.

"Will you get me Michael Mason?"

Sir Michael Mason was the Chairman of Bannister Ellis. He

was one of the old school of London Market brokers. He had started in the market in the mid 1950s as a filing clerk and was one of the few people in the market that Jennings truly respected and trusted.

The intercom buzzed and Mary cheeped, "Sir Michael for you."

"Allan, how are you?" Mason's deep voice reflected the genuine pleasure of speaking to a friend. "Long time, no see."

"That's why I am phoning you, Michael. It's much too long since we had a bite of lunch. I wondered if you would like to sample the fare of our new chef."

Mason replied that he would be delighted and lunch was arranged for the next week. Jennings then rang Cross and Pinter and invited them for the weekend.

***

The sky was a watery grey and the windows were speckled with a fine drizzle. Jennings was in the study reading Collins' report. His focus was interrupted by the singing of the door bell.

"Bloody November, I hate it," Pinter's voice echoed from the hall. Jennings put the file away and went to greet his old friends.

Charlie rushed down the stairs and jumped into Pinter's arms crying, "Uncle George." Jennings looked on, remembering feeling the same excitement as a boy at the arrival of Uncle George. Pinter was now well in his sixties but still retained the infectious enthusiasm of youth.

"I suppose you will tell me what favour you want sometime." Pinter turned to Jennings and spoke over the boy's shoulder.

Jennings protested only to be stopped. "I know you want something. I've known you since you were Charlie's age and can still read you like a bloody book," Pinter laughed boisterously.

Jennings gave up thoughts of declaring innocence and said, "Later when Jim and Jane arrive."

Pansie ushered them into the lounge and Jennings produced drinks. The sound of the Daimler pulping the gravel drive indicated that Cross had arrived. The door was opened, more greetings exchanged and extra drinks produced.

"I think these three want to play silly men's games." Gwen had no time for the little schemes that seemed to fascinate the male of the species. She found all the little intrigues that her husband was involved in a trifle tiresome. "Shall we girls take Charlie out for lunch?"

The question was actually an instruction. Both Pansie and Jane were somewhat peeved but bowed to the inevitable out of respect for Gwen. They collected the boy and piled into Jennings' Jaguar.

The ministry driver sat quietly in the Daimler until the three men left the house. He then jumped out and opened the doors for Cross and his guests. The car and driver were one of the fringe benefits that Cross received due to his exalted position in the security services.

They ordered drinks and lunch and settled at a quiet table in the corner of the bar of the Haycutter.

"Shall I go first?" Cross started. The others agreed.

"I have had a strange reaction from my connections in the States." he began. "I was given full chapter and verse on the Cirrolla, Umbari and Carpessa families. When I asked about Scorsi, Carter and Pedrosa I drew a virtual blank. I was told that Scorsi used to be connected with the Mafia but they did not think he was now active. They said Carter was involved with an insurance scam, had done his time and was now living on the results of his crimes. They also said that there was no connection between the two."

"What about Pedrosa?" Jennings interrupted.

"He's a pillar of the bloody community, if you believe what I was told."

"Who's your contact?" Pinter asked.

"Tom O'Connell," was the response.

"You can't go a lot higher than number two at the CIA," mused Pinter.

Jennings shook his head, unable to believe what he was hearing. "I just don't believe what you're being told."

"Oh neither do I," smiled Cross. "The way Tom gave me the information was as though he was quoting from a book. He knows much more but is under orders not to co-operate. MI5 and

CIA do not always see eye to eye in certain areas."

"That actually fits in with what I've been told," Pinter interjected. "An old friend of mine, who was with OSS when I was with Special Operations, is now quite high in the FBI. He tried to access the files for Carter and Scorsi and found everything, apart from the basic information, classified at the top security level. He runs all the administration for the southern states but was barred from the computer system."

"Did you get anything else, George?" Cross asked.

"A couple of other sources had Scorsi still active as a money man for several of the big families. They also thought that he was the actual finance behind Carter but didn't know for certain."

"Anything on Pedrosa?" Jennings queried.

"Only suspicion. He, apparently, is so bloody clean he can't be true. No records of him until four years ago when he appeared in Miami as an insurance expert."

"At least I have some factual information," Jennings sighed. "I know that of the five claims I looked at, three were nonexistent and the other two were not insured by Pedrosa."

"I presume you can pass that snippet on to your reinsurers and watch the shit hit the fan," Pinter smiled.

"I am not sure that it will. I have a suspicion that Freddie Jarvis and those three bastards from Lloyds are in on the deal. If they are and I let them know what we're doing they'll bury the whole thing."

"What makes you think that they are in on it?" Pinter queried.

"Only that the night before the explosion in my office Jarvis was entertaining an attractive woman in his office. Her name was Penny Hacker."

Pinter whistled through teeth. "Do you think she planted the bomb?"

Jennings shrugged. "It's a hell of a coincidence if she didn't, and if she did Carter would have been the only one to know about her special skills. That ties Carter in with Jarvis."

"What about the Lloyds people?" Cross wondered whether Jennings was beginning to see a conspiracy around every corner.

"They got very upset when I started to question Comet as a

company. I was virtually told to keep my nose out or lose all their business."

"Do you think that the Hacker woman will try again?" Pinter's voice reflected his anxiety.

Jennings shrugged and replied, "Probably, based on her past record."

"What about the police, have you told them?"

"What can I tell them?" Jennings' frustration was reflected in his tone. "All we know is that she was there. There's no other proof connecting her with the explosion. If Jarvis is part of it he will just say they were in the office bonking. Apart from that, do we want to show our hand at the present?"

They finished their meal under a pall of gloom. They had some information, which indicated that a money laundering operation was being channelled through Lloyds but no proof. They would have to get substantiation from somewhere, but how? The emergence of a skilful assassin in the background complicated everything even further.

They left the Haycutter, their mood still dispirited, and drove to Jennings' home. Jennings showed them the list of reinsurances Collins had produced.

"What's their involvement?" Cross asked, pointing to Mutuelle Avionique.

"I don't know," Jennings replied. "That deal seems to be slightly different from the rest but the overall design of the package is the same. Why do you ask?"

"Mutuelle Avionique produce guidance systems for the French space industry. They are one of the leaders in the technology." Cross seemed surprised to see their name.

Jennings shrugged. "I don't think that they are part of the whole, it's probably just there by coincidence. I asked Collins to set fixed parameters for the report. There are bound to be one or two that are pukka reinsurance deals. I was going to send this lot to Richard Sutcliffe to see if he could get some more background, which would sort out the wheat from the chaff."

"I think we need some help." Cross knew that the three could not control this by themselves. "I think you will find that John Hubbard is at a loose end. He's just finished a little job for me."

Pinter smiled. "So it was the big hairy bastard who got Hans Graf out of East Berlin for you, was it?" The story of the physicist's defection from East Germany had made all the front pages.

"Did I say that?" Cross winked. He turned to Jennings, "Shall I contact him?"

"If he can help, yes," was the reply.

The sound of mirthful laughter spilled in from outside. The three wives and Charlie burst into the room. They were laden with bags, all emblazoned with designer labels. Charlie sported a new baseball cap which declared, 'Liverpool, Up the reds.'

Jennings picked the boy up and said, "Arsenal are the best." He took the cap and, playfully, threw it across the room, much to the Charlie's chagrin. The boy struggled from his arms shouting, "Arsenal are rubbish," and retrieved his headgear.

***

LE HAVRE, FRANCE

The rain cut through his clothing driven by the fierce wind. On the rusty deck the Vietnamese hands panted as they stowed the heavy wooden cases. Mersonne looked on from the dockside, the wind tearing tears from his eyes. Even the heavy anorak could not hide his lack of physical stature. He watched with noticeable disdain as the skipper half-stumbled down the gangplank, his breath reeking of cheap cognac.

"Is everything to your satisfaction, monsieur?"

Mersonne watched as the last of the crates were lashed down and took the envelope from his pocket. "Everything is fine," he answered, passing the envelope.

Martinez took the package, checked its contents and stuffed it inside his duffle coat. "Au revoir, monsieur. Perhaps we do business again." He lumbered up the gangway and started shouting at the crew. Moorings were cast off and black acrid smoke belched from the engine's exhaust. The *MV Astrid* eased away from its moorings.

Mersonne watched as the grimy ship slid out of Le Havre. He pulled the collar of his coat tight around his neck as he walked back to the Citroen. He watched the *Astrid* lurch through the waves and said quietly to himself, "Perhaps we will *not* do business again, monseiur."

The pilot had disembarked and the course was set. Martinez sat in his cabin, glass in hand. The *MV Astrid* was back earning money for her owner.

She was registered in Panama but now did little work in her home waters. Her misdemeanours were too well known by the coastguards of the Pacific coastline.

Martinez had purchased her ten years before, with thoughts of making his fortune, only to find her too small for high-earning legitimate cargos and too big for the smaller, less honest kind. He had scraped a living until he discovered a highly profitable trade in white powder from Medellin which needed discreet transportation to Los Angeles, Miami and places north.

It was two years before he had his first encounter with the authorities. It was night and they were two miles off the coast in the Gulf of Santa Catalina. Out of, what seemed, nowhere the spotlights appeared accompanied by the throbbing of a high powered diesel. Fortunately for him, Martinez was on the bridge when the coastguard materialised. The illicit cargo was ditched before the *MV Astrid* was boarded. From that day, however, the ship was an automatic target for the forces of law and order.

It was inevitable that Martinez and the cocaine trade would part company. The sellers were intrinsically unhappy on the occasions that their product was fed to the fish, and Martinez knew that their ways of expressing displeasure could be uncommonly distressful. He had looked for other cargos.

This cargo was one of the best. He was having a nice trip to Madagascar with heavy machinery aboard plus a very profitable meeting off Mozambique for which he had received a bonus of 500,000 francs. He patted the envelope and poured another large cognac.

***

Mersonne threw his sodden coat on to his visitor's chair. It was nine in the evening and the office was empty and in darkness. He picked up the phone and dialled. The earphone

127

whined the single rings particular to ITT. A voice answered giving the number.

"The cargo is in transit," Mersonne stated and replaced the receiver.

***

Michael Mason arrived in Jennings' office just before one. The two greeted each other with genuine pleasure. Their two companies were competitors in virtually every field but they separated business rivalry from friendship.

The waiter had already poured Jennings beer when they entered the Chairman's private dining room. Mason asked for the same.

"Is no one joining us?" Mason asked, noticing the table was set for two.

"No," Jennings responded, "I want to have a private chat."

"Very intriguing," Mason smiled.

The meal was served. Smoked salmon mousse followed by beef Wellington. The conversation had been of the market, football and anything else which interested both. The discussion was easy and relaxed. Mason knew that the real reason for the lunch would be raised in Jennings' own time.

Once the cheese board had been dispatched and coffee and a decanter of vintage port deposited on the table, Jennings elected the time to be right.

"The reason I asked you here, Michael, is that I have seen one or two contracts we handle that may not be what they seem." Jennings chose his words carefully.

"What, some sort of fiddle?" Mason guessed. The business of insurance where large amounts of money changed hands in exchange only for a promise of indemnity was bound occasionally to attract the odd fraudster.

Jennings looked at his guest. He wanted to trust him but should he? He knew that some time he would have to put his faith in someone's honesty. He decided this was the someone and now was the time.

"I think it is a lot more than that. I don't have proof, but it's more than a wild guess. It looks as though some of the contracts running through us are laundering money, not taking risks."

Mason smiled. "It won't be the first time it's happened. It's bound to occur in any money business."

"I know that, Michael," Jennings replied, "but not drugs money for the Mafia."

Mason put his glass down. "You'd better tell me more."

Jennings went through the tale from his first suspicions onwards. He noticed Mason's eyes widen when he mentioned the name of Comet.

"Are you suggesting that Jimmy Wilkes may be involved?" he asked when Jennings had finished.

"If my suspicions are correct, yes."

Jennings handed a copy of Collins' report to Mason. "This is a schedule of all the contracts we have that fit the criteria of an overseas front reinsuring into London who then chutes it to a captive in a tax haven. Not all are necessarily crooked but they all follow the same pattern."

Mason took the list and read it. "Some of these names look familiar to me," he commented. "What do you want me to do?"

"If you can produce the same information from your books we can then share notes to see if a similar pattern is there. If there is, we have to decide what to do."

Mason agreed.

***

To see an African sunset is an indulgence that all humans should luxuriate in some time in their life. The sky is ablaze with hues of red and orange from the furnace red of hell to the softness of a Spanish orange grove in a misty sunrise. As the fiery orb sinks below the horizon the vista changes from second to second. It can never be captured on film or canvas. Each brain will capture the particular moment when time stood still, the moment when nature's tinting of the sky was flawless to their eyes.

Martinez watched as the sunlight quickly became darkness and the stars flickered their greeting. The *Astrid* was meandering, making only four knots. She was ten miles off Xai Xai idling along towards her meeting.

In the distance a light flickered. Martinez turned his

binoculars in its direction. The light flashed, four short, two long. Martinez took his Aldis lamp and replied. He ordered the crew to start removing the tarpaulins.

The pulsation of the twin diesel engines came closer. The boat bumped alongside and four men were aboard the *Astrid* before the engines cut. They dropped to their knees, the Kalashnikovs held ready for action. Each wore a uniform of jungle camouflage.

Martinez watched as a tall man with a back as straight as a Roman road boarded. He carried a riding crop. A Browning automatic nestled in a holster at his waist. His ebony skin shone in the moonlight.

"This is the *MV Astrid*." His accent could only have been born and nurtured in Eton and/or Oxford.

Martinez confirmed it was the *Astrid* and moved forward proffering his hand. The tall stranger ignored the overture and snapped, "Where is our equipment?"

Martinez pointed to the containers neatly stacked on the deck. Orders were issued in a tongue that was alien to Martinez and the cases were transferred from *Astrid*. Another instruction was shouted and four men disappeared below decks.

"Where are they going?" Martinez shouted.

"We are just checking that we have everything, captain. Please indulge us." Each word was enunciated perfectly and disavowed any questioning. The four returned and alighted on to their own vessel.

The man now took Martinez' hand. "Thank you for your assistance, captain. We will detain you no further." He jumped from the deck. The diesels roared into life and *Astrid's* visitor was gone.

Martinez ordered the mate to set another course and went to his cabin to celebrate.

The *Astrid* had been two hours in the Mozambique Straits, or one and a quarter bottles of cognac by Martinez' measurement, when the whole structure shook. The explosions holed *Astrid* in three places below the water line. She sank within two minutes. The radio operator only transmitted one Mayday before the cold ocean dragged *Astrid* to her final rest.

Two days later, deep in the African bush, the containers

were being opened and their contents examined. On that same day the *MV Astrid* was listed as missing by Lloyds of London.

Chapter 10

With over eighty per cent of the company's contracts being renewed on 1st January the last two months of any year are frenetic. This year was worse. There was much new underwriting capital in the market place needing to be fed premium. Several new brokers had been formed and were trying to take business from their elder rivals. Prices were dropping and still rapacious innocents were accepting the business. Hurricane Alicia, the latest windstorm to assault America's East Coast, had stiffened one or two underwriter's backbones but not enough.

Jennings sat in the daily meeting of the brokers forcing himself to concentrate. Every broker at the meeting told the same story. Prices were under the hammer and as a result commissions would drop. Corby Manning, even if it held its whole account, would undoubtedly suffer a heavy loss in turnover.

Jennings mused on the lunacy of an insurance broker's life. He will expend enormous amounts of energy trying to reduce the premium of his client. By doing so, as a commission agent, he also reduced his own earnings. Brokers are the only profession who delight in cutting their own income.

"It's not all doom and gloom." Jarvis' voice was smug. "I have several new connections and estimate that over the next year my brokerage will increase substantially."

"In what sort of fields, Freddie?" Jennings asked, trying to sound casual.

"I have a number of captives in different territories who are desperate for non-captive income. The American Revenue are tightening up so much on tax havens that all of them must have non-captive business. If they don't, they lose all the tax benefit of having the captive."

"Well, at least there is some good news." Jennings decided

the meeting should close. "Same time tomorrow please." He closed his folder and stood.

Jennings paced his office looking at his Rolex every two minutes. Pansie had telephoned him soon after he arrived in the office that morning. A package had arrived from Sutcliffe in Hong Kong. Jennings had dispatched one of the chauffeurs to collect it. Mason had completed his investigations and arranged a lunch for that day.

The package arrived at the same time as his morning tray of coffee. Jennings watched as Mary poured the coffee and arranged the chocolate biscuits, which he never ate, neatly on the Doulton plate. He asked Mary to close the door and hold all his calls. He tore open the heavy Manilla envelope, still hoping that his suspicions were unfounded.

Dear Allan,

Investigation of Various Companies

Following your instructions I have instituted studies in order to ascertain the antecedents of the companies on your list. I apologise for taking so much time but the exercise was substantial.

I attach an individual report on each of the companies giving all the detail we have been able to glean from our sources.

There appears to be a pattern among the majority of them. Of the ten captive companies you listed nine are financed by investment trusts in the USA. These trusts are managed through three banks.

We have investigated the actual investors in the original trusts. The sources of funds appear to be Mafia, Triads and Yardies, all organised crime syndicates.

The exception is Mutuelle Avionique Insurance in Jersey. This is a bona fida captive insurance company who take part of the insurances of their owners. The capital of this company is subscribed, quite openly, by the mother company.

I also enclose my invoice for the production of this report.

Should you need any further enquiries made please contact me.

Yours sincerely
Richard Sutcliffe

Jennings scanned the individual reports. The picture on each was depressingly similar. The investors were all part of organised crime and all the companies had lost substantial sums of money. He knew, from his own records, that money had found its way through his company and back to the USA for onward transmission.

Jennings arrived at Mason's office just before twelve. He was shown into the boardroom and offered a drink.

"Allan, good to see you," Mason greeted him. "I am not sure that the reason for seeing you is so good," he continued.

"What did you find out, Michael?" Jennings asked.

Mason placed a file on the table and opened it. "I have had our records searched and nine out of the ten companies on your list appear on ours. In every case but one an agent in the States finds a front, reinsures it into London who then reinsure it to one of the captives. In nearly every case there is not a lot of premium but a number of fucking great claims."

Mason passed the computer print to Jennings. It showed thirty-five contracts with American agents. These were insured into five companies who reinsured them with O'Sullivan, Green and Payne. They then reinsured them into eight companies in Bermuda, the Caymans and the Turks and Caicos Islands.

"It's exactly the same as we have," sighed Jennings. "Are these all the contracts that fit?"

"The one exception is out of Israel to a French-owned company."

"I presume that is from Sharom in Israel to Mutuelle Avionique in Jersey." Jennings hoped it was not. He saw from Mason's expression that it was.

"You told me that you had suspicions that these contracts were being used to launder drugs money." Mason voice was uneasy. "All I see is eight captives with bloody lousy underwriters."

"I wish it were so," replied Jennings. "I have followed the path of the money on one of our contracts. I discovered that three of the claims paid did not even exist and two others were not insured by our scheme. Next the payments were made by the captive to Pedrosa and paid out, as claims, to the bank accounts of several different recipients. Each of those bank accounts had a facility that automatically transferred the money to one account in Panama. The account was in the name of Barrancabermeja Investments. They are Colombian. The final point is that Comet, the company concerned, is owned jointly by Mafia families in New York, Chicago and Miami. Need I say more?"

Mason's brow furrowed as he looked at the papers Jennings had passed him. "Is Jimmy Wilkes a party to this or an innocent who is being used?" he asked.

"I am not certain, but I would put my money on him and Jarvis being up to their necks in it. I wouldn't bet against O'Sullivan, Green and Payne being involved as well."

"We have to put a stop to it," Mason snapped, anger seething inside. "If it comes out that we are mixed up in this type of thing it will ruin both our companies."

"Just hold on, we only have supposition." Jennings tried to calm Mason's rage. "We can't rush into anything. You sack Wilkes and he will go off and start somewhere else. What we have to do is get the proof, both here and in the States, and then nail the whole bloody chain. If we just take out one link another will be put in."

"And how are you and I supposed to get this proof?" Mason asked.

"I have already involved Jim Cross, an old friend of mine. He is very senior in the security services. With his connections we can close the whole operation down with the minimum of fuss or fall out. There is no way our government is going to want to publicise that Lloyds, the flagship of the London insurance market, is laundering dirty money."

Mason thought for a moment. He knew that he had no choice but to go along with Jennings. "What do you want me to do?"

"We have to pool all our information and make it available to Jim. You will have to check everything that Wilkes is involved with and I'll do the same for Jarvis. I also have someone else who can do a bit of ferreting for us. I suggest we have a meeting away from the City."

Mason nodded. "I own a hotel on the Tweed just outside Berwick. Why don't we have a weekend up there with your two cohorts?"

***

The restaurant was virtually empty. During the summer Boulogne is seething with tourists streaming off the ferries to stock up with cheap beer and wine. On a dull November day the bargain hunters make for the out-of-town supermarkets.

"Was everything to your satisfaction?" Smith asked.

Mersonne raised his glass. "The money is safely in our hands and totally unconnected with our small transaction. We also have the benefit of a nice insurance claim for the junk that was lost with the *Astrid*. I think that is entirely satisfactory."

"When will you be ready for the next shipment?" Smith, being American, wanted everything done today rather than tomorrow.

"You hurry too much, my friend." Mersonne studied the hue of the Chablis. "My stock situation must be managed. I have to designate what I sell you as rejects, so they will have to be a small proportion of the production. Our records have to show all perfect equipment and to where it is sold. To put your needs together will take time. Remember, this was only a test run."

"What about our main customers? We have a deal already agreed. Why can't you manufacture a batch and reject the bloody lot? That way we can supply to both your and our needs."

"Monsieur," Mersonne spoke sardonically, "our main customers are the government. If we are seen to have a major failure in quality control I will be buried under a hoard of civil servants and, even worse, newspapers. That is an inhibition I do not want."

"I want my twenty systems within two months." The European way of conducting business was as frustrating to Smith.

"I am sorry." Mersonne smiled, knowing that Smith's need to buy was greater than his desire to sell. "Twenty weeks is the best I can do. Also the price will be fifty per cent more."

"What the hell are you talking about?" Smith blustered. "We

136

have a deal."

"We had a deal and that contract is now finished. The price is now $1,500,000 for each unit. You have missiles that won't hit anything and I have guidance systems that will make sure that they will. I do not need you but you do need me."

Smith clenched his teeth trying to suppress his anger. He knew the Frenchman had one of his balls in each hand and would not hesitate to squeeze. "OK, you have a deal."

"Let me have details of the monetary and the transport arrangements when you have them." Mersonne stood, bestowed a Gallic bow and left.

***

HAYCUTTER INN, SURREY

The flecks of grey on his temples gave Hubbard the appearance of a distinguished barbarian. The jet-black hair on the back of his immense hands was untainted by the onset of middle age. Jennings' hand was engulfed by one of the gigantic paws and violently shaken.

"The only time I see you is when you've got a problem," Hubbard smiled.

Cross had contacted him two days before and arranged a meeting with Jennings. Hubbard's rosy complexion showed that he had arrived at the Haycutter some time before the designated time.

Having finished greeting Jennings he enclosed Pansie in the gentlest of bear hugs. "Haven't you got rid of him and found yourself a real man?"

"You never asked," she chided him.

They ordered drinks and sat at their usual table in the corner.

"Jim tells me that you think there is a little chicanery going on," Hubbard stated casually. Chicanery was the lifeblood of his business. After serving with the Special Boat Service he had slipped easily into being a freelance agent for whoever paid the best money.

Jennings filled him in on the facts and suspicions he had.

"It does sound like funny money being shifted," Hubbard

mused, "but what do you want me to do?"

"We were actually hoping that you might have some ideas."

"As I see it," Hubbard continued, "you have a lot of circumstantial evidence but bugger all facts. What you have to do is to rattle a few cages and see who growls."

"How do we start to rattle?" Pansie asked, caution in her tone.

"Penny Hacker is the handle. She knows from Cobra that we are not keen on taking prisoners when the chips are down. We play on that."

"How do we play on it?" Jennings was becoming interested. He knew that Hubbard's solutions to most problems included an element of violence or, at the minimum, the threat of it.

"I'll go and warn her off. You know that she was in your office the night before the bomb, but does she know that you know? If I have a little chat to her she might go running off in a panic. We just follow the frightened rabbit and see where it goes."

"What if she doesn't?" Jennings doubted that Penny was so easily alarmed.

"We look for another who might be the weak link. Given time we will find one. The one thing we are not short of is subjects." Hubbard was warming to the task. He had spent the previous three months skulking in a grimy cellar in East Berlin waiting for the right time to escort out a dissident physicist. Action was his motivation and patience not one of his major virtues.

***

MORE THAN A PENNY FOR 'EM CLUB

At first Penny did not recognise him. She saw a man who seemed to be wider than he was tall with his head fixed directly into thick-set shoulders without the intervening need for a neck. The glass looked like a thimble inside his mammoth palm. As he walked towards her she recognised him but knew not from where.

"Well, if it isn't Penny Hacker." His voice was ominously

quiet. "I haven't seen you since the wedding that you tried to make a funeral."

Recognition leaped into the frontal lobes of her brain. This was Jennings' friend. The dangerous one.

"I wonder if we could have a chat." Hubbard's tone was even. "Preferably in private."

"Of course," she responded. "Shall we go upstairs to my flat?" She indicated to the barman where she was going. The barman realised that she was unhappy with the company she was about to keep.

She opened the door and let Hubbard into the flat.

"Very nice," he commented, noting the soft colours and lighting. "If I had come here for a fuck this is the place to do it." He sat in one of the luxurious armchairs.

"What do you want?" she snapped.

"I want to know why you are still after Allan's hide?" A hard edge had appeared in Hubbard's voice.

She moved to the small bar and said, "I don't know what you are talking about." As she leaned across the bar to retrieve a glass she pushed a small button.

"You know exactly what I am saying. You were in Allan's office the night before the bomb went off. What were you doing there?" Hubbard's voice was calm but menacing.

The door opened and was filled by eighteen stones of the club's number one bouncer.

"Is there a problem?" The question was polite but carried a threat to the problem.

Penny smiled. "This gentleman is about to leave, Gordon. Would you escort him from the premises."

Hubbard sat, unmoved, the soft leather hiding his true size.

"I am sorry, sir, but you have heard the lady. I think you should go." He moved towards Hubbard and leaned forward to lift him from the chair. Hubbard waited until the angle was perfect. His fist was clenched with the centre knuckle protruding. He drove it upwards, like a Stone Age spear. The blow was just below the rib cage but above the solar plexus. The vast bulk of the bouncer emitted a gasp of air and collapsed to the floor. Blood seeped from his mouth.

Penny had never understood true fear. She had felt the

adrenaline-filled fear of failure, but never real terror for her own well-being. Hubbard had changed that in seconds. Her throat was dry and her intestines knotted.

Hubbard did not wait for her panic to subside. "If I hear of you being anywhere near Allan or his family, I'll be back."

Tears of pusillanimity filled her eyes. She had never seen herself as weak but this animal had found the frailty in her. She turned her head away as he rose.

Hubbard knew he had accomplished what he came for. He went to the bar and poured a drink. She would not look at him. He fixed the listening device to the underside of the table.

"I hope we do not have to meet again Penny." The door closed.

"I think your friend upstairs might need a little assistance," Hubbard remarked quietly to the barman as he left.

It was an hour before Penny Hacker regained enough control to leave the seat where she cowered. The bouncer had been taken downstairs still nursing his bruises.

Hubbard sat in the car. The case on his lap contained a small receiver and recorder. The earpiece picked up the sound of a telephone dialling.

"Cameron, it's Penny Hacker." The small bug could not pick up the reply.

"I am sorry but I will have to return your payment," Penny's voice trembled. "Jennings knows that it was me who planted the bomb."

Again there was silence whilst a reply was given.

"I don't know but he does. I've just had a visit from one of his friends."

The earphone went quiet.

"It was John Hubbard. The thick-set one with the evil eyes."

Hubbard smiled to himself. His visit had the effect he hoped for.

***

WOLDINGHAM, SURREY

"She rang someone called Cameron," Hubbard sat at the kitchen

140

table with Jennings. "That has to be Carter. Perhaps I should go over to the States and shake a few skeletons over there."

"If it is the Mafia we are dealing with, you might be taking on more than we can deal with." Jennings knew that he and Hubbard could look after themselves but had to consider Pansie and Charlie.

"It's your call, Allan. I'm the piper, you are paying so tell me the tune."

"He's being the English gentleman and worrying about the little wife." Pansie's voice came from behind them. "You don't have a choice, Allan," she continued. "If you ignore what you know it could end up ruining the company and you. That means me and Charlie as well."

Jennings put his arm around her waist. "I know you're right but I can't put you and Charlie at risk."

"You do that whether you act or not. They've already tried to kill you once. Do you really think that they will give up?"

Jennings shook his head. Every potential gain carries a commensurate risk. The hazard to himself was acceptable but the thought of imperiling his family eroded his resolution.

"Just do it, Allan," Pansie scolded. "Tell Jim what you are planning. I am sure, with the resources he has, he will make sure we are safe."

***

CORBY MANNING'S OFFICE

The document had caught Jennings' eye as he scanned through the morning post. It was a bordereau of risks that had been ceded to Corporate Credit and Surety from Sharom. It showed that twelve policies had been reinsured under the facility with a total premium of $6,500,000. It also revealed that all the original risks emanated from South Africa. Jennings was perplexed. Sharom was a domestic Israeli company, albeit Palestinian owned, and yet was producing huge volumes from South Africa. He picked up the telephone and dialled.

"Michael, how are you?"

Mason confirmed his health and well being to be excellent.

"When we had lunch you told me that you handled a facility from Sharom in Israel," he continued. "Have you had any premium ceded under it yet?"

"Actually, there was a bordereau through yesterday. I noticed it because it was sent for Jimmy Wilkes."

"What was in it?" Jennings asked.

"There was about $4,000,000 of premium for six or seven performance guarantees. Why do you ask?"

"Can you remember where the original risks were located?"

"I think that most, if not all, were from Southern Africa." Mason's voice reflected his puzzlement at the question. "Is there a problem?"

"I don't know, but something feels wrong." There was nothing that Jennings could put a finger on. "I have a bordereau here under our facility. All the cessions are from South Africa and none of them seem to have any connection with Israel. I can't see why Sharom should be involved."

"It does look a little strange," mused Mason. "It could be politics. South Africa is a bit of a leper at the moment. As Sharom is only fronting the account, it's possible that the real insurers don't want to be seen dealing directly. Who are the reinsurers, I've forgotten."

"It goes to Corporate Credit who then pass it on to Mutuelle Avionique," Jennings responded.

"That's probably the reason," Mason laughed. "The bloody French are devious bastards. They will trade with the devil as long as they don't think they will get caught. Their government is very anti-South Africa at the moment. If Avionique were seen to be dealing with the bastion of apartheid they would probably lose all their government contracts. By hiding their connection the French civil service can now turn a blind eye."

"You are probably right," Jennings commented. Mason's reasoning was logical and certainly in character with the French ethics, but doubt still niggled at the back of his mind. Common sense told him that this account was not the same as the others. The premiums were substantial and it would be almost impossible to fabricate claims under performance and solvency guarantees. "I think we should still monitor them." Mason agreed and the line went dead.

The Lime Club was quiet. During the renewal season the lunch hour would be bedlam, with fraught brokers and underwriters demanding food and drink in the minimum time. By half past two the place would be empty except for the odd committed drinkers.

Jennings was sitting at the bar when Cross arrived just after four. Drinks were delivered and taken to a table in the corner.

"I had a meeting with the Permanent Secretary at the Foreign Office this morning." Cross' expression showed that the tryst had not been to his liking. "He was extremely interested in my friendship with you and my enquiries about Carter and Scorsi."

"What have the Foreign Office got to do with them?" Jennings' expression was mystified.

Cross shrugged. "I haven't the faintest idea, but I was told that such matters were not within the ambit of the security services. I was told that, if they were crooks, it was a matter for the American law enforcement agencies not me."

"Did you tell him what we think is going on?"

"Only in general," Cross replied. "That bastard leaks worse than a cullender. If I told him everything it would be all over Whitehall and the newspapers within a day. All I told him was that there was a possibility that certain leading financial institutions may, unwittingly, be laundering drugs money."

"How did he react to that?"

"He questioned that this type of thing had any connection with the functions of MI5. He suggested that I give what I have to the police and then mind my own business."

"Are you going to?" asked Jennings.

"What do you think? I am not going to have some fairy Whitehall mandarin ordering me about. What intrigues me is where he got his information and why the Foreign Office doesn't want me nosing about."

"As John said," Jennings quipped, "rattle a few cages and see who growls. Well, someone has growled and all we need to find out is who and why."

"I will, and when I do I'll have that pompous bastard." Cross spat the words with venom.

"It's an interesting episode so soon after John's little chat with Penny Hacker." Jennings could not see any connection but the coincidence of timing disturbed him.

Cross and Jennings had not met since Hubbard's talk with Penny. Cross' eyebrows rose as Jennings related the tale of Hubbard's visit and her subsequent conversation with Carter.

"I think we should have a council of war," Jennings said solemnly. "I have had to involve Michael Mason and he has suggested that we get together at his hotel in the borders. Can you make the weekend after next?"

Cross checked his diary and confirmed he could.

***

HILTON HEAD ISLAND

"I thought you told me that the broad was reliable," Scorsi was shouting. "I don't give anyone a contract and let them pull out because they are panicky."

Carter tried to interrupt but Scorsi stopped him. "That fucking slag is dog meat and if you try to interfere you will be." Carter knew that the threat was actually an assurance.

"Now, what about this asshole Jennings?" Scorsi ranted. "Is the bastard a problem or not?"

"According to Freddie Jarvis he doesn't know anything." Carter spoke calmly, hoping to placate Scorsi's fury.

"Can we trust his judgement?" Scorsi was now screaming. "The Hacker woman is his bit of tail and he doesn't even know that Jennings has her fingered. I'm beginning to think that your whole fucking operation is falling apart."

"Don't you speak to Cameron like that." Karen's temper became unleashed. "You need him more than he needs you. He has the connections to do the job and does it. All you do is pick up the trade and take a cut."

Scorsi caught the side of her face with a stinging blow. "Shut up, you whore."

Carter moved to intervene and found himself facing a snub-nosed revolver. "Just try me, Limey." The words were whispered. "Just remember who pulled you out of the shit and set you up. If you ever cross me you're dead." The words sent a

144

shiver of fear down Carter's spine.

"You go and pack a bag. I want you in New York to talk to some people."

Carter obeyed, knowing that if he didn't his life-span could be considerably shortened.

Karen sat up. Blood seeped from the cut where Scorsi's ring had struck her. Scorsi leaned across and lifted her chin. "That mouth of yours is for cock-sucking not giving opinions. Just keep it that way."

As Scorsi and Carter walked across the hallway of Hilton Head airport they passed, but did not notice, a heavy-set man with the backs of his hands covered in jet black hair.

Hubbard, however, did recognise Carter. He watched as they boarded the flight for Charleston.

Crystal Sands Hotel sits in the middle of the Shipyard estate. Hubbard asked for a map of the island at reception and found the location of Carter's condominium.

The Trans Am eased down the drive as Hubbard checked the numbers. The Americans are extremely information-conscious and each post box declared the number and the occupant's name. He stopped by the box that announced '85 Cameron Carter.' Inside he saw a blond with an hourglass figure. He drove back to the hotel and asked them to reserve the last tee time of the day at the golf club for the next afternoon.

***

Make-up could not fully conceal the purple bruise on her face. The cut looked like a glowing red smile in the centre of the bruising. She lay by the pool, catching the last rays of the sun before it sank below the horizon at the centre of a fiery orange halo. She heard the golf ball land about twenty yards away, but took little notice. Errant golf balls were a fact of life when your home is situated next to a fairway.

Hubbard had three attempts before he managed to hit the three wood with enough slice to carry the rough and reach the manicured lawn.

"Excuse me, madam." Hubbard spoke in his premier English accent.

Karen looked up and saw a heavy-set man standing on the boundary of her garden. She saw that his arms were thicker than her own legs and were covered with fine black hair. Lust stirred in her momentarily. Carter was her man, but an occasional dalliance could be satisfying and he had let that animal Scorsi knock her about.

"I am terribly sorry but my drive has ended up on your lawn," Hubbard continued.

The accent further aroused her. She had always had a penchant for the English. She found that once their in-bred reserve was overcome they could become intensely fervid. She stood and walked towards the barrel-chested stranger.

Hubbard did not take his eyes from her. She wore a bikini if it could be described as such. The top was no more than a strip of material designed to just cover her nipples. Her breasts were firm and swayed gently as she walked. The bottom, a thong with soft pubic hair peeping from the sides.

She picked up the ball, walked across to Hubbard and gave it to him. "Don't be sorry," she smiled, "it often happens." She looked him up and down and saw only solid muscle.

If he had asked, he could have laid her there in the garden. Carter had let her down. The Italian scum had slugged her and he had done nothing. At that moment she felt alone and unprotected.

Hubbard saw the look in her eyes. He noticed that her nipples had become hardened with sexual arousal, but he knew that now was not the right time for his purposes.

"Thank you very much, madam." He doffed his hat and turned back to the golf course.

She watched as he played his shot. He jumped into the buggy, gave her a cheerful wave and was gone. She sat in the jacuzzi, her eyes closed, imagining that the jets massaging her body were huge hands covered with fine black hair. Later, she decided, she would go over to the hotel to see if there was any action.

Hubbard watched as she walked across the car park into Crystal Sands. She went to the bar and perched on one of the stools. The barman greeted her as if she was an old friend and produced a martini without being asked. Hubbard knew the time

146

was now right.

"If it's not the angel of mercy who rescues the balls of straying golfers." Hubbard chose his innuendo carefully.

She recognised him immediately, the fantasy in the jacuzzi still fresh in her mind. "It's all part of the service," she responded.

Hubbard noticed a slight flush tinge her cheeks. "Can I buy you a drink?" he asked. She nodded to the barman for a refill.

"I'm Gerry Croft." Hubbard used one of his usual aliases. She reciprocated the introduction.

There was a small stage and dance floor in one corner of the bar and a large banner was being erected proclaiming, 'Hilton Head Shag Club.'

"What the blazes is that?" Hubbard asked, thinking that shag could only mean either pipe tobacco or sex.

She winked at him, knowing the English connotations of the word. "It's not what you think. It's a dance club, the shag is somewhere between ballroom and jitterbug. Maybe the Limey shagging comes after the dancing," she laughed.

They took the drinks to a table far enough away from the music to allow conversation. A couple more drinks had been consumed and the complimentary buffet raided before Hubbard asked her to dance.

She moved lissomely, allowing their bodies to brush against each other. "Are you as big all over as you look?" she whispered.

Hubbard's genitals became independent and took control of themselves.

She pressed her abdomen to him. "I think you've answered my question." Her eyes shone with the ire that coursed inside her. The drinks were left unfinished.

Hairy men have always aroused her. She ran her hands across the fine black hair that covered his belly. His penis was large and stood erect. She took it in both hands and gently massaged it.

Her breasts were not small but his mammoth hands enveloped them. He caressed them with a tenderness that was unexpected.

She ran her tongue from his navel to his chest. His hands

147

were on her waist and she felt herself being delicately lifted and lowered on to him. As he entered her the most delicious pain filled her abdomen. He was deep inside her and she gyrated as the explosion rose from within her.

They lay in each other's arms. "You're one hell of a lay," she panted.

"You're not at all bad yourself," Hubbard reciprocated.

Hubbard awoke two hours later. He stroked her face and her eyes opened. A smile lit their corners.

How did you get this?" he asked, touching the partially healed cut.

Her eyes blazed anger. "That greasy Italian bastard hit me," she snarled. "And my man did fuck all to stop him."

Hubbard knew now was the time to strike. "What Italian?" he asked innocently.

"Joe Scorsi, Cameron's partner," she spat.

Slowly Hubbard wheedled the tale from her. Her man, Cameron, did deals where money was moved using insurance. His partner dealt with the people who wanted the money shifted. Recently he had found a new customer who needed to move a lot of cash. Both Cameron and Scorsi seemed frightened of the man and his cohorts, but she did not know why. She had tried to intervene and Scorsi had belted her. Cameron had not tried to stop him.

Hubbard whispered comforting words, saying that if she was his nobody would touch her. She held him tightly and their bodies fused again.

For the next two days, before Hubbard had to leave, they played golf during the day and made love at night. It brought a new meaning to the term 'under cover' for Hubbard.

***

SHERATON TOWERS, NEW YORK

Carter had always known that Scorsi had a streak of malice in his character, but never expected the venom to be aimed at him. His guts still churned when he remembered the revolver aimed at his face. On the flight to New York Scorsi had said little and

Carter had not wanted him to.

Smith had arrived soon after lunch and his eyes had gone cold when the tale of Penny Hacker's conversation was related to him.

"Who suggested this broad in the first place?" he snapped.

"The Limey," sneered Scorsi, ignoring Carter's presence. "But don't worry, I will take care of her myself now."

"Just be sure you do." There was a chill in Smith's tone. "There is another Limey who seems to be getting too nosey."

"Jennings?" volunteered Carter.

"I don't know the asshole's name, but the wrong people are asking questions about the both of you. I don't know why but I want it stopped."

Scorsi assured him that the matter would be taken care of.

"Let's get down to the proper business." Smith opened his briefcase. "In the next three months I want $30,000,000 ready to go the same place as the last deal."

"From South Africa again," Carter interjected.

"No," Smith replied. "This will come from Central America and the Middle East. There are funds that can be used in Honduras, Costa Rica, Panama and Jordan."

Carter thought for a moment. "I think that it would be best to use all four. $30,000,000 is too noticeable an amount to put in one deal in one of those countries. I presume that the same rate of costs are to be charged?"

"I want another five per cent to go here." Smith handed Carter a sheet of paper containing details of an account at the Swiss Bank in Geneva.

"This is not a problem. I will use a nominee shareholder in the agencies." Carter smiled inwardly. It seemed that Smith wanted his snout in the trough as well.

"I want the deals set up in three weeks. I will contact you if and when I want the money to start moving." Smith closed his case.

"What do you mean if? Is this deal on or not?" Carter did not like the idea of setting up a programme that subsequently collapsed. He wanted no suspicions raised.

"I will know for certain in a couple of weeks, that's all I can tell you."

Chapter 11

Lomobo and his companions took little notice of the European, who was obviously drunk, at the other end of the bar.

Martinez may have been drunk but the sight of that straight back and the sound of the clipped English accent sobered him.

On the night the *Astrid* had sunk he had, in a drink-enticed fit of duty, staggered to the bridge and relieved the helmsman. The ship was six miles off the coast of Mozambique, near Mogincual, when the explosions ripped the soul from the old ship.

The rules of the sea, such as the Captain going down with the ship, had never been instilled in Martinez. As soon as he sensed the degree of the damage he made for the one serviceable lifeboat and launched it. The cries of the Vietnamese crew were ignored as he pulled away from the rapidly sinking ship. He had spent three days in the lifeboat, drifting in the Mozambique Channel, before a tramp steamer had come across him.

The only saving grace was that he had been wearing his jacket with Mersonne's envelope in the pocket. The tramp had delivered him to Xai Xai and from there he had made his way to Maputo. Now sitting at the end of the bar was the bastard who had obliterated his ship. He waited and watched.

Lomobo and his cohorts were talking animatedly. Martinez could not understand their tongue but, from their demeanour, he knew it was of the utmost importance.

When they left he asked the barman who they were. The man was reticent until the sight of hard currency dented his resolve.

"They are fighters. They fight to free their country from the white oppression." He spoke of them with awe.

That afternoon Martinez had been intending to report his

lost vessel to his embassy. The conversation decided him against this course. He wondered how much it would be worth to Mersonne and his company for him to stay silent about their connection with terrorists.

***

It took Lomobo and his men three days to reach their destination south of Pietersburg. The equipment was mounted on the back of a four-wheel drive flat bed. They set up camp and waited. The bush was their home and they were elated, both for being there and for what would happen.

***

"Ladies and gentleman, we have begun our descent for Pretoria. Would you please fasten your seat-belt, ensure your seats are in the upright positions and the trays stowed away. Thank you for travelling with South African Airways." The purser's voice was calm and soothing.

"I'll be glad to be back. I'm a soldier and should be on the ground fighting." General Van Damen spoke to his aide. He had for the last three years commanded the counter-insurgency forces of the government. The command had been a huge success and the number of terrorist attacks had fallen by two thirds.

Pieter Bootha, the Minister for Internal Affairs, sat in the row opposite. He ordered another cognac. The three senior diplomats who accompanied him sipped dutifully at their water. One looked idly out of the porthole and saw a flash on the ground. "A trick of light," he thought.

Lomobo watched as the twelve-foot rocket sped from the launcher. It did not appear to be moving fast and seemed to spiral idly upwards like a petal caught in an updraught.

"Turn left to heading 165." The air traffic controller was enjoying a few moments of relief. Whenever a ministerial flight was arriving all other flights were held outside the control area of Pretoria. To have only one flight on his monitor was a blessed relief from the usual chaos he watched.

151

"Thank you, Pretoria, confirm heading 165." The Captain eased the stick to port to make the correction. "Are you going to give that new stewardess a seeing-to tonight?" he smiled and looked at the co-pilot. Suddenly the port wing disintegrated. Before the pilot could call Mayday the fuel tanks exploded.

Lomobo and his men watched with satisfaction as the fireball crashed to the ground like an errant meteor. They loaded their equipment into the transport and bumped away through the thorn bush.

"I don't know what has happened," the air traffic controller could not believe what he had seen. "One moment 165 was on the screen and then it wasn't."

"Get a strike team scrambled from Pietersburg," Colonel Curren shouted the order down the telephone. "And I want two gun ships on standby."

He paced his office, his mind imagining the worst but hoping for the best. The worst was soon confirmed when the oxidised remains of SA 165 were spotted by a search aircraft.

"We have a report from the strike team, sir."

Curren looked up at the Sergeant standing in front of him. "And?" he snapped.

"There were three medium to heavy vehicles, sir, and about twenty men. It seems that they are heading for the border with Mozambique."

"Thank you, Sergeant." Curren now regretted his terseness. "Please let me know when we have a contact. Oh, and move the gun ships to the base in the Kruger park. We can cut them off there if we have a contact."

It was the next afternoon that contact was made.

"I have a contact," Captain Callard shouted over his radio. "They are approximately three miles ahead of us. We will be unable to catch them before they cross the border."

"Fuck the border, Hunter one." Curren had now taken direct command and bawled into the radio handset. "I'm ordering a hot pursuit. I want those bastards. Two gun ships will be with you shortly."

"Understood, hot pursuit in progress, Hunter one out." Callard wanted to leap with joy. So many times had he nearly had a group of bandits only for the border to save their necks.

This time there was no escape. Now he could follow and destroy. Both his parents had been killed in a bomb attack in Johannesburg and he viewed his job with the army as his own personal vendetta.

The dust swirled like a mini tornado as the two gun ships flew overhead. "We have your bandits in sight, Hunter one. We will stop them, you pick up the pieces that are left. Eagle one out." The noses of the two Wessex helicopters dipped in unison and they roared away.

Lomobo had heard the choppers before they appeared over the horizon. The two rockets sped away leaving a dust storm behind them.

Callard watched as the gun-ships climbed ready to swoop down on their prey like authentic eagles. He yearned to be aboard one behind a 50mm cannon. Then two fireflies buzzed from the ground. The eagles that had risen ready to destroy their quarry disappeared in a flash that seemed brighter than the sun. The men of Hunter one looked on dumbfounded.

"Report situation of engagement," Curren's voice snapped across the radio.

"Both Eagles destroyed. The bandits have missile capability." Callard could still not believe what he had seen and reported.

Curren thought for a few moments. Until now the bandits had missiles but never hit anything. Now, in one engagement, they had three hits with three shots. "Hunter one, call off hot pursuit." Curren took the decision that it was more important to find out about this new surface-to-air capability than a limited vengeance on a few bandits. "I want you to guard the wreckage of Eagles one and two and the surrounding area until a crash team arrives."

He telephoned the Ministry for the Interior to report. The ministry was in a state of chaos. The Minister was aboard SA 165 and it seemed that nobody had yet assumed command. Eventually he was passed through to the Premier's office and reported. Two crash investigation teams were dispatched. Details of only one were given to the media.

That evening the Ministry for Information announced the tragic death of the Minister and some aides in an air accident.

Within an hour the Anti-Apartheid Consortium claimed responsibility for the crash from their headquarters in Zambia and Smith telephoned Carter and told him to go ahead with the money transfers as agreed.

***

MANOR HOTEL, BERWICK-ON-TWEED

It was a crisp December evening as they sat in the lounge of the Manor at Berwick. Mason had acquired the hotel several years previously. He was an avid lover of field sports and both the Tweed and the Till ran through the thirty-acre grounds. During the fishing season guests with more money than sense paid between £700 and £1,000 per week to fish the Tweed. It was a superb financial investment for Mason. The cash poured in and he had the extra benefit of keeping the Till, which was better for both salmon and sea trout, as his own private water. Additionally he also had thirty acres of fine shooting.

"What a wonderful place you have here, Michael." Cross was fully at ease with life. He had bagged several brace at the shoot in the afternoon, eaten a gastronomic extravaganza and was now enjoying a seventy-year-old Courvoisier with his Havana.

"I love it here," Mason replied, "I can shut the rest of the world out and enjoy my own little private paradise."

They had all driven up on Thursday evening and decided to use Friday for relaxation. Tomorrow would be down to business.

"What do you know about the accident involving Bootha, Jim?" Pinter, always a journalist, wanted the inside story.

"The same as you, George," Cross replied diplomatically. "Air accident, reason not known until the investigation is finished. I don't think that they have recovered the flight recorder yet. It's probably been eaten by a hyena."

"You'll get eaten by a bloody hyena if you give me that bullshit," Pinter chided. "Bootha wasn't the only big wig on that plane was he?"

"You know I can't comment on that," Cross replied amiably.

"Off the record, just tell me if I'm wrong," Pinter smiled.

154

Cross nodded. He knew that Pinter was in the old fashioned mode of journalist. If he said 'off the record', it would be.

"General Van Damen was also a passenger on that flight," Pinter started.

Cross did not dispute the statement.

"They had both been to a secret conference in Lusaka to discuss whether there was some way of ending the running conflicts in Southern Africa."

Cross nodded.

"The conference was a complete shambles with all the black Africans telling Bootha that there would be no peace until apartheid was dismantled."

Again Cross affirmed the accuracy of Pinter's information.

"When the flight left Lusaka it was routed over Zimbabwe rather than Botswana, which in itself is most unusual." Pinter did not wait for confirmation. "And that route change was only known to Lusaka and Pretoria control."

"Ten out of ten so far George," Cross laughed. It had long been a irritation to the security services that Pinter's sources were both unknown and unimpeachable.

"Lastly is it true that, until then, the AAC had never had surface-to-air capabilities?"

"Not quite true." Cross could not resist the opportunity to prove one of Pinter's sources wrong. "They do have SAMs but they are Yugoslavian. They are surface-to-air in that they leave the surface and go in the air, but the guidance systems are either crap or non-existent. They have trouble hitting the bloody sky, let alone something in it."

"Do you know if the AAC have new missiles?"

"We will not know that until the pieces are all put together. On your past record you will probably know before I do."

"Bloody difficult place to do business now," interjected Mason. "Have you got much there, Allan?"

"We have some," replied Jennings, "but it's getting smaller all the time. Too many bloody underwriters only write business so that they can visit the place. With the problems, South Africa is not as popular as it used to be. I suppose the biggest account we have from there is out of Sharom in Israel."

"You city slickers do talk a lot of crap." Hubbard was

dragged from his daydream inside Karen's knickers. "How can it be South African if it comes from Israel?"

"It's quite simple John," Mason took it upon himself to explain. "An agent in South Africa accepts business on behalf of an overseas company who happens to be licensed in South Africa. So Sharom has its own domestic business plus other business from branches in other countries."

"Sounds too bloody complicated for me," muttered Hubbard, his mind reverting back to Karen's erogenous zones.

"Did you say the account from Sharom is still mainly South African?" Mason continued.

"It's not mainly, all of it is," Jennings responded.

"That's interesting," mused Mason. "So is all of ours. The contract we have is supposed to be for all agents' business world wide."

"Same as ours," Jennings commented. "As it's a new account for Sharom it may be that the South African is the first agent to be signed up. Let's keep an eye on it and see what else comes in."

"Maybe this one is just a red herring." Mason was not convinced that this particular deal was part of the problem. "What about the ones we have more information on? What do we do about them?"

"I think that we have to investigate them to see if all of the claims are fictitious. If they are, then we have to go to the Committee of Lloyds." Jennings knew that suspicions were not enough. Proof had to be obtained.

"If I can put in my halfpence worth," said Cross. "Once you have investigated and found that the claims were chimerical, all you have is an insurance fraud. You do not have money laundering. If you want to go the whole hog you have to tie in payment with delivery."

"How are we supposed to do that?" Mason was an insurance man not a policeman. "We can't. If, however, we can prove a fraud, we shut the operation. Isn't that enough?"

"You will only close it temporarily." Cross tried to hide his exasperation. "There will be a scandal and it is possible that some of the perpetrators might end up in the slammer, but with the sort of money these bastards are dealing with they'll find other routes and other people."

"I'm afraid he's right," Jennings sighed. "Carter's pulling the strings and he has already done six years in a Carolina jail. Being caught hasn't stopped him."

"Why not do the simple part first and then think about the rest of your strategy?" Hubbard's mind had replaced Karen's attire and now wished to join in the general conversation. "The first thing you have to do is confirm that the claims are dodgy."

"John's right," Jennings muttered. "And it's best if he does the investigation." The group nodded in general agreement. "Can you get a list of the locations and amounts paid that have gone through your company, Michael?"

It was agreed that the information would be produced within the next week and Hubbard would then look at each site.

***

The Iberia flight was about an hour from Madrid when Martinez awoke and rang for the stewardess to re-supply him with cognac.

He had spent seven days in the small bar in Maputo before Lomobo and his group returned. They were in ebullient mood and the beer and whisky flowed. The celebrations carried on for several hours and the company became more and more intoxicated.

Martinez had read the reports of the demise of SA 165 and hoped that this event and the celebrations in the bar were not entirely unconnected. He waited until the alcohol had induced both wellbeing and camaraderie. He picked one of the company, who was sober enough to talk but drunk enough to have lost any reticence.

"What is the celebration for?" he asked innocently.

"Now they know what a Kaffir can do," the man slurred.

Martinez said nothing and waited for the man's brain to fight through the alcohol and re-connect with his tongue.

"One shot and that big bird fell from the sky," the rambling continued. "They thought we couldn't get them in the sky but we could."

"Why did they think you couldn't?" Martinez asked obliquely.

"Our rockets were bad, man. They flew but never hit anything. Then we get new eyes from a ship and our rockets can see."

Martinez smiled inwardly. The cargo he had carried had been the key to the attack on the aircraft. This information would be worth many francs.

Martinez had found the Spanish Embassy and told them the story of the *Astrid* being lost with all hands except himself. He had given his name as Manuel Cossador, who was the Spanish mate of the *Astrid,* now at rest in the Mozambique Channel.

It had taken the Embassy three days to verify the existence of Cossador. Once this had been confirmed it had been easy to obtain new papers from them. He was now on his way to Paris and then Rouen.

It was a damp, drear December day when he finally arrived in Rouen. The boarding house was warm and comfortable and run by a plump middle-aged woman who smelt of rough red wine and garlic. The anonymity of the place was perfect for Martinez' plan. He intended to ascertain as much as he could about Monsieur Mersonne before he squeezed him.

***

By the time Hubbard reached Charleston his view that insurance was the most fatuous business ever created had been confirmed. He had spent the last ten days visiting the addresses given to him by Jennings and Mason. At every location he found that either there had been no fires or, if there had been, they were not insured with the insurer on his list. He wondered how an industry where fraud was so easy to perpetrate had survived as long as it had.

He caught the courtesy bus outside the terminal to Mr Thrifty's emporium and rented a Mercury Cougar. He had decided that a few days' break was needed and maybe Carter would be away on one of his regular jaunts. His loins stirred in anticipation as he turned off Highway 17 towards Hilton Head Island and the Crystal Sands Resort.

She was sitting at the bar nursing a martini. He put his hands on her shoulders and whispered, "Look who's here to surprise you."

She turned and her face lit up with genuine pleasure. "Gerry, what are you doing here?"

"I was in the States on business and thought I would finish with a couple of days' rest and some golf, or possibly something else." He winked at her and she responded by brushing his groin with her knee.

"Your timing is perfect" she pouted. "Cameron is leaving for New York tonight."

"Well, not quite perfect," he laughed. "I should have come a day later."

"Oh no, it is perfect. Cameron was busy getting papers ready. He will have left by now. I told him I would go to the Shag Club. I didn't think that I would get both the American and the English versions." She giggled like an impish schoolgirl.

***

"I think I prefer the English version," she whispered, her head resting on the soft hair of his chest and her heartbeat slowly returning to normal. "If sexual athletics were an Olympic sport," she thought, "Gerry Croft would be a contender for a gold medal."

They had only had one drink before the reciprocal needs of their bodies had taken command and they had withdrawn to Hubbard's room. The disrobing had been frantic, but the coupling that followed had been long and sensitive.

She went to the mini-bar, her firm round buttocks swaying gracefully from side to side, and poured drinks.

"How long are you been in the States?" she asked, handing him a glass of foaming beer.

"I arrived in Miami ten days ago." He took a long pull at the amber liquid.

"Business or pleasure?" she queried.

"Until an hour ago it's been business. The last hour has been more than a pleasure." She nuzzled up to him on the bed and he felt the beginnings of desire re-awakening at the feel of her smooth delicate skin against his body.

She rested her hand on his thigh and whispered, "You've

never told me what you do. I can't believe it is something boring."

Instinct told Hubbard that this was the prologue he needed. "I buy things for people who want them."

"What sort of things?"

"Whatever is wanted," he replied non-committally.

"You're not a crook are you?" Her lips brushed his ear and her hand caressed his reviving manhood.

"Only when it's absolutely necessary."

"You're a bad man, Gerry Croft," she sighed and pushed him into the prone position. Her hands and lips caressed him. He lay there, eyes closed, stroking her lissome body as she ministered to him. When satisfied that his arousal was satisfactory she climbed upon him and thrust him deep inside her. She groaned with gratification as his hardness grew in her loins. She gasped in both pain and ecstasy as they climaxed together.

They awoke in each other's arms. Beams of bright sunlight flooded the room through the chinks in the curtain and danced on the wall like an animated ballet. They made love again as the shafts of radiance illuminated their bodies.

It is worth travelling to America simply to experience their breakfast. Both Hubbard and Karen were ravenous after their athletic exertions of the night.

The buffet was laid out offering a selection of delights ranging from fresh pineapple to grits. In one corner a rotund lady dressed in an immaculate white chef's coat was preparing eggs and waffles in whatever form the customer required.

They both returned to the buffet several times before their hunger was sated. Over coffee she lit a long cheroot and let the smoke drift from her lips like an emission from a near-dormant volcano.

"What sort of things do you really buy and sell?" she asked.

"I sell anything that people want. I find out what there is a market for and buy it." He was deliberately evasive, wanting her to draw the information from him.

"How do you pay for what you buy?"

"That depends on how open the payment is allowed to be." This was the line he needed her to pursue.

"You wouldn't be trying to defraud the IRS would you?"

The question revealed that she, also, had no wish to reveal too much.

"Some deals I don't want anyone to know apart from me and my customer. I have no desire to end up in a cell." His ace was down. Would she trump or not?

"How much money is involved?" she asked coyly. "Are you very rich?"

"The people I deal for are," he replied. "Some transactions run to well over £1,000,000."

"I think we might be able to help each other." She put her hand on his. "It would be nice to do business with you, I like the fringe benefits."

"How can you help me?" Hubbard's tone became earnest.

"I can't tell the full detail, but, suffice it to say, you invest in a commercial business venture and lose all your money. The amount you lose, less a little fee, ends up in the hands of the people you wish to pay."

"Are you saying that, not only do I buy and sell dodgy goods, but I can get tax relief on a capital loss as well." Hubbard knew the bait had been taken.

She nodded. "I feel very tired after all that food. Shall we go to your room and have lie down?" He felt her toes tease him under the table.

***

SOUTH AFRICAN BUSH

The African sun beat down mercilessly as it reached its apex in the sky. Callard and his platoon had been dug in for two days waiting to spring their ambush. His arms were torn where the spiteful thorn bushes had ripped at them as he prepared the concealment.

Their intelligence had been that a bandit group had been operating in the area and would use this route returning to their base in Zambia. They would travel through the Okavanga and cross the border near Maramba.

Callard's frustration was boiling inside him. This was the third time in succession that he and his men had fried by day and frozen by night hidden in the bush waiting for non-existent bandits to appear. He was now seriously questioning the parenthood of the intelligence officer who briefed them. He decided to wait one more day and night and then abandon the fruitless exercise.

The radio crackled into life. The look-out was perched in a Bayabab tree, its bulbous trunk squatting in the earth like an acned Buddah.

"Vehicles two miles to the west," the tinny voice called.

Callard peered through the binoculars but could only see the dust storm created by the four-wheel drive land cruisers. He looked around his positions and saw that his men were now alert, hoping for a fight. Twice in the last days vehicles had approached and twice the adrenaline had started to flow. Each time the arrival had been tourists, armed with cameras and wide-eyed at the wonders of nature they had seen in the Okavanga Delta. Would this be third time lucky?

The diesel engines roared as the vehicles negotiated the rutted track.

The voice on the radio sounded elated. "Bandits, I say again, we have bandits."

The land cruisers bounced into sight, the cloud of dust following them like a mystic demon from the *Arabian Nights*.

Simultaneously two sheets of flame burst from the back of the hand-held rocket launchers. The anti-tank missiles leapt and pounced on their targets, disintegrating their bonnets.

The fire fight was brief and savage.

Callard's shouted orders were short and succinct.

"Two men guard the prisoner."

"Radio for return transport."

"Bury the dead, quick as possible." Even as he hated these butchers he could not leave their bodies for the hyenas and vultures to scavenge.

Dust filled the air as the Chinook settled its fat belly on the ground. Lomobo half ran and was half dragged to his impending destiny, grime clogging his throat.

The mission had, until then, been highly successful. They had skirted the Kalahari to the West and crossed the border near Tshabong. Three farms near Vyberg had been burned and their owners liberated from the yoke of life. The return journey had been a celebration. They had drunk maize beer and toasted twenty fewer boots on the neck of the black man.

Now he lay, face down, on the adamantine metal floor of the Chinook, a Boer boot on his own neck. Now his future was clear to him. He would be questioned by internal security and there could only be two possible outcomes. He would break or he would die. He prayed for death.

He raised his head and tried to look around. A boot smashed into his cheekbone.

"Grovel down there, you Kaffir bastard." The words were spat at him.

"Cut that out." Callard's voice rose above the roar of the rotors. "We want him in one piece for questioning." Callard had no time for the cruel and arrogant ways of the Boers, but since the death of his parents he had even less time for the black. South Africa was a beautiful country, but could the despised ever live in peace with the hated?

***

HAYCUTTER INN, SURREY

"She goes like a rattlesnake. If I was off guard for a minute she was jumping on me." The Haycutter was quiet as Hubbard waxed lyrical on Karen's virtues. "What's even better is we can set up a dummy deal and get the proof we need."

"Just a minute, John," Cross interrupted. "We don't just want the money laundering, we want the tie-in with drugs as well."

Hubbard's two days at Hilton Head had been fruitful, both for self-gratification and his real objective.

"I realise that," Hubbard said patronizingly. "If you had let me finish I would have told you that we can probably get Carter to set up the cocaine buy."

Cross nodded resignedly. He should have known that whenever Hubbard had information to reveal it would be invariably presented in titillating titbits like a carrot on a stick.

"I gave her the notion that cocaine was one of my interests as a buyer," Hubbard proceeded. "I was given the distinct impression that she or her connections could either supply or put

163

me in touch with a supplier."

"That will be Scorsi's end," Jennings commented.

"What we need to have…" Cross' mind raced, "…is where the drugs come from, how they are imported and how the money is laundered. If we can get all that we can break the whole thing."

"I think that I can organise all that for you." Hubbard sat back looking as smug as a teenager gloating after his first sexual conquest. "The only minor problem is that I have got to put together a guarantee for £2,000,000. I have to have either cash or an acceptable letter of credit. The other minor matter is that everything will have to be in the name of Gerald St John Croft. I'm sure the head of MI5 can organise that."

"It's all very well to bait the trap." Pinter noted that ebullience was beginning to overwhelm common sense. "Before you do anything you have to sure you can spring it as well."

"Let's run through what is likely to happen," Jennings mused. "John sets the deal up with his sleeping partner. If the usual pattern is followed, either my company or Bannister Ellis will get orders to place the reinsurances. Following that the claims will appear. That's when we strike. We question the losses and have them investigated. We find out that they are fraudulent and dig back from there."

"I'm sorry, Allan, but that can't work." Pinter saw the flaw in the idea. "The drugs are not going to be supplied before they are paid for. That means that someone is going to lose £2,000,000. You might be able to break the ring but not before the money has disappeared to Colombia."

"I'm afraid he is right," Cross muttered. "We have to be prepared to lose the money if we want to hit both the supply and the laundering."

"You're loaded, Allan," Hubbard laughed. "You've got a lot more than that floating about."

"Piss off," Jennings chuckled. "I might be rich but I'm not bloody stupid. As far as I'm concerned the main thing I want is to stop my company and my market being used. If we can only do half the job, so be it."

"You may not even be able to do that." Pinter decided to be the devil's advocate. "The Umbari, Cirrolla and Carpessa families all run through one company. All they have to do is to add John to that deal and you have no control at all. What I suggest is that we go public with what we know. I am sure my editor would kill to run the story as we know it now."

"That's only going to put a temporary stop on it, if at all." Frustration echoed in Jennings' voice. "We know that they are not just using the London market from Peter Huber's deal in Hong Kong."

"There may be one alternative." Cross tried to lift the descending gloom. "Both the FBI and CIA have monstrous budgets. If they could break a massive drugs ring then, maybe, they might be prepared to finance the sting."

Cross agreed to contact his connections in the USA and put the proposal to them. The melancholy was, at least temporarily, lifted from the four friends and replaced by circumspect anticipation.

***

Jarvis arrived at the More than a Penny for 'em Club just after midnight. The last month of the year was frantic. Huge volumes of business had to be renewed and, at the same time, the coming of Christmas was being celebrated.

That evening he had attended two cocktail parties followed by the annual Christmas bash of his department at a Chinese restaurant in the Commercial Road. His ears had been assaulted with inane conversation all evening and he had consumed too much food and nearly too much alcohol.

He sat with Penny at the bar, his eyes lusting after her body and his mind bemoaning the fact that the club would not quieten until at least two.

An underwriter, somewhat the worse for wear, clapped Jarvis on the back and wished him compliments of the season as he left. Jarvis noted the blond hostess with him who would supply the services for which the underwriter's company credit card had been despoiled.

By two the upstairs bar was empty and only a few remained in the downstairs salon. Penny told the barman she was going to her flat and did not want any disturbance. He winked knowingly.

165

The lovemaking had been unsatisfactory due to Jarvis' alcohol-impaired functions. He was sleeping beside her when the door burst open and smashed against the wall. Jarvis woke and peered through the haze that filmed his corneas. The nebula lifted and he looked into the gaping eyes of a sawn-off shotgun. Penny shrieked and his bowels moved involuntarily.

"What's going on?" he blustered. The words were ridiculous but popped out as a pure reaction.

"Shut up, fat boy." The words came from within a ski mask and were delivered with a mid-Atlantic accent. "It's not you I want to talk to."

"Who are you?" Penny's voice croaked.

"I work for a friend of yours. He tells me you don't carry out your contracts. I do." The voice made Jarvis' skin crawl.

Flame erupted from both voids. Penny was thrown backwards and gore covered her body. Her eyes stared but took in no light.

"Just remember what a contract is, fat boy." The ski mask spoke to Jarvis and then was gone. Jarvis sat in his own excrement, his body convulsing with terror. Then he screamed.

When they arrived, the police found the doorman with a deep stab wound in his abdomen, the barman lying with blood seeping from a depression in his skull and Jarvis quivering like a sapling in an earthquake beside the insensate body of Penny.

"Christ, guv, it looks like there's been a bloody war in here," the young constable gasped.

Paramedics were busy ministering to the two injured men before transporting them to hospital.

"Who else is there?" To Inspector Boyd, who had seen it all before, this was just another job.

"The owner's dead upstairs and her boyfriend is sitting there quivering like a jellyfish. Also he's shat himself."

Jarvis was beginning to regain control of himself when Boyd entered the room. He was suddenly conscious of his nakedness and the stench. Boyd grabbed a dressing gown that hung behind the door and passed it to Jarvis. "Go and have a shower, sir. You'll feel better for it." The voice was kind.

Jarvis stood in the shower, trying to wash away the last hour. He could only cleanse his reaction to it. He knew who had

166

ordered the atrocity he had observed, but there was nobody he could tell.

It seemed like many hours, but was only one, by the time Boyd allowed him to leave. He was sure that Boyd had not believed him when he said he knew nothing. To an extent it was true. He knew nothing he could tell. Fear and rage tore at his insides, each battling for precedence.

Back at his flat his hand shook as he dialled the area code for Hilton Head.

"Do you know what the time is here?" Carter's voice was indignant.

"I don't care what fucking time it is." Jarvis' anger was temporarily in the ascendency. "Penny's been murdered. Did you arrange it?"

"Of course I didn't," Carter tried to placate him. "It must have been Scorsi or, possibly Smith."

"Why?" pleaded Jarvis.

"She took a contract and reneged on it. They don't like that," was Carter's simple reply. "If they did not need me they might have me killed as well."

"But Jennings knew about her. If she had carried on she would have been caught." Jarvis expected logic to have some precedence in the thinking.

"They seem not to think like that, Freddie. If there is a loose end they cut it off rather than tie it in."

"I'll tell you one thing, Cameron. That bastard is going to regret what he's done." Jarvis' anger erupted.

"Don't do anything stupid," said Carter trying to calm the fury.

"I wont," Jarvis responded icily. "I'll wait for the right time and place."

***

CORBY MANNING'S OFFICE

"I knew that Freddie's genital desires would get him into trouble eventually." Collins was waiting for Jennings in his office.

"What are you on about, Geoff?" Jennings knew the

167

statement to be correct but not the reason for it being made.

"You haven't heard then?" The question was rhetorical. "Freddie was giving his bit on the side a seeing to last night and someone trots in the bloody room and shoots her. He phoned me at home this morning."

"Where was this?" Jennings asked.

"At a club that she owns, or should I say owned." Collins found Jarvis' plight highly entertaining. All the producers seemed to spread their favours like elephants in must. It was nice to see one get his comeuppence. He had long been jealous that such fringe benefits only ever fell to the outside men in the company rather than the real workers like himself.

Jennings knew that it was Penny Hacker who had died, but let Collins continue.

"The club is called More than a Penny for 'em. It's a bit of a clip joint but very popular."

"I know the club," Jennings interpolated, "I think you will find that we have it blacklisted on the entertainment roster."

"Anyway," Collins continued, "Freddie has been giving the owner one for some time now. He went there after his departmental do last night for a bit of nookie. They had just finished bonking when a bloke in a mask bursts in and lets her have two barrels from a shotgun. Blood and coppers everywhere apparently."

"Who else knows about this, Geoff?"

"Only you and me for the moment, but it won't stay a secret for long in this place," Collins replied gleefully.

"Just say nothing for the time being." Jennings statement was an order not a request.

Jennings' private line shrilled and he picked up the receiver. He recognised Cross' voice and covered the mouthpiece.

"Excuse me, Geoff, this is private."

"Have you heard about Penny Hacker?" Cross asked.

Jennings confirmed that he had.

"I've spoken to the investigating officer," continued Cross, "and it would seem that it was a professional hit. He took out the bouncer, who is an ex-pro boxer, the barman and Penny in about two minutes flat. It appears that your man Jarvis was the only witness and he says he knows sod all."

"Who do you think did it?" asked Jennings.

"It's only a guess but I would surmise that she had taken a contract on you and reneged on it following John's little talk with her. The Italians don't like people who break contracts."

"What are the chances of catching whoever did it?" Jennings could already guess the answer.

"About the same as Screaming Lord Sutch becoming Prime Minister. The hit man will be long gone by now. The only good thing is that it looks as though John's cage-rattling has stirred them up a little storm."

"Should we meet and talk over our next move?" Jennings was uneasy at this latest twist.

"I'll have to leave it until next week. I am off to Los Angeles tomorrow to see if the FBI or CIA will fund a little scam for us."

Within a few minutes of Cross hanging up both Pinter and Hubbard rang to transmit the details of Penny's demise.

The morning progress meeting with the brokers had been a waste of space and time as the topic of Jarvis took over the meeting. Carol Jarvis telephoned as Jennings was drinking his fourth coffee of the morning. He could hear tears of both anger and sorrow in her voice.

"How could he do it?" she sobbed. "Why was he sleeping with a whore?" The usual bounce was missing from her voice.

Jennings tried to placate her but initially only succeeded in making her more distraught. After twenty minutes she sounded calmer but Jennings knew that she should not be alone. He telephoned Pansie and asked her to drive over to stay with Carol.

An hour and a half later Pansie pulled into the U-shaped drive of the Jarvis' house in Kent. A van was parked in front of the house, its side proclaiming White Star Security. A locksmith was busy at the front door.

"That bastard is never coming in this house again." Carol launched straight into the tirade, by-passing the formalities of a greeting. "I've found out more about that conniving little shit in one hour this morning than I have in the last thirty years."

Pansie decided that calm should be restored and was about to suggest the soothing ministrations of hot sweet tea when she noticed the half-full tumbler standing next to the Jack Daniels bottle.

"All done, Mrs Jarvis." The locksmith appeared with two sets of shiny new keys in his hand.

Pansie sat in the lounge while Carol inspected and paid for the work. The room was spacious with oak-beamed ceiling matched by chunky oak furniture. An immense Chinese rug, some twenty feet by ten, adorned the floor, its deep blue background complementing the upholstery.

Carol returned, picked up the tumbler and downed its contents in one. "I've been through his study." There was a sob in her voice, "I thought we shared everything, but he's been hiding things from me for years."

Pansie sat silent, letting Carol talk in her own time.

"There's a statement from a bank in Switzerland. It has 15,000,000 francs in it, look." She passed Pansie a bank statement. "Where did he get it from?" She broke down and the tears flowed.

It was two hours before Carol's frustration and anger had subsided. Most of the time Pansie had listened as the wrath of the spurned woman was vented.

Eventually Carol went to the bathroom. When she returned she was calm, and appeared to be in full control.

"I've made an appointment to see a solicitor tomorrow." Her voice was icy. "In the meantime I must go through all his papers to see if he's been hiding anything else. I'm all right now. Thank you for coming." With that Pansie was dismissed.

Jarvis did not arrive in the office until after lunch. His face was drawn and his eyes sagged with lack of sleep. His clothes were dishevelled and he was unshaven.

"It's a bloody nightmare, Allan." He sat at the coffee table in Jenning's office nursing a Scotch.

"What happened?" Jennings asked.

"I was asleep. The next thing I know is Penny's covered in blood and someone in black is disappearing out the door."

"So you saw nothing?"

"A shadow flitting out of the door, that's all," sighed Jarvis.

"Have you spoken to Carol?" Jennings knew the answer but still asked.

"I'm in deep shit," Jarvis nodded. "She's told me she's changed the locks and seeing a solicitor. I've booked into the

Tower Hotel for a few nights until I can get things sorted out."

"I think it would be best if you took a few days off. I presume the police will need to see you again and you have to try and repair your marriage with Carol." Jennings wanted Jarvis out of the office for a while.

"I am afraid that is not possible," Jarvis answered with unexpected vehemence. "There are one or two covers at a critical stage and I must see them through."

Jennings could only wonder whether these covers were genuine or arrangements involving Carter. "It's your choice, Freddie," he commented non-committally.

***

WOLDINGHAM, SURREY

Jennings was only half listening as Charlie told him of his adventures at school that day. The boy had been given the starring role of Joseph in the Nativity play and proceeded to recite his lines. "I have travelled far and my wife is with child," he trilled. "And then Barry says there is no room at the inn, you must sleep in the stables."

Jennings remembered the story as he was taught. The innkeeper was kindly and offered the stables as the inn was full. The 'You must' in the offer of the stables sounded more like a statement from a Spanish hotelier who had over-booked.

Pansie, who had seen that Jennings was more than distracted, returned with a beer for him, a glass of wine for herself and a squash for the boy. Charlie, as is the way with the young, ignored his own drink and began to solicit for a sip of his father's beer. Persistence won and a mouthful of bitter was consumed with the usual face-pulling at the unacceptable taste. No matter how much anything is disliked, children will always want something that they are not supposed to have. Charlie was no exception.

"Come on, Charlie," Pansie ordered, "upstairs and in your bath."

Charlie considered rebellion, but his mother's tone told him that such action could be met with severe reprisals. He

171

scampered upstairs to sit in the bath whilst resolutely ignoring the soap.

"Carol was in a terrible state when I arrived," Pansie commented. "She had a man changing the locks and had rifled through some of Freddie's papers in his study."

"The $64,000 question is did she find anything of interest?" Jennings asked.

"Actually she did." Pansie was aware of his initial disinterest. This sort of marital disharmony was not unknown in the reinsurance industry, even if the method of Carol's discovery was unique.

"She had details of a bank account in Switzerland with 15,000,000 Swiss francs in it," Pansie continued, knowing that this information would guarantee Jennings attention.

"What!" Jennings exclaimed. "That's well over £4,000,000. His little sideline seems very lucrative."

"You don't want to know the account number at Union Bank in Berne then?" she smiled.

"You know it?"

"She showed me the statement and I memorised the number." She went to the writing desk and produced a sheet of paper.

Jennings took the note. "Mrs Jennings, you are a genius as well as being georgeous. I think I might ask Richard Sutcliffe to see what he can find out about this account."

"I spoke to him today." Pansie was enjoying herself. "He said he should be able to report in a couple of weeks. He did say that Swiss banks' systems were some of the hardest to break into."

"He probably said that so he could charge a lot of money," Jennings chortled. He took Pansie in his arms. "I'm so lucky to have a wife who is not only beautiful but very very bright."

She slapped him playfully on the arm. "Go and see if Charlie has got the soap wet yet."

***

NEWPORT BEACH, CALIFORNIA

172

The Sheraton in Newport Beach was smaller, but friendlier than most hotels in the chain. The barman chatted amiably to Cross about his one visit to England. He apparently saw more in one ten-day trip than Cross had in his forty years plus lifetime.

The time difference was slowly catching up with Cross. The journey had been uneventful. The flight to Los Angeles had been on time and it was only a short hop to Newport Beach. The CIA chauffeur had met Cross and transported him to the hotel. He had been booked in a suite which struck Cross as a little ostentatious for only two nights.

Tom O'Connell and Morgan Alexander were due to arrive early the following day. Cross had known O'Connell, who was one of the four Assistant Directors of the CIA, for several years. He had yet to meet Alexander. He, so O'Connell had advised, headed the FBI team, which constantly crossed swords with organised crime.

The bartender's tour had now moved east of London to a 'Wunnerfull' little town called Canterbury and it's 'cute' cathedral. Cross' watch told him that it was ten in the evening, his body advised five in the morning. He ordered one for the road. Courtesy required that he allow the barman to get back to Heathrow and the end of his journey before Cross abandoned him.

Cross was breakfasting when the others arrived to join him. Alexander was introduced. He could be recognised as FBI from fifty paces. The crisp white shirt, dark blue suit and sombre tie looked out of place in the holiday atmosphere of the hotel. After the introductions the two made for the buffet and returned with plates piled high with food.

"I've booked one of the conference rooms for our meeting," Alexander mumbled through a mouthful of corned beef hash. "I have a secretary from the local office to take notes, but I didn't bother with recording facilities." He raised his eyebrows awaiting Cross' approval of the arrangements.

Cross indicated that the logistics were perfect. Privately he had not wanted the formality but accepted it as part of the deal when communicating with the exalted in the FBI.

"If I understand what Tom has told me..." Alexander's drawl emanated somewhere south of Georgia, "...you may be able to help us nail the Umbari family."

"More than just them." Cross had decided that, if he wanted the catch, he would feed the bait slowly. "If we have full co-operation we may also get the Cirrolla and Carpessa's as well. It's also possible that some Triads and Yardies could be caught up in the same net."

"Please go on." Alexander's eyes lit up at the thought of such a coup. He had long had his eye on the job of Director of the FBI, which would be vacant in the next year. To inflict damage on such a breadth of organised crime would be a headdress, not just a feather, in his cap.

"I believe that we have discovered how certain payments relating to drugs importation are being made."

"Can you tie the money directly to the drugs?" O'Connell interjected.

"Not at the moment," Cross continued. "But, if we have the finance, we may be able to. We do know that substantial amounts of capital have been invested by the families, via certain investment trusts, in off shore reinsurance companies. It appears that dummy insurance operations are set up in the States which are then reinsured into London and other markets. This is then reinsured into the companies owned by the families through the trusts. Claims are made under the original insurances and eventually collected from the off shore company. The claims are paid into numerous bogus bank accounts. From there they all transfer to one company in Panama."

"I presume that the claims are authenticated." One of Alexander's many talents was that he was qualified as an accountant. "If the original insurance is located in the USA it would have to be audited by a CPA and be reported to the State Commissioner for Insurance. Any document could be inspected at any time."

"You're perfectly correct in that presumption." Cross would now throw more ground bait. "A lot of the claims seem to be genuine. If our guess is right, there are loss adjusters who produce two identical reports. They investigate a genuine claim and prepare a report for the insurer. They also do another for the company involved in the laundering, sometimes they change the location, but the report is totally credible as it actually gives detail of a genuine fire. The latter sets up a policy starting some time before the claim and then presents the claim."

"Surely someone is going to notice that claims keep happening soon after the policy is issued. I know that you need not be very intelligent to get into insurance but even they're not that dumb." Alexander was starting to regret wasting his time.

"Not so." Cross knew that the fish was now nearly on the hook. "I am not an expert but, the way it works is that the insurances usually come from an agent. He accepts business under agreement with the insurance company on behalf of the insurer. He only advises the insurer of what he has accepted in a bordereau each quarter. This is usually presented a couple of months in arrears. So when he has a loss that can be used he sets up a dummy policy starting three or four months before the claim. This gets lost among the other insurances which do not have claims. By the time the information works its way through the first and second reinsurers it's probably nine months to a year old. All the companies are audited but their documentation always appears to be in order."

"If the whole scam is so well covered, how did you unearth it?" Alexander was still sceptical.

"A complete accident," Cross responded. "Someone had remembered a particular fire because the address included his birth date and his name. He happened to be in Miami and had some spare time. To while it away he went to look at the site of the fire and found that there had not been one."

"What did he do about it?"

"Well actually, nothing. He was killed in a mugging the following day. What he had done was to note his query in his trip notes. The whole thing was picked up from there."

"As I see it…" Alexander's interest was now reviving, "…you have only got insurance fraud at the moment. How do you leap from there to drugs and organised crime?"

"First we know that there have been fraudulent claims presented and paid. Second we know that the parties who eventually pay are three Mafia families. Third we know that the cash ends up in Colombia. If the Mafia had lost the kind of money that is involved here a lot of people would, at least, be minus their kneecaps. What actually has happened is that when money is lost it is replaced by new funds from the same people. Drugs is the obvious reason for the anomalies."

"I agree," Alexander commented reluctantly. "What do you propose?"

"An associate of mine has got close to one of the people behind the insurance side of the scam. He thinks that he can set up a purchase of cocaine and tie the payment directly into it."

"How does that get us the families?" Alexander could almost see the headlines beatifying him.

"As I see it, once you can break one deal and get the money men the floodgates open. It gives you the authority to investigate bank accounts and investments. Once you know where to look and what to look for the whole can be ferreted out."

"I presume that your associate is Allan Jennings," O'Connell had been silent until then.

"Actually it isn't." Cross was taken aback by the identification of Jennings. "What makes you think that?"

"We have our sources," O'Connell responded.

"I'm afraid your sources have added two and two and come up with five. The associate I have is a freelance, but one of us."

"From what I hear we could have a deal." Alexander could feel his feet standing on the Director's lush carpet. "We will set up a co-ordinating unit so that we all hit the targets concurrently."

"There is only one small problem, and that is why I'm talking to you now. My budget cannot be used to finance the sting. I need £2,500,000 which may have to be written off."

"Go on," Alexander urged.

"That's it. I can get them for you but you would have to finance it. It's virtually certain that the finance would have to be given before the drugs are supplied. You may not be able to retrieve it."

"My opinion is that if we can nail that amount of drug importers in one operation, it's a small price to pay. We spend more than that trapping the small fish."

For the rest of the day Cross detailed how the operation would work and what participation was needed as the sting progressed. Alexander made copious notes and questioned each step in detail. Finally they agreed that the proposal would be put to the Director of the FBI with the recommendation to proceed.

***

"Why did you say that Jennings was not involved?" O'Connell paused and sipped his martini. The bar was empty apart from a young couple in the corner whose interest did not extend beyond the physical attraction of the other.

"I didn't say Allan was not involved," Cross replied defensively. "I said he was not the associate who could set up the buy. Why are you interested in Allan?"

"We did some initial investigative work on this operation before this meeting and his name seemed to be linked quite closely with you. When you mentioned insurance I knew that he was in that business and put two and two together."

"As I said, you made five." Cross was relieved by the answer but a small doubt still nagged inside him. "Allan and I are old friends. I have picked his brains but that is about all."

O'Connell took another sip from his drink and switched the subject to the current machinations in the communist bloc.

HILTON HEAD ISLAND

"It was you who got us tied in with the bastard." Carter was shaking with rage. "Now he just pulls the plug and tells us to piss off."

Scorsi had just informed Carter that Smith had severed his relationship with them and no longer wanted to use their services.

"What bloody reason did he give?"

Scorsi shook his head. "He just told me that his principals wanted a cheaper method of moving the cash."

"He could stop taking an extra five per cent for himself for a start," Carter snapped. "Apart from that we could cut a couple of points off our margin. All in all we could easily carry on for a total of ten points. He won't do it any cheaper if he wants the same level of secrecy."

"I told the asshole that," Scorsi shrugged. "He thinks he can and there was no persuading him."

"So we end up processing fifty million only when I've geared up to do ten times that amount. How did you find this shit?"

"His credentials were good." Scorsi was definitely on the back foot. "The money sources were perfect and he could virtually guarantee the volume."

"Virtually isn't good enough. That's fucking obvious now," Carter raged. "I've got three companies set up and ready to run, there are business plans lodged and no bloody business to give to them."

"It may not be as bad as you think, honey," Karen interjected. She had been waiting for the right moment to introduce the subject of Gerry Croft.

"What do you know about how fucking bad it is?" Carter was ready to vent his wrath on any target.

"I met this guy a few weeks ago and he could be a customer for our services." Her loins tingled at the thought of Gerry Croft.

"What are you talking about?"

"We only deal with Americans at the moment. This guy is English. He needs to move money unobtrusively. I guess that he has other connections with the same needs."

"Who is he and how did you meet him?" Scorsi was now becoming interested.

"He was holidaying over here a couple of months ago. We got to talking in the bar and, after a few drinks, he told me he was into buying and selling things. Things that the authorities should not know about."

"Why should he tell you that? People don't meet a stranger in a bar and tell them that they are crooks," Carter remarked scornfully.

"You underestimate me, Cameron," she pouted. "A few drinks, a look at a bit of thigh and cleavage and most men will start to think with their cocks. It worked with you."

Carter flushed, remembering how he first became involved with Scorsi. "What's his name?"

"He's called Gerry Croft. He lives in London."

"Can you check him out?" Carter spoke to Scorsi.

"My connections can. Leave it with me."

CITY OF LONDON

The Chez When Club was crowded with brokers and underwriters beginning to enter into the festive spirit. Jennings, Cross and Hubbard sat at a table in one of the booths. Hubbard had demolished his devilled crab almost before the other two had begun their starters.

"That was very palatable," he commented, mopping up the sauce with the remains of his bread.

Three more pints arrived at the table. Jennings was a regular customer and the waiter knew that near-empty glasses should be re-filled unless instructed to the contrary.

Cross pushed a file across the table. "You can read that while we finish our food, John."

Hubbard studied the contents of the folder, laughing occasionally. "I must have some bloody good lawyers. It seems I've been charged seven times and only found guilty once, and that was only for possession of cannabis. I appear to have got away with three counts of grievous bodily harm, one of manslaughter and two for trading in illegal substances."

"Have a look at the security services file on you," said Cross, spooning more chutney on to his curried prawns. "They think you are a very bad man."

"Jesus," exclaimed Hubbard, "I deal in arms as well as drugs. I really am a shit."

Cross finished his food and placed the fork in the empty plate. "From a week ago Monday you were Gerald St John Croft of 64 Knightsbridge. The police record is stored in the Metropolitan Police computer and is flagged to see if it is accessed. There are also paper files on you in their offices and MI5 as well as Customs and Excise. If anyone checks on you that's what will be found. Also, in there, you will find your passport with the US visa and entry stamps for the times you were in the States."

"You are most efficient." Hubbard offered a mock salute. "If MI5 are that good how come you keep letting spies work for you?"

"Stop the pissing about," Jennings intervened. "I take it that everything is set up now."

Cross nodded. "The money is ready and John can start the whole process moving after Christmas."

"Just a little thought." Hubbard was re-reading the file. "Why don't I see if I can get arms as well as drugs from them?"

"I was going to raise that with you. I think it is worth a try but I would have to clear that with Alexander at the FBI."

Jennings raised his glass, "Here's to success, but first let's enjoy Christmas." As he drank Jennings noticed that Jarvis, Larry Payne, Kieron O'Sullivan, Jimmy Wilkes and Jack Green were lunching in the private annex.

***

"I wish I'd never got involved in the whole bloody thing." Jarvis still had nightmares of the blood-soaked body of Penny lying beside him. Tomorrow, at the funeral, it would be worse.

"It's too late now." Payne could see that Jarvis was close to breaking point. "She was not the same as us. We are needed by them. If they try anything with any of us the whole structure collapses. As long as we stick together we're alright."

"Absolutely right," O'Sullivan retorted. "What we have here is a nice little operation. We all have a lot of money stashed away with more to come. It was most unfortunate that you had just given the woman one before they did her, but it was her they were after not you. She didn't do her job, we do. It's as simple as that."

"I never expected murder to be part of the package," Wilkes said nervously.

"For God's sake," O'Sullivan sneered. "We are dealing with people who shift multi-millions of illegal money about. Do you really expect them to be gentlemen who slap her wrist and say, 'You're a bad girl.' Just forget about her and concentrate on our own business."

***

OXTED, SURREY

180

Jennings had not expected many people to attend the funeral, but All Saints Church was full to overflowing. He had thought long and hard whether to go or not. In the end she had been the wife of his oldest friend, until he was killed.

He looked around the church, which contained a true cross section of society. All the hostesses from her club were there. Each was vying with the others as to how much pink flesh could be made to peep from under the black at such a melancholy occasion. Some had elected to raise their hems to make the thigh the theme and others allowed cleavages to peep above black silk blouses.

There were many businessmen in sombre black suits. This was the first occasion when they would visit Penny without their credit cards being molested.

Penny's parents were at the front, her mother weeping profusely. The boy and girl standing beside them could have been Tony Hacker and Penny before they married. Danny was nineteen years and tall and slender, as his father had been. Jennifer, a year younger, had her mother's voluptuous figure and eyes that smiled.

The mass was sung, partly in Latin, which took Jennings back to his boyhood with Tony Hacker at John Fisher School. The priest gave a soliloquy which hardly mentioned Penny but spoke obliquely of there being good in us all. He was aware of Penny's occupation and felt her to be a sinner who was doomed to burn in the fires of hell, but her parents had made a very generous monetary gesture so he attempted to make the funeral an occasion to be remembered.

Following the interment Jennings felt a tap on his shoulder.

"Thank you for coming, Uncle Allan. I didn't think you would." Danny Hacker looked Jennings straight in the eye.

"What happened was a long time ago and your mother was ill," Jennings lied. "Apart from that your father was my oldest friend."

"Do you know my mother's club?" he asked.

"I'm afraid not, Danny. I've never been there."

"Jennifer and I are going to run it now. You must call in some time." He shook Jennings' hand and left.

SECURITY HEADQUARTERS – PRETORIA

Joshua Lomobo lay on the dirt floor of the cell, his wounds beginning to fester from the filth that encompassed him, and wept. He had wished to die, and soon that craving would be granted, but too late. He had been broken. He had screamed for mercy and told them everything. Soon he would die and a kangaroo inquest would hear about his weak heart that had failed, despite the most compassionate treatment he received as a prisoner. His body would be burnt and his ashes discarded. No one would know how they had ravaged his mind and body.

He had been thrown in this six by eight hovel when he was captured. There was nothing in the box other than himself. The floor ran with urine and excreta. The stench of deprivation and death filled his nostrils. Then the beating had started.

At first they had punched and kicked him. "Where are the missiles? Where did they come from?" they screamed as boots and fists smashed into his body. He could take this. Many times he had been beaten. Then they changed.

Four men came to his cell, each carrying a zambok – a wicked hide whip, sharp as a razor and stiff as a cane. His tattered garb had been ripped from his body and he was smashed to the floor. Then it started.

At first there were three sensations. He heard the hiss as the zambok cut through the air, then the crack as its coarse hide cut into his body. Finally the searing pain that was like nothing he had ever experienced. Soon the three had melded into one. His whole being was engulfed with torment. All the time they shrieked, "Where are the missiles?"

When fatigue made them stop they spat in his face and urinated on his body. For two weeks the floggings continued. His body was a mass of cuts and weals. The older wounds festered until beaten clean by his tormentors.

For two weeks he fought them. He prayed to God for death to rescue him from this living hell. Each day the anguish seemed to last longer. The passing of time slowed and his resistance weakened.

At last his resolve crumbled like a cliff eroded by a

persistent sea. A swarm of locusts were consuming his soul.

"The camp at Gwanda," he blubbered. His body cried out for them to stop. "The camp at Gwanda! The camp at Gwanda!" Now he was screaming. Why did they not stop? He could feel the flesh being torn from his bones.

"Speak up, Kaffir, I can't hear," the voice snarled and another blow crashed into his face. Others ripped into his torso and legs.

"The missiles, the camp at Gwanda," now he whimpered like an injured buck surrounded by hyenas.

"What's my name, Kaffir?" The hide whips thudded into his body like a hailstorm.

"The camp at Gwanda, boss. Don't beat me any more, boss." All dignity had now deserted him.

The beating stopped. "That's more like a good Kaffir," the voice spoke and a boot drove deep into his stomach.

Now he lay in the filth and grime as the fever burned inside him. He shook with fear at the sound of approaching boots. His bowels moved as if controlled by an outside force. He had told them everything, but was that enough?

"No more, boss, please don't beat me again, boss," he mumbled as the last embers of his life were doused.

***

GWANDA, MOZAMBIQUE

The two Chinooks swept low across the border. No one spoke. Each had only his task in his mind.

"There," cried Callard to the pilot. "That small hangar."

A platoon had disembarked before the first Chinook had rested its bulbous gut on the ground. They formed a defensive ring around the hangar.

A second platoon disgorged from the other and moved into the hangar. Four shots echoed and a voice shouted, "Clear."

Two gun ships hovered above, pouring fire into the tented camp. Tracer rounds buzzed like fireflies kicking up spurts of dust around the camp's startled occupants.

Six men emerged from the hangar carrying long heavy

boxes. They pushed them into the first Chinook.

"Charges set, go, go, go." The order was heard above the din.

The two platoons disappeared inside the bellies of the helicopters. Dust swirled as the machines rose clumsily into the air. Their noses dipped to salute the horizon and they were gone. It had been barely four minutes from arrival to departure.

The gun ships stayed longer. Cannon fire hailed down on the camp until the hangar erupted in a ball of fire. Then, suddenly, all was silent. The helicopters were now only a whisper on the wind.

Chapter 12

WOLDINGHAM, SURREY

Charlie had woken the whole house before six. He had decided that not a moment of Christmas day should be wasted. He had taken Jennings and Pansie a mug of tea in bed. The minor problem was that he had not mastered the rudiments of having to boil the water first. The tea bags had been placed in the pot and covered with water from the hot tap.

Both sipped the noxious liquid and told their son how delicious the concoction was. He jumped up and down clasping a huge stocking that had appeared on his bed overnight.

"Father Christmas has been," he chortled. "Can I open my stocking?"

The coloured wrapping paper was shredded to find the goodie it concealed. Each present was inspected briefly before being discarded at the thought of more to come.

Jane Cross, woken by the commotion, appeared in the doorway.

"Don't you wish you were six again?" she smiled, enjoying the boy's excitement.

Hubbard and Cross appeared together. Both their eyes still showed signs of the residual damage from the previous night's revelry.

"Is there tea in the pot?" asked Hubbard, noting Jennings nursing a mug.

"I wouldn't try it," Jennings laughed.

Charlie had now finished his voyage of discovery through the stocking and was ready to assault the major presents that resided under the tree in the lounge. He threw a minor but unsuccessful tantrum when told that the paper must be cleared up first and then he would have to await the arrival of Uncle George. After realising that his point was lost he dutifully began stuffing the paper into a plastic bag.

Christmas breakfast in the Jennings household was a tradition. It consisted of thick juicy slices of honey roast ham accompanied by warm hard boiled eggs served out of their shell. This was washed down with Bucks Fizz, made using only freshly squeezed oranges and Bollinger. The menu owed more to convenience than gastronomic excellence, but it was invariably consumed with much relish. The binding effect of the eggs was much appreciated by the males following their previous excesses lauding the coming of the festive season.

Breakfast was finished soon after eight and Charlie had to suffer the interminable wait for the arrival of George and Gwen Pinter. After an hour, which to Charlie lasted several lifetimes, his lust for the colourful boxes was sated. Pinter arrived bearing Dom Perignon in one hand and a bouquet of carnations in the other.

The Dom Perignon was deposited in the refrigerator to cool and two more bottles of Bollinger were opened. Charlie was given the responsibility of distributing the presents, much to his chagrin, as it delayed the opening of his own for more vital seconds.

When the ritual opening of all the presents had been completed Charlie was taken through the kitchen to the garage. Standing there, the light glinting from its shiny paintwork, was a new Raleigh bicycle. Charlie whooped with uncontrolled delight and ran forward to touch it shouting, "Can I ride it now?"

The men were designated as instructors in the art of cycling and the wives repaired to the kitchen and the freshly brewed coffee. After an hour the youngster had mastered the rudiments of starting, stopping and turning corners and the team of tutors became surplus to his needs. The driveway had become the Alps and Charlie was now leading the Tour de France.

The four males dutifully offered assistance in the kitchen and were peremptorily rebuffed. Left with no choice they elected to test the quality of the polypin of Shepherd Neame bitter which awaited them in the utility room.

"Here's to the health and wellbeing of Gerry Croft." Jennings raised his glass to Hubbard. The others repeated the toast and all four laughed.

AMIENS – 27TH DECEMBER 1984

Martinez' Christmas had been relatively enjoyable. Since his arrival he had spent his days tracking the movements of Mersonne and the nights in the fulsome embrace of his landlady. Before Christmas he had decided that his knowledge of Mersonne was now complete and elected to concentrate his energies on his landlady for the duration of the holiday. He had been sumptuously fed and his other bodily needs attended to with great enthusiasm. Today, however, would be the first day of his new life as a rich man.

Martinez watched Mersonne leave the offices of Mutuelle Avionique. Mersonne was a fastidious man and watches could be set by his actions. He was, notionally, the Director responsible for quality control in the partially state-owned company. Every day just before eleven he would leave the office for a small café opposite. There he would order an espresso coffee and a large cognac. These were taken to a corner table and consumed, along with three Camel cigarettes, whilst he studied the financial pages of several papers. Today would be different.

"We meet again Monsieur." Martinez sat in the chair opposite Mersonne.

Mersonne looked up, somewhat startled at the interruption to his routine. There was a familiarity about the face but he knew not from where. "I am sorry, do I know you?" he asked politely.

"We last met on the dockside at Le Havre," Martinez replied. "You gave me an envelope containing Frs 500,000 and I carried a small cargo for you on my ship."

Mersonne paled visibly as the recognition dawned on him. "I have never met you in my life," he blustered.

"Do not insult me, Monsieur," Martinez spoke quietly. "I know what the cargo was and I know what it was used for."

"What do you want?" Mersonne snapped, deciding that his bluff of ignorance had failed.

"I require to be compensated. I lost my ship and my crew. I am sure that many newspapers would bid for my story. I am giving you the chance to buy the sole rights."

187

"What story do you have to tell?"

"The little cargo that was unloaded at sea in the Mozambique Channel," Martinez smiled. "The little cargo that was taken by the man who shot down the plane carrying the South African Minister for the Interior. The little cargo that helped him perpetrate that act. That is my story."

"We cannot talk here." Mersonne realised that any pretence of innocence would be fruitless. "I have to talk to other people. Where can I contact you?"

Martinez laughed aloud. "You cannot contact me, Monsieur, nor can any of your associates. My price is Frs 10,000,000 in cash." He passed Mersonne a piece of paper. "Insert that advertisement in the personal column of *Le Figaro* on Friday if you are willing to pay. If I see the advert I will contact you, if not I go to a newspaper."

Mersonne watched, clutching the paper, as Martinez left. His heart palpitated and his guts churned at the thought of Martinez' story becoming public knowledge.

***

'The fly will swot the spider.' Martinez' heart leapt as he read the words in *Le Figaro*. Soon he would be rich.

"I see that you have decided to be sensible." Mersonne immediately recognised the voice of Martinez. "At three on Saturday afternoon you will go to the offices of Muller Navigation on the docks at Le Havre. They will show you to a motor launch which you will take out to sea and steer due north and maintain a speed of fifteen knots. The radio will be operational so listen for further instructions. You will have the money and be alone."

"I am an engineer not a sailor," Mersonne protested.

"Just keep the compass needle pointing at north and the speed constant," came the reply.

***

He had been bouncing through the waves for thirty minutes. The icy spray seemed to burn his face and numbed his hands. The

188

English Channel was at its least hospitable. The radio crackled into life.

"Stop your engine, Monsieur." Mersonne complied with the instruction.

"There is a small rubber dinghy in the rear of the launch." Mersonne looked and saw it under the seat. "I want you to inflate it, place it in the water and put the money in it."

He pulled the toggle and oxygen hissed into the tiny rubber boat. He dropped it over the side and threw the attaché case in.

"That is good," the voice echoed. "Now start your engine and head due south. You will be back in Le Havre before you know it."

Mersonne fired the engine and turned the launch. As he crested a wave he caught sight of another launch standing off about eight hundred yards. He pushed the throttle forward and surged away.

He watched over his shoulder as the other boat approached the dinghy. It was dragged aboard. He waited for the occupant to inspect the contents of the attache case. The sea reflected the hues of red as the explosion tore the small craft apart. Mersonne smiled and turned to a compass heading of south.

SECURITY HEADQUARTERS, PRETORIA – 28TH DECEMBER 1984

"I don't understand all this technical bullshit," Curren snapped. "Just give me a simple answer to the question, where do the bloody missiles come from?"

Mike Wellard was becoming flustered. He was an electronics engineer and weapons specialist. He was unused to the abrasive way in which the security services operated.

"It's all in my report, sir," he replied limply.

"I haven't time to plough through a load of technical mumbo jumbo," Curren retorted. "Just tell me what the fucking thing says in English."

"The missiles actually come from more than one place," Wellard said timidly. "The actual missile is the Yugoslavian model that the AAC have had for some time. The difference is that the original targeting system, which, as we know, was disfunctional, has been replaced with a highly sophisticated radar-controlled and heat-seeking guidance system."

"Where the hell do they come from then?"

"That is the problem, Colonel. There is no way of knowing with certainty. All we can say is, based on the overall design, we do not think they emanate from either America or the USSR. Our best guess is that they are European in origin."

"For Christ's sake, man." Curren's frustration was now beginning to overwhelm him. "Europe is a bloody continent. Can't you be more specific than that?"

Wellard nervously adjusted his glasses. "The technology to produce these systems is available to any country that contributes to the European Space Agency. We guess, however, and I must stress that it is only an educated guess, that only France, Germany and the UK have the production capability to manufacture these systems."

"How the blazes are these terrorists getting hold of this sort of equipment?" Curren blazed. He motioned to Wellard to leave.

He started to read the report, hoping a strategy would spring from its pages. If the AAC had the ability to bring down any aircraft over his territory it could tear at the jugular of his country. Sanctions were an inconvenience that could be overcome but not without communications.

The report told him that six complete missiles had been taken. Were there more, and if so where were they? How did they get the guidance systems and from whom? All questions and no answers. He desperately needed help. He checked his watch which told him it was nearly noon. It would be ten in London.

The line buzzed only once before the voice answered.

"Cross speaking."

"Good morning, Jim, it's Matthew Curren."

"Matthew, good to hear from you," Cross replied. He was genuinely pleased to hear from an old friend. Whilst his masters had, in their wisdom, classified South Africa as a demi-pariah, the security services of both countries had many common interests.

"I have a problem and I need your help." Curren's voice was unusually grave. "Can I talk openly?"

"I hope so," Cross laughed, trying to inject lightness into his tone. "I am the head of MI5. If my line is not secure then nothing is."

"You know that those bastards from the AAC shot down a civilian airliner." The telephone accentuated his accent.

Cross grunted acknowledgement.

"A couple of weeks ago we raided one of their camps," Curren continued. "We captured six of their missiles in tact."

Cross remained silent, waiting for the tale to unfold.

"As you know they had been supplied with those toys from the Yugoslavs which couldn't hit a skyscraper at twenty paces. It now seems that someone has given them a sophisticated guidance system and the bloody things are lethal. Apart from SA 165 we also lost two assault helicopters in the pursuit."

Cross whistled through his teeth. "Christ, that means that any bloody terrorist organisation can get hold of them, even our Irish friends. Where do the guidance systems come from?"

"That is where I need your help. The best our people can come up with is that the technology is most likely from a member country of the European Space Agency. Their best guess is French, German or British."

"You think that someone in Europe is selling anti-aircraft weapons to terrorists?" Cross could not give credence to what he was told. All the companies involved in such research and development had been screened. "I can't believe that. Security on the space agency is as tight as a fish's arsehole."

"That was my first reaction," Curren responded gravely. "But my people seem fairly sure."

"What do you want from us then?" asked Cross.

"I would like to send you one of the guidance systems. What I need is for your boffins to study it and tell me who made it. Once I know that I can stop the bastards."

"You stop them!" exclaimed Cross. "If what you say is true, I'll have them myself. How soon can you get the hardware to me?"

"I will arrange for it to come through the diplomatic channels in a couple of days."

AMIENS – 5TH JANUARY 1985

"Perhaps you would tell me why there has been a delay in payment." Mersonne studied Smith's eyes.

"The route we have been using for the transactions cannot be relied on as secure. The money will be sent in the same manner as previously but we have to set up a new operation. We will resume the transfers in a couple of months."

"You realise that there will be no shipments until payment is received," snapped Mersonne.

"I understand that," replied Smith. "Payment will be forthcoming. We just need a little more time."

The telephone shrilled into life.

"You were very foolish, Monsieur." Mersonne immediately recognised the voice. "The price is now Frs 50,000,000. Pick up your pen. You have to take some notes."

"Are you OK?" Smith asked as the colour drained from Mersonne's face.

Mersonne ignored Smith and spoke to the handset. "I have a pen."

"The bank is the Union Bank in Zurich. The account number is 11354423. I want you to deposit fifty million into that account within seven days. If you do not I will have to tell my story." The telephone clicked and went dead.

Martinez replaced the receiver and smiled. The departures board told him that Swiss Air flight 809 to London was boarding at gate 14.

His many years of dealing with the cocaine barons had instilled a deep distrust of anyone he dealt with. In his heart he had hoped for Mersonne to renege on the deal. His first price had been too low.

It had only taken a few thousand francs to persuade the brother of his buxom landlady to make the collection from Mersonne. His last instruction to the fat idiot was not to open the case but simply collect it and bring it back.

The transfer had gone perfectly. He had watched the launch pick up the dinghy and seen Mersonne disappear towards Le Havre. The 8 by 40 lens binoculars gave him a clear view from the deck of the fishing trawler. Then the lard-covered fool had become inquisitive.

Martinez' scream of, "Don't open it," remained unheeded. As Martinez watched the case was opened and a sudden flash ripped the small launch apart.

That night he took a train to Paris and then a flight to Zurich.

Now he would travel to London. He reasoned that, if he had to tell his story, Britain would be the place to obtain the maximum financial return. The saga of the destruction of a civilian flight in a former British colony by equipment supplied by the perfidious French would earn him many dollars. He smiled at the stewardess and ordered champagne.

Chapter 13

KNIGHTSBRIDGE, LONDON

Hubbard was beginning to suffer from terminal boredom. He had been Gerald St John Croft for two weeks since the enquiry into Croft's criminal record from a precinct in New York and nothing had happened. The local hostelries were full of chinless wonders sipping tequila sunrises, which were, apparently, the 'in' drink for the chattering classes. He was beginning to doubt whether any normal people actually resided in the West End of London.

The intercom buzzed. "Who is it?" Hubbard asked, pressing the control.

"I have a package for Mr Croft." He recognised the voluptuous voice immediately.

"Please bring it up," he answered, pushing the button that opened the entrance.

She was dressed in a full-length silver fox coat. Her eyes sparkled with a desire that was reciprocated in Hubbard's loins.

"Is that the package?" he asked, pointing to the small case she carried.

"No I am," she giggled. "Shall I unwrap it for you?"

The coat slipped from her shoulders to the floor. Beneath the coat she was totally naked apart from her high-heeled shoes.

"You can examine the merchandise, in fact, I think you should," she laughed as Hubbard stood open-mouthed.

He picked her up and carried her into the bedroom. They made love that was tender yet violently passionate. They became one as the craving rose and engulfed their beings.

"You are one fantastic lay," she whispered as they held each other. His heartbeat was beginning to slow from the machine gun speed it had accelerated to.

"You're not too bad yourself," he said, stroking the firm

curve of her breast.

She kissed him and sat up. "I'm supposed to be here on business, and I could eat an elephant. You can take me out for a business lunch." The sudden change from the soft yielding siren to efficiency personified did not surprise Hubbard. It had the first time, but now he knew that Karen could be two people; the seductress in your arms or the astute wheeler dealer in a negotiation.

The restaurant was small and the tables covered with bright red check tablecloths. The pasta sauce titillated the taste buds. Karen devoured hers like an Italian soldier who had been on field rations for weeks.

"What's the business you have to talk about?" asked Hubbard.

"How did you ever get to have a name like St John?" she asked pronouncing the name as two words from the Bible.

"It's actually pronounced 'Sinjen' not like the Baptist," Hubbard laughed. Now he knew that it was she or her associates who had accessed his criminal record. "I think that my mother fancied a priest with the same name."

"Well then, St John." This time she enunciated it correctly. "You told me that you could be interested in buying some goods and using my friends' services to process the money. Is that still the case?"

"Well, it could be," he replied non-committally. "What I really need is someone to sell me what I want as well as move the money."

"It may be that I can arrange for that as well." She looked straight into his eyes. "What is it that you want to buy?"

"I have two clients with different needs. One wants a regular supply of a fine white powder that makes people very happy and for which they will pay a lot of money. The other lives in the North of Ireland and has a passionate dislike of republicans. He is a violent man and wants the suitable equipment to allow him to exercise that streak in his character."

She looked around the restaurant, noting that they were the last two customers. "In other words you need cocaine and weapons." She touched his hand saying, "You can trust me. We don't have to play games."

195

He nodded, indicating that her précis had been totally accurate.

"I think that we can do business together," she smiled. "I'll need a couple of days to let you have definite ideas." She placed a credit card on the bill and held it up for the waiter. "I'll buy the lunch if you promise to fuck me for the rest of the afternoon."

***

"Hello, Pansie, is Allan there?" Hubbard lay on the sofa recuperating from the exertions of the afternoon.

"It's the hairy one for you," Pansie shouted up the stairs to Jennings.

Jennings picked up the extension in the bedroom.

"Mr Croft, how nice of you to telephone. How are you?"

"I've just spent the afternoon trying to satisfy a nymphomaniac. I feel like someone has dragged my balls through a mangle. Apart from that I am fine."

"So they have been in touch." Jennings tried to suppress his excitement at the chase to come. "Was it just bonking or do they want to deal?"

"It looks like they want to deal," Hubbard answered. "I told her I wanted cocaine and arms. She said to give her a couple of days."

"Have you spoken to Jim Cross?"

"No, I'll leave that to you. Tell him to have the finance ready for when I need it." Hubbard replaced the receiver, closed his eyes and drifted into a deep sleep.

***

HILTON HOTEL, LONDON

"What's so special about this guy?" Carter snapped. "Are you rogering him?"

"If I am it's got nothing to do with you," Karen retorted, slapping his face. "He's got money and wants what we have got to sell. That's what matters. If I want to lay him it's up to me."

"Just shut up, the pair of you," Scorsi cut in, "unless you

want everyone in the bloody Hilton to know what we are doing."

Carter went to the bar and poured himself a large scotch.

"What exactly does this guy want?" Scorsi continued.

"He has got outlets for coke and also for arms, if you can supply him," Karen rejoined.

"What sort of arms?"

"I don't know that. He said he had connections with the anti-republicans."

"What the silly cow means is the loyalist para-militaries," Carter interjected scornfully.

"And what arms would the loyalist para-militaries want, if you are such an expert?" she snapped back.

"At a guess, I would say they want hand guns, automatic rifles and explosives." Carter knocked back the whisky and poured another.

"If that's so we can supply," Scorsi commented. "You had better fix up a meet with this Croft. I want to check him out myself." He turned to Carter. "I have to see a few people tonight. I want you both to stay here and cut out the brawling." The door crashed shut as he left.

"Look, honey, you know it's you I really want." Karen sidled across to Carter. Her passion always rose when tempers frayed. "Sometimes I have to give the odd favour for business," she lied, "but you're the real one."

She knelt and slowly unzipped his trousers. His erection grew hard as her tongue teased his penis and her hands caressed his scrotum. She looked up at him and smiled. "Lay down and if you get hungry while I'm busy you can eat my pussy."

***

Hubbard tried to concentrate on Scorsi. His concentration had to be Herculean. Karen sat across the small table and her stockinged toes were exploring his inner thigh.

"How do you intend to import the goods?" he asked, pushing his chair back, needing to escape her amorous designs but not really wanting to.

"That has got nothing to do with you," Scorsi replied ungraciously. "I tell you where and how to take delivery in this country. How they get in is my problem."

"If you think I am dealing that way you can get stuffed," snapped Hubbard. "The last time I left anything to someone else the shipment was being trailed by Customs. I lost three good men who were knocked by the fucking excise people, and a quarter of a million pounds' worth of heroin was impounded. I want to know every move that is to be made or I'm out. I can get plenty of suppliers so my only interest in you is the money washing. You either do it my way or not at all."

"Now look here, you Limey asshole," Scorsi retorted. "You don't tell me how to run my operation and I won't tell you how to run yours."

Hubbard knew he nearly had Scorsi on the hook. He moved forward, allowing Karen to resume her game, and said, "I am not telling you how to run your side of the deal. All I want is to know how and when the goods are being transported and delivered. I have connections in customs and can find out if they are suspicious. If I don't know I can't warn you and I could find myself walking into a set-up."

"My people have been running this type of deal for years in the States." Scorsi was more placating and Karen's toes more insistent. "We're experts at it."

"Bringing goods into the UK is a lot different to the States." Hubbard pressed closer to the table. "You have thousands of miles of uncontrolled border. Over here it is a small island and most points of entry are limited and controlled. It's a bloody sight harder to import dodgy goods into the UK than it is to the States. I've got the connections and I can help you. That is the only way I will deal." Hubbard's king was on the table. Was the ace in the pack or in Scorsi's hand?

"OK, Limey, you have a deal," Scorsi sighed. "But if you step one inch out of line you're dead."

"The same applies to you, Yank," Hubbard replied coldly.

"Point noted," Scorsi nodded. "Can you take Gerry home Karen? I need to talk to Cameron for a while." Scorsi knew that this would aggravate Carter and took vindictive pleasure in belittling the plum-in-the-mouth Englishman.

"How soon can you have the financial operation running?" Scorsi asked.

"It's ready now," Carter replied sulkily. "I can start to shift the cash within two months. You know that. Why did you send her off with him?"

"Because she is going to screw him. A man's brains go soft when his cock is out and if he has a weakness she can find it. It worked with you."

"Bollocks," stormed Carter.

***

She sat astride him, her torso sliding backwards and forwards rhythmically. His enormous hands cradled her breasts, his thumbs massaging her nipples. She could feel his eruption coming but wanted more. She stopped moving and leaned forward, her breast tantalising his lips. "Why did you kill Tommy Apson?" she whispered.

Surprise showed in Hubbard's eyes. Tommy Apson was a fictional character in Croft's criminal record. "I didn't kill him, I was found not guilty." He bit her proffered nipple.

"You beast." She slapped his chest and resumed her gyrations, but now with an urgency to satisfy her own rising desires.

She lay in his arms. "You did really kill him, why?"

The cover that Cross supplied was always comprehensive. "You remember I told Scorsi about three of my people being knocked by customs. Apson was the arsehole who cocked up the operation. He never did it again."

She had heard what she wanted to hear.

***

WEST LONDON

Martinez slammed the receiver down and swore aloud. The Union Bank had told him that there had been a transfer, but only for Frs 10,000,000. Mersonne was trying to take him for a ride. He picked up the receiver and dialled.

"You are being very stupid, Monsieur," he said.

"The money has been transferred as you requested,"

Mersonne blustered.

"I told you the price had gone up to 50,000,000."

"We cannot move that amount of money in one." Mersonne was buying time. "The payment we have made is to show our good faith. The rest will take longer to organise. If you tell me where I can contact you I will tell you when the rest will come."

"If I tell you where to contact me someone will arrive and blow my head off. I am not stupid, Monsieur, you have two weeks to produce the rest." Martinez replaced the receiver and stared idly out of the window.

The hotel was small but comfortable. Outside the Cromwell Road was seething with traffic either going to or escaping from the West End of London.

Dozens of newspapers were piled on the bedside cabinet. He had studied all the national papers since his arrival and his back-up plan was formulated. If he were to break the story he needed a paper with a huge circulation and consequently much money to pay him. If it became necessary, it would be either the *Express* or the *Record* that would get his scoop.

He re-dialled the number in Zurich and gave his account number. The bank were polite, but seemed a little disappointed when he requested them to transfer the bulk of the cash to Mexico. As his current resources were starting to dwindle he also asked them to put an amount into London where he had opened an account. Now all he could do was wait.

***

"It looks as though the deal is on," Hubbard said quietly.

The four sat in their usual corner in the Haycutter. It was Wednesday and the bar was quiet.

"What are the arrangements?" Cross asked.

"I am meeting them for dinner and Scorsi will give me an outline of the procedures he'll use. Provided I am happy with them the whole thing will be go."

"Where are you meeting them?" Pinter enquired.

"The organisation has been left to me. I need somewhere that is quiet. The other thing is I should push the boat out a bit. We are setting up a big sale so the surroundings have got to be

200

right."

"Let's sort out a venue later." Cross' mind was sorting priorities. "Firstly will you be able to wear a wire. I will need a full record when I bring Customs on the scene."

Hubbard laughed aloud. "I can, but on one proviso. I have to get rid of it before we leave the restaurant."

"Why?" Pinter asked innocently.

"You're getting old, George," Jennings chuckled. "There is a fair chance that Romeo here and the salacious Karen stop off on the way home and she will savage the poor bastards' body."

"How come I never get jobs like that?" sighed Pinter.

"What we need then…" Cross bought the conversation back to a dignified level, "…is a venue that is quiet and discreet where we can site the listening equipment nearby. We also have to get it off John before he leaves. Any ideas?"

The germ of an idea rose in Jennings mind. "I might have the perfect solution. How big is the recording equipment and could it be installed discreetly in a car?"

Cross nodded. "You can get it the size of a briefcase. Why do you want to know?"

"John wants to lay on something that looks a bit flash. I suggest that he goes out of town. That way he will have to use a chauffeur-driven car. The chauffeur will be one of your people and can monitor the conversation. Before they leave he can get the wire off John."

"What about the venue?" Pinter interposed.

"If you really want to impress it must be the Waterside Inn at Bray," Jennings mused. "It has three Michelin stars, is out in the sticks and the car can park right by the building. That means the listening equipment need not be too high-powered, thus it'll smaller."

"There is one problem," Cross frowned. "At the moment this whole thing is not official. If I start organising limousines I have to set up a formal enquiry file to charge the costs to. If I do that Customs and Excise are in straight away. I want to run this without internal politicking at the start."

"Bloody civil servants." Jennings dug Cross in the ribs. "You don't have to worry about that. I can provide the car if you supply the equipment and driver. You forget that I am Chairman of Corby Manning and any time I want I can commandeer the company Rolls."

"I've always wanted to drive a Roller," said Cross. "Can you borrow a chauffeur's hat for me?"

***

HILTON HOTEL, LONDON

The doorman sprang to attention and opened the door of the Rolls as it drew up. He bowed, showing a suitable degree of deference as Hubbard alighted. "Good evening, sir," he gushed. "Have you any bags?"

Hubbard shook his head and placed a suitable reward in the man's extended hand to thank him for his exertions. "I'm just picking up some guests for dinner."

The doorman rushed ahead and opened the door hoping to double his money. His hopes were dashed. He turned to the bearded chauffeur and ordered, "Wait over there." The ideal training for a doorman at a large hotel is to have served as a Lance Corporal in the Catering Corps. Lance Corporal is the first tiny step on the ladder to authority. Whilst he must show total subservience to any person who outranks him, he may treat all those perceived to be lesser mortals with scorn and disdain.

Cross, who was desperately anxious to scratch the false foliage on his face, complied obediently with the instruction. He checked that the radio receiver in the briefcase was operational. As Hubbard and company approached he alighted from the driver's seat to open doors.

"I've never travelled in a Rolls-Royce before," Karen giggled. "Is this yours, Gerry?"

Hubbard grunted, which could indicate either yes or no, but was taken as an affirmation.

Cross watched her firm round buttocks disappear into the car and a tinge of jealousy of Hubbard's secondary roll flitted across his mind. He resumed his place and eased the car into Park Lane. He could see the four talking animatedly in the back but the soundproof glass that separated them denied him entrée to the conversation.

The drive out past Windsor to Bray took about forty minutes. Scorsi spent most of the journey in a churlish mood. He was a New York city dweller and pathologically hated the country. Karen was the opposite. When she saw signs for places such as Windsor and Henley she cheeped with delight and demanded to know why she was never taken to all these famous places when she visited London. This made Scorsi even more Neanderthal.

"Where are we going, Gerry?" Carter asked, more to calm Scorsi's growing petulance than to ascertain where they were eating.

"The Waterside Inn," Hubbard replied casually. "Do you know it?"

The conversation changed to the merits of different eating houses and the atmosphere relaxed.

Cross pulled up outside the restaurant. The Rolls had the right effect and the doors were opened and the valued guests ushered inside. Cross parked the car and sat back to listen.

Inside, drinks were taken at the bar and menus duly supplied.

"How am I supposed to order from this?" Scorsi snapped. "It's all in French and there's no damn prices."

Carter, who still retained his English reserve, explained that the waiter would offer whatever help was needed, and that only the host had a menu with prices, so the guests would not be embarrassed if their meal was particularly expensive.

The waiter maintained his aplomb when Scorsi stated that he did not want food covered in crap sauces. He smiled and wrote down Scorsi's order for a man-sized steak and fries and a green salad with Thousand Island dressing. Carter squirmed with abashment through the whole charade. Dinner was served in the private room that had been reserved. The room had an ambience of its own. Father Thames meandered lazily by the picture window.

Cross was listening outside. It was after the first course had been finished before they got to the reason for the dinner.

"OK, Limey, what do you want to know about how the operation will work?" Scorsi was assaulting his mouth with a toothpick.

203

"Start with how the payment is made." Hubbard knew that the hounds were now gathered and the fox was about to break cover.

"It is a relatively straightforward exercise," Carter said. "We have an insurance company in the Turks and Caicos Islands which has a capital of $500,000. The ownership of that company will pass to your nominees at cost."

"You want me to fork out half a million dollars before we even start?" Hubbard queried.

"No," Carter replied. "The capital is financed by a letter of credit. All you do is replace our guarantee with yours. The actual cost will be about one and a half percent."

Hubbard nodded. "Go on."

"Once you have ownership of the company you will have to increase the capital value, again with an evergreen letter of credit, by the value of the transaction."

"Surely if I put further capital into the company it then could get locked into a liquidation?" Whilst Hubbard was not an expert in financial management of companies he did understand the rudiments.

"The finance that you inject will not be capital." Carter's tone reflected a schoolmaster talking to an errant pupil. "The additional investment is made in the form of a contributed surplus to the company. That means that it has the benefit of being available as a free asset, it does not have the restraints which apply to capital. As long as the unencumbered reserves of the company are greater than the original capital the company will remain solvent."

"So what you are saying is that the capital of the company is in two forms. First the amount authorised and issued by the board, which is the half million, and second the additional that goes into the profit and loss account." Hubbard wanted the record of the conversation to be clear and unequivocal.

"Correct," Carter sighed. "The tranche of money you put in will be part of the capital asset but not the capital base."

Hubbard said nothing and motioned for Carter to continue.

"Once the contributed surplus is in the company it will commence to accept reinsurances from Lloyds of London. Certain of these will suffer large claims, which will be paid by the company. The total cost of the claims, less the premium that has been paid, will be equal to the cost of your transaction with Joe's associates plus, of course, the commission payable on the monetary transaction."

"Are you telling me that the supplier is someone in Lloyds?" Hubbard knew the answer but asked the asinine question for the tape.

"Don't be such a bloody fool," Scorsi interjected. "The dollars go through Lloyds in another transaction. They are just a staging post to muddy the trail. All you need to know is that your payment reaches the right place."

"Do you want this deal or not?" snapped Hubbard. He didn't wait for affirmation. "Because if you do I want chapter and verse and understand exactly how it works."

"I'm sorry," Carter placated him. "You have to realise that the transaction is commonplace to us. The original insurance comes from an agent in the US who places it with an American insurer. That insurer reinsures it with Lloyds in London who, in turn, then reinsures it to your company in the Turks and Caicos. When the claims are put through there is a set of documentation between the agent and the insurer. Then another set between the insurer and Lloyds. The third set is between you and Lloyds. All three are self-contained and self-sustaining. If any queries are raised relating to your company they only run to Lloyds through your contract with them. Whilst we know there is a chain it cannot be traced backwards by a third party."

"I think I understand," Hubbard mused. "What about the claims that are put through? Do they actually exist?"

"Of course," Carter smiled. "They are now all real and can be seen. We have arrangements with one or two loss adjusters who will supply us with a duplicate report on claims they investigate. This means that our insurer had a bona fide loss adjuster's report and, if needed, the actual site of the claim can be inspected. We end up with an actual claim, properly documented, right through the chain."

"What do you mean, they are now all real?" Hubbard stressed the now.

"A small problem we had in the past. One of the associates was sloppy and used bogus claims. The situation will not recur."

Carter smiled.

"Too fucking right," Scorsi grunted. "That bastard's feeding the fishes."

"So far I am impressed," Hubbard smiled. "The only problem I can see is, what do I want an insurance company for once I have the goods and have paid for them?"

"You don't." It was obvious that Carter had anticipated the question. "When you buy the company there will be a contract of sale. There will be a clause in that contract allowing you to sell the company back to its original owners at the same price you paid for it. So, if it is a one-off purchase, you buy the company, pay the money and then sell it back to us. If, however, you want to continue your relationship with Joe's principals, you keep the company and contribute more surplus."

"You seem to have thought of everything." Hubbard made himself sound suitably impressed. "The last question is how much will it cost?"

"I wondered when you would get to that." Carter could see that a pledge was coming. "To move this sort of money through other channels would cost about thirty per cent. This will cost you twenty. Ten for my end, four each for Lloyds and the American insurer and two for the adjusters."

Hubbard raised his glass. "I think that we are halfway there. Now how about the goods?"

"You will get the goods, that is all you need to know." Scorsi was boiling inside. Croft already knew more than any of his other customers and still wanted more.

"OK, no deal." Hubbard replaced his glass on the table. "It's a pity, I like what I have heard so far."

Before Scorsi could reply the door opened and a bevy of waiters appeared with the main courses. The plates were placed in front them and the silver covers removed, simultaneously, with a flourish.

The lull in the discussion gave Scorsi the time to realise that his masters could become unhappy if he blew several millions of profit because of his own personal antagonism. He knew that Carter would not hesitate to put his balls in a grinder.

The waiters disappeared as quietly and efficiently as they had materialised.

"I don't see why you have to know, but if it stops your asshole twitching I'll tell you," Scorsi started ungraciously.

"Please carry on," Hubbard forced courtesy into his voice. He would have delighted in embarking on a bout of extreme violence with this pig, but knew the narrative to come would be more important than his personal feelings.

"I can only talk about the coke. The other will depend on what is wanted and where," the American continued. "All you have to do is to set up a small fruit importing company and we will deliver to them. After that you are on your own."

"Are you some sort of idiot?" Hubbard interrupted. "Bring the stuff in boxes of fruit and our Customs people will have you. That's been tried and it doesn't work. One lot even tried filling the cases with bloody spiders to frighten off the Excise. He got done for both drugs and breach of quarantine."

"Don't you ever let anyone finish before you interrupt?" Scorsi's anger was beginning to boil again.

Hubbard realised that Scorsi's growing rage was an accessory to be used. If he could be wound up enough every detail would be extracted. "I'll let you finish as long as you are not giving me crap," he said.

"Let me tell you a story," Scorsi continued. "There was a guy in Detroit who worked as a security man on the gate of a factory for twenty years. Every Friday one man came out with all his working gear in a wheelbarrow. The security man knew he was on the fiddle and every week he searched him and never found a thing. When he retired he met the other in a bar. 'I know you were stealing when I worked at the factory but never could catch you,' he said. 'Now I've retired please tell me what you were taking?' The guy smiled at him and said, 'Every week for twenty years I stole a wheelbarrow.' That's how we bring the coke in."

The others sniggered at the story but Hubbard elected to continue his unwanted criticism. "So who pushes the barrow?" he snorted sarcastically.

"If British Customs are all as dumb as you, Mac, I could use a wheelbarrow." Scorsi was beginning to feel the intellectual superior. "The point of the story is that the security man looked inside the barrow but didn't look at it. That's how we fetch the gear in."

"You mean the containers?" Hubbard put on his most incredulous expression. "The coke is part of the container not in the contents."

"At last the Limey's got it," Scorsi addressed the group as a whole. "That is exactly it. The fruit that is loaded into containers is kosher. Dogs can sniff it to their heart's content and never find a thing. The containers are made with hollow posts at each corner. We shrinkwrap the coke to the exact size, it drops inside and the ends are soldered. When you get the container you sell the fruit, then take off the seals with a hacksaw and out pops your real import. Once you've got the coke out you put the ends back and solder them in place. We even give you a small tin of matching paint to cover where you've worked."

"That's very ingenious, but where does this start its journey? What's the security like at source?" Hubbard knew that Scorsi would answer, if only to put him down.

"The source is Colombia and it is routed through the Caribbean."

"I thought they were really starting to clamp down there?" Hubbard needed to know more and played innocent.

"They are on the major islands like Jamaica and Trinidad." Scorsi was now beginning to enjoy putting the Limey right. "What we have is a company that distributes from St Martin. We operate from the Dutch part of the island. It's actually a genuine business that brings in various fruits from the surrounding islands, like Anguilla and Barbuda, packs it and exports it to the US and Europe. When we have a special customer he gets his own distinctive packaging."

"How does the stuff get to St Martin?" Hubbard forced himself to sound dispassionate.

"If you have ever been to St Martin you would know." Derision oozed in Scorsi's voice. "I could walk through the god-damn airport with an atom bomb in the trolley and the bastards would never notice."

Hubbard had all he wanted to know. He forced the smile that tried to invade the corners of his mouth, into a frown. "I think we have a deal," he whispered quietly. "Who do I work with setting it up?"

"You had better deal through Karen, she's better in the sack than Lord Fauntleroy over there." He indicated Carter. Scorsi's venom was now redirected at his usual whipping boy.

Coffee arrived and was consumed. Hubbard stood. "I'm just going to the khasi, the john to you," he bowed to Scorsi. "I'll tell Justin that we will be about half an hour."

***

Where did you get Justin from?" Cross laughed as he disentangled the microphone.

"I just want them to call you Justin on the way home and see your face when they do. Did you get everything?"

Cross patted the briefcase. "All in there."

The journey back to Park Lane was considerably more relaxed. The deal was set and money was to be made. Scorsi could not resist the final twist of the knife in Carter's side, and told Karen to escort Mr Croft to his flat and see to his needs. Karen obliged with much enthusiasm.

Chapter 14

<u>M15 HEADQUARTERS</u>

Cross could not believe what he was reading. The report had been prepared by the boffins who had dissected the guidance system sent by Curren. He skimmed through the technical jargon that constituted the bulk of the report and read the conclusion.

"Our conclusion, based on the layout of the unit, is that it was originally manufactured in France. The overall design has similarities, which, in our opinion are conclusive, with equipment manufactured for the French military, in particular, the Exocet. This equipment is produced by one of two companies. These are Mutuelle Avionique in Amiens and Electronique de France in Lyon. We are unable to say with any degree of certainty which of these two produced the unit we have inspected."

Cross knew both companies. They were both partially state-owned and, between them, they supplied most of the electronic gizmos for the French military. What perturbed him was that somewhere in the back of his mind he knew something else about Mutuelle Avionique, but could not recall what. He forced his mind away from the subject, hoping that the automatic recall button in his brain would function some time.

He replaced the report in its folder and put it to one side. He knew it was a time bomb and it was ticking. He had evidence that lethal military equipment from a state-run company in one of the country's European partners was being supplied to terrorists trying to overthrow the government in one of Britain's former colonies. The political ramifications were monstrous. He went to the safe and placed the folder inside. The decision on what was to done would take time.

The wall clock told him it was gone six. That night he was meeting with Hubbard and the others. It seemed that matters were now beginning to move.

It was as he drove up Woldingham Hill towards Jennings' home that his brain decided to search its files for Mutuelle Avionique. The name had appeared on Jennings' list of deals that could be suspicious. He remembered asking about them and being told that they did not fit the overall pattern. Mason had said the same when they were at his hotel. Could they be wrong?

Hubbard and Pinter had already arrived and were sitting in the study chatting about football. Jennings poured Cross a drink, saying, "It looks as though things are about to start moving."

Cross took the glass and sat opposite Hubbard. "What has happened, John?" he asked.

"In a couple of days I will be the proud owner of an insurance company in the Turks and Caicos called Oasis Reinsurance and a small fruit importer in Forest Hill. Karen has now given me all the details for the insurer and the formal transfer of ownership should be made within the next week."

"How is the financial deal set up?" Cross asked.

"I've organised that," Jennings interjected. "As you know, your contact in the FBI has given a bank guarantee from Credit Swiss which we can use. That guarantee has been used to set up a trustee account in Liechtenstein. They, as trustees, are putting up the letter of credit for $500,000. Once ownership has been transferred a further $2,500,000 letter of credit will be issued as contributed surplus to the company.

"What is the next step?" Cross knew that soon he would have to involve Customs. Every part of the transaction would have to be monitored.

"The first thing will be the reinsurance deal will have to be set up. I am monitoring all new business from Freddie Jarvis and Michael Mason is doing the same for Jimmy Wilkes. If things follow the past pattern the interlinking reinsurances will be set up within a couple of weeks."

"What about the cocaine? When does that come?" Cross knew that they would have to co-ordinate with the Dutch authorities.

"The first shipment will arrive at the end of next month,"

Hubbard replied. "My fruit company will have to put in the order by the fifteenth. The goods then come by sea to Harwich. British Road Services has been contracted to collect the containers and deliver them to Forest Hill."

"What about the arms? Is anything happening on that front?"

"One deal at a time Jim," Hubbard laughed. "I have given them a shopping list. I said I wanted Uzis, Kalashnikovs and Semtex. Karen has told me that they can be supplied but Scorsi and his supplier want to talk direct. I presume the supplier doesn't want too many people in the know."

"That's a pity," Cross mused. "It would have been nice to have had both transactions running at the same time. It means that we will have to follow the drugs but back off on closing the net until the arms are bought in."

"Is that a problem?" Pinter spoke.

"Not really," Cross commented. "All it means is I have to restrain the publicity-conscious Customs people from shouting about their coup. I'll have to play either the diplomat or the bastard. They normally like to do their own thing without anyone else interfering. I'll start the ball rolling tomorrow."

Jennings looked at his watch. "The taxis should be arriving in half an hour," he remarked. "I thought we could take the ladies out for a meal."

Pansie, Gwen and Jane sat in the lounge. This was in deference to Gwen who held the firm opinion that plottong and schemeing was something for the silly men to do. Both Pansie and Jane would have much preferred to be directly involved. They both knew, however, that all would be revealed to them later. The bottle of Bollinger was some consolation and now nearly empty. All three were giggling.

"Have our heroes sorted out the troubles of the world?" Gwen chuckled.

"Not yet," Pinter replied with mock admonishment. "But we will soon." He turned to Jennings. "You had better get me another drink so I can catch up with these three piss artists."

The building that housed the restaurant had originally been the country retreat for William Pitt the Younger. It had all the accoutrements of an ancient listed building. The wooden floors sloped and creaked in a true antediluvian manner. Between each of the rooms was an archway of a height that meant only the diminutive did not spend the evening crushing various parts of their cranium as they passed through. The food was as solid and English as the original owner of the property.

It was nearly midnight by the time they arrived back at the Jennings household. Charlie was sleeping deeply in his bed as was the babysitter in front of the television. She was woken, paid and sent off in a taxi.

The three wives, under Gwen's instruction, made for the kitchen to make coffee. Jennings opened the cocktail cabinet and produced a bottle of Courvoisier and seven brandy bowls.

"There is something I wanted to ask you, Allan." Cross swirled the brandy in his glass. "When all this business first came up was it you that mentioned a company called Mutuelle Avionique?"

"Yes," Jennings nodded. "They were involved in a reinsurance package that was placed by Freddie Jarvis. Why do you ask?"

"This is totally and absolutely off the record." Cross looked directly at Pinter who shrugged understanding. "You remember that airliner that came down in South Africa?"

"That one with the Minister and the General on board," Hubbard interjected.

"That's the one," Cross continued. "As George knows, it was not an accident. It was shot down with a surface-to-air missile. It was the first time that the AAC had demonstrated the ability to bring down any aircraft. Prior to that they had Yugoslav missiles but the bloody things could not hit a barn at five paces. Suddenly they fetch down an airliner and a few hours later two helicopter gun ships."

"I never heard about the gun ships." Pinter's voice reflected surprise.

"Nobody did," Cross answered. "The South African security services hushed that up."

"What has that to do with Mutuelle Avionique?" asked Jennings.

"Maybe something or nothing," Cross replied. "Following the loss of the aircraft the security services captured one of the leading lights in the military wing of the AAC. He told them there were more missiles and where they were."

213

"Then, I presume, he had a heart attack." Pinter was no lover of the regime. "I guess that the person you are talking about was Joshua Lomobo."

Cross nodded. "Whatever the rights or wrongs, the South Africans raided an AAC camp in Mozambique and captured a number of the missiles. What seems to have happened is that the Yugoslavian missiles, which are very good at exploding but couldn't do it in the right places, had been fitted with a new, highly sophisticated guidance system. From the information I have it is probable that the new targeting devices were manufactured in France by one of two companies. One of them is Mutuelle Avionique. What I wonder is whether there is any connection with those reinsurances you showed us?"

Jennings whistled through his teeth. "If there is, it means there is a whole new game out there. Drugs is one thing but sophisticated armaments is somewhat different."

"Do you think it is possible?" Cross asked.

"That's what worries me." Jennings' mind was racing. "Both my company and Michael's had that deal coming through our books. The company reinsured was Sharom in Israel but, as you probably remember, the original business came from South Africa. It looks too much of a coincidence not to be true."

"Have you got any way of checking whether your deal is kosher or bent?" Hubbard asked.

"I may have." Jennings contemplated. "I think that I'll have a word with Richard Sutcliffe when I'm in Hong Kong next month."

The wives burst in with a tray laden with coffee and accoutrements. Gwen scolded the men for looking too serious and sent Jennings to fetch their cognacs. For the moment the topic of Mutuelle Avionique was closed.

***

"I love you, Allan Jennings, what's on your mind?" she whispered as she snuggled close to him. He had been tossing and turning for several hours. It had been after one o'clock before the others had left. Jennings had wanted to talk, but she was both tired and a little tipsy. "Wait till tomorrow," she told him, "when we are both awake and compos mentis."

Cross' revelation about Mutuelle Avionique troubled Jennings deeply. He had not considered this contract to be a part of his problem. If it was, the predicament was much greater than the others realised. In his mind's eye he could see the computer report on insurances through the facility before it was cancelled. Initially the only sources were in South Africa, but later both South America and the Middle East figured prominently.

He turned and took her in his arms. Tomorrow he would share his apprehension with her. Now he needed her to hide him from the world. "It's nothing for you to worry about tonight," he whispered. "Just make love to me."

***

AMIENS, FRANCE

"Have you managed to trace where the bastard is yet?" Smith's fury was apparent, even through the telephone line.

"We think he is in London," Mersonne replied.

"What do you mean, you think?" Smith began to sound apoplectic. "Is that the fucking best you can come up with? I'm hanging my arse over a precipice and you think he is in London."

"You know the position," snapped Mersonne. "Officially Martinez is dead. He was lost at sea when the *Astrid* was sunk. The only survivor was a Manuel Cossador, who we know is actually Martinez. We have found out that Cossador flew to Zurich from Paris and then on to London. There, the trail stops. We are trying to find one man in a city of eight million."

"You only have a few days left," raged Smith. "If you don't find him we will have to pay the bastard."

***

WEST LONDON

Martinez was becoming bored and frustrated. The weather was typical for late January. Every time he ventured out the freezing

215

drizzle that seemed to fall perpetually from the sky assaulted him. He was from a climate more allied to the equator than the Arctic. The cold and damp burrowed into the marrow of his bones. It was still seven days before his deadline with Mersonne expired.

As he shuffled along the pavement, which shone through its permanent film of rainwater, a poster caught his eye. All it portrayed were sun and sea. The memory of the sun on his back, its warmth soaking through his body, pervaded his mind. He stopped and looked in the window.

Young women in smart red outfits sat behind desks. Pictures of sun-drenched beaches adorned the walls. The urge inside him for the warmth of the sun's rays became overpowering. He already had $1,500,000 in an account in Mexico. If Mersonne failed to produce the rest of the money, retribution could always wait for a few days. He pushed the door and stepped inside the travel agent's.

**

"We have him!" Mersonne's voice was elated. "A Manuel Cossador has booked a flight from Heathrow to Port of Spain in Trinidad. He flies out on Saturday."

"Where is he now?" Smith asked.

"We do not know that," Mersonne replied. "The booking was paid for with a Master Card. The address given was care of a branch of a bank."

"I thought you said you had him?" Exasperation returned to Smith's voice.

"Don't worry we will have. Not only is he flying to Trinidad, we also know that he is stopping at the Hilton. Trinidad is a dangerous place and it is likely that he will be attacked by a drug crazed mugger." Mersonne was smug and elected to endow Smith with his grasp of the English vernacular.

"Just make sure he is." Smith replaced the receiver. He thought for a moment, then picked the telephone up and dialled.

"I have another contract. This time you will only be a back-up in case something goes wrong. How do you fancy a trip to the Caribbean?"

216

***

HILTON HOTEL, PORT-OF-SPAIN, TRINIDAD

The receptionist greeted Martinez courteously and enquired politely about his journey. The reply was mumbled due to the numbing effect of the more than ample supply of free liquor on the British West Indies flight. The bellhop took his bags and escorted him to the lift. In his room Martinez collapsed in a drunken slumber on the bed.

"Mr Cossador has arrived and is in room 321." The receptionist replaced the telephone and patted his wallet that now bulged a little more. He had no idea why the two heavy-set men had wanted to know when Cossador arrived and cared less. The money would buy his wife a new dress and him a night with an extremely proficient whore.

Martinez awoke. His mouth felt as though it was occupied by a large furry animal and there was a dull ache behind his eyes. He showered and changed which made him feel a little more human. The bar was unoccupied apart from a barman who stood idly polishing glasses.

"Give me a large rum," Martinez asked gruffly.

He drained the glass in one and ordered another. A trip to the sun had seemed a good idea but this place was like a morgue. "Is there any life around here?" he asked.

"We are very quiet at the moment, sir," the barman replied politely. "You may find a little more excitement down the town. There are a couple of clubs where it is always lively." The barman winked, guessing that his customer was looking for a combination of sex and booze in whatever order they were most conveniently found.

Martinez showed considerable interest and the barman started to tell him details of where to go. "Excuse me a moment, sir. I will just serve these gentlemen." Martinez ignored the two men and waited for further detail on how his evening should be spent.

After five large rums the jet lag and hangover had both dissipated. He was now in the mood to follow the bartender's advice. The taxi dropped him in a street where a number of neon signs advertised their ability to satisfy most lusts and desires.

By the time he left the third, alcohol had heightened his sexual needs. She stood on the corner, her long legs were accentuated by a microscopic skirt. Her shiny black cleavage peered rather than peeped from the top of her blouse.

"Are you looking for a good time?" Her teeth shone pearly white in the lamplight.

"I could be." His mind was already undressing her.

"Come with me then, man," she smiled, "I'm the best fifty dollars in town."

She walked into a side street beckoning him to follow. Lasciviousness and booze are a combination that most males of the species find difficult to resist. He followed her.

He did not see the two men as he passed them, nor did he feel the blade enter his back. He was dead before any pain could be transmitted to his brain.

"Looks like a ganja victim." The policeman stood over the blood-soaked corpse of Martinez. "Better get a suit out here. They always like to look as though they investigate these things." He knew the detectives would make a cursory examination of the scene and then file the whole matter with all the other unsolved muggings.

The other clicked his radio on and relayed the detail of what lay in front of him.

The police investigation was thorough by normal standards to the extent that they identified the body as 'a Manuel Cossador', a Spanish citizen. They had found enough ganja on the body to be fairly sure he was dealing rather than using. From that point it would be an unsolved drug-related murder.

The Spanish consulate was lumbered with a body, which had no traceable next of kin. Neither the credit card Company nor the bank in London could offer any real assistance as to the origin of Manuel Cossador. All anyone knew was that the passport he carried had been issued in Mozambique and he had several thousand pounds in a London bank account. The body was eventually buried in Port of Spain, initially at the expense of the Spanish tax-payer, and what little belongings he had were sent to a bank in London.

218

"The minor problem has now been eliminated." Mersonne raised his glass.

"It shouldn't have happened in the first place." Smith did not join the toast. "If we go ahead there is not going to be any more fuck-ups, are there?"

"You pay us the money and we will deliver the goods to wherever you wish," Mersonne replied. "By the way, when will you be resuming payments? I have so-called defective stock in the factory. It cannot remain there for too long."

"I should be organised within a few weeks."

Chapter 15

"I think I might have what you were looking for." Mason's voice was its normal cheery self.

Jennings picked up the handset. This was a conversation not to be broadcast on the squawk box. "What do you have, Michael?"

"One of Jimmy Wilkes' facilities has suddenly come to life and it involves Oasis. It has been set up a few months for business produced from an agent in Houston. The insurer is Carlos Pedrosa and he is reinsured with Lloyds."

"Let me guess," Jennings interjected, "Larry Payne."

"Yes," Mason replied, "and Kieron O'Sullivan and Jack Green. All three have a reinsurance with Oasis. The cover has been in place for six months and suddenly business is being declared to it, most of it incepting several months ago."

"We have been waiting for this." Excitement set an edge in Jennings' voice. "Can you get copies of what you've got?"

"Already in my briefcase."

"Can you meet for lunch tomorrow? How's the City FOB sound?" Jennings was already formulating the next move.

Mason confirmed that he could.

The FOB was designed to look like an old London ale house. The wooden floor had a covering of sawdust to add authenticity. Jennings had reserved the private room known as the Office.

Cross and Pinter were already a third of the way through their first jug of Davy's Old Peculiar Ale when Jennings and Mason arrived. There was an air of expectancy. Not only had the fox broken cover, now the hounds had the scent.

"What have you got?" Cross ignored the niceties of formal greetings.

Mason pulled a file of papers from his attaché case and placed it on the table.

"This package was set up several months ago. It has stayed dormant for some time. Last week we received a batch of declarations on the cover, some dating back to the time it incepted. What someone needs to do is to find out if any of the locations shown here have had a fire."

"How many are there?" Jennings asked.

"See for yourself." Mason passed him the file.

Jennings studied the documents before him. The total premium amounted to just over $200,000. Pedrosa's company, as the insurer, kept the first $10,000 of any claim and $50,000 of the premium. The Lloyds underwriters had the next $10,000 of the claim and another $50,000 of the premium. The numbers fitted exactly.

"This is definitely it," he exclaimed. "Look at the figures. The cocaine buy is for $1,000,000. That means that the fee for washing the money will be another $200,000, of which Pedrosa gets forty and Lloyds forty. This matches exactly. If I am right, Carter takes his share as the claim passes. That means the claim will be…" he frowned as the mental arithmetic spun around his head, "…in the region of $1,320,000."

Pinter looked totally perplexed. "How do you get to that?" he asked.

"John has to pay $1,000,000 for the drugs." Jennings wrote the figure down on his notepad. "That means the costs of moving the money are another $200,000. Of that $80,000 goes to Pedrosa and Lloyds, that is the four per cent each that Carter mentioned to John. They get that at the start." He pointed to the two reinsurance transactions. "They both get $50,000 of premium and pay $10,000 in a claim leaving them $40,000."

"I'm with you so far," nodded Pinter.

"As it stands at the moment John has got $100,000 in premium but has to pay that back plus the $1,200,000 for the drugs and fee. Lloyds and Pedrosa have got $50,000 but should only have $40,000. The claim has to adjust all three back to their correct position on the whole deal."

Pinter smiled, like St Paul on the road to Damascus, as the numbers fell into place. "Of course," he cried, "John has to pay

$1,200,000 for the total deal, but he also has got $100,000 extra in premium, so he has to pay that back as well. That makes his payment $1,300,000. The two in the middle have got $10,000 too much so that has to be returned. They each pay $10,000 towards the claim. So the claim is the deal, plus the premium and the rebate from the middlemen. Hey presto $1,320,000." He grinned inanely, like an economist who had actually made a correct prediction, if ever such a thing could actually happen.

"What do you intend to do next, Allan?" Mason asked.

"If you let me have the list of locations I will pass it on to Richard Sutcliffe. His people can look and see where there has been a fire."

"That's a copy for you." Mason passed a sheet to Jennings.

He studied the schedule. There were seventeen insureds listed with properties at thirty locations in Texas. As he ran down the addresses and sums insured he mentally discarded those where the value was too small to be used. He surmised that a single claim would be used to move the cash. There were six possibilities for Sutcliffe to investigate.

***

That evening Hubbard received a visit from Karen. After the initial, most physical, greeting, she wanted to talk business. The consignment was now on its way to St Martin and the money was to be paid. Hubbard was required to set up an evergreen letter of credit for Oasis amounting to $1,200,000. Once this was done the process would be automatic and he would be told when to expect his consignment.

Hubbard's libidinous desires had not wanted Karen to leave when she did, but her efficient character had, for the moment, ousted the siren in her. He dialled Jennings' number.

"Karen has been here," he began.

"I can hear that. You're still panting," laughed Jennings.

"Piss off and listen," Hubbard replied aggrieved. "She came to tell me that the delivery has started its journey. I have to set up the finances within twenty-four hours. I will be flying out to Switzerland tomorrow to sign the papers."

"I'll pass the information on to Jim." Jennings replaced the receiver.

He picked it up immediately and punched in a number in Hong Kong.

"Sutcliffe," a voice said.

"Richard, it's Allan Jennings. I have a job for you." Jennings gave Sutcliffe the list of addresses. "I have to know if any of them have had a fire in the last four months and, if they have, who were the insurers. I also have to know within the next couple of days."

"It's only the impossible that we find difficult," Sutcliffe chuckled. "I can have this for you within a day."

Jennings next phoned Cross and told him the project was moving.

He went upstairs and into Charlie's room. The boy was sleeping the slumber of the innocent. The corners of his mouth twitched occasionally as the fantasies of the dreamworld flitted across his mind.

Jennings sat on the bed watching, wishing he still retained such innocence. He knew that a tiny snowball was just starting to roll down the mountain. Who would be engulfed in the resulting avalanche?

MI5 HEADQUARTERS, WHITEHALL – 16TH FEBRUARY 1985

"I realise that importation of controlled substances is usually a matter for Customs and Excise." Cross was becoming exasperated. "What you have to realise is that this may also involve matters of national security."

Cross had called the meeting to co-ordinate the actions of the interested parties. Both Customs and the police had immediately demanded to take overall control as the matter came within their particular sphere. Tony Westhead, the senior Customs officer, was practically drooling at the publicity, and potential promotion, he would get from a drug capture of this size. Eric Malcolm from the drug squad was starting to see himself as a future Chief Constable of Essex on the same premise.

"We are not simply following an illegal importation of cocaine. There are much wider implications." Cross tried to put authority in his voice.

"We cannot have that amount of cocaine passing without seizure," Westhead interjected. "On the streets that could kill hundreds of youngsters."

"For fuck sake." Cross' temper had finally snapped. "It is not going onto the streets. The importer is working for us. What we are after is the whole chain including the money laundering and the arms."

"I understand that, sir," Malcolm saw an opportunity to score a point. "It is absolutely vital that we break the whole business up. In view of the substantial surveillance that will be needed I believe that the policing authorities must be responsible for co-ordination."

"No they will not," Cross sighed. "I will be responsible for co-ordination. You and your people will do exactly as they are instructed. If you wish me to get written authority to that from the Prime Minister, then I will." He passed a folder to each. "There is an outline of exactly what I need from each of you. I want you to take it away and study it. If you have any problems, tell me."

The two took the documents and left like sulky children whose lollipops had been taken away. Cross watched them leave with relief. Inter-departmental arguments on one's authority over the other were always the most wearing of disputes.

Over the last week matters had started to move. The Dutch authorities had advised him that a container had been shipped to Markem's Importers of Forest Hill in London. The cargo was tropical fruits. The container had been shipped four days previous, on route to Harwich via Amsterdam.

The evening before, Mason had informed him that the claim they had been expecting had arrived in the offices of Bannister Ellis. The adjuster's report on the fire was known to be genuine as Sutcliffe had discovered it two weeks before. It was not insured with Pedrosa but the report stated it was. The claim was for $1,320,000 as expected. Cross had sat up half the night formulating his plans.

Customs and police would combine to follow the shipment to its destination. Anybody involved in its movement would be filmed and identified.

Sutcliffe, with his skills at interrogating other people's computers, would follow the payment. Now all he could do was wait.

His private line buzzed. He picked it up and said, "Cross."

"John has a meeting with the arms suppliers tonight," Jennings' voice said.

"Where and what time?" Cross asked urgently.

"They are going to his flat," came the reply.

Cross' mind buzzed with conflicting questions. 'Have I got time to set up proper observation?' 'Can I risk bugging the flat?' He was suddenly aware that Jennings had not finished talking. "Say that again," he asked.

"John has already bugged the flat so we can have a record of the conversation," Jennings continued. "And George will have one of his photographers across the road, using a fancy lens, so we have snaps of who goes in and out."

***

The man that arrived with Scorsi had Arabic features and spoke with a mid-Atlantic accent. The dark brown tone of his skin was partly genetic. Blue skies and clear sunshine had also contributed. Scorsi introduced him as Ray Burns. He greeted Hubbard warmly, as one would a friend.

"I understand that you may wish to purchase some equipment from us." Burns spoke as he accepted the Scotch proffered by Hubbard.

"That is the purpose of this meeting, I believe." Hubbard elected to be both blunt and offish.

"Straight to business," Burns mused. "I like that. Joe tells me you want Uzis, Kalashnikovs, Semtex and, of course, ammunition. Is that correct?"

Hubbard nodded but said nothing.

"Can you tell me the quantities you require?"

Hubbard opened the folder on the table and gave Burns a sheet of paper. Burns took the document and read it.

"It looks as though you or your associates want to start a small war." He looked at Hubbard.

"I think you will find that my associates have been involved

225

in a small war for the last twenty years. However, the use that they will be put to is not your affair. All I need to know is, can you supply and, if so, how, where and how much?"

"Oh, I can certainly supply you with what is listed here. I would suggest that the Browning machine pistol is superior to the Uzi should you prefer it." He smirked at Hubbard like a life assurance salesman.

"My client prefers the Uzi," Hubbard replied brusquely. "How do you intend delivering the order?"

"I presume that I am right in assuming that the merchandise is to go to Northern Ireland." The smile never left Burns' face. He continued without waiting for affirmation. "They would initially come in by ocean-going trawler to Kinlochbervie on the north east coast of Scotland. There they would be transferred to a smaller fishing vessel and be moved to Ireland. Larne would be one possibility, but I would prefer Ballycastle."

"You talk as though you have done this before," Hubbard commented.

"Mr Croft." He leaned across and patted Hubbard's arm. "Your clients may abhor republicans, but there are also parties who find loyalists an abomination. Their needs are much the same as yours. Their deliveries usually go to Ballbriggan or Drogheda. What you are getting is only a small detour from a well used route."

Hubbard suppressed a smile. He was getting more than he had hoped. "How soon can you deliver the goods?"

"Once I have the money, that is one million dollars, I can deliver in three weeks."

"Then we have a deal." Hubbard stood, indicating that the meeting had now concluded.

"Karen will be in touch," Scorsi said as he left.

***

"Who was that greasy little bastard?" Hubbard asked.

The four were sitting in Jennings' study. Photographs and papers were spread across the desk.

"He is actually a Lebanese by the name of Ahmit Doron," Cross replied. "He has interests all over the world. He spends

226

most of his time on his yacht in the Mediterranean. Most of his business is run from Monte Carlo."

"How the hell is he connected with the Mafia?"

"We didn't know he was until now," Cross answered. "He may simply be a one-off supplier. We certainly suspected him of being behind some of the arms in the hands of the IRA but could never prove anything."

"You can now," laughed Jennings. "You have the bastard by the balls if you want him."

"The problem is…" Cross' brow furrowed, "…there is no way we can tie Doran in with the missiles in South Africa. His sources of supply are mainly lunatic dictators in the Middle East. None of them could have access to the sort of guidance equipment that was in those missiles."

"It may be that there is not a connection," Jennings broke in. "It is still possible that the business in South Africa was simply coincidental."

"I do not like that sort of coincidence," muttered Cross. "Anyway, what is the next step?"

"It would seem that things are moving." It was Jennings who spoke. "Michael rang me today and told me that the Oasis cover is now getting declarations from Syria and Lebanon. I should have the details tomorrow and I will pass them on to Richard Sutcliffe."

"What about the cocaine?" asked Pinter.

"That's on its way," Cross responded. "It will off-load in Amsterdam tomorrow. The Dutch Customs will inspect the container as part of what will look like a random check. They will put a homing beacon inside so that we can follow it if it deviates from the route we have been given. Our Customs will pick it up at Harwich and follow it to its destination."

"When do you intend to close the net?" Pinter's enquiry was more related to when he could emblazon the front page of the *Record* with his exclusive than an actual interest in the timing.

"Don't worry, George." Cross read Pinter's motive. "You will get your exclusive. At the moment we will have to wait for the arms deal to go down before we move. Then we have to co-ordinate with the agencies in the other countries involved. To use the Custom's term, we all have to knock at the same time."

227

"Is there anything else we need to talk about?" Hubbard looked at his watch. "I have the lovely Karen calling on me tonight and I should get some rest in first." He winked at Jennings.

***

ZURICH, SWITZERLAND

"I thought you looked a good lay when you came looking for your golf ball in my back yard." She nuzzled her head into his furry chest. "But I never realised that you would be phenomenal."

She had reversed her roles this time. When she arrived she had been the efficient businesswoman. The arms transaction had been arranged and the weapons were to be delivered within three weeks of the money being transferred. She had decided to accompany Hubbard to Zurich and indulge her ire. Carter had objected but he could never take her body to the heights that Croft elevated her to, so his entreaty fell on deaf ears.

The flight to Zurich had been uneventful and the meeting with his attorney short and efficient. The Liechtenstein bank would set up a further letter of credit for Oasis for $1,200,000 within twenty-four hours. The documents were prepared and signed in half an hour. They could have returned to London that afternoon but chose to stay.

They took a room at the Ascot and made love for the afternoon. That evening they went to the old town and feasted on *Zurcher Geschnetzel* and *Rösti*. Several bottles of local wine accompanied the meal. They returned to the hotel and made love for most of the night.

"I need a new partner," she whispered, her body still on the plateau of her last orgasm.

"Why, wasn't that good enough for you?" Hubbard joked.

"I mean business partner, you idiot." She slapped him on the chest. "I know how Cameron's scams work and can do them myself. What I need is a big strong man to look after me," she tweaked his biceps, "Like you."

"Who will you deal with?" he asked. "Carter seems to have

228

a pretty tight hold on his end of the business. Do you think that Scorsi will drop him for you?"

"No." Her mouth was set firm. "Cameron knows too much. If Joe wanted to change his operation he would have to remove Cameron permanently. I wouldn't want that."

"Who would you deal with then?"

"There is one guy who Cameron dealt with until he fucked up. He was talking really big money. The operation was set up and running when the plug was pulled."

"Why was that?" Hubbard tried to keep his voice calm.

"I don't really know why, but I think it was a hit on some guy in London that went wrong."

Hubbard's mind was now racing. The 'guy in London' had to be Jennings. "Have you a contact with Mr Big Money?" he asked casually.

"I got it out of Joe Scorsi's files. His name is Tom Smith or that's what he uses. I have already spoken to him and told him that I know another source that can handle the money. All I need is for you to contact him and we can set up an arrangement using a man called Jarvis. It was him who designed the original deal."

"He must be one of Carter's men if he was in on the first arrangement," Hubbard inquired innocently.

"He is out of it now. It was his bit of tail that fucked up the hit. He was bedding her when she was blown away."

"What use is he if his bottle has gone?"

She looked at him disdainfully. "He might have been scared shitless but he is still a greedy bastard. If the money is right he will do it."

"It looks as though we are partners." He took her in his arms.

That morning they both boarded the Swissair flight to New York.

***

"If I find that either Scorsi or that po-faced English asshole have anything to do with this you are both dead meat." Smith's face was expressionless. "How does that big-assed broad know you?"

"She's good in the sack and, obviously, has some good

229

connections." Hubbard smiled.

Hubbard and Karen had arrived in New York and checked into the Vista in the World Trade Centre. The meeting with Smith had been arranged for the following day. To pass the time away he had succumbed to the persistent ministrations of his new partner. He had never before been the recipient of a blow job whilst telephoning a business connection and found the experience both perplexing and stimulating.

Karen had stayed in the bedroom of the suite when Smith arrived. Hubbard could see her in his mind's eye. She was dressed in only a tiny lace bra, just large enough to cover her nipples, silk French knickers and a translucent negligee. When he had finished with Smith she would undress him, her lips following her fingers as she disrobed him.

"How soon can you begin to move the cash?"

Hubbard dragged his mind away from the enticing crotch that awaited him in the adjoining room. "Once I know the source of the funds and their destination, it should be only a few weeks," he replied.

"There are two sources." Smith produced a file from his attaché case. "One is in Jordan and the other Honduras."

"And the destination?"

"An insurance company in Jersey. It's in that file."

Hubbard opened the file. The name jumped at him, Mutuelle Avionique. He continued looking at the file, waiting for his heartbeat to return to normal.

"I see that you are looking to shift $10,000,000 from Jordan and $15,000,000 from Honduras. That, plus our commission, is a lot of money from two small countries." Hubbard's brain was dredging all the scattered knowledge he had accumulated from Jennings about the business of reinsurance. "Do we have to limit ourselves to just those countries?"

"I don't give a fuck what you do. All you have to do is get the dollars to Jersey without any waves appearing." Smith stood to leave. "I need an address where I can contact you."

Hubbard produced a card from his wallet. Smith took it and left.

The bedroom door opened. He had been almost right about her attire. The negligee was loosely fastened and her dark brown nipples peeped through the fine lace. The negligee dropped to the floor and Hubbard realised that he had slightly overdressed her in his mind. The french-knickers had remained in the bedroom. Her dusky blonde pubic hair glistened with the desire that was within her.

She tore at the buttons of his shirt. She was on her knees, her lips caressed his chest and navel whilst her hands removed his remaining clothing. She looked up at him and smiled voluptuously. "We've just made five million bucks," she whispered. "How do you want me to thank you?" Her tongue teased his manhood and his passion rose. He picked her up and carried her into the bedroom. They coupled like the last survivors of an endangered species.

They spent two more days in New York. During the day they played the part of wide-eyed tourists. The Empire State Building was climbed, the Statton Island Ferry was travelled on and the Statue of Liberty inspected. In the evenings they dined at the finest restaurants and returned to the hotel to discover every nuance of the other's body that gave physical gratification.

Finally reality forced its unwelcome snout into their temporary licentious world. If $5,000,000 was to be made they had to return to London, and Hubbard was expecting a shipment of fruit the following day. Karen telephoned Jarvis and arranged to meet him at Hubbard's flat the day after they returned.

Chapter 16

Both Jennings and Cross were becoming perturbed at the extended absence of Hubbard. He had intended to go to Zurich for one day to set up the new financial arrangement with the bankers. That had been four days previous.

The cocaine container had arrived at Amsterdam. The Dutch Customs had made what appeared to be a cursory inspection. They had the container opened and one had squeezed between the boxes of fruit and fixed the small beacon to the container wall. They had then ordered the container to be re-sealed. Three days later it was loaded onto a ship destined for Harwich.

"Where the hell has he got to?" Cross was agitated. All the documentation for the import of the fruit was complete but Hubbard would have to confirm delivery. "If he fucks this up I will kill him."

Jennings leaned back in his chair. "Give him a chance. The delivery is not scheduled until tomorrow. He will contact you or me."

"I hope so." Cross was unconvinced. He knew that occasionally Hubbard's sense of responsibility could evaporate if his crotch became inflamed. Three years previously an operation had nearly collapsed because Hubbard, the undercover man, had been getting his leg over a Soviet agent.

The intercom buzzed on Jennings' desk. "I have a Mr Hubbard for you," trilled Jennings' secretary. Relief showed visibly in Cross' eyes.

Jennings picked up the receiver.

"Jesus Christ, I'm knackered," Hubbard's voice echoed in the handset. "If she's not asleep she is wanting to bonk. I've been at it for the last three days, non-stop."

"So you get all the lousy jobs," Jennings chuckled. "We were worried about you. The fruit has arrived and is waiting to be delivered."

"Shit!" Hubbard exclaimed, "The bloody stuff's here a day early."

"Can you sort it out?" Jennings asked.

"I will authorise collection with BRS this afternoon," Hubbard confirmed. "I also have to see you and Jim as soon as possible. It looks as though I am now handling a money laundering deal from Jordan and Honduras to Mutuelle Avionique."

"Just a second," said Jennings. He indicated to Cross to pick up the other extension. "Go on."

"It would seem that Carter," Hubbard continued, "was originally shifting a lot of money for a guy who says his name is Tom Smith. For some reason they fell out and Smith is now looking for someone else to do the job for him. Karen contacted him and it looks as though we have a deal. I'm seeing your Freddie Jarvis tomorrow night to discuss it."

"How is Freddie involved?" Jennings questioned.

"It would seem that Karen is declaring independence from Carter. Jarvis handled the initial package with this guy Smith so Karen is going to offer him a piece of the action to work with us."

"Do you think he will go for it?" Cross interjected.

"That is anybody's guess," Hubbard responded. "If he doesn't we'll have to find someone else. I don't know what these bastards are flogging, but whatever it is it will be high tech and probably bloody nasty."

The three arranged to meet that evening at the Prospect of Whitby in Wapping. Hubbard suggested that Pinter would be interested and Jennings agreed to call him.

***

DAILY RECORD'S OFFICE

George Pinter had been staring at the contents of the letter that had arrived on his desk that morning. It had been addressed to him and marked 'Strictly Private'. The covering letter was from the Manager of the Cromwell Road branch of the National

Westminster Bank. It read:

Dear Mr Pinter,
 Re Manuel Cossador
 The above gentleman was a customer of this branch and I have recently been advised by the authorities in Trinidad that he has died following a mugging in Port of Spain.

 Following extensive enquiries by the Spanish consulate, it appears that he has no surviving relatives. The only traceable connection of this gentleman was this bank. I was approached by the Trinidad Authorities to see if I could assist them in any way.

 Mr Cossador had a current account with us and a safety deposit. The current account offered no assistance other than a transfer of monies which had been received from Union Bank in Zurich. They would not supply any details without an order from the court.

 In view of the difficulty it was decided to open the safety deposit. This, of course, is not an action undertaken lightly by this bank, but in the circumstances seemed justified.

 The only item in the safety deposit was the attached, which is a sealed envelope addressed to you and marked confidential. We did not consider it to be correct to open the attached, so have elected to forward it to you in the hope that you may be able to assist us in tracing the next of kin of the deceased.

 I would be most obliged if you could let me know if you have any information relating to the late Mr Cossador.

 Yours sincerely

 Paul Rhodes
 Branch Manager

Pinter looked again at the contents of the envelope.

There were several photographs of the same man. Some were taken as he entered or left an office. Others were in ordinary places such as cafés and bars. The only thing that could be deduced from the pictures was that they were taken somewhere in a French-speaking country.

There was only one which featured someone other than the main subject. He was dining with a heavy-set man with black curly hair that tinted grey at the temples. Whilst the face was unclear, somewhere in the depths of Pinter's brain the features were familiar.

The only other item in the envelope was a letter addressed to Pinter.

Dear Señor Pinter,

If you receive this letter it will mean that I am dead.

I have, for many years, been involved in the transportation of various less than legal goods across the seas. I was the owner of my own ship named the MV Astrid.

I had an agreement to transport machine tools from Le Havre to Madagascar. There was also a second cargo, which was off-loaded in the Mozambique Channel. For transporting this second cargo I was paid F.Frcs 500,000 in cash. The second cargo was taken from my ship, at night, in the Channel. The men who took the cargo were, I now know, members of the Anti-Apartheid Congress. Several hours after unloading the cargo there was an explosion aboard the Astrid *and the ship was lost with all hands apart from myself. I was rescued at sea and taken to Mozambique where I adopted the identity of my first mate, Manuel Cossador, who was lost with the ship.*

Whilst in Maputo, awaiting papers for my new identity, I came across the group of men who unloaded the cargo from my ship. They were celebrating the destruction of the South African airliner with the Minister for the Interior aboard.

One of the group, who was very drunk, told me that they had obtained eyes for their missiles. I guessed that my cargo had supplied these eyes.

I came to Europe to find the man who had given me the cargo, with the intention of making him pay for the loss of my ship. He is the man in the photographs attached to this letter. He is named Thierry Mersonne and is a Director of a Company called Mutuelle Avionique.

I have studied the English papers and you seem to be an expert on all matters of security. This letter has been written for you to avenge my death by uncloaking the bastards for what they

235

have done to me.
With kindest regards

Pablo Martinez

There was a bizarre un-English formality about the letter as Pinter read it. The writer had his own opinion on how the English corresponded and had elected to adopt it. Pinter tried to imagine Martinez struggling to write the letter in proper English whilst contemplating his possible demise. It was the last paragraph that revealed the true Pablo Martinez. If his attempts at blackmail were to fail, retribution would still be his.

The telephone chirped into life, interrupting Pinter's musing.

"It looks as though things are starting to move," said Jennings' voice. "We are meeting for dinner at the Prospect tonight at seven thirty."

"I'll be there," replied Pinter, "I'll most definitely be there."

***

The Prospect of Whitby still retained much of the character of the old smuggler's inn which had been its origin. The modern accoutrements, a requirement for today's tourists, had been added but the long oak bar and the sawdust-covered plank floors had been leaned on or trodden by many a scoundrel in the past.

Jennings and Cross were at the bar when Pinter arrived. They greeted him warmly and a pint of ale was duly produced.

Jennings looked at his Rolex saying, "John will be about half an hour."

"What is happening then?" Pinter asked. The letter from Martinez was in his briefcase but he wanted the full audience in attendance before producing his surprise.

"The drugs are being delivered tomorrow," Cross began. "Customs have been tracking the container since it left St Martin. They have full surveillance equipment at the Forest Hill warehouse and will have photographs of anyone who has any contact with the container."

"Will I be able to get any copies or do I need my own photographer?" Pinter enquired.

"I will let you have some photos for your story when you publish it," Cross smiled. "He's like a ferret down a rabbit hole if he thinks he's got an exclusive." The aside was directed at Jennings.

"Just make sure you remember that I want the arms as well," Cross proceeded. "Once we have got the arms delivery we can close the net on all the bastards at once. I don't want a whisper of this to get out before then."

"Can you keep the lid on it?" Pinter inquired.

"The FBI are keeping tabs on their end and waiting on my instructions. Interpol can move on Doron any time I ask them. My only problem is the local police and Customs. Both the bastards see this as a leg-up for their next promotion."

"Can you keep them in line?"

Cross winked at Pinter. "If they get out of line they will be standing in a bloody dole queue."

"What about John's new connection?" Jennings queried.

Pinter raised his eyebrows. "What new connection?"

"It would seem that John's sensual prowess has so impressed the lovely Karen that she wants to set up in business with him and drop Carter," Jennings responded. "He will tell us all the details when he gets here, but it looks as though Mutuelle Avionique are not as innocent as we imagined."

Pinter's eyes widened. "What's this about Mutuelle Avionique?" he asked.

"It would seem that a former connection of Carter wants money shifted from Honduras and Jordan to them. The trouble is we don't know why."

"Shit," Pinter muttered. "I know why." He opened his case and produced copies of Martinez' letter which he gave to Cross and Jennings.

"God in hell, this is fucking dynamite," Cross murmured as he read the letter. He turned to Jennings. "Am I right in thinking that the deal you and Michael Mason thought was kosher came from South Africa through Israel and London and ended up with Avionique?"

Jennings nodded sombrely. "If this is true, and these bastards are supplying guidance systems, where are the next lot going to?"

"Take your pick," Cross replied. "You have the Palestinians and the fundamentalists in the Middle East, and South and Central America are hotbeds of potential revolution. Whoever this stuff goes to, a lot of shit is going to hit a lot of fans." He looked at Pinter. "Have you got the photographs here, George?"

"These copies are for you." Pinter passed an envelope to Cross.

Cross flicked through them and suddenly stopped. "What about this other guy here?" He pointed to the picture of Mersonne and the stranger. "What has he got to do with it?"

"Buggered if I know," Pinter snapped. "You have got the same information as me. Do you know him?"

"I know him." Cross' voice reflected his apprehension. "His name is Tom O'Connell. He's with the CIA."

"He also calls himself Tom Smith and likes to shift illicit cash." Nobody had noticed Hubbard arrive. He leaned over Cross' shoulder and looked more closely at the photograph. "That is definitely the Tom Smith who wants me and Karen to do a bit of money laundering."

"It looks as though we have a real problem," Cross mused. "O'Connell is closely tied in with the operation we are running with John. Whether he is working on his own or this is a CIA operation, he's going to have to throw a spanner in the works before we close the net just to protect himself."

"I thought you were co-ordinating with the FBI," Pinter interpolated.

"I am, but the CIA are also being kept fully informed by the FBI."

"Tell the bastards to lie to them then." Hubbard, as ever, suggested the uncomplicated solution.

"I wish it were that simple," Cross sighed. "Just put yourself in their position. I would have to go to them and tell them to mislead their own security services, and not give them any sound reason, just a suspicion. Even if they believed me they would have to take the matter higher. If this business with Avionique is actually a CIA covert operation we blow the whole thing. If it isn't they will jump on O'Connell straight away and we still end up stuffed."

"What do you want to do then?" Jennings asked.

"God in hell knows," Cross muttered. "I need some time to think the whole thing through."

"Time is one thing we haven't got," Hubbard broke in. "I am supposed to be taking a delivery of cocaine tomorrow. Apart from that, there is a load of weapons and ammunition which will soon be on its way."

"Look." Cross' mind was searching for a way around the problem. "We go ahead tomorrow as agreed. The police and customs will have enough evidence after tomorrow to pull in all the people from London and the FBI will have the same their end, but we want the whole thing absolutely watertight. That means that nothing will happen until after the arms are shipped, so we have a little breathing space. That's the best I can suggest for the moment."

"What about John's position?" Jennings interposed. "This O'Connell knows that we have someone working under cover. If he puts two and two together and actually manages to make four, John is up to his neck in a cesspit."

Cross looked at Hubbard. "I am afraid that's a chance we are going to have to take."

"Don't worry, Allan." Hubbard slapped Jennings on the shoulder. "Independents like me are always classified as dispensable by the security services."

"What time is the shipment arriving tomorrow?" Cross addressed Hubbard.

"It's expected some time after ten," was the reply.

"Someone else is going to have to take the delivery, John. You can't be there."

"Why the hell not?" Hubbard retorted indignantly.

"Westhead, from Customs, and Malcolm, from the drug squad, have got the whole place neatly set up," Cross proceeded. "Customs people will be there acting as workers at the warehouse. Video cameras have been set up so there is a full record of the delivery from the time it arrives until the cocaine is impounded. A copy of that film will go to the FBI, which means that the CIA and O'Connell will probably see it. If O'Connell recognises you, your cover is blown."

Hubbard nodded sagely and turned to Jennings. "What about this little shit Jarvis I am seeing tomorrow? Anything I need to know?" he asked. Hubbard was totally practical. He knew he would have to miss the kill but a greater target awaited him.

"You will probably have to lean on him a bit," Jennings responded. "Ever since someone blew Penny Hacker away two minutes after he had given her one, he's been like a frightened rabbit."

"That's not a problem," Hubbard smiled. "I think I might enjoy meeting your Mr Jarvis." The ability to instil terror into another human being had always been one of Hubbard's major attributes.

A waiter appeared and presented each with a menu. The conversation turned, temporarily, to the topic of food and drink. The food was ordered and they made their way to a table with a view of the river.

Over dinner the arrangements for the following day were finalised. It was decided that Jennings would act as Hubbard's stand-in for the purposes of the delivery as both Cross and Pinter's faces were too well known to possible viewers of the video.

Hubbard quizzed Jennings, in depth, about the operation of insurance and reinsurance in readiness for his tryst with Jarvis.

By the time the spotted Dick, which was a unanimous choice as a sweet, arrived all plans had been finalised.

FOREST HILL, LONDON – 8TH MARCH 1985

The entrance to the warehouse was from a narrow side street. The driver made several attempts before successfully reversing his trailer into the yard.

"Can you reverse it inside the warehouse?" a voice shouted.

The driver realised that this was not actually a request but an order and edged backwards until the trailer was inside the sliding doors. He switched off his engine and alighted from the cab. He saw that the source of the voice was a tall man dressed in jeans and a grey sweater.

"Morning, guv, sign here," he said cheerily and presented Jennings with a delivery note in duplicate. "I am supposed to collect the trailer and the empty container tomorrow morning. Is that right?" he queried.

240

"That's right," Jennings nodded and returned the delivery note signed.

"I'll see you then," the driver said jovially. "By the way…" he now spoke quietly. "…I can put you in touch with someone who will give you a nice deal on any of the pallets you don't want." He winked at Jennings. Many drivers in the heavy haulage industry had their small sidelines, which were always treated as a fringe benefit.

"No thanks," said Jennings brusquely, "I have already got a buyer."

"Never mind, maybe another time," the driver commented breezily. He busied himself disconnecting the trailer. He waved airily as he drove from the yard, shouting something that was inaudible.

"Get those bloody doors shut and start unloading all this fruit." Westhead had decided to take control of the proceedings. The other Customs officers reacted dutifully. Westhead was ambitious to a fault and possessed all the management skills of Attila the Hun.

It took an hour to unload the pallets that were piled high with boxes of exotic fruits. Finally they were all stacked neatly along one wall awaiting inspection. That would be a pointless, but necessary, exercise.

A ladder was placed against the corner of the container. Westhead climbed the ladder and inspected the corner-piece.

"It has been soldered," he shouted and started cutting with a hacksaw. After a couple of minutes the end of the corner stanchion slipped from its mounting. He reached inside and his fingers grasped heavy-duty plastic. There were several layers. He gripped the first and pulled. A white package emerged, about a foot long and two inches square. "Got the bastards," he shouted triumphantly. He grabbed the second layer and another neat chalky parcel emerged. Soon there was a pile of ten solid blocks of cocaine standing neatly atop the container.

"What the blazes is this?" Westhead muttered as he drew the last package from its hiding place. "It's a tin of bloody paint." He held it up for those below to see.

The packets were passed down to the ground and Westhead descended the ladder. "Check the rest of the stanchions," he

241

ordered one of his assistants. He had the glory of discovering the cocaine so a minion could finish the job.

Each corner post of the container yielded ten packages.

"There must be about twenty kilos here." Westhead addressed Cross as they watched the last of the cocaine being removed. "I'd like to thank you for the information."

Cross realised that Westhead's brain was now ringing with the plaudits he would receive for the haul that had been discovered. He had already relegated Cross to the position of a useful informer and nothing else.

"Get onto headquarters and organise some transport for the container," Westhead shouted to one of his associates.

"You will do no such thing," Cross interjected. "I want those ends replaced, sealed and painted. The container is being collected."

"I am sorry, Mr Cross, but that is not possible." Westhead put on his comptroller's voice. "That container is evidence and has to be retained with Customs."

The other officers stood, waiting to see Cross' reaction.

"I don't give a toss whether it is evidence or not, Mr Westhead," Cross exploded. "I want that container sealed, re-painted and ready for collection tomorrow."

"But it is evidence," Westhead's voice quavered slightly as he repeated himself. "It has to be retained by Customs until a prosecution is brought. If we do not present full and proper evidence for the defence to examine, a prosecution could be thrown out."

"Fuck your proper evidence, Westhead" Cross' anger had now reached boiling point. "I am running this operation and this is only a part of it. I am not having an officious little shit like you bugger it up because it is more than your job is worth."

The other Customs officers tried to hide their glee at the strip that was being torn from their less-than-beloved leader.

"You will reinstate that container to its original condition." Cross now spoke quietly through gritted teeth. "Then you will remove the other evidence you have to a safe place. You will say nothing to anyone about today's operation until you have my written permission to do so. If any word of what we have found here today leaks without my approval you will spend the rest of

242

your career at Luton Airport searching tourists for their illicit bottles of booze. Do I make myself clear?"

Westhead nodded disconsolately.

"Thank you," snapped Cross. "Can I leave you to tidy up here?"

Again Westhead acquiesced compliantly much to the concealed delight of his subordinates.

"I want copies of all the photographs and film you have on this to be in my office by lunchtime tomorrow." Cross left the order in the air. He did not bother to wait for a reply as he left with Jennings.

"You were a bit hard on that poor bastard," Jennings commented as he eased the Jaguar from the yard.

"He's a pompous prat with a typical Civil Service mentality," Cross commented, making no attempt to hide his disdain for Westhead. "I lost two good agents last year because of an idiot like him in a consulate in Minsk. If he fucks this up I'll have his balls in a vice."

Jennings changed the subject, hoping that he would never get on the wrong side of Cross.

***

HILTON HOTEL, LONDON

Freddie Jarvis had a narcissistic view of how the opposite sex viewed him. When Karen had contacted him to say she wanted to meet him, a vision of her in the skimpy white bikini she had worn in La Manga leapt into his mind. He automatically assumed that Karen's desire to meet with him stemmed, at least in part, from an aspiration on her part to be bedded by him. He had arranged to meet her in the bar of the Hilton in Park Lane. As a sensible precaution he had also reserved a suite on the executive floor in expectation of an assignation after dinner. The fact that she arrived accompanied by a bull-necked man with hairy hands the size of shovels disturbed him, but did not dispel his anticipation.

"I'd like you to meet Gerry Croft," she smiled. "He is my new partner."

Jarvis' hand disappeared inside Hubbard's monstrous paw and was shaken. He extracted it and asked them to sit. A waiter appeared and drinks were ordered.

"What can I do for you then, Karen?" he asked, his eyes studying her cleavage rather than her face.

"Do you remember Tom Smith? We met him in Spain at Cameron's villa," she started.

Jarvis' insides began to churn. The sight of Penny, her body ripped apart from the blast of the shotgun, sprang into his mind. He gulped down half of his gin and tonic to stop himself gagging. "I remember him." His voice was hoarse.

"He was unhappy at dealing with Cameron and Joe," she continued. "I don't know what they did to upset him, but the whole deal was stopped."

Jarvis could almost feel the warm sticky blood that had burst from Penny and covered him.

"It appears," she pressed on, "that he still wants to carry on the deal but not with those two involved. He is prepared to do business with myself and Gerry, and, of course, you."

It took a moment for the words to sink into Jarvis' conscious mind. Then fear, or anger, or both, took him over.

"If you think that I am getting involved with that bastard, you are wrong," he snapped. "You know what happened to Penny, and I know that Smith was behind it."

"We all know what happened," the man's voice interjected. It was quiet and menacing. "What we don't want is for the same thing to happen again. Particularly to you."

The threat was left in the air. The terror that Jarvis had felt that gruesome night returned. "I work with Cameron not anyone else," he spluttered.

"But Cameron is out of the picture now, honey," Karen touched his hand. "This is something he can't do, and there is at least one million dollars in it for you."

The greed that a million dollars generates is enough to overcome all but the most raging panic. Jarvis sat still for a moment. Penny's shattered body had been replaced in his mind by the beach at Sandy Lane in Barbados. "What's involved?" he finally asked.

"It is the same as we were doing before." Karen knew she

244

now had Jarvis on her side. "He wants to take twenty-five million from Honduras and Jordan and repatriate it to the same French company."

Jarvis' brow creased for a moment. "Mutuelle Avionique, was it not?" he asked.

"That's it," nodded Karen. "He is happy for me and Gerry to handle the detail, but we need you. Our total cut is three million," she lied, "and we will split it three ways."

"What about the agents I have to use? They will have to be paid." Jarvis' avarice had now consigned thoughts of Penny to the dustbin of his mind, at least temporarily. "Will that have to come out of my share?"

"No, there is another half a million for them apart from our shares." Penny smiled. She had read Jarvis perfectly. "How soon can we shift the money?"

"I don't have anyone I can use in Honduras at the moment," he mused. "Jordan is alright, I could have that running within a month. Honduras will be about ten weeks."

"Make that six weeks," the hairy man commented. "That is where we can be contacted." He gave Jarvis a business card. "We will meet there a week today and you can let us know how things are developing."

Jarvis watched as they left. The secluded table, the flowers and the room for the night seemed to have been an unnecessary expense.

He had not been to the More than a Penny for 'em Club since Penny's murder. He decided that an executive room at the Hilton would be a waste without someone to share it with. The taxi pulled up outside the club ten minutes later and Jarvis alighted.

The bar was quiet as it was still early in the evening. The company credit card holders would not appear until after they had dined at their company's expense at a suitably extravagant restaurant.

Jarvis, without thinking, went to the end of the bar and sat on the stool he had occupied many times prior to tasting the exotic fruits of Penny's body.

"Good evening, Mr Jarvis. The usual?" the barmen greeted him. Jarvis nodded and returned the welcome.

"It's Freddie Jarvis isn't it?"

The voice came from behind him. He turned to see who it was and his heart leapt into his mouth. She could be Penny Hacker, but twenty years younger. She wore the turquoise dress that had been her mother's favourite. The tops of her firm young breasts peeped above the rich azure silk. The sombre black suit she had worn at her mother's interment had done her less than justice.

"Why haven't we seen you since the funeral?" she asked.

"Too many bad memories," he answered truthfully. "I needed time to assuage them. How are things going?" He asked the question simply to change the subject.

"Very well indeed," Jennifer replied. "We both miss our mother, but what happened has given the place a notoriety and that attracts custom."

Jarvis was taken aback by the easiness in the way the statement was presented. Jennifer noticed the shock register in his eyes.

"Come now, Freddie," she laughed. "You musn't be shocked. Mum always told us that life was for the living. You only look back on the dead for one day, then you look forward again. That's what she would have wanted. She spent the last six years teaching Danny and I about her business interests and how to run them."

"All her business interests?" Jarvis asked.

"Oh yes," she answered blithely. "We both can run this club with our eyes closed, but Danny has developed quite an expertise at Mum's secondary business." She winked at him. "You know, the one she called her removals trade."

"Are you saying that Danny takes on the sort of contract that your mother carried out?" he asked incredulously.

"Oh yes, he's very good at it," she commented congenially. "Anyway, enough of us. What are you doing here tonight?" The question seemed delivered innocently.

"I had what I thought was a long business meeting tonight, so I booked in at the Hilton. As it turned out the meet lasted less than an hour so I was at a loose end."

"You have an empty room and wanted a bit of company for the night." She shifted on the stool revealing a long smooth

246

thigh. "I'm sure I can help you there." She smiled demurely.

Jarvis was unsure of the signals he was being given. He stirred uneasily in his seat as his crotch reacted to the thought his brain was processing. She was the image of Penny and his thoughts swung to the nights he had spent in the flatlet above the club. "I hope *you* can help me," he replied, hoping the inflection on the 'you' was subtle enough to indicate his desire for her but would not be seen as a suggestion.

She touched his knee. "There is no need to play games," she smiled impishly. "From what Mum told me you deserve to be treated as a very special customer."

Jarvis hoped he knew exactly what was meant. Penny had told him that, occasionally, valuable customers were given the favours of the proprietor as a thank you for their patronage. He looked across at the door to the flat.

"Not there." She squeezed his thigh. "That is now part of the ambience of the club. We have some very weird customers who are willing to pay five hundred pounds to hump in the bed where a murder was committed. The flat is now an extremely high-earning facility of the club."

Disappointment flickered momentarily across his brow. Perhaps he had misunderstood.

She noted his chagrin. "I will finish here about one," she pouted. "I would love to have a nightcap with you at the Hilton."

***

Jarvis noted that his telephone instructions had been followed as they entered the room. The Bollinger stood proudly in an ice bucket and a selection of canapés sat on the table beside it.

"I'll slip into something more comfortable while you open the champagne." She left the comment in the air as she went into the bedroom of the suite.

Jarvis was pouring the champagne when she returned. She made the towelling robe, supplied by the hotel, look like a designer outfit. She sat opposite Jarvis and leaned forward to pick up the glass. He breasts were round, full and the creamy white of a perfect natural pearl.

She saw his gaze transfixed on her bust, and remained still

for a moment. She felt the warmth of lust flood into her loins. Her mother had told her of his prowess and now her body wanted to taste the fruits of that virility.

He knew she wanted him and carried her into the bedroom. She undressed him slowly. He closed his eyes and could feel Penny's hands and Penny's lips caressing his body. Her robe fell to the floor and his hands enveloped her breasts. Her hands caressed his inner thighs and slid gently around his erection. She lay on the bed and he thrust himself inside her. Their ire rose in unison as they crushed their bodies together. Their snowball of passion grew into an avalanche of carnality when their orgasms detonated together.

He lay there, his eyes closed, a panorama of visions filling his mind. One spectre kept returning. The flash from the shotgun blinded his eyes. He heard the sickening sound of the pellets tearing at her body. Her blood splashed upon him like warm treacle. He convulsed with horror.

"What's the matter, Freddie?" her voice was gentle.

He turned and wept on her shoulder. Guilt racked his brain. Smith had her murdered in front of him, and yet he was going to take the bastard's shilling.

She waited until his sobbing subsided. Her arms were strong around him, bringing comfort. "What can I do?" he cried. "If I don't work for the bastard he will kill me, the same way he killed her."

Jennifer's body stiffened. "Who will kill you, Freddie?" she asked urgently.

"That bastard Smith." He spat the name.

"Who is he?" She tried to keep her voice steady.

"Cameron introduced him to us. We were moving money for him."

"Who is Cameron?"

"Cameron Carter," he replied. "He and I used to be colleagues. We have been running reinsurance transactions to cover large movements of cash for some time for a man called Scorsi. He introduced us to Smith who had a very big deal on offer. We met him in Spain at Cameron's villa. He knew Penny and made it clear that he did not like her being involved. A few weeks later she was murdered." Jarvis did not know why he was telling her. He had to confide in someone. The dam holding back his pent-up guilt had burst and she was there.

"Are you sure this Smith was responsible for the death of my mother?" she asked.

"As sure as I can be," he sighed.

"How do I find him?" There was a hard edge in her voice.

"I don't know," he lamented. "I only ever met him once and that was with Cameron."

"Where does this Cameron Carter live?"

"He had a condo on the Shipyard Estate on Hilton Head Island in South Carolina. Why do you want to know?" he asked.

"I'm just interested." She enfolded him in her arms and whispered, "Make love to me again."

Chapter 17

"The shipment of arms is on their way," Hubbard's voice sounded jubilant. "They are to be brought ashore on an insignificant fishing boat. There is a small beach a mile south of Ballycastle."

"When?" asked Cross.

"A week Tuesday at two in the morning," Hubbard replied. "I am supposed to have my people there to take delivery."

"Good," Cross intoned. "Give me a day to organise my people and I'll give you the arrangements." He replaced the receiver and muttered, "Got the bastards."

It had been two weeks since Jennings had contacted him and told him about the claim that had been presented to Oasis. The figures matched with the arms deal. He opened the file and thumbed through it. The report from Sutcliffe had confirmed that the claim, which was the payment for the cocaine, had been paid through SeaShores in Miami. Sutcliffe had traced it through three transactions to its final destination. Barrancabermeja Investments was confirmed as the ultimate resting place for the cash.

The second report from Sutcliffe had only arrived the previous day. The payment for the arms had been paid through Lloyds of London. The money had initially been paid to a company in Switzerland and then transferred to a bank in Monaco for which Ahmit Doron was the trustee. Once the arms were seized the net could be closed.

He picked up the telephone and dialled a Belfast number.

"Conon O'Brien," a voice replied. The accent had the soft lilt of the borders without the harshness of a Belfast brogue.

"Conon, it's Jim Cross."

"I presume this means you have some news for me," O'Brien interrupted. He was head of Customs investigations in Northern Ireland. Cross had briefed him three weeks previously on the

250

possible arms import. The exercise had been somewhat easier than his dealings with Westhead. O'Brien was neither young nor rabidly ambitious. The secondary advantage was that Customs and the security services had always been forced to work closely with each other in the six counties.

"I have a location and a time for you," Cross carried on. "Tuesday the 20th at 2am a shipment will be landed from a fishing vessel on a small beach a mile south of Ballycastle."

"I know it," O'Brien commented. "What do you want us to do?"

"We need you to intercept the arms and arrest the vessel and everyone on her. I want them all held incommunicado until noon on the Wednesday."

"That will be no problem," O'Brien replied cheerfully. "What do I do with them after that?"

"I'll take them off your hands," said Cross. "By that time we should have the buggers we want in the bag in Monte Carlo and the States."

"What about the people in the UK?" queried O'Brien.

"I've not quite finished with them," Cross answered evasively. "There may be other irons in the fire as far as they are concerned."

"You bloody security people, you love your little games," O'Brien laughed. "Don't worry, I'll take your men and the weapons and won't ask any more embarrassing questions."

FBI HEADQUARTERS, WASHINGTON – 14TH MARCH 1984

"Neat, don't you think?" Alexander switched off the video. "Our people search the contents and the coke is actually part of the packaging." This was the third time he had watched the record of the drug delivery to Forest Hill.

"Have you got enough to arrest the people this side of the water?" O'Connell asked.

"Oh, more than enough," Alexander replied. "We have direct evidence from Cross' undercover man, including tapes of the conversations. The monetary transactions can all be traced from the source to the final destination. With that we can then investigate the rest of their operations which should put Cirrolla,

251

Umbari and Carpessa in the frame. I would say that everything has gone perfectly so far."

"What about Cross' man? What do we know about him? Will he come through when the chips are down?" O'Connell seemed to be acting as the devil's advocate.

"I presume so," was the reply. "I don't know who he is. We have to trust Cross on that one. The first I've seen of him was on that video."

O'Connell had watched the film with more than a simple professional interest. He had other fish to fry and did not need this operation to taint the fat. He had bitten his tongue when he saw Jennings sign for the delivery of the merchandise. He was relieved that there seemed no connection with his own sideline, but remembered that Cross had assured him that Jennings had no involvement. The thought, 'Liar', had sprung into his mind when he recognised Jennings in the video. This was a complication he would rather be without. "When do you mean to arrest them?" he asked, hoping that he would have time for some damage limitation.

"It will be a few days yet," Alexander responded. "Cross has an arms deal running through the same sources. He wants the arms in the bag before any plugs are pulled. I'm just waiting on his OK."

"Good," said O'Connell rising to leave. "Will you send me a copy of that tape?" Plans were already forming in his mind.

HILTON HEAD ISLAND, SOUTH CAROLINA – 14TH MARCH 1985

It had been three days since his sister had telephoned Danny Hacker. The lead to his mother's murderer was tenuous but better than nothing. He had flown out to Charleston that night, hired a Mustang at the airport and driven the hour to Hilton Head. It had only taken him a short time to ascertain the location of Cameron Carter's condo. For the last two days he had watched.

Carter either lived alone or was alone for the moment. Both lunchtimes he had made his way to the clubhouse of the Shipyard Golf Club. There seemed to be a group of people living locally who met there on an ad hoc basis. In the evenings Hacker

252

had followed Carter to the Crystal Sands Hotel. He had a few drinks in the bar and made libidinous eyes at any female tourist with long legs or prominent busts, to little apparent avail.

Danny Hacker had been taught well by his mother. "Planning is all," she had told him. "Equipment like explosives and guns let you do the job," she had said. "But remember it is planning that lets you get away undetected."

In the two days he had watched it appeared that he was not the only one observing Carter. All day and all night an inconspicuous car with an equally inconsequential inhabitant had been parked a few yards from Carter's home. The car and the driver had changed from time to time but their apparent interest in Carter remained. This was an intrusion that Hacker would have preferred not to exist. As it did, his plans were made accordingly.

Hacker watched as Carter left the hotel bar just before ten. He had made several unsuccessful attempts to converse with attenuated legs or abundant bosoms and given up for the night. Hacker knew that it would take Carter a quarter of an hour to walk home. He looked around and saw the other observer follow Carter out.

He finished his drink and left, walking towards the golf course. As he crossed the second fairway he saw the lights go on in Carter's condominium. If Carter was true to the previous nights he would close the curtains at the front and open the patio doors to let in the cool evening breeze. He reached the back of the house and saw the curtains wafting gently in the night flurry. He removed the Walther from his shoulder holster and screwed the silencer to it.

Carter was sitting, a glass in his hand, with his back to him as he entered.

"Good evening, Mr Carter," he said quietly.

Carter, shocked at seeing an uninvited visitor in his home, leaped to his feet. He had only managed to enunciate the words, "Who the hell," before the back of a hand smashed across his face, knocking him back into the chair. The muzzle of a pistol was forced into his mouth and a voice said, "Just be quiet and I won't pull the trigger." Carter nodded acquiescence.

Hacker removed the silencer from the terrified Carter's

mouth. "I have a few questions for you, Mr Carter." His voice a menacing whisper. "I believe you know who was responsible for the murder of my mother."

Carter shook his head like a rag doll being shaken by a toddler. "I don't know anything about any murder," he whimpered.

"Her name was Penny Hacker."

Understanding and foreboding flooded into Carter's conscious mind. "I had nothing to do with it," he croaked. The pistol barrel cracked into the side of his face.

"I didn't know he was going to have her killed." Carter was now beseeching for his life. "I swear to you I didn't know."

"Who had her killed?" Hacker asked.

"It was Smith. It was nothing to do with me."

"Where do I find this Smith?"

"I don't know," Carter blubbered as the silencer rent open his cheek. "It was Joe Scorsi who introduced us. I only met him a couple of times in New York."

"Where do I find Scorsi?"

"He has an apartment on 44th and fifth. I don't know the number." Carter was now so terrified that he would have betrayed his mother. "The details are in that file over there." He pointed to the desk.

Hacker grabbed Carter by the collar and dragged him across the room. "Which file? Show me."

Carter scrabbled through the papers on the desk. "Here it is."

Hacker threw him back in the chair and looked at the papers. He folded the file and put it in his pocket.

"Thank you, Mr Carter. You have been most accommodating." The Walther spat, the sound was like an acorn falling in a lake, and Carter slumped forward, a neat hole in his forehead.

Hacker was an hour out of Atlanta, on his way to New York, before the FBI investigated Carter's failure to appear.

LONDON 16TH MARCH 1985

"It looks as though we have a major problem." Cross was agitated when he arrived in Jennings' office. Alexander had telephoned him that morning to advise him of Carter's demise.

254

"Carter has been murdered."

"What!" exclaimed Jennings. "Who by?"

"I wish I bloody well knew," Cross retorted. "The FBI found him this morning. Someone had knocked him about and then made a neat round 36-millimetre hole in his head."

"Who would want Carter out of the way?" Jennings asked.

"The only one person I can think of is O'Connell," was the half-expected reply. "If it is him, then it is likely that Scorsi is next on his list."

"What about John?" Jennings queried.

"If I am right and O'Connell was behind Carter's death," Cross continued, "then John could be next in line after Scorsi. It depends on what they got out of Carter. Neither Alexander nor O'Connell know who my front man is. The trouble is that Carter did."

"Have you spoken to John?" Jennings asked.

"I've asked him to meet us today at twelve in that boozing club of yours. He knows about Carter so he will be watching his back."

"Shall I see if George can join us?"

"It might be an idea," Cross responded. "The way things are going we may have to resort to a Pinter scoop to bring this whole mess into the open."

Hubbard and Pinter were already seated at one of the tables in the Chez When Club when Cross and Jennings arrived. Two pints stood on the table awaiting their arrival.

"What is all this panic about?" Hubbard began. "Someone blows Carter away and you reckon that I'm on a hit list. That's a load of balls. Anybody could have shot the bastard. I don't think he was Mr Popularity."

"The likelihood is that O'Connell wanted Carter out of the way," Cross replied tolerantly. "He is setting up an illegal arms sale with you, having initially worked with Carter. If Carter was pulled by the FBI, and spilled all the beans, it could put both Mutuelle Avionique and himself in the frame."

"Bloody hell, Jim," Hubbard retorted, "you have been so long with MI5 that you are looking for intrigue where it probably doesn't exist. All we know is that poor old Cameron has been knocked about and shot. It could have been anybody."

"Who else would you suggest?" Cross asked sarcastically.

"Scorsi, for a start," Hubbard retorted, "he hated the pompous bastard. And what about the people who got ripped off in the scam that Carter went to jail for? A lot of people lost a lot of money on that."

"I still say that O'Connell is the most likely," Cross snapped. In his position as Controller of MI5 he was unused to his wisdom being questioned.

"How about you two calming down and applying a bit of logical thinking to this," Pinter interjected. "There is not a lot of point in slagging each other off. What we need to do is decide where we go from here. Do we abandon the operation or do we go on?"

"Well spoken, George," exclaimed Hubbard. "The fact that Carter is no more does not affect our deal with O'Connell. He knows I knew Carter. The contract is nearly set up. We have to go ahead and wait and see what happens."

"And if O'Connell has put out a marker on you?" Cross looked pointedly at Hubbard.

"If he has," Hubbard smiled, "I'll just have to keep an eye on my backside, won't I?"

"It's up to you," Cross conceded ungraciously, "its your arse in the cauldron."

"Good," said Hubbard smugly. "Now, what we need is a watch put on Mutuelle Avionique and Mr Mersonne. The money from Jordan should start to move in the next couple of weeks. Once that happens the equipment will have to be despatched. We have to know how it is done and where it goes to."

"I already have three people in Amiens," Cross responded. "One is working at Avionique and the others are keeping tabs on Mersonne."

"OK," Hubbard nodded. "We also need to trace the source of the money that is being processed." He turned to Jennings and asked, "Can Richard Sutcliffe help us on that?"

"He should do," mused Jennings. "I know the names of the agents in Jordan and will know who we are dealing with in Honduras from Freddie's files. I can ask Richard to delve into their banking arrangements and see if he can find where the funds come from."

"If we can get that and follow the guidance systems to their source, we can have the bastards," Hubbard chortled.

"Provided we are allowed to," Cross intervened. "If these deals are actually covert government operations we could find ourselves gagged." Cross suspected that both the US and the French administrations were either directly involved or at least turning a Nelsonian eye. O'Connell was too senior in the CIA to be running his own private agenda. The involvement with Mutuelle Avionique, a state-owned arms manufacturer, strengthened these suspicions.

"I hope you are right," interjected Pinter. "If they are I will have a monstrous scoop on my hands. I could make a million on the book rights alone."

"Thank you for that, George," Hubbard laughed. "We know that you would share your new-found wealth with us."

"If we are going ahead..." Jennings returned the party to matters in hand. "...what is happening about the arms?"

"They are coming in next Tuesday morning in County Antrim," Cross responded. "Customs, the Royal Ulster Constabulary and the military will be there to meet them. Once the arms are in the bag the FBI will pick up Scorsi, Pedrosa, the agents and adjusters and put them under wraps. The French police will do the same with Doron. We will have to leave the Lloyds people until after we get the evidence on Mutuelle Avionique, if we can."

AMIENS – 19TH MARCH 1985

"If we are not careful, Monsieur, this whole thing could explode in our faces." Mersonne spoke quietly. O'Connell had arrived earlier that day and told him of Carter's demise and Scorsi's mysterious disappearance. "I do not like the way this matter is developing," he continued. "I have the units ready for delivery and very little of the money has been received. Unless something happens quickly I will have to destroy the equipment. We do not normally keep so-called defective stock this long."

"I agree with you whole-heartedly," O'Connell responded. "The problem is you seem unwilling to accept my word that the finance will be forthcoming."

257

"It is our way, Monsieur," Mersonne shrugged. "When we have the money, you can have the goods."

"You bastards wouldn't trust your own mothers, would you?" O'Connell's exasperation showed. Mersonne shrugged again. "The situation is that payments from Jordan will commence within the next two weeks and the full amount will be paid over three months."

"Three months is too long," Mersonne interrupted. "I must have the goods off my hands within six weeks. In the past our partners simply handed over cash in a suitcase. That was somewhat more efficient."

"It is also much more dangerous," snapped O'Connell. "The way we are handling this will leave no trace of the transaction. You will have destroyed defective units and your insurance company will have made exceptionally good profits. No comebacks and no scandals."

"Very well, Monsieur." Mersonne held his hands up in mock surrender. "I have the units to fill the order for the Middle East. Provided that half of the payment has been received in Jersey within six weeks I will arrange for delivery to be made. I will not, however, make the same agreement with your friends in South America. The Arab is shrewd but his word is good. I cannot say the same for your other clients."

"That will have to do," O'Connell replied. He stood and proffered his hand to seal the agreement.

Back at the hotel O'Connell dialled a number in London. He recognised Karen's voice when she answered.

"Hi, Karen, its Tom Smith." His tone was light. "Is Gerry there?" he asked.

"Not at the moment. He should be back in a couple of hours." She was expecting Hubbard any moment but would need the desire in the pit of her stomach to be adequately satisfied before attention was given to anyone else. "Can I ask him to call you?" she asked.

He gave her the hotel number, telling her that he needed confirmation that certain time limits could be adhered to. He replaced the receiver and stood looking idly out of the window. He paid no attention to the man huddled in the doorway opposite.

Karen did not bother to await Hubbard's return. She telephoned Jarvis and told him to 'Get off his fat ass and get the money moving.' Jarvis, though a little taken aback at he bluntness, confirmed that the timing would be adhered to. She then passed the information to Tom Smith.

BALLYCASTLE, COUNTY ANTRIM – 20TH MARCH 1985

It was a dank, end of winter's night. The rain drizzled relentlessly searching out every tiny weakness in the construction of his rainwear. It dripped from his hair and down his back. Waves with foaming tips clattered onto the beach and then slid back out to sea as the next swell rushed over their retreat. Conon O'Brien was cursing his own enthusiasm. Why was he lying on a sodden dune, soaked to the skin, trying to peer through the misty haze across the beach? He could have been in a warm control centre listening to reports from younger men. Beside him was a Captain of the Green Jackets, who looked young enough to be his son.

"Not long now, sir," the young man commented.

O'Brien ignored him as he was not in the mood for social conversation. He peered through the binoculars at the sea. Then he caught a sight, just a glimpse of the bow of a dinghy struggling through the breakers towards the beach. It rose above the boiling sea and a light twinkled in its prow. He looked towards the beach below and another light flickered a welcome.

"This is it, Captain," he said as he rose and tried to restore some feeling to his frozen limbs. "Have your men ready in case we need you."

The young Captain barked some orders into his radio and gave the thumbs up.

The four occupants of the skiff jumped from the vessel as its bottom caressed the sand, and heaved it towards a more secure base. Suddenly it was as though it had become morning. A blaze of lights illuminated the beach. A tinny voice ordered, "Her Majesty's Customs and Excise. Stay where you are." The four men tried to reverse their efforts from tugging to pushing. A gunshot rang out and they heard the zing as the projectile passed above their heads. They ceased their efforts and raised their hands above their heads.

Aboard the ocean-going trawler the Captain ordered full ahead and full right rudder as soon as the darkened beach had become a panorama of light. Then he heard rumbling, deeper than his own engines.

"This is Her Majesty's cruiser *Arganout.* Heave to or I will open fire." The source of the instruction abruptly appeared as the flares burst overhead. The Captain had no choice but to obey. In less than three minutes a squadron of Marines boarded his ship.

***

O'Brien sat in his office, both hands clasping the steaming mug, trying to transfer some of its warmth to his torpid joints. The telephone jangled and he picked up the receiver.

"Everything go as planned, Conon," Cross' voice sounded as though he was in a warm comfortable place.

"We have ten men, a trawler, four cases of Kalashnikovs, twenty Uzis, ten kilos of Semtex and five thousand rounds of ammunition in our custody. I think that is what we planned," was the passionless reply.

"Is everything alright?" Cross asked with concern.

O'Brien took a pull at the whisky-laced coffee. "I'm sorry, Jim," he replied, as the whisky began its warming journey from inside to out. "I'm just bloody wet and freezing." He took another slug from the mug. "We took the arms on the beach and the *Arganout* arrested the trawler and crew. We have the prisoners in the barracks at Coleraine for the night, or what's left of it. We will transfer them to Belfast in the morning. Everything was exactly as expected."

"Thank you, Conon." Cross' tone revealed genuine pleasure. "That was a first class job."

Two hours later, in the harbour at Ville France, Ahmit Doron's yacht was boarded by officers from Interpol and the French police. Doron was arrested and taken into custody at Nice to await extradition.

FLOODS HOTEL, ENNISCORTHY, EIRE – 20TH MARCH 1985

He sat at the bar, his Guinness untouched, reading the *Irish*

Times. The headline blared, 'IRA arms intercepted'. He knew that the weapons were not intended for the IRA. If arms were being brought in they would not bring them in by sea to the six counties.

He was not a man that many would notice. His weight and height were average as was his dress and demeanour. Only if you looked into his eyes would you see the steel that was within him.

He had been born in Clonroche, a small village nearby. His upbringing had taught him to hate the English and abhor their occupation of the North. The hate had been endemic in his family since an uncle had been shot by the Black and Tans in 1916. Over the years the tale had been embellished to the point that the uncle was an innocent who was brutally murdered in his bed. The actual truth, now lost in the passing of time, was that the uncle had tried, and botched, an ambush on a British army patrol. He had been killed in the ensuing firefight. The 'so-called' culprits were not even the Black and Tans, but a platoon of the Kings' Own Light Infantry.

His recruitment by the IRA was a formality, soon after his seventeenth birthday. He had joined the British army and been taught exemplary skills with both weapons and explosives with the Rifle Brigade. Those who had trained him were now his enemies.

"A bit slow with the Guinness tonight, Sean." The voice came from behind him.

Sean Murphy turned to the new arrival, and then smiled. "Mr O'Connell, how nice to see you again."

O'Connell sat on the stool beside Murphy and ordered a pint. He took a bulky envelope from his pocket and passed it to Murphy. "A very neat job you did in South Carolina. Worth every penny," he said.

"I'm afraid I was a little too late for that one," Murphy responded. One of the services offered by the IRA was the removal of unwanted individuals from the hair of people willing to pay a handsome fee. Cameron Carter had been such a task. The problem was that Carter's remains were already inert when he had entered the condominium.

"Some bastard had got there ahead of me," he continued. "It

was a very professional job though." He took a long pull at his drink and pushed the envelope back towards O'Connell. "Apart from that your man Scorsi had already done a disappearing act before I could get to him. Expenses only this one, I'm afraid."

"Keep it," replied O'Connell. "I have another problem to be sorted and need your help. Let's call that a down payment." The fact that Murphy had nothing to do with Carter's death and Scorsi's disappearing trick disturbed him. Murphy, however, was not the man to confide in.

Murphy picked up the cash and put it in his pocket. "Double money," Murphy mused. "Must be a difficult one."

O'Connell passed him two sheets of paper and a photograph. "I understand that there have been previous attempts. They all failed."

Murphy read the documents, occasionally whistling through his teeth. He finished and studied the likeness of his next victim.

"I would have done this shit for free," he snarled. "Anyone who won the sword of honour at Sandhurst and served with the SAS in the six counties doesn't deserve to stay alive."

"I hoped that is what you would say," chuckled O'Connell, "because I want this one out of the way as soon as possible."

"You want this fucker badly don't you." Murphy saw a bargaining position opening. O'Connell nodded. "You want this one a little more than usual," Murphy continued. "You promised us missiles. Where are they?"

"They are on their way." O'Connell was becoming exasperated. "I told you that my source would not supply direct to Ireland. I will have delivery in six weeks to Cyprus. Once there, it will take another two to three weeks to get them to you. That is, unless," he jabbed the photograph of Jennings, "he has the chance to fuck the whole thing up."

"I understand." Murphy picked up the papers and photograph and put them in his pocket. He drank the remainder of his Guinness and turned to O'Connell. "It's nice to see you again, Mr O'Connell. Consider the job done." He shook O'Connell's hand and left.

O'Connell peered into the frothy head of his drink, small worry lines creeping across his brow. He had contracted Murphy to organise the demise of Carter and the disappearance of Scorsi.

When both had happened he had assumed that the contract had been performed. It seemed that someone else had the same agenda, but who and why?

THE BRONX, NEW YORK – 20TH MARCH 1985

The apartment was no more than a filthy hovel. Scorsi, alone for the first time in three days, struggled with the bonds that held him to the chair. It was to no avail, the only result being that the hessian dug deeper into his wrists and ankles. His face was a mass of weals and half-healed lesions, his body covered in bruising.

He had been in this predicament for three days. He remembered answering the door to a deliveryman and then nothing until he found himself shackled to a chair in this lice-infested room. It was then that Danny Hacker had introduced himself. Somehow Hacker knew that he and Smith were the causes of his mother's death.

At first Scorsi had denied all knowledge of both the murder and Smith. Hacker had not believed him. After three days, during which Hacker had demonstrated his abilities at inflicting pain, he had been broken. He had told him all he knew, which was little, other than that there was money in abundance.

The original approach had been from Smith. Scorsi's only contact was a telephone number. The area code was Denver, but he guessed that the calls were not received in that State. He had contacted Smith, on that number, and they had met, in New York, within an hour. Hacker had taken the number and left him alone. His body was racked with pain and fear tore at his insides. His struggle with the bindings was fruitless and he surrendered to whatever was to come.

***

Hacker sat in a dingy bar, toying with a Bourbon on the rocks. It was clear that Smith was well hidden. He had rung the number, forced out of Scorsi, and a machine had answered. The voice of Smith had told him that he was not there but would return his call. He left no message.

His mind wandered over the possibilities. Who would be able to receive a call in New York directly from a Denver number? The possibilities were too great. Any large corporation would have a network of tied lines to all their locations. The difference was that corporations would operate through a switchboard. On this line a call to Denver had been received thousands of miles away. To have that facility on a single line would indicate someone of importance, but important in what and to whom?

He needed Scorsi to lure the man from his cover. A trap would have to be set. He threw the drink back and left, a plan forming in his mind.

Scorsi heard the footsteps as they approached the door. His guts knotted with fear.

"I want you to make a call for me, Joe." The quietness of Hacker's voice was menacing rather than calming. Scorsi nodded vigorously. He would now do anything to escape alive from this hell hole.

The machine on the line bleeped. "It's Joe Scorsi here," he read, "I have to see you urgently. I will be in Ryan's Bar on Fifth Avenue and 52nd between four and five for the next three days." The receiver was taken away and replaced.The adhesive tape was replaced around his head and mouth.

"That was very good Joe," said Hacker scornfully. "Now I have a present for you."

Hacker rummaged in his holdall and produced a small square package. "This is specially for you, for being so nice to my mother." He placed the carton on Scorsi's chest and started to affix it with tape. He wound the tape around his victim, constricting his movement even more than the rope.

"You can have an hour to make peace with whoever you feel you need to." He turned a dial on the top of the package and a faint ticking began. "You can watch your life ebbing away if you wish."

Scorsi looked down. The dial was set to sixty. He tried to struggle but was unable to move.

"It's alright, Joe." Hacker's face showed no emotion. "It's an explosive incendiary device. It should be quick and quite painless. It will probably take quite some time to find out who you were." He picked up the holdall and was gone.

The explosion in the Bronx, which killed one unknown person, warranted two column inches in the *New York Times*.

Chapter 18

There was a feeling of spring in the night air as Jennings walked to his car at Woldingham station. The air was invigorating with no trace of the dank of winter. The fresh, clean air served to lighten the gloom that had descended on him during the day.

First thing that morning, one of his Directors had told him of an error by one of the younger brokers. An underwriter had been supplied with information that was basically incorrect. A massive claim had occurred and the underwriter was now refusing to pay. Unless the matter could be resolved amicably, his company would be plunged into a multi-million dollar lawsuit in California. He had endured a meeting with the underwriter which was both fruitless and unproductive. The matter would now be a honeypot for numerous lawyers to plunge their snouts into.

He had subsequently lunched with an underwriter who spent the whole meal castigating Jennings for his poor results from business offered by Jennings' company. Jennings tried to point out that his company only offered the business and it was up to the underwriter to decide whether or not to accept it. This was taken as a personal attack on the man's expertise and he had stamped out of the restaurant.

In the afternoon Cross had telephoned. He had just heard that Scorsi had been identified by the New York police as the body that had been blown asunder in a Bronx apartment.

"First there was Carter and now Scorsi," he had said. "It has to be O'Connell that is behind both of the killings."

"It does seem too much of a coincidence to be someone else," Jennings had replied.

"The whole thing makes me very nervous of John's situation," Cross continued. "If O'Connell finalises all his connections in the same way, then John has got problems down the line. I'm beginning to think that I should pull the plug on the whole operation."

"What does John think?" Jennings asked.

"He thinks he's the modern day Rockfist Rogan and can handle anything that comes along. The trouble is that Rockfist Rogan was in a comic and John's not."

"Can't you let it run for the moment?" asked Jennings. "Surely O'Connell is not going to take any action until the business with Jordan and Honduras is finalised."

"That's what I've agreed to do, but only for a week or so. If we can't get any solid evidence by then we will have to pull in the Lloyds people and forget about Mutuelle Avionique and O'Connell."

"You can't do that," Jennings protested. "Those bastards are supplying missiles to bloody terrorists."

"Keep your hair on," laughed Cross. "When I say I will pull the plug, I mean officially. Unofficially, I do have available some off the record sanctions I can apply, but don't ask me what or how."

Jennings had left the office in a despondent mood. He popped into the Bunch of Grapes to see if a couple of pints before catching the train, would cheer him up. There two other underwriters who had spent their afternoon over coffee and liqueurs had confronted him. By the time Jennings arrived they had both decided that their poor results had nothing to do with their own inadequacies as underwriters, but simply that those bastard brokers had conned them. As Jennings was available, and a broker, their venom was immediately directed at him. He had tried to placate them for the time it took to drink a couple of pints to no avail. After the day he had endured, the last thing he needed was to be berated by two inebriated underwriters. He wished them a cheerful goodnight and made for London Bridge station.

As he walked across the station car park his melancholy slowly lifted. Waiting at home was the most desirable woman in his world. Whatever happened during the day would be stored away until the morning. Tonight he would make love to Pansie, his alluring seductive wife.

As he turned the corner at the top of the hill his headlights picked up an agitated movement in the distance. Jennings peered, trying to make out what it was. It seemed to be somebody waving their arms on the side of the road. As he got closer he could see that the figure seemed distraught. Then he recognised who it was. What was Charlie doing out there at that time of night?

He pulled into the side and the boy tore at the door. He was both screaming and sobbing. He calmed the boy down and asked what was the matter.

"There is a man in the house with mummy, and he has got a gun."

Pansie's scream had broken into Charlie's sleep.

"Who are you? What do you want?" Her voice had a ring of fear.

Charlie had crept onto the landing and peered through the bannisters. A stocky man was pushing his mother across the hall. In one hand he held a gun, like those he had seen in action movies. She was propelled into the lounge.

"Is there anyone else in the house," a voice had shouted.

"My son." His mother's voice sounded calmer. "He is upstairs asleep for the night." Charlie recognised the edge that came into her voice when her hackles were rising. "You lay one finger on him and I'll kill you." Her articulation was as calm as the eye of a hurricane. It was not a threat but a statement of fact.

"Show me. I want to see for myself," the other voice had said, a little less assuredly than before.

Charlie had scampered back into his room and buried himself in the bedclothes. He heard voices at the door.

"Is he asleep?"

He had felt his mother's comforting hands tucking the blankets around him.

"Fast asleep," he had heard his mother reply.

He heard the door being closed and footsteps move across the landing and down the stairs. He had lain there, his brain spinning. His mother was in trouble but what could he do? He knew that his father would be home soon, and would walk into a trap. Through the curtains the shadow of the old tree waved like a finger beckoning him. His father had told him many times of how he had climbed down that very tree from the bedroom

268

without his parents knowing. Charlie had never plucked up the courage to try. Now he must.

He pushed one pillow and some clothes into the bed to make it look as though it were still occupied. The window slid quietly open. The nearest branch was just beyond his reach. He would have to jump for it. It was only a short way but seemed a chasm. He leaped and landed astride the bough. His hands were torn by the rough bark but he held himself steady. Climbing down the tree was easy. He crossed the back garden, away from the house, and followed the hedge to the road. Once there he ran towards the station to where the road was straight. He recognised the twin headlights of the Jaguar and waved his arms frantically shouting, "Stop, Dad, stop."

The car eased to a halt and the door opened. He climbed into the car crying, "There is a man with mummy, he's bullying her."

Jennings let the boy calm down. He extricated the story, what little there was, piece by piece. A man was in the house and he had a gun. That seemed to be all that Charlie knew. Jennings started the car and drove slowly down the road. As he passed the house he peered, trying to see something, anything. He saw nothing. A hundred yards down the road he pulled into a small lay-by. He told Charlie to stay in the car and lock the doors until he or mummy returned for him.

He approached the house from the rear. Lights were blazing in the kitchen, the lounge and the upper landing. He squinted through a crack in the curtains into the lounge. A chill of panic ran down his spine. Pansie was sitting, venom spitting from her eyes, as she watched the stranger inspect the room. Jennings knew the stranger. He was the one that got away.

It was seventeen years before that Jennings and his section had lain in wait at the arms cache in Armagh. They were there, in hiding, for three days before the Provisionals came to collect their instruments of mayhem. There were eight Provisionals and, waiting for them, six members of the SAS. Jennings waited until the arms were taken from their hiding place.

"You're under arrest," he had shouted. "Lay down your weapons."

Only one of the Provisionals reacted as a trained soldier would. He went to ground and rolled away as far as possible. One of the others fired in the direction of Jennings' voice. The return of fire was instant and fatal. Within three seconds seven terrorists were dead. The eighth had disappeared. Sean Murphy was the one they had wanted most and they had missed him.

Pansie watched as the stranger paced the room. At first, when he had forced his way in, panic had temporarily invaded her senses. It was not fear for herself, but that of a mother for her offspring. Now she was angry. She focused her anger on the interloper who had invaded her domain. Her demeanour seemed calm, but inside her rage was fuelling a need for retribution.

She had felt this way only once before. Her unit of the People's Freedom Party had been caught in a jungle ambush by a British patrol. Her friends were torn to pieces in a vicious crossfire. Somehow the bedlam had missed her. The soldiers laughed and joked over the bodies of her comrades. She watched, rage growing inside her like a malignant abscess. It had taken five days, shadowing the group, before her need for vengeance had been sated. By then only three of the twelve remained alive.

Murphy paced around the room. There were pictures and mementos of Jennings and his antecedents. It seemed that the family had a long history of serving the usurpers of his country. Above the fireplace were two photographs, one of Jennings and the other his father. Both showed them receiving the sword of honour at Sandhurst. He was going to enjoy the arrival of this man Jennings.

Jennings moved away from the house and rounded the garage. He heaved a sigh of relief as the side door opened noiselessly. At the end of the garage a small cupboard was bolted to the wall. The padlock slipped open. The moonlight glinted on the polished blade of the kukri. The kukri was the personal weapon of all Gurkhas. His two years serving with the regiment had given Jennings a colossal respect for the ways of these tiny Nepalese fighting men. Like any Gurkha, he could never discard the kukri. He kept it locked away but every month it had been polished and honed. He slipped it into his belt.

Around the back he started to climb the old cherry tree. As a child he knew each branch and bough, but time and man had reshaped it. The limbs of the tree creaked with his weight. Now he was opposite the window of Charlie's room. At full stretch he leaned across and grabbed the sill. In his head it sounded like an explosion as he swung across and his feet crashed into the wall. He pulled himself up and dropped into the bedroom.

"What was that?" Murphy looked up towards the sound.

"It's just the old tree," Pansie replied, hoping, but not believing, that it was something more.

Murphy pulled the curtain back and peered out of the window. The boughs of the tree quavered in the breeze as though offering an apology for disturbing those inside the house. He pulled the curtains together.

"What time is your bastard husband home?" he snapped.

Pansie saw a hint of agitation in his manner. "I don't really know," she replied meekly. "If he gets caught with the wrong client they may go to dinner and, maybe, a club afterwards."

He slapped her around the face. "Don't try to be bloody clever with me," he shouted.

Jennings clenched his fist around the handle of the kukri when he heard the slap. "Hang on, Pansie," he thought, "just for a few more minutes."

He made no sound as he crossed the room to the doorway. He pressed himself flat against the wall. Many times he had mimicked his son when he was having a tantrum. Was his imitation good enough?

"Mummy, Daddy," he cried in a high-pitched whine. "It's the Troll, he's coming to get me."

Pansie started to move and Murphy slapped her down. The voice cried out again from upstairs.

"It's my son." Her eyes pleaded to be allowed to go to him.

"Just walk slowly in front of me." Murphy waved the Uzi towards the stairs.

"Mummy, Daddy," Jennings whined. He heard footsteps on the stairs. They moved across the landing.

Pansie went straight across the room towards the bed. Behind her, Murphy followed, the Uzi extended towards her back.

There was just a hint of a flash of light. The curved, razor sharp blade cut through his jacket. Tendons, sinew and muscle separated as the kukri sliced through his forearm. Only the bone stopped its progress.

The Uzi fell to the floor. Murphy had no time to react before a rock-hard fist smashed into the nape of his neck. He pitched forward, unconscious. Jennings stepped forward from the shadows and stood beside the prone body. He knew that this man was more dangerous than a cornered tiger. He raised his knee and drove his heel, with all his strength, into the base of Murphy's spine. Vertebrae parted from vertebrae. Splinters of bone slammed into the spinal cord, the super highway of the body.

Pansie turned and saw her husband. She fell into his arms sobbing with relief. "Are you all right?" he asked quietly. "Did he hurt you?"

"Not as much as I was going to damage him," she muttered defiantly, "the bastard. Who is he?"

"His name's Sean Murphy. He's a member of the IRA," Jennings responded.

"Why was he after you?" she questioned.

"I'm buggered if I know."

Pansie was now fully in control. She looked down at the prone body of Murphy. "I'd better get a towel. That bastard is bleeding all over Charlie's new carpet."

She returned and started to bind it around the wound in Murphy's arm. Suddenly she realised that her son had not moved in the commotion. "Charlie!" she screamed.

"It's alright." Jennings took her in his arms. "Charlie is in the car, parked in the lay-by up the road. He climbed out of the window to warn me."

"He what?" she whispered incredulously.

"The little sod saved our lives. He saw what happened and came to warn me."

"I'd better go and get our little hero," Pansie grinned with maternal pride.

"Here are the keys," Jennings handed them to her. "The car's in the lay-by up the road. Take him into the kitchen until I can sort this bastard out."

He pulled the towel away from the wound. No bright red blood spurted from the open gash. The artery was still intact. He wrapped the towel back around Murphy's arm and taped it. He picked up the inert body and carried it down the stairs. The

272

basement door creaked as it opened. He satisfied himself that Murphy was secure and went upstairs to his study.

"Hello?" Jane Cross' voice sounded chirpy.

"Jane, it's Allan." Jennings forced his voice to sound bright. "Can I speak to Jim?"

"Allan, what can I do for you?"

"I need your help." Now there was urgency in Jennings' tone. "I have a damaged body here. I think it is someone that you may be interested in talking to. Does Sean Murphy ring any bells?"

"What are you talking about? Are you taking the piss?" Cross half thought that this was one of Jennings' jokes. Murphy had been one of the most wanted terrorists for ten years.

"I wish I were, Jim. He was waiting for me with a fucking great Uzi when I got home. Fortunately I was warned. I've got him trussed up in the basement. By the way, he needs a doctor."

"I'm on my way." Cross realised that this was no prank. "Don't do anything until I get there."

***

Murphy peered into the darkness. He remembered following the woman upstairs and into the boy's bedroom and then nothing. Now he was in pitch blackness. A searing pain engulfed his right arm and his left was tethered tenaciously to something. A dull ache spread across his back.

He tried to move but his legs failed to respond to his brain's bidding. Slowly, as his eyes realigned themselves to the darkness, shadowy shapes appeared. There was a steep staircase. A glimmer of light crept from underneath the door at the top. Spread around the room were an assortment of old furniture and nick-nacks. He racked his brain, trying to remember what had happened. All he knew was that something had gone badly wrong.

A shaft of light shot downwards as the door opened. The figure of a man was framed in the opening. A hand reached up and the room was flooded with brilliance. As the silhouette descended he recognised it as Jennings. He tried to move but was unable to do so.

273

"Don't try to move," Jennings said coldly. "You may damage your spine even more."

Murphy said nothing. He looked at his plight. His left arm was bound to a heavy-duty pipe attached to the wall. His right was swathed in a blood-soaked towel. The ache in his back had become a withering pain.

"Perhaps you would like to tell me who you are working for?" Jennings now stood above him.

"Fuck off," Murphy spat back.

"Suit yourself." Jennings turned towards the stairs. "You will tell me though," was left as a parting shot.

Jennings closed the door and went to the kitchen. Charlie was, by now, into the excitement of the moment. His fears had been removed when his mother had told him that everything was alright. He had rushed up to the bedroom and seen the blood. Now he had to know the full tale. He would make his friends at school sick with jealousy that they were not part of his adventure.

"Where is the bad man, Dad?" he cried. "Did you kill him?" He saw the Uzi, which now rested on the kitchen table. "Did you let him have it with the gun?" he asked breathlessly.

Jennings picked him up and sat him in a chair. "The man is locked up and won't cause any more trouble."

Charlie was a little disgruntled that he was not to witness some more action. "Can I see him, Dad?" he asked.

Jennings shook his head. "Uncle Jim is coming to take him away," he said quietly. "I want you to promise me something." Charlie nodded his head vigorously in affirmation. "You must not tell anyone about tonight."

"Not even my best friend?" The boy's chagrin showed in his face. "He'd be jealous as hell."

"No one," his father replied firmly. "If you do tell anyone there could be a lot of trouble for Mummy and me," Jennings lied.

Charlie promised, although his reluctance was clear by his grimace.

The wheels of a car scrunched into the drive. Cross and three others alighted.

"Will you show the doctor where he is?" Cross instructed

rather than requested. "You two check the grounds are secure," he continued. The other two moved swiftly towards the rear of the house.

Jennings took the doctor towards the basement entrance. "Don't move him, will you," he remarked. "His cervical spine is damaged, probably fractured."

"Thank you," the doctor replied as though such an injury were a minor scratch.

Cross took Jennings by the arm and steered him into the lounge. "What the fuck has happened here?"

"He forced his way into the house before I got home. Charlie was in bed and heard Pansie scream. He climbed out of the back window and came to warn me. Lucky he did." Jennings shivered at the thought of the damage that the Uzi could inflict.

"Do you know why?" Cross had his suspicions, but hoped that they would not be confirmed.

"I've no idea," Jennings shook his head.

The doctor returned. "He has to be hospitalised immediately." He moved towards the telephone.

Cross stopped him. "I have to know why he was here first."

"Look, sir," the doctor said. "That man has a five-inch wound across his right forearm. The tendons are severed and there is severe muscle damage. Apart from that he has two or more vertebrae fractured and probable damage to his spinal cord. He has to be treated immediately."

"I don't care what is wrong with the bastard," hissed Cross. "He has already murdered at least sixty people. As far as I'm concerned he has about the same rights as a rabid dog, which is all he is. If he wants treating he will have to answer my questions first." Cross stormed out of the room.

The other two had completed their search of the grounds and now waited in the hallway.

"With me, you two," Cross ordered. They followed him downstairs.

Murphy looked up as they descended. Now fear invaded his pain. Cross' face was as familiar to him as his own. Since MI5 had become involved in the anti-terrorist operations, under Cross' command, near mortal wounds had been inflicted on the IRA. Cross' operatives offered no quarter and took no prisoners.

Cross sat in an old armchair and looked at Murphy for what seemed a lifetime. "Well, Mr Murphy," he started, "I have been waiting a long time for this."

"Fuck you." Murphy, even in his predicament, attempted defiance.

"Thank you," smiled Cross. "Let me tell you a few facts."

Murphy turned his head away, attempting indifference.

"That wound in your arm," Cross carried on, "has damaged the tendons and if it is not treated soon you will lose the use of your hand."

"Bollocks," was Murphy's retort.

"Not that it matters too much." Cross seemed to be enjoying himself. "Because you have also broken your back. If that is not treated you will never walk again."

Murphy turned to face his tormentor.

"All you have to do, Mr Murphy, is to tell me why you were here and who gave you the orders. If you tell me that I will ask the doctor to call an ambulance and take you away to see if your body can be put back in working order. If you don't tell me then I will have to wait until I can get some Pentathol delivered. One injection and you will tell me what I want to know. Unfortunately for you, if you choose to force me into the second course of action, your treatment will be delayed and you will never walk or use your right hand again. It's up to you."

Murphy's back felt as though white-hot shards were being driven into his spine. His arm pulsated with spasms of agony. He knew what Cross had said was true but refused to accept it. He said nothing.

Cross turned to one of the two that accompanied him. "Get on the blower will you, Collins. I want a psycho-doctor and Pentathol down here as soon as possible." He stood and made towards the steps.

"Alright, you bastard," Murphy accepted the inevitable. He had seen the truth drug used on others. "I'll tell you what you want to know."

Cross resumed his seat. "Just remember one thing, Murphy." Cross' tone was venomous. "I will still use the Pentathol after the quacks have finished with you. If you give me shit now, I *will* find out. If I do, I promise you that whatever the doctors mend I

276

will have broken again."

Murphy nodded.

"Why were you here?"

"To finish that arsehole upstairs," Murphy replied sulkily.

"Who sent you?"

"A connection of ours from NORAID."

"Name?" quizzed Cross.

"He calls himself O'Connell. I don't know if that is his real name."

Cross' fears were being confirmed. "Have you done anything else for him recently?"

"I was supposed to but I was too late. Someone else got there first."

"Who were the targets?"

"A man called Carter in South Carolina and another named Scorsi in New York."

Cross stood over Murphy. "Are you saying that you had this O'Connell's contract for Carter and Scorsi and someone else took them out before you?" Murphy nodded his head.

Cross turned to one of the others. "Go and tell the doctor that he can have this lump of shit now."

Forty minutes later a butcher's van arrived. The inside was a fully-equipped ambulance. Murphy was taken away, accompanied by the doctor and Cross' two associates.

Pansie had, eventually, calmed Charlie down enough to put him back to bed. He was put in one of the spare rooms although he would have much preferred to sleep in the room where the adventure both started and finished. Jennings had poured three large Courvoisiers and they sat contemplating the events of the night.

"This whole bloody thing is getting out of hand," mused Cross. "I had a suspicion that O'Connell might suss out that John had a foot in each camp, but I know he can look after himself. The last thing I expected was that he would go after you."

"I thought about that when that animal was parading around this room," Pansie interjected. "At first I though it could be something from Allan's time in the army. Then it struck me. If O'Connell saw the video of the cocaine being delivered, who did he see on film?"

"That's it," exclaimed Jennings. "You had to keep John out of the delivery because you couldn't risk O'Connell seeing the film. I signed the driver's docket. If O'Connell was going to put out both Carter's and Scorsi's lights, he would also want to remove any unwanted connections this end. He saw the video and there I was."

"Shit!" Cross ejaculated. "I should have foreseen that. It's bloody obvious that he would have to clean up both ends. That means that you will still be a target. I think that we are going to have to pull the plug on this operation. It's getting too bloody dangerous for too many people."

"You can't do that now that we're so close." Jennings' frustration began to show. "The payments to Avionique are running through merrily and it can only be a short time before the guidance systems are dispatched. Without that you have no case. You have to wait."

Cross took a pull at his drink. "The situation is that I am putting people in danger who are not supposed to be. What we have at the moment is the money laundering and we can tie that in with both arms and drugs. Once we open up the investigation we should be able to trace the whole thing from source. That's what we were initially after. The business with Avionique was discovered by accident. It could be political dynamite."

"Can't you let it run just a little longer?" This time it was Pansie who entreated.

Cross shrugged his shoulders. "I am going to have to talk to my masters about that. With what we now know I can't run it covert any longer."

The following morning the *Daily Record* headlined a scoop.

'MOST WANTED IRA TERRORIST CAPTURED'

Cross had given George Pinter both the true story and the one for publication. Under Pinter's byline the nation was informed that:

'Last evening, acting on information, officers of the anti-terrorist squad arrested Sean Murphy in Surrey. Murphy was surprised at his hide-out late last night. He fought ferociously to escape from the police and several officers were injured restraining him. He is now being held in a secure hospital where

the injuries he sustained were being treated.

Police also recovered an Uzi machine pistol and a number of rounds of ammunition. A spokesman for the anti-terrorist branch said that Murphy's capture had caused a huge hole to be made in the IRA's chain of command.'

The article went on to detail the atrocities that Murphy was thought to be responsible for. The opinion column of the paper congratulated the police on their success.

Chapter 19

"It was not until last evening that I was certain that a member of the CIA and a French Government arms manufacturer were involved." Cross shuffled uneasily in his seat.

That morning, at his weekly meeting with the Prime Minister, he had reported the facts, which had been given by Murphy. He also advised him of the undercover operation with Hubbard.

The reaction of the PM had been somewhat unexpected. No surprise had been expressed at the disclosures. All the PM had done was to make notes and tell Cross that this was a matter he must consider carefully. At lunchtime Cross had been instructed to attend number ten at three that afternoon. On his arrival he was faced with, not only the PM but the Foreign Secretary and his top Civil Service mandarin.

"I don't know if you realise how potentially embarrassing this situation could be," the Foreign Secretary began. "It would seem that you, as head of MI5, have instituted a covert operation with the avowed intention of entrapping a senior member of our most loyal allies' security services."

"That is not so," Cross interpolated.

The Foreign Secretary held up his hand. "Let me finish," he continued. "Not only that, but you appear to be trying to ensnare a state-owned company of another member of the EEC. This is totally unacceptable conduct for a servant of Her Majesty's Government."

This reaction only served to bemuse Cross.

"I am sorry that you see it that way, sir," Cross replied. "That is not a true representation of the facts. Initially I received information relating to laundering of illegal monies through certain of our major financial institutions. I instituted an operation to ascertain whether the information I received was true. That operation ran as planned and we have ample evidence to bring prosecutions relating to the import of both drugs and arms, and those people who were involved in the illicit movement of the money. During the undercover action my operative was approached about managing the financial end of another deal. It was then that we discovered, mainly by accident, there may have been a connection with the illegal export of missile guidance systems. At the outset, the only possible entrapment was against people trading in drugs and arms."

"If this was only a matter of drugs and arms," the mandarin interjected, "why was MI5 involved? Surely such matters fall under the brief of Customs and the Police?"

"They were both involved." Cross was beginning to become disturbed at the underlying nuances. "I acted in a co-ordinating role because the original source was mine and mine alone."

"That is not the situation as represented by either Customs or the Essex Police," the mandarin retorted smugly.

Cross realised that he was being herded into a corner, but knew not why. "It was necessary to co-ordinate two separate operations, one on the mainland and the other in Northern Ireland. I was the only person who had a full overview. Consequently it was vital to ensure that no peremptory steps were taken which would be out of synchronisation with the overall objective." Cross realised that he was slipping into Civil Service-speak.

There was silence for what seemed like an age, but was merely a minute or two. Finally the Prime Minister spoke.

"Ignoring any rights or wrongs in this matter we must primarily consider what the consequences will be. At the present time we need the support of the United States within the United Nations on certain matters which I am unable to reveal. Apart from that we are entering very delicate negotiations relating to the future of the European Community. In these we must have the ongoing support of the French Government. If we allow your covert dealings to run to their natural conclusion, we run a serious risk of losing the goodwill of both the French and the Americans. In addition we would also bring into the open a huge scandal in one of this country's most revered financial institutions. Do we wish to take this step?"

Cross sat back, aghast at the implication that the matter could be suppressed. Inside he was beginning to boil with anger.

"The guidance systems," he tried to select his words carefully, "have, so far, been given to the Anti-Apartheid Congress and used to shoot down an aeroplane containing over one hundred and fifty people, including a minister of the South African government. We also guess that they will next be supplied to factions in both the Middle East and South America. What sort of havoc can they reap in those two zones?"

"Neither of those areas," the mandarin said smugly, "are in our direct spheres of influence. South America is left strictly to the Americans and the Middle East is, in the main, the Soviets and the Americans. Our only real influence there is Saudi and that is more commercial than political."

"Are you saying," Cross responded incredulously, his angst breaking through his exterior calm, "that whilst we know that equipment is being supplied that will, almost certainly, fuel unrest and result in hundreds, maybe thousands, of people dying we should ignore it. Simply because we are trying to re-negotiate the bloody common agricultural policy of the EEC?"

"I do not believe that sort of vitriolic comment will take this discussion any further, "the mandarin commented contemptuously. "This is a political matter and requires political judgement. If all our decisions were made using your sort of simple philanthropic ideals government would be an anachronism."

Cross' rage had now overtaken him. He was about to reply when the Prime Minister raised his hand.

"I don't think we need to carry this matter any further. I believe some of us are becoming a little vexed," he began. "I am afraid that, in this case, we must take the course that is most beneficial to this country. Your operation must be terminated and the file closed without any further action, Mr Cross."

"That could be a little difficult, sir." Cross had two cards left. "I have been working closely with the FBI, who actually supplied the finance. They will want to see some result from their investment."

"That has already been taken care of before this meeting," the mandarin said coyly.

"The other matter is that one of my sources was a journalist. He will probably still publish what he knows." Get out of that, you bastards, thought Cross.

"There is no need to worry about that either." Again it was the mandarin. "D notices have already been served about all matters pertaining to this affair. If your man wishes to go ahead he will be prosecuted under the Official Secrets Act."

"Shit," thought Cross, wishing he could say it aloud.

The Prime Minister rose. "I am sure you realise that matters of state sometimes conflict with more localised interests Mr Cross. In these circumstances the interests of the State have to be paramount. He offered Cross his hand saying, "Thank you for coming." With that Cross was dismissed.

Cross was seething as he was shown out of number ten. He had been involved before where potential actions could produce goals which were contradictory, but never such as this. His initial reaction was to go to his office and tender his resignation, but that would serve no purpose. He would still be bound by the Official Secrets Act. He knew something would have to be done, but what?

His mood had not improved by the time he arrived at his desk. He snapped, unnecessarily, at his secretary, simply because the afternoon post was not on his desk. It mattered not that he had not been there to see it. He thumbed through the pile of reports that arrived daily, until one caught his eye. The envelope was sealed with wax and marked 'Secret – J.Cross only'. The report inside was headed 'Subject Thierry Mersonne'. He pushed the other papers to one side and read.

Amiens – 10th April 1985

The subject Mersonne was followed to a private airfield outside Le Havre. He accompanied a Renault van, which had been loaded with approximately thirty cartons at the warehouse of Mutuelle Avionique. The warehouse was closed for all other matters when the loading took place. At the airfield the cargo was transferred to a small aircraft owned by a company called Air Transporte.

As a result of subsequent enquiries I ascertained the following.

1)   Air Transporte is a one man, one aircraft company specialising in small, high value cargoes. It is suspected that part of the operation involves the transportation of illicit shipments.

2)   The flight plan of the aircraft was direct to Famagusta in Cyprus.

I advised Nicosia station of the flight and asked them to institute surveillance on the cargo when it arrives.

Cross put the brief report down. The first shipment was on the move and he had been told to close the operation down. He put the report in his briefcase. He would start to dismantle the various facets tomorrow. It could take several days to get to his people in Amiens or Cyprus. Perhaps a few days would be enough.

He telephoned Jennings and arranged to meet later that evening. He also asked him to ensure that Pinter and Hubbard would be there.

***

Cross arrived at Jennings' home soon after eight. Pinter's Bentley was already in the drive. Cross had no idea of what he wanted to say. He simply needed to release his frustration to someone who would listen.

Jennings opened the door before Cross rang the bell.

"Come in, Jim," he said. "The others are inside."

Pinter and Hubbard were settled in easy chairs and Pansie was pouring the drinks. The usual greetings were exchanged. Pansie produced a beer for Cross without the need of being asked. Cross sat and then wondered how he could start.

For the benefit of Pinter he started, "Firstly I must stress that this is totally off the record."

Pinter smiled at the necessary charade. "OK Jim, that's the bullshit over. What's the problem?"

"I was called to a meeting this afternoon with the P.M. and the Foreign Secretary," Cross began.

"Let me guess," Pinter interjected. "Because of our need for the support of the Americans in the UN, and the French in the

284

EEC negotiations, you have been told to can this whole operation with O'Connell and the French."

"Who are your sources, George?" Cross asked, perplexed that Pinter already knew the tale.

"A little bit of information and a lot of logic," replied Pinter. "I've been observing the Foreign Office for years. The chances of them letting you blow the whistle on the CIA and the French arms industry are not too high."

Cross turned to the others. "Basically George has it correct. I have been ordered by the PM to shut the whole thing down and close the file."

"Do you mean to say," Hubbard laughed, "that I have been giving Karen a good seeing-to for bugger all reason?"

The comment broke any tension that was developing.

"Is that really it," Jennings asked, "or do we make our own agenda?"

"That is exactly what I wanted to talk about," Cross responded. "I have to, officially, close the file, but unofficially I still want to see those bastards done. What I have to know is whether it is feasible."

"How is your relationship with Matthew Curren in South Africa?" asked Pinter.

"We get on very well, but it would have to be a last resort to involve him."

"Why?" Pinter enquired.

"At present the South Africans are feeling a little bit like pariahs and convinced that everyone hates them. They currently have the same siege mentality as Mossad in Israel, an eye for an eye and all that. If I fed them the facts we know, they would probably leave a trail of human debris across three continents."

"But they are there as a last resort," commented Pinter.

Cross nodded in affirmation. "What I need to know is whether there is another way in which we can bring this mess into the open."

"These reinsurance contracts. Are they fairly standard wordings?" It was Pansie who raised the question. She had been a top underwriter in Hong Kong before she became a wife and mother.

"I think so, love," he husband replied. "Why?"

"If the contracts are standard, then they would contain a clause allowing the reinsurer to inspect the records of his client at any time. Can't you use that and dig back from there?"

"We could," said Jennings, "but the only person who can invoke the clause is the reinsurer. The problem we would have is that both of the reinsurers, Lloyds and the off shore company, are a part of the laundering chain. They are not going to blow the gaff on themselves."

"What about me?" Hubbard interjected. "Technically I own Oasis. Can I stick a spanner in the works from them?"

"You could," Jennings mused, "but it is likely that the people who manage Oasis are part of the conspiracy. It would make you a target for a lot of people."

"I've been one of them all my bloody life," Hubbard retorted.

"Can Peter Huber help us at all?" Pansie's mind was searching desperately. She was sure that Huber's company had been offered a deal but the details stayed locked in her subconscious.

Jennings picked her up and hugged her. "Pansie, you are a genius. I had forgotten all about that."

"About what?" the other three questioned.

"One of Peter Huber's people in Hong Kong was offered a package that looked suspiciously like the deals we have here. The company was called Armitage Reinsurance. Peter told me that they had eventually accepted it. The business came from Thailand and was reinsured into Hong Kong and then out to London. Larry Payne if I am not mistaken. If Peter institutes an inspection he will find out that the original insurances are fakes. He can then tell me or Michael Mason of his worries and we take it from there."

"Why should Huber tell you or Mason?" Pinter knew little and had even less interest in the machinations of the City.

"Because we are the brokers, you dozy old sod," chuckled Jennings. "He can raise suspicions in our minds, on which we have to act. We will have to dig out all similar deals and investigate them, in conjunction with Lloyds themselves."

NEW YORK – 16TH APRIL 1985

Hacker was beginning to admire him. He had taken a beating for two days and still refused to name his principal. Only one other had resisted Hacker's particular form of persuasion for that long, and he had died before saying a thing.

Hacker had waited in Ryan's Bar for three nights. He noticed him on the first evening. The bar was practically empty when the man arrived. He had sat and nursed one drink for an hour. All the time he kept looking at his watch as though expecting someone. When he had appeared the second and third nights Hacker was certain that this was his man. He had followed him from the bar and forced him into an alleyway. When he found the Magnum in the shoulder holster he guessed that the stranger was there to hit Scorsi rather than talk to him.

Hacker had rented an apartment in a converted warehouse. Its main benefit was the fact that it had been soundproofed. He had taken the interloper there so that they could talk in peace. There was no identification in the man's wallet, but it did contain a piece of paper with a familiar Denver telephone number and a photograph of Scorsi.

Hacker decided that he needed one last desperate throw of the dice.

"Seeing as though you don't want to tell me anything, I suppose that we must part company." Hacker opened the can and began to pour the petrol over the tethered stranger.

"What the fuck are you doing?" the man cried, the acrid fumes stinging his eyes.

"You know what I want. You tell me who you are and why you were going to hit Scorsi and I won't strike this." He held the Zippo to the man's face.

"I don't know any fucking Scorsi," his voice pleaded. Fear shone from his eyes.

"Then I have made a terrible mistake," Hacker grinned. "The problem is nobody else can know I fucked up."

He flicked open the lid of the lighter and rolled the striking wheel. The flint spat and a flame danced.

"For Christ's sake don't," the man implored, his guts knotting with horror. "I'll tell you what you want to know. Just shut that thing off."

"That's better," Hacker smiled. "Who are you working for?"

"The CIA," was the reply. This was the last answer that Hubbard had expected.

He struck the lighter again. "Don't try to bullshit me," he snarled.

"I'm not," the man was now begging. "Tom O'Connell gave me the contract. He's CIA"

"Why did the CIA want Scorsi hit?" Hubbard was beginning to believe the man.

"I don't know. I just carry out instructions."

"Whose is this Denver telephone number?" Hacker held up the paper with the number scrawled on it.

"That was where I was to contact O'Connell after the contract was finished. It connects directly through to his office in New York. He uses the name Smith when he is there."

"That is extremely interesting, so you are not the elusive Mr Smith?" Hacker mused. "Where is this office?"

"It's on 42nd and Broadway, the fifth floor. The front is an investment company. Now, for God's sake put that thing out." Cold sweat glistened on his forehead.

"You've been very co-operative." Hacker smiled benignly. "Even though we were not properly introduced it has been very nice meeting you."

He threw the lighted Zippo onto the man's lap. The flames leaped into life, making a sound like an express train passing through a tunnel. The screams lasted only a few seconds before the searing heat oxidised his larynx into silence.

ZURICH – 30TH APRIL 1985

The bar in the Schplugenschloss Hotel was empty, apart from the barman. He had started to pour a glass of Hurlimann as soon as he saw Jennings. This man was a regular and only ever drank the beer.

"Good evening, Mr Jennings," he smiled. "The usual I presume?" He placed the drink on the bar.

Jennings thanked the barman and took the drink to a table in a quiet corner. He checked his Rolex. Huber, as always, was late. It was not a Swiss trait to be dilatory, but Huber had developed the habit during the years he had spent in Australia and the Far East.

Huber bustled into the bar, bellowed, "Same for me, Heinz," to the barman, and shook Jennings' hand with the usual vigour.

"Sorry I'm late." He offered the obligatory apology which was as sincere as a pledge of celibacy from him. "Got tied up in the office." The beer disappeared down his gullet in one. A second arrived before the glass was replaced on the table. The barman knew Huber well. Half of the new drink disappeared before the initial quenching was completed.

"Well, Mr Jennings, what can I do for you and why did you not want to see me in the office?" Huber questioned.

"This whole matter is a little delicate and I wanted your full attention, without your bloody phone ringing and your minions crawling up your arse," Jennings replied.

"Go on then." The second half of the Hurlimann followed the same route as the first. "What's your problem. Have your firm fucked up and you want me to get your balls out of the fire?"

"Nothing like that, Peter," Jennings responded. "It's about that reinsurance of Armitage Reinsurance that your company did out of Hong Kong."

"I remember the one. It was offered to Schmidlin. That's where we only fronted for Lloyds and got paid a million dollars for the pleasure of it." One of the major assets of any underwriter is a memory like an elephant. "The results were not too good last time I looked, but we still make a nice turn on it. Is there a problem?"

"I don't know, but I think there may be." Jennings chose his words carefully. "I think that you should invoke the inspection clause and audit the records of the Armitage."

"What the fuck should I do that for? We have one hundred per cent of it reinsured. Why should we piss money up against a wall?" Huber was somewhat surprised by Jennings' proposal. There was no way that his company could lose any money on the contracts. Only Armitage could lose. His company was sitting in the middle with no liabilities and one million dollars and, the icing on the cake, protected by a guarantee from a bank with over a billion dollars in assets. Why should he pay to have the company's books and records inspected?

This was the initial reaction that Jennings had expected. Huber had developed many Anglophile traits, but still retained his Swiss values where non-essential expenditure was involved.

"If I told you that I have good grounds to believe that there are no actual insurances," Jennings continued, "and that the whole thing has been set up to launder money for drugs and arms, would that change your opinion?"

Huber looked dumbfounded. His company was the largest and one of the oldest reinsurers in the world. It had an unrivalled reputation for honesty and integrity. "Are you pulling my plonker?" he asked incredulously.

Jennings shook his head. "I'm afraid not, Peter. I have discovered that certain people in London have been setting up dummy reinsurance deals to disguise money laundering. I also know that the cash is for both drugs and arms."

"Have you got proof?" Huber asked.

Jennings spent the next hour telling Huber as much as he could. Huber's eyes became wider as the tale progressed.

"How do I know that Armitage is part of this?" Huber asked, still hoping that the whole thing was untrue.

"If my guess is correct, firstly you will be reinsured with Larry Payne, Kieron O'Sullivan and Jack Green." Jennings responded. "Secondly, the results of the contract will have been bloody awful or fantastically good, depending on who is buying and who is selling."

Huber raised his eyebrows quizzically.

"I've seen both." Jennings noticed the implied question. "In some cases the finance is shifted by collecting on dummy claims, in others huge premiums are ceded with no losses. If the Thais are selling, Armitage will be paying and vice versa."

"Let me make a call." Huber rose and walked towards the door, pausing only to ask the barman to replenish the Hurlimann.

He returned after a couple of minutes. "Bloody computer people," he muttered. "They think that they are bloody gods." Half a glass of beer sank down his throat before he sat. "The information will be on my desk in an hour."

They spent the next hour talking over old times together. Huber's usual exuberance was temporarily defunct.

Huber's office was large enough to hold a junior basketball match in. A huge Persian rug adorned the floor. At the far end a desk the size of a table tennis table dominated the room. Huber picked up the plastic folder that sat in the middle of his pad and read. He muttered, "Shit" and passed it to Jennings. The printed report showed that Payne, O'Sullivan and Green were the reinsurers of Huber's company, and that over ten million dollars had been paid in premium and fifty million dollars in claims. "If what you say is right, it looks as though the Thais are selling," muttered Huber.

"I'm right," Jennings said emphatically. "My information is that the finance behind Armitage comes from Chinatown in San Francisco. If Triads are paying that sort of money to a source in Thailand it has to be for heroin."

"Shit!" Huber repeated and took back the report. He folded it and put it in his pocket. "I'm taking you up to the old town and we are going to get horribly pissed."

***

Jennings flight back from Zurich arrived at Heathrow early the next afternoon. The drive from the airport seemed interminable. The chauffeur was at his most buoyant and chattered inconsequentially for the whole journey. Jennings, who was still recovering from Huber's ministrations the previous night, merely grunted. He arrived back at Woldingham soon after four.

Pansie seemed subdued when she greeted him.

"Are you all right, love?" he asked.

"Jim is coming down tonight. He has been pushed out of MI5."

"He's what!" Jennings exclaimed.

"He was called in yesterday to number ten and sacked," she replied. "He has been replaced by someone from the Foreign Office. I've asked John and George to come down as well."

Cross was seething with rage when he arrived. Since his peremptory dismissal his replacement had been busy. Hubbard had been contacted and told that he was no longer working for the agency and whatever he was involved in was closed down. It seemed that all files relating to the Lloyds matter, as it had been named, were to be re-classified as inactive.

"I'll have those bastards if it is the last thing I do," Cross muttered as Jennings poured him a drink.

"What actually happened?" Jennings asked as he gave Cross a tumbler half full of whisky.

"What happened!" Cross spat. "Politics and the old school tie happened, that's what."

Jennings said nothing as Cross emptied the glass.

"I was called into the Prime Minister's office yesterday. I had a meeting with his Private Secretary who told me that the PM had developed serious doubts about my judgement, and that it would be better if I offered my resignation. I would, of course, still receive my full pension and a handsome severance payment. He then handed me a fucking cheque for a hundred thousand quid."

"What did you say to that?" Jennings guessed that the reply would not be in the Civil Service manual of acceptable responses.

"I thanked the bastard for the cheque and told him to tell the PM to bugger off."

The doorbell rang, heralding the arrival of both Pinter and Hubbard.

"If you farted it would smell of bloody roses," Hubbard commented after Cross had repeated the tale of his demise, in particular the severance settlement. "All I got was an earache from some prat about the Official Secrets Act. It seems now that I am undercover, living with a nymphomaniac, and no bugger to report to."

"Every cloud has a silver lining," Pinter chuckled. "How is the voracious Karen?"

Hubbard did not reply, but simply offered a single digit salute.

"What did you mean when you talked about the old school tie?" Jennings addressed Cross.

"One of the PM's old school friends from Eton was Stuart Tierman. For the ignorant among you he is the Chairman of Lloyds. If my information is right, they had dinner a couple of nights ago. You can probably guess what was discussed."

"But, Tierman is one of the old school." Jennings knew him

292

well. "He would not be a party to the sort of thing that has been going on."

"According to my sources, he is more worried about Lloyds' standing than he is about a few dodgy deals by certain individuals. I am told that three underwriters and a couple of brokers will be warned off. They won't get the elbow, they will just be told to desist from participating in this type of deal. That way there will be no scandal, and no future transactions."

Jennings whistled through his teeth. "So it doesn't matter how many bodies the drugs and guns have, and will kill, as long as Lloyds' reputation remains in tact?"

"That's about the score," sighed Cross.

Pinter rose to pour more drinks. As he filled the glasses he asked, "Do you have any good news, or should I turn into a manic depressive?"

"I don't know whether it is good or not," Cross responded. "Just before I was called to number ten I had a report from the observation in Cyprus. It seems that the shipment from Avionique has been split in two in Cyprus. Half of it was loaded on a small freighter bound for Tripoli and the rest onto an ocean-going tug called named the *Christina*."

"Where was that bound for?" asked Hubbard.

"Nowhere in particular," was the reply. "It's one of those bandits that roams the seas waiting for vessels to get into trouble. If it is first on the scene and puts a line on board it gets the salvage. It's a sort of sea-going ambulance chaser. If I had still been in the job I would have had an electronic tracer planted on the bloody thing."

"We can still follow its course." Jennings perked up a little. "All movements will be reported to Lloyds register of shipping. I can arrange for all its activity to be reported to me."

There was little else that could be achieved that night. They agreed that Hubbard would continue his charade until such time as the South American transaction was completed. Jennings had doubts that this would ever be so, as Jarvis would certainly be one of the brokers to be targeted by Tierman.

BANGKOK – 15TH MAY 1985

The air conditioning and a long cool drink were beginning to correct the fault in Huber's body thermostat. The flight had been both long and drear. He had seen both films shown on the aeroplane several times. The tedium was increased by the tardiness of the cabin staff in replenishing empty glasses, a cardinal omission in Huber's consideration.

The journey from the airport had been hot, bumpy and uncomfortable. It had taken him past the best and the worst of this amazing city. He had passed stunning dainty oriental edifices, and other places that openly advertised their desire to sate the depraved needs of paedophiles or any other sexual perversion a twisted mind could imagine.

Whilst another long cool drink was being produced he wondered what he would find the following day. He had written to Armitage in Bermuda telling them of his trip to the Far East. He had expressed his concern at the results of the business his company had received. He went on to say he would like to meet their agent whilst he was in Bangkok to find out what action was being taken to improve the situation. He had left them little choice by naming a date and time for his visit.

He had a couple more drinks before he succumbed to the inevitable fact that his body was still operating on European time and a night's sleep had been lost.

A very pretty young lady bearing his breakfast, which he ate with relish, awakened him the following morning. He left the hotel just after ten. The taxi stopped at the address given. The driver babbled incoherently and pointed to the blackened hulk of what had been a building.

"One-four-seven, one-four-seven," jabbered the man, pointing at the smoke-stained remains. This had been the offices of the Armitage's agent.

Huber paid the taxi driver and alighted. The premises had been a two-storey building, with a shop below and offices above. Three policemen stood idly studying the burnt out residue. Huber approached them, only to be vociferously waved away.

Across the road was a small bar. Huber decided that, if anyone would know all the local gossip, it would be the bar owner. He ambled across the road and into the dimly lit saloon. There were no other customers.

The bar owner seemed a little surprised to see a European favouring his establishment. It did not appear exactly tourist friendly. Huber ordered a cold beer.

"I was supposed to visit someone over there today," Huber pointed to the scene of the fire. "What happened?" he asked casually.

"Big fire last night," the bar owner replied. "Building and owner burnt to a cinder."

"Not Paulo Mandingo?" Huber asked, looking at his itinerary.

"That's him," the man nodded vigorously.

"How did it happen?" Huber asked.

The man shrugged his shoulders. "Someone did not like him."

"What business was he in?" Huber was now becoming intrigued.

"If there was money in it, he did it." Again a shrug. "He was tied up with some bad people."

Huber paid for the beer and left.

Over the next two days he had meetings with all the dignitaries of the local insurance market. He asked each about the insurance activities of Paulo Mandingo. None had ever heard the name.

How could Mandingo control millions of dollars of premium and yet be unknown in the local market? The question was one to which Huber had to know the answer.

On his return to Zurich he telephoned Jennings and told him about his attempt to see the Bangkok agent. They arranged to meet in London.

***

Huber had met Cross, Pinter and Hubbard previously, the first time at Jennings' wedding. Jennings had invited them all to lunch in the boardroom at his office. He allowed the preliminary banter to run out of steam before he mentioned the *Christina*.

That morning Lloyds registry had advised that an ocean-going trawler had lost power in the Atlantic. It had sent out an SOS and a salvage tug called *Christina* had taken her in tow.

The crippled vessel was being taken to a small fishing port in Donegal for repairs.

"Shit," gasped Cross when Jennings told them the story. "Those guidance systems are going to the IRA."

"What are you talking about?" Huber was bemused.

Jennings related the tale of the shooting down of SA 165, the connection with Mutuelle Avionique and how it was connected with the *Christina*.

"Why do you not tell the authorities?" Huber asked.

"Actually, I used to be the authorities," Cross answered wryly. "Unfortunately the authorities above me had a different agenda to myself."

"You are not telling me that your government knows of this and is ignoring what is happening?" Huber found this untenable. It was not the Swiss way, unless the contraband happened to be gold bullion.

"They know that guidance systems are being illicitly exported from France," Jennings interjected. "They also know that a senior member of the CIA is involved, and that Lloyds and the international reinsurance market has been used to launder the money for this and other deals. Apart from that they are in total ignorance."

"Something must be done to bring this into the open." Huber had problems accepting what he was being told. "If my company is being used I intend to stop it."

"Before we do anything, we have to stop the *Christina* delivering what she is carrying." Jennings knew, from his time in the province, that the IRA armed with surface-to-air missiles would be Armageddon to any thoughts of a peaceful solution. Wounds could be opened that would not heal for a century or more.

"I agree," Cross commented. "I think I may have an answer. Can I use the phone?"

He took out his pocket-book and punched the numbers into the pad. He recognised O'Brien's soft brogue as soon as he answered.

"Conon, how are you?" The English must always begin any conversation with the required civilities. O'Brien offered a suitable reply and enquired the reason for the call. The news of

296

Cross' demise in the security services had not yet reached him.

"What sort of relations do you have with your opposite number in Eire?" Cross asked.

"We have a very good working relationship," O'Brien responded. "We have worked quite closely together in the past, particularly on drugs, why?"

"What about arms?" Cross ignored O'Brien's question for the moment.

"Never happened so far." O'Brien's puzzlement was becoming intrigue. "Do you know something?"

"I have received some intelligence information. If it is accurate, and I am certain it is, you will have to act jointly with the Irish Customs. I have to know whether that is going to be a problem."

"We meet on a regular basis and whenever we have run combined operations there have never been any problems." O'Brien guessed that what was about to be revealed to him was big, very big.

"My sources tell me…" Cross knew that he had to trust this man, "…that guidance systems for anti-aircraft missiles are presently in transit. They will arrive in County Donegal within the next few days, if they are not intercepted."

"Are you certain?" O'Brien asked incredulously.

"As certain as I can be."

"How are they arriving?" O'Brien's tone changed from affable to efficient. "And how are they being brought in?"

"A salvage tug called the *Christina* is presently towing a crippled trawler into a port in Donegal. My sources confirm that the guidance systems were loaded on *Christina* in Cyprus. Since then *Christina* has not entered any other ports. The only possible conclusion is that the cargo is illicit and intended for the IRA."

"How good is your source of information?" O'Brien enquired.

"Impeccable," was the reply.

O'Brien repeated the story back to Cross to confirm that he had all the facts. "I'll contact the people in the South immediately and keep you fully informed on progress."

"Don't do that, Conon." Cross knew that this was the moment of truth. "The politicians want to keep a lid on this

297

whole thing. I've been running an operation on this for months and yesterday the Foreign Office closed the file and had me fired. When you go to the Irish it has to be on the basis of information you have received from one of your sources." Cross stressed the 'your'.

"So it will be my arse in the flames," O'Brien said ruefully.

"It's either that or the Provisionals start to shoot down aeroplanes."

"I take your point." O'Brien had decided that a warm rear was preferable to the alternative. "Where can I contact you?"

Cross gave him Jennings' telephone number.

"The immediate problem is in hand." Jennings was speaking as Cross turned his attention back to the group. "But where do we go from here?"

"As I see it," Pinter was busy packing his pipe as he spoke, "we are going to have to drag this whole thing out bit by bit."

The others said nothing, waiting for Pinter to continue.

"We will have to do what politicians do."

"What is that?" Huber interjected. "Bury our heads in the sand and wait to be re-elected?"

"A little more pro-active than that, Peter," Pinter laughed. "What I mean is we start to leak."

"Who to and what?" Cross asked.

"The first step would be the *Christina*," Pinter had the embryo of an idea. It would mean his losing an exclusive, an anathema to a journalist of his standing, but needs must.

"I have an old friend at the *Irish Times* who would chew glass to get hold of this story. I can nudge him in the right direction."

"Then what?" This time it was Huber who spoke.

"Then I think that you Peter should air your suspicions, in a general way, about business your company has."

"You want me to tell the whole world that my company is staffed by imbeciles instead of underwriters. Bollocks," Huber snorted.

"You don't have to be that direct," Pinter responded. "You arrange an interview with someone from the insurance technical press and voice your suspicions about certain reinsurance packages. Give them the example of the agent, who was not, in

298

Bankok as an example. All these people in the technical press think that they really should be investigative journalists. Offer them a snippet and the Pulitzer Prize will flash before their eyes. Just feed them enough to send them in the right direction and they will blunder off and start creating waves. Once that is done the real investigators will latch on."

Chapter 20

'SECURITY FORCES INTERCEPT MISSILES'

The headline blazed from the front page of the *Irish Times*. Underneath the story was told. Padraig Corchoran had his exclusive and his byline.

> *Yesterday afternoon the Irish Navy intercepted and boarded the ocean-going tug* Christina *off the coast of Donegal. The* Christina *was towing the trawler* St Patrick *back to its home port after it had suffered engine failure.*
>
> *Acting on information received from the security forces in the six counties the* Christina *was boarded and searched. It was discovered that equipment for use in anti-aircraft missiles was being carried. The captain and crew of both vessels have been taken into custody by the Garda.*
>
> *The equipment impounded is said to be highly sophisticated guidance systems. It is thought that similar equipment was used to destroy the South African Airlines flight SA 165. The South African Government has always denied that the flight, which was destroyed whilst carrying the Minister for Internal Affairs, was bought down by a missile attack, but rumours to the contrary still persist.*
>
> *It is presently thought that the impounded equipment was intended for the Provisional IRA.'*

Corchoran continued giving more detail of the loss of SA 165 and then surmised at the potential calamities that could result if such equipment became available to paramilitaries in the north.

Following the publication of the story all the major newspapers in Britain and many from the United States and Europe dispatched reporters to Eire. George Pinter was among them.

NEW YORK – 24TH MAY 1985

"Whoever is responsible for this security breach is going to be dead meat." O'Connell slammed his fist onto his desk. "I want you on the next flight to Ireland, and don't come back until you find the leak and stop it. I want you to have a very close look at Croft and that slapper he is fucking."

Martin Dolan said nothing. He had seen O'Connell in this sort of frenzy before and knew that it would only abate with time not words. He simply commented, "Yes, sir" and made a hasty exit. He appreciated that O'Connell was looking for blood and had no wish to offer his.

PRETORIA – 24TH MAY 1985

"This is the first real lead that we have." Colonel Curren addressed the remark to Callard. "I want you over in Ireland tomorrow. See what you can find out."

"I might pay your friend Jim Cross a visit whilst I am over there," Callard replied. "Now that he is out of MI5 he might be a little more amenable to telling us what he knows."

"Good idea," Curren responded. "I am sure that he knows who supplied those bastards with the missiles. Do whatever you have to but find out who supplied them to the AAC."

DONEGAL – 26TH MAY 1985

Pinter sat in the corner of the bar jotting down some words to keep his editor happy. It was the first time in his life that he had a massive exclusive and could not use it himself. His brilliance as a wordsmith had allowed him to produce reports that seemed to say more than the other newspapers but actually didn't.

He knew that the story was now running out of steam and needed an injection of life from him. As he pondered how to kick-start the incident back into newsworthy life, he noticed a new face at the bar. Among the hacks who were trying to wheedle snippets of information from each other was a heavy-set young man with a deep tan. Pinter knew the face but for the moment could not put a name to it.

He put his notebook in his pocket, downed his drink, and

wandered across to the bar.

"I do apologise, clumsy old fool that I am."

The other mopped the spilled drink from his sleeve and said, "That's all right. Accidents happen."

The accent was the jolt that Pinter's memory bank needed. What was South African intelligence doing in Donegal?

"Let me buy you another drink." Pinter smiled at the man he now realised was Captain Callard of the South African counter intelligence unit.

Callard accepted his offer. He had recognised George Pinter of the *Record* immediately. Pinter's reputation was known world-wide. He was generally accepted as the journalist with the highest knowledge and connections in matters of international politicking and intrigue. If a lead was there, Callard knew that Pinter would either have it or be in close pursuit.

"There is a space over there," Pinter said affably. "Shall we sit down?"

"I haven't come across a South African accent until today. Are you a journalist?" Pinter wondered what Callard's cover would be.

Callard nodded. "I am with the *Rand Daily News*."

"I would not have thought that arms to the IRA were of much interest to your readers," Pinter said innocently.

"The original story linked the arms find with SA 165. My editor told me to come over here and see what I could find out," Callard replied affably. "So far, I have got sod all to report."

"Do you think that there is a link?" Pinter asked.

Callard shrugged. "There may be."

"By the way, I am George Pinter." Pinter proffered his hand.

"I know who you are, Mr Pinter," Callard responded. "Your work is well known in my country. I'm Bob Callard."

Pinter smiled inwardly. If Callard was using his own name rather than a pseudonym, he must think that South African security services personnel were not known outside his country. This could be an opportunity to stir the pot.

He saw Padraig Corchoran pushing his way to the bar. He waved at him and shouted, "Over here, Paddy."

Corchoran ordered a Guinness and brought it across. Corchoran not only was, but also looked Irish. His eyes seemed to twinkle with fun and his face had the slightly ruddy complexion of someone that had and would enjoy a 'good crack'.

Pinter introduced Callard and initial greetings were exchanged.

"Did you get anything out of Lloyds Register of Shipping?" Pinter addressed the remark to Corchoran even though the object was to feed the information to Callard.

"Not much," replied Corchoran, "other than that the *Christina*'s last port of call was Larnaca."

"Is that where you think that the missile systems were loaded?" Pinter asked.

"It's a fair guess that they were," Corchoran replied. "*Christina*'s previous job was in the gulf towing a rig into place. It could not have been carrying extra cargo weight doing that."

"Are you saying that the illicit cargo came from Cyprus?" Callard interjected.

"It was probably loaded in Cyprus," Corchoran responded, "but I would guess that was only a transit point. The gear must have come from somewhere to Cyprus. What I want to know is where that somewhere is?"

"Any ideas, Paddy?" Pinter asked knowing that he had Callard's interest.

He shook his head. "Not really. The boffins are still studying it, but even if they identify the source we may never know. It could be bad politics to bring it into the open if it originates from a friendly country."

"They couldn't hush that sort of thing up, could they?" Callard asked trying to appear naive. "I know it could happen in Pretoria but not here. You have a completely free press. They would never get away with it."

"Anything related to the Republican movement in the six counties is outside of the normal rules over here," Corchoran responded. "The whole topic is so bloody emotive no politician will grasp any nettles. There are two simple facts that everyone knows but won't admit to knowing. The first is that the majority of the people in the six counties do not want to be part of a united Ireland. The second is that the south could not afford the north if the UK withdrew all its financing. It would cripple our economy. Even though we know that, we still keep that bloody silly clause in our constitution saying it's ours. If the UK said to the Irish government, 'You can have the six counties. We don't want them any more,' the Irish Government would have to say thank you, but only if you give us lots of money as well.

"To answer your question, if my government found out that the missile systems came from the Americans they would not say a word. If they came from Libya they would broadcast it world-wide.

"That's enough of the lecturing," Corchoran smiled. "Whose turn is it to buy the next round?"

Callard offered, a little too enthusiastically, and made for the bar.

"A little guileless, your young friend, George," Corchoran commented.

"Not as much as you think," replied Pinter. "My young friend is an intelligence agent for the South African Government. His innocence is all a front."

"What is his interest?"

"My guess would be vengeance," Pinter replied. "If Pretoria ever find out who suppled the AAC, retribution will be both swift and severe."

Corchoran nodded sagaciously. "That should be a good news story."

"Are you following up on the Cyprus connection?" Pinter changed the subject.

"One of my people is on his way there now," Corchoran replied.

"Tell him to look at air cargo imports." Pinter took out his notebook and wrote 'Air Transporte'. He passed the paper to Corchoran. "That is a name which might be worth taking a close look at."

Corchoran took the paper and put it in his wallet. "You know a lot more than you are letting on, don't you, George?" Pinter made no comment.

"What I don't understand is why are you feeding me the story? Why aren't you running with it yourself?"

"I have my reasons," was all Pinter said.

Callard placed the drinks on the table. He had caught the tail end of the conversation and seen, as Pinter intended, the name

'Air Transporte' when the paper was passed. He said nothing.

SHERATON HOTEL, KNIGHTSBRIDGE – 30TH MAY 1985

Dolan sat in the bar, a large vodka martini in front of him. He thumbed through *Business Insurance* searching for the article.

He had spent three days in Donegal and then another in Dublin. All his attempts to find any further information had been fruitless. He had flown to London and contacted Croft to arrange a meeting. He then telephoned O'Connell to report his lack of progress.

O'Connell seemed not to have recovered from his bout of angst. He had questioned Dolan's parenthood several times when told that no progress had been made. "My nuts are in the fireplace and some bastard is about to strike a fucking match," he had screamed. Dolan, guessing that something new had arisen to fuel O'Connell's disenchantment, had asked whether there had been any further developments.

"Further developments?" he had raged. "Get yourself a copy of *Business Insurance* and see for your fucking self."

Dolan flicked through the pages until the headline caught his eye.

ARE WE MONEY LAUNDERING?

Dolan opened the magazine and read. The article reported on an interview with a man called Peter Huber who was a General Manager of a major Swiss company. In the interview Huber had expounded at great length about there being reinsurance contracts placed, which were, in fact, money-laundering deals. He expressed deep concern at this and said he intended to root out the truth, no matter what the cost to him or his company. The article gave Huber's background and that of his company.

Dolan finished and whistled through his teeth. The whole plan was falling to pieces. First one of the cargos is intercepted and then a billion dollar multi-national company says it will delve into the sort of financial arrangement which has been used. It was little wonder that O'Connell's fury was unabated.

Dolan looked at his watch. Croft should arrive soon. He ordered another martini and placed the paper, open at Huber's interview, on the table in front of him.

"Mr Johnson?" The voice came from inside a body that most men would give their right arm to sleep with.

As Johnson was a cover name he had not used before Dolan took a moment to react. He stood and said, "Yes. And you are?"

"My name is Karen." She leaned forward to take his proffered hand. The two white breasts that appeared when her neckline succumbed to the forces of gravity transfixed his eyes. "Gerry is getting the drinks," she smiled. "He won't be a moment."

She sat down and crossed her long slender legs. Dolan sat opposite and his attention moved from her bust to her upper thigh.

He dragged his attention back to business when a man with enormous hairy hands appeared. Hubbard introduced himself as Gerry Croft and asked courteously, "And how is Tom Smith?"

"He is spitting razor blades and wants to know what the fuck is going on."

The reply was close to Hubbard's expectations. The interception of the cargo in Donegal put O'Connell's neck firmly on a chopping block. He feigned ignorance and commented mildly, "What's the problem? Everything is running smoothly. The finances are flowing nicely and the whole transaction should be completed within the next couple of weeks." He smiled benignly.

"What about this then?" Dolan stabbed at the *Business Insurance* sitting on the table between them.

"About what?" Hubbard asked innocently.

"This goddamn article." He threw the paper at Hubbard. "Read that and then tell me everything is sweetness and fucking roses."

Hubbard made to read the magazine that had been tossed at him. He had no need as he had already seen the proof that Huber had sent to Jennings. He did, however, need time to think. He had not expected to be confronted with it by O'Connell or his associates.

Hubbard studied the article for several minutes, closed the

306

magazine and smiled. He had decided that attack would be more effective.

"I don't see that there is any problem here," he began. "This is just Peter Huber ranting on about his favourite hobbyhorse. He does it from time to time."

"You know this bastard?" queried Dolan.

"Great big fellah and a major piss artist," Hubbard nodded. "Every so often he jumps on his high horse and his mouth gets out of tune with his brain. He's been on about money laundering in reinsurance for years to any bugger who will listen."

"Read what he says about rooting out this type of deal. He's got big money and resources behind him." Dolan was somewhat relieved at Hubbard's comments, but his anxiety were not fully assuaged.

"He is not even involved in our package," Hubbard said amiably. "Every link in our chain has got a finger in the honeypot. The people I deal with run their own operations and don't answer to anyone. The whole procedure is tight as a drum."

"What about someone outside? Could they unearth anything?" Dolan wanted to be convinced.

"There is nothing to raise anyone's suspicions. To the outsider all we have is a simple commercial transaction. It runs through Lloyds of London, the most prestigious insurance market in the world." Hubbard leaned back and waved at the waiter to bring more drinks.

"How come we lost a shipment?" Dolan bit his tongue. He knew he had said too much.

"Was that crap in Donegal yours?" Hubbard sat forward showing renewed interest.

"It's nothing to do with you." Dolan tried to extricate himself from the hole into which he had just jumped. "You just stick to the financial transactions." He looked at his watch muttering, "I have to go." He made hasty farewells and left, hoping that his indiscretion would go no further than Hubbard.

Hubbard and Karen finished their drinks. "You handled him very well," Karen whispered in Hubbard's ear. "I think you deserve a reward." She squeezed his thigh.

On the way out Hubbard stopped at the concierge's desk. "Did you get it for me?" he asked. The concierge handed him back the Polaroid and four photographs. "Many thanks." Hubbard exchanged a ten-pound note for the photographs.

Back in his room Dolan poured himself a stiff drink. Croft has eased his mind on the security of the financial operation, but would his indiscretion come back to haunt him? On the positive side he felt that he had some good news. He picked up the telephone and dialled the Denver number.

"Yes!" O'Connell's tone indicated that his mood had not improved.

"Martin Dolan here, Tom," he began. "I have had a meeting with your man Croft and I don't think that there is a problem with him or his operation."

"Are you sure?"

"As sure as I can be," Dolan continued. "All he is running is the financial side. He would not have known anything about the cargo or its destination."

"What about that crap in *Business Insurance*?" snapped O'Connell.

"We talked about that and it does not seem to be an obstacle to us." Dolan had his fingers crossed.

"Then it has to be those French bastards. I want you over there and find out what is leaking and plug it. Do whatever you have to."

Dolan replaced the receiver.

SAVOY GRILL LONDON – 30TH MAY 19845

"Well, gentlemen, it was most rewarding while it lasted. I suggest that we toast the memory of Cameron." Larry Payne raised his glass.

Jarvis, Wilkes, Green and O'Sullivan lifted their champagne flutes and said, "Cameron Carter," in unison.

"What a pity it all has to end," Wilkes commented as he re-filled his glass with Dom Perignon. "It was, to put it in the vernacular, a very nice little earner. The violence was a little disturbing. Fortunately it was not connected to or directed at us."

"You never know," Payne responded. "We all know that amnesia is a perennial part of this market. I certainly intend to keep my little company in the Caymans. I think that we can revive the scheme in a couple of years and nobody will notice."

"You reinsured yours into the Caymans?" questioned Wilkes.

"Well, it was easy for you Jimmy," Payne responded. "All you had to do was watch. Yours and Freddie's cuts were taken off the top and paid straight into your Swiss accounts. I had premium paid into and out of the syndicate. I had to set up a small reinsurance arrangement with a company I owned to get my share out. Otherwise all the other names on the syndicate would have shared in the deal. The same applied to Kieron and Jack."

"Jack and I used the Turks and Caicos rather than the Caymans," O'Sullivan interjected.

"If you want to revive the package in the future you can count me out." Jarvis had stayed silent until then. The memory of Penny's blood-spattered body lying beside him still haunted his dreams. "I have got several million dollars tucked away in Switzerland. That's enough for me."

"You're too bloody squeamish, Freddie," Payne laughed. "Have another drink." He waved at the waiter for another bottle.

LARNACA – CYPRUS 2ND JUNE 1985

Corchoran was surprised at how hot it was as he left the aircraft. Islands are surrounded by sea, which usually cool the excessive heat. Today, however, the temperature was in the high eighties.

When Paul Kendrick, the ferret he had sent to Cyprus, had telephoned him from Larnaca to tell him the results of his investigation he had booked the flight immediately. Kendrick looked hot and flustered when Corchoran exited the Customs area.

"He's waiting in the hotel." Kendrick ignored the courtesy of a greeting. "He remembers the Air Transporte flight. The cargo was held in the transit hangar."

"Can we tie in the arrival and the departure?" Corchoran asked.

"That's where the story is," enthused Kendrick. "The man waiting in the hotel controls everything that is shipped through Larnaca. He can tell us exactly where the cargo originated and where it was transhipped to from Larnaca."

Corchoran's nose was beginning to sniff a global scoop. He sat in the taxi, his mind envisioning the plaudits he would get. If his suspicions were right he could prove that major arms manufacturers were supplying terrorists.

The man sat in the corner of the bar at the hotel. His complexion was that of aged parchment. He smiled when Kendrick approached. Corchoran was introduced. The man bowed graciously, but failed to return the full introduction. He simply said, "I am Panos."

"Well, Panos, what have you got to tell me?" Corchoran smiled and placed the envelope on the bar. It contained $5,000.

Panos' eyes glowed at the bulk of the envelope. "Can I check?" he asked. Corchoran slid the envelope across the bar. Panos flipped through the crisp fifty-dollar bills and nodded approval.

"The cargo your friend talked of arrived on a chartered flight from France. It was split into two before it was re-exported. Part was loaded onto the tug called *Christina*. Its destination was stated to be Marseille. The other half of the consignment was designated for Tripoli."

"And the name of the ship?" Corchoran asked.

Panos held his hands in the form of surrender, palms upwards. "I cannot recall," he replied simply.

Corchoran picked up the envelope and placed it in his pocket. "Tell me something I don't know and I will pay you," he snapped.

Panos looked perplexed. "I have told you all I know." His tone changed from officious to meek. "I can try to find out the name of the vessel."

"You do just that." Corchoran picked up his glass and tossed the drink back. "When you have something worth this," he patted his inside pocket, "come and see me." He strode out of the bar, followed by a confused Kendrick.

"I don't understand," Kendrick was pouring two large whiskeys from the mini-bar in his room. "We have the story. The missiles came from France and were sent to Ireland and Tripoli."

"I know we have the story," Corchoran sighed resignedly.

"What we don't have is factual substantiation. I know, and you know, that some bastard is supplying terrorists with missiles, but we have to have immutable proof before we publish. I have to be sure before I will go to press."

"What if Panos doesn't come up with the goods?"

"He will." Corchoran smiled. He had been through many situations akin to this. "If he doesn't, we feed the story as we can confirm it. The truth will be dug out eventually."

Chapter 21

The sky was clear. The Mirage skimmed across the ground at two thousand feet. The cameras in the belly of the plane whirred as they recorded the landscape below. Benny Levy whistled to himself. It was a routine daily mission. The Americans supplied them with satellite pictures of Southern Lebanon. The only need for Levy's flight was the paranoiac distrust his military command had of all outside help.

He had studied the morning's pictures from the American satellite and the ground was a mirror image of them.

Suddenly his radar screen bleeped. A missile had locked on to his plane. He chuckled to himself. The Palestinians had obtained a supply of Yugoslavian missiles, which were supposed to bring down aircraft. They could not even bring down a roof if fired from the inside of the building.

"Missile locked on," he reported, and released two flares. "Diversion released." The missile would pursue them until it ran out of steam. He turned to fly over the site of the launch again. 'Later that day it would be destroyed,' he thought.

His radar screen hissed a warning. Its colour changed from green to red. The missile was still tracking him.

"Missile still locked on," he reported. "Releasing secondary diversion." His eyes were now locked on the screen in his cockpit. The dot that was attacking him came closer and closer. "Missile locked on. Cannot avoid. Ejecting!" The Mirage was a fireball before the ejector rockets finished firing.

***

"Pilot down. Scramble!" The tannoy screamed at the troopers in the ready room. Within seconds they had donned their equipment and were sprinting towards the Chinook. In less than two minutes the helicopter was airborne. It crossed the border at Jbail and headed north.

"I have the pilot's signal," the co-pilot shouted to the Captain. "Ten miles due north." The Chinook's nose dipped as it accelerated to full speed. "Ground radar shows two vehicles approaching from the west," he reported.

"Bandits on the ground!" the Captain shouted through the intercom.

Two troopers manned the heavy machine guns set on each doorway.

The pilot and co-pilot surveyed the ground. "There he is. Straight ahead."

Levy saw the Chinook appear over the horizon and waved frantically. To the west he could see the dust of approaching vehicles.

The helicopter swooped down, like a kestrel protecting its nest, and hovered. "Recovery team away," the captain shouted.

Ropes spiralled down from the belly of the aircraft. In moments ten troopers were on the ground.

"Bandits sighted!" the co-pilot bellowed.

The Chinook turned and swept towards the approaching lorries. The heavy machine guns spat tracer rounds towards the approaching enemy. Hcavy white-hot rounds smashed into the oncoming vehicles. They spluttered to a stop as fire burst from beneath their bonnets. Men spilled from the back of the lorries. Their attempts to return fire were greeted by a withering hail from both of the Chinook's guns. Several fell, their temporary existence on this earth terminated. The remainder ran.

"Bandits dispersing. Cease firing," the Captain ordered. The cacophony ceased. Only the whirring of the rotor blades could be heard. The helicopter landed, was loaded with the pilot and recovery team. It was airborne again within three minutes.

***

MOSSAD HEADQUARTERS, TEL AVIV

"I don't know what it was, sir, but once it locked on to me I could not shake it." Levy was being debriefed by Simon Zeltner.

313

Zeltner was a veteran of the 1967 conflict. He had commanded the tank regiment that had pushed the Syrians off the Golan Heights. Now he controlled the counter insurgency arm of Mossad.

Prior to this incident the Palestinians had never had any effective surface-to-air missiles. The odd plane that they had brought down owed as much to luck as intention. It now seemed that things had changed.

"What evasive action did you take, Flight Lieutenant?" Zeltner asked.

"Everything I had, sir," Levy replied. "Flares and anti-radar. When they failed I tried to outmanoeuvre it. I had about as much chance of that as Yassar Arafat becoming Chief Rabbi. It hung onto me like a leech on an artery."

"Any thoughts on what sort of missile it was?" Zeltner asked.

"No, sir," Levy replied. "It certainly wasn't one of those crap Yugoslavian things and I don't think it was Soviet either. We've come up against Soviet equipment before and never had any real problems. This was different."

"Thank you, Flight Lieutenant." Zeltner watched as Levy departed. Ominous concern welled inside him. Israeli air power had always been its ace in the hole. If this was nullified, potential disaster was staring him in the face. He paced the room, his mind searching for something half-forgotten.

Then it flashed into his mind. He picked up the telephone and dialled.

"Simon, good to hear from you. How are you? What can I do for you?" Mathew Curren was genuinely pleased to hear from his old friend. Over several years Israel and South Africa had forged close links. Both countries, in their own way, had been ostracised by much of the international community: South Africa because of Apartheid and Israel because its enemies had oil and she did not. Whilst not ideal bedfellows co-operation between the two had been effective.

"I am well," Zeltner replicd. "I am hoping you can help me with a problem. Yesterday we lost a Mirage to a SAM. I have just debriefed the pilot and it seems that the PLO have got hold of a missile that is a lot more sophisticated than anything we

314

have come across before. If I remember correctly you had a similar predicament with your AAC. I just wondered if you had managed to get any information that might be of help."

"You mean the loss of SA 165," Curren responded. "We are still working on that. Following the attack on SA 165 we actually captured the remainder of the missiles. All we know, thus far, is that new, highly sophisticated guidance systems have been made to fit the Yugoslavian missile and warhead. The guidance systems are Western European in origin. In fact, we are pretty certain that they are either German or French." Curren's Anglo Saxon roots caused him to dismiss any thought that the offending items were British.

"We don't know how the AAC got them, but we intend to find out. I have a man in Europe at the moment working on it. If my hunch is correct, the gear that was intercepted by the Irish security forces is part of the same problem."

"I see," mused Zeltner. "Is there anything else you can tell me?"

"I sent one of the boxes to an old friend of mine, Jim Cross, to see if he could have it identified as to source. To date I have had no comeback."

"I know Jim Cross," Zeltner commented. "Do you think that his demise at MI5 has anything to do with your request?"

"I think it is very likely," was Curren's response. "You know how much the British Foreign Office worships the ground that we have got coming to us. If Jim found something that was detrimental to an EEC member and favourable to us they would do their utmost to suppress it. I should know more in a few days. My man is going to contact Jim."

"I would be grateful if you could keep me informed of any developments." Zeltner hoped that more would be offered.

"Why don't I send you everything I have to date? As we both seem to have had the same problem we may as well work together." Curren gave the affirmative response that Zeltner had hoped for.

Chapter 22

Cross threw the paper onto the table in front of Pinter. The headline blazed:

'ISRAELI PLANE SHOT DOWN BY MISSILE'

"We don't have any more time to piss about," he shouted. "It's obvious that the PLO has got the French equipment. We have to blow the lid off the whole thing now, or have another war start in the Middle East."

The four friends sat in Jennings' study. Events were beginning to overtake them.

"I think you are right Jim," Pinter replied. "I am going to have to give Paddy a little shove."

"A little shove," stormed Cross. "He wants a bloody great boot up the arse."

"There is no point in shouting at each other," Jennings interjected. "We all know how serious this is. We also have to have irrefutable proof that we can show. At the moment we have only circumstantial evidence."

"Circumstantial evidence," snapped Cross. "We have got laundered money paid to Mutuelle Avionique. We know that they exported certain goods to Cyprus and the Irish police intercepted that part of that consignment. What they intercepted was parts of missiles almost certainly made by Avionique. I think that I would accept that as proof beyond reasonable doubt."

"Yes, we have good factual evidence." Pinter was trying to placate Cross' wrath. "That is not enough. You know and I know that the politicians are running on their own self-interest. The Foreign Secretary is a Europhile and to make matters worse he is in love with the Arabs. If we put a thesis forward, without substantiated proof, he will ignore us. Then whatever we have will be fed to the French and a cover-up will be organised. We have to prove what we know."

The jangling of the telephone interrupted them. Jennings picked up the receiver. He listened for a moment. "It's Paddy Corchoran for you, George." He proffered the handset to Pinter.

"George, its Paddy Corchoran."

"I know that, Paddy. What have you dug up?" Pinter's response was abrupt. The machinations of the last few days preyed on his mind.

"I'm keeping you informed, just as you asked!" Corchoran was taken aback by Pinter's response. "If you don't want to know I won't tell you."

"I am sorry, Paddy." Pinter realised that his reaction was to the circumstances, not the call. "We have got shit flying into all sorts of fans."

"I understand," Corchoran replied. "What I have may produce even more crap for general circulation. I've traced where the rest of the cargo went after it left Cyprus."

"It was bound for Tripoli, wasn't it?" Pinter asked.

"It was," Corchoran answered. "The thing is that the freighter it was on made an unofficial stop. The cargo was supposed to be machinery for drilling, but part of the cargo was off-loaded when the ship had to put into port for repairs. The port it went into was Tyr in South Lebanon. I've found someone who will confirm that. As I see it, whatever was being supplied to the Provisionals was also going to the PLO."

"Have you got proof?" Pinter asked.

"I have more than that." The reply lifted Pinter's spirits."I also know that the original source of the export was Le Havre."

"What do you deduce from that?" Pinter asked, half-expecting the reply he was about to receive.

"Mutuelle Avionique in Amiens," was the anticipated reply. "They are the only company within reasonable proximity with the technology to manufacture these bloody things."

"Are you going to publish that?" The net was closing and Pinter needed to know by how much the diameter of the neck had been fastened.

"You know I can't," Corchoran responded. "We both know

317

that those bastards supplied fucking terrorists, but we have to prove it. I will go ahead with the story, but I can't finger Mutuelle Avionique by name. All I can do is hint."

"That will have to do," Pinter commented. "Thanks for the call, Paddy. I look forward to seeing your scoop."

"Well?" Cross looked quizzical.

"It seems that Tripoli was a red herring," Pinter began. "The ship that left Cyprus made an unscheduled stop en route to Tripoli. How does Tyr sound?"

"He has proof of that?" Cross asked.

Pinter nodded. "The other thing Paddy has found out is that the cargo started its journey at Le Havre. Not a million miles away from Amiens."

"Is he going to publish in full?" Cross guessed that this was unlikely.

"Yes and no," Pinter responded. "He is going with all the factual information, but can only bring in Mutuelle Avionique by implication."

"At least that is a step in the right direction," Jennings interpolated.

Cross looked at his watch. "I have to be away in a few minutes. I am meeting an old associate from South African intelligence. He telephoned this morning asking for a meet."

"That would be Bob Callard?" Pinter quizzed.

"How do you know that?" Cross was always amazed at the accuracy of Pinter's information. "I did not know he was in the country until this morning."

"He wasn't, he was in Donegal," Pinter smiled. "And it is very likely that he has also made a little trip to Cyprus. If he is as good as his reputation, all he will want from you is confirmation of what he already knows."

"How do you know, George?" Cross enquired.

"I spoke to him in Donegal. His cover was that he was reporting for the *Rand Daily*. I also fed him a little lead to Cyprus."

"You cunning old sod," Cross laughed.

"Where are you meeting him?" Jennings interjected.

"In the Hoskins Arms," was the reply. "I told him I was stopping down this way for a while. He's booked himself into the

318

hotel for the night."

"Do you need any back-up or possible eavesdropping?" enquired Jennings.

"That is probably a good idea," Cross responded. It would not do any harm. Why don't you and John get there ten minutes or so before me, have a drink at the bar and then grab a table adjacent when I arrive?"

"I suppose I sit in the car and stay sober?" Pinter spoke in a tone that reflected the slight he felt.

**

Hubbard and Jennings made for the bar. They ordered two pints and surveyed the other occupants. There was a small crowd playing darts and a couple of courting couples looking deeply into each other's eyes. The only other occupant was deeply tanned and sitting at a table in the corner. Hubbard nudged Jennings. "That's our man," he whispered.

Jennings took the glasses and strolled across the room. He placed the drinks on the table adjoining that at which the tanned stranger was sitting. Hubbard joined him and started to talk animatedly about football. Neither appeared to take any cognisance when Cross arrived.

Callard stood and walked across to greet Cross at the bar.

"Shit," Hubbard whispered. "The bastard has fucked off."

"Jim, good to see you." Callard extended his hand. "What'll you have?"

Callard ordered a Guinness for himself and a Fremlins for Cross. "Do you want to go and sit with your minders or on the table next to them?" Callard asked casually.

Cross raised his eyebrows quizzically.

"Come on, Jim," Callard continued. "South Africa may have been ostracised but we still have our own intelligence sources. John Hubbard is too big, hairy and bloody ugly to stay incognito."

"You know John," Cross sighed.

"We have a file on him," Callard replied. "He's not exactly someone that blends into the background."

Cross picked up his drink and walked across to where

319

Hubbard and Jennings sat, followed by Callard. He placed his beer on the table and introduced Callard.

"Well I never. The mongoose, as you are known in intelligence circles." Callard smiled at Jennings.

"I don't understand," Jennings blustered.

"Come now, don't be so modest," Callard chuckled. "We know what actually happened with Cobra even if Charlie public doesn't. The only thing is, there is one missing. Where's George Pinter?"

"Go and get him," Cross nodded to Hubbard.

"Bob Callard of the *Rand Daily News*, is it not?" Pinter bowed extravagantly.

"Nearly right," Callard commented. "Can I suggest that we stop the fencing and talk about surface-to-air missiles."

"OK," sighed Cross. "I suggest that you tell us what you know and we reciprocate."

"I have had a long talk with Mathew Curren this morning. As you've probably guessed, Mossad are now mightily interested in the same subject. Mathew and Simon Zeltner have agreed to work in unison to get to the bottom of the whole affair."

"Zeltner!" exclaimed Cross. "He has got a better intelligence network than George here."

Pinter ignored the jibe and motioned Callard to proceed.

"By combining what we and Mossad know we are beginning to build a picture from the jigsaw. The problem is we still have too many pieces missing." He took a pull at his drink whilst deciding where to start.

"What we do know is that SA 165 was brought down by a Yugoslavian weapon that had been customised using a new Western European guidance system. We also lost two gun-ships to the same type of missile.

"We also know that the Israelis have lost a Mirage. Their pilot reported that the weapon that attacked him was much more sophisticated than anything he had ever encountered. He went through his whole range of defences and was still hit.

"Our guess is that the same or similar missile was used against both SA 165 and the Mirage."

"It doesn't exactly take a leap of faith to get to that conclusion," Hubbard said under his breath.

320

"I realise that, John," Callard retorted. "I am simply running through the facts as I know them."

"Sorry. Go on," Hubbard murmured apologetically.

"If our thesis is correct identical missile systems have been supplied to the AAC and the PLO, and judging by what I have heard over in Donegal they have attempted to supply the IRA as well. What we don't have is a connection across the three. We don't know whether there are one, two or three sources of supply."

"There can only be one source of supply," Cross intervened. "The guidance systems are basically the same as the Exocet. The only differences are in the functional communications within the unit. They have been customised to operate with the Yugoslavian design."

"How long have you known that, Jim?" Callard asked.

"A little while," was Cross' reply. "Unfortunately my political masters did not think it opportune for such information to be made available to your people."

"Bastards!" spat Callard. "So not embarrassing the French is more important than hundreds of South African lives?"

"That is about the political reality at the moment, Bob," Cross sighed.

"There is another consideration," Jennings interposed. "You say you don't have a connection between the AAC, the PLO and the IRA. How would it be if you added dissidents in Central America, such as the Contras in Nicaragua to your list?"

"You mean they are getting the same equipment?" Callard asked.

"We think so," replied Jennings.

"Why?"

"Initially I started to dig into some reinsurance arrangements, handled by my company, that looked questionable. I had my suspicions that they were vehicles for laundering money. My fears were not unfounded. I discovered a number of contracts of a similar type. In essence the money passed through an insurer and then one or two reinsurers using three or four separate and independent contracts on the way. Basically there were no original insurances and the claims that were paid were non-existent. The end result was that substantial amounts of cash crossed several borders without raising any eyebrows."

"How did you discover this?" Callard asked.

"That's a long story. Suffice it to say, I found, by accident, one dubious claim and started digging."

"How does this tie in with the missiles?"

"One of the contracts which seemed to fit the pattern involved business emanating from Southern Africa. The original premium was generated there and passed through a West Bank insurer to a reinsurer in London and then ended up with the captive insurer of Mutuelle Avionique in Jersey. At first we ignored it. We were looking for drugs and arms money and it did not fit the pattern. Then Jim received a report on the guidance unit you sent him. That concluded that the manufacturer was Mutuelle Avionique."

"So where do the IRA, PLO and Contras come in?" To Callard the tale seemed convoluted.

"Luck," Cross interpolated. "We knew that dubious money was passing around the world using international reinsurance markets as a route. What we did not have was proof. John put on one of his many disguises and became someone who wanted to buy cocaine and guns. It just happened that the nymphomaniac who had the right connections also wanted his body. She made the contacts and two deals were set up. The payment was routed through an insurance company in the Turks and Caicos Islands, then through Lloyds of London and out to Miami."

"I still don't follow," Callard said, exasperated.

"Following that, the lady in question decided to become an independent. She knew how the scam ran and cajoled John into being her partner. The next thing we know is they are being asked to set a package involving Mutuelle Avionique. The sources of the money were Jordan and Honduras."

"What about the Irish?"

"We are not certain about that at the moment." Jennings took over the story. "My guess would be that one of the parties changed the rules of the game. I think that part of the shipment that was designated for the PLO was re-routed to Ireland."

"What makes you think that?" Callard asked.

"If our guesses are right the affair is being sponsored by governments not individuals. We know that one of the people implicated is a senior US intelligence officer, and he also has close connections with NORAID."

"Are you saying that the Americans are involved?" Callard was incredulous at the suggestion.

"We know a member of the CIA is," was the reply.

"Jesus Christ!" Callard exclaimed. "This isn't *shit* hitting fans, it's a bloody sewage works."

"Can I put a little thesis forward?" Pinter interjected. "We know that the Americans have close ties and probably supply the Contras. We also know that the French are desperately trying to strengthen their ties with certain oil-rich Arab countries. If we put those two facts together it is not illogical to envision the Americans supplying the finance for the French to produce and supply the missile equipment."

"But the Americans would have nothing to do with the PLO. No American administration could afford to antagonise the Jewish vote." It was Cross who spoke.

"If they had no choice they might," Pinter responded. "Whilst they support the Contras, and indeed finance them, they could not put such sophisticated American equipment into that area. If it were captured, and that is very likely with that bunch of ragtag mercenaries, there would be such a furore that American influence could be destroyed in the whole of Central America. If, however, the missiles are Yugoslavian with French guidance systems, the Americans are seen to be clean."

"And the French could insist that supplying the PLO had to be part of the whole deal." Hubbard took up the thesis.

"That's all very well," Callard responded. "Where does South Africa come into the picture?"

"My guess was the supply to the AAC was simply to test that the equipment worked." Pinter shook his head as he spoke. "That is the only explanation. Neither the Americans nor the French gain any benefit from supplying the AAC, unless it is simply to test equipment they intend to give to their clients."

"Bastards," snapped Callard. "There were one hundred and fifty people on that fucking aeroplane."

"It's only a theory." Cross needed to calm Callard's ire. "What we don't need is anyone taking precipitous action."

"We have had a civilian airliner blown out of the sky, a

minister and several top ranking army officers killed and you don't want us to take precipitous action," snapped Callard. "Bollocks! You've spent too long pussyfooting about with the British Foreign Office looking over your bloody shoulder."

"All I am saying…" Cross tried to sound calm and sympathetic, "…is that you take some time out to think about your next step. We are well down the road to bringing the whole matter into the open. Just give us a bit of time to do it. That's all I ask."

"I hear you." Callard had calmed down slightly. "But, I cannot answer for my masters."

Back at Jennings' house Cross was pacing the lounge. Things had to be pushed forward. If they were not, the South Africans and the Israelis would take the law into their own hands.

"Well! What has he got to say?" Cross spoke as Pinter returned from the study.

"Paddy's story is being given the full treatment in *the Irish Times* tomorrow." Pinter had telephoned Corchoran hoping to speed up the bleeding of information that would eventually prove terminal to the conspirators.

"Is he bringing in the French and American connections?"

"He's reporting the facts he has got so far," Pinter responded. "Firstly that the shipment arrested by the Irish came originally from Cyprus. Second that it was part of a larger consignment and the rest was shipped out, allegedly on course for Tripoli. Third that the ship carrying the freight to Tripoli made an unscheduled stop at Tyr in the South of Lebanon. Finally that the cargo originated in Le Havre."

"Is that all?" Cross sighed.

"No." Pinter had been at his most persuasive to get Corchoran to widen his story. "I managed to inveigle him into drawing some possible conclusions based on reliable sources, namely me."

"And they are?" Cross enquired.

"He will conclude that if the equipment is French that the most likely source is Mutuelle Avionique. The publicity will force the French government into some sort of action."

"A cover-up you mean," Hubbard interjected.

324

"Quite possibly," was Pinter's reply. "The point is that it will not give them much time. Any cover-up will have to be quick rather than elaborate. The less time they have the easier it will be to break down whatever tale they give out."

"I think there is another way we can stir the pot a little." Jennings had only listened up to this point. "Why don't we give them the financial operation?"

"How?"

"Freddie Jarvis," Jennings replied. "Since Penny Hacker was shot he has been like a rabbit in a light beam. You can see it in his eyes. He is scared witless and doesn't know what of."

"I agree with that," Hubbard commented. "Karen and I hardly had to raise a sweat getting him to dance to our tune."

"That's the point," Jennings continued. "We have all the evidence we need to have him put away for the rest of his natural. All we have to do is offer him a choice. He either comes clean to the police or we feed him to O'Connell."

***

CORBY MANNING'S OFFICE

It was as though the sword of Damocles had been returned to its scabbard. Jarvis looked at the computer report and relief flooded through him. The last accounts had been processed and the premiums transferred. He had received formal cancellation of the facility from both Honduras and Jordan. It was over. He had money enough sitting in Switzerland to disappear and never be found again. Negotiations for the purchase of the small estate in Brazil were well advanced. A couple of months and he would be gone.

The telephone on his desk jangled.

"Freddie, it's Allan here," Jennings' voice echoed through the intercom. "Can you spare me a minute? I'm in the boardroom."

Jennings was standing by the bar when Jarvis entered. There were two others, both with their backs to him, pouring drinks. One looked familiar to Jarvis, but he knew not why.

"What can I do for you, Allan?" Jarvis adopted a lighthearted tone.

"It's just a couple of people I would like you to meet," Jennings replied jovially.

The thicker-set of the two turned and proffered a drink to Jarvis. "Gin and tonic as usual, Freddie," Hubbard said.

Panic flitted across Jarvis' face. What was this man doing in Jennings' boardroom?

"Thank you," was all he could say.

"How are you, Freddie?" Hubbard enquired. "I haven't seen you since we set up that authority in Honduras and Jordan."

Jarvis' mind was racing. What did Jennings know, if anything? "I am well, Gerry, and yourself?" He decided to bluff the situation out.

"Why are you calling John, Gerry?" Jennings voice now had an edge.

"His name is Gerry Croft," Jarvis blustered. "I placed a couple of facilities for him. That's right, isn't it, Gerry?"

"I am afraid you are wrong, sadly wrong." Jennings' voice was now as cold as an Arctic wind. "The correct name is John Hubbard, and he was working for me."

Jarvis' mind was now a pot-pourri of conflicting thoughts. Had he been set up? Was Jennings a sleeping partner in the scams? Would he make his green haven in Brazil?

"You told me your name was Croft," he said accusingly to Hubbard.

"I lied," Hubbard replied simply.

"What the blazes is going on here?" Jarvis elected to attack.

"What is going on is that you have been using this company to launder dirty money." Jennings' face now showed anger. "And what is going to happen is you are going to the police to make a full statement of your and everybody else's involvement."

Jarvis' heart sank into his hand-made shoes. Moments ago the nightmare had ended for him and the future looked bright. The incubus had suddenly returned.

He slumped in a chair, knowing that he had no means of escape from what was now inevitable. Hubbard or Croft, whatever his name, had all the evidence needed to incarcerate him for the rest of his life. He had looked along a tunnel of light. Now bleak clouds obscured his vision.

"What do you want?" he sighed.

"My name is Jim Cross," Cross intervened. "I set up the operation with John. I was head of counter espionage and security for Her Majesty's Government."

Jarvis appeared to twitch as he took on the fact that it was more than a simple felony that embroiled him. "What are you talking about?" Bluster seemed to be his only defence. "Am I supposed to be a spy of some sort? Rubbish, all I did was to launder some money."

"Some of the money you laundered paid for surface-to-air missiles."

Jarvis' thoughts were now in a frenzy. "I know nothing about any missiles."

"I doesn't matter," replied Cross. "You knew about drugs and you knew about arms. What do you think Avionique make other than aerospace products, French letters?"

Realisation dawned on Jarvis. He had thought the contracts with Mutuelle Avionique seemed out of pattern, but never questioned why. "If I had known I would not have got involved."

"That's by the by, I'm afraid," Cross answered. "The simple facts are you have been directly involved in the sale of anti-aircraft missiles to a number of terrorist organisations across the world. You are going to be put away for the rest of your life, unless…" Cross left a pregnant pause.

"Unless what?" Jarvis would now grasp at any straw.

"Unless," Cross proceeded, "you go to the police and volunteer all the information you have on what you have been doing, including names."

"If I don't?" Jarvis asked even though he could guess the answer.

"Then I put forward what I know and you get arrested, Freddie," Jennings interpolated. "Either way you are in deep shit. It may just be a little more shallow if you go in voluntarily."

"I need time to think about it." Jarvis never gave up on a negotiation until it was totally lost.

"The bloke's a prat," Cross snapped. "I said you were wasting my time, Allan. I'll phone a friend of mine at City of London Fraud." He picked up the telephone and began to dial.

"All right, all right." Jarvis knew that he had no choices left.

"I'll do it."

"Good." Cross winked at Jennings. "Who was the senior officer investigating Penny Hacker's murder?"

"His name was Boyd." Jarvis' spirit was now broken.

Cross pulled out his address book and looked up the number for West End Central police station. He wrote it down and passed it to Jarvis. "Tell him you have to speak to him urgently this afternoon, and that you want a colleague and your solicitor to come with you."

AMIENS – 4TH JUNE 1985

The cognac was excellent. Dolan sipped from his glass, his eyes studying the man opposite.

Mersonne had gulped his brandy down in one swallow and ordered another. His eyes darted from side to side as though he thought he was being observed. Corchoran's story had brought the world's press to Amiens, like a pack of jackals scrabbling over a kill. "How did that Irish newspaperman get to know?" he muttered, as much to himself as to Dolan. "And what were those units doing there? Northern Ireland is part of the European Community. My masters are furious."

"To the first question I do not have an answer," Dolan replied. "As to the second, that was a decision of my masters. To supply the PLO are not exactly in the spirit of my government's foreign policy. That was agreed at your government's insistence. Our sweetener was a little bonus to the Irish vote at home." Dolan knew that the latter statement was untrue. He and O'Connell had made a private, independent arrangement to help those they perceived to be fighting for the rights of their long-forgotten ancestors. It did no harm, however, to let the French think something else.

"What I am more interested in," Dolan continued, "is where the information is leaking from. It's not from our end, so it has to be here."

"That cannot be so," Mersonne responded indignantly. "Our security is sound."

"Wherever it is we have to move quickly." Dolan was still convinced that the leak came from France. "We still have not moved the units for Nicaragua."

"They are ready, and payment has now been received in full. We will start to transport them tomorrow."

"How?" Dolan asked.

"In view of the security situation I am not prepared to say, Monsieur." Mersonne replied. "Just make sure your vessel is at the rendezvous off the Bahamas on 23rd of the month."

"It will be."

NEW YORK – 4TH JUNE 1985

Danny Hacker checked and re-checked his notes. He had been observing O'Connell for many weeks now. His mother had always stressed the need for planning. "Every human being is a creature of habit to some degree," she had told him. "It is when they are carrying out an habitual action that they are at their most vulnerable. If they are in routine surroundings doing something that is a repetition of previous behaviour the expectancy for anything unusual is diminished." He had always followed this counsel.

"Never act in anger or passion," was her other advice. She had only once chosen to ignore her own rule. She had let her hate for Jennings overcome her. When she had heard that Jennings was responsible for her lover's death, an anger such as she had never felt gripped her whole being. Retribution could only assuage her if it was immediate. It was a mistake and she had spent several years incarcerated as a result.

Hacker looked at the photographs of O'Connell. He would have his retribution, but on his terms and at his time. He would look into the eyes and see the fear that manifests itself when death is inevitable.

In the weeks he had been following O'Connell he could have struck many times, but with risk. Now he knew the time and the place to avenge his mother.

O'Connell's Achilles heel was baseball, and in particular the New York Yankees. He went to every home game. He sat in the same seat with the same friends surrounding him. Afterwards they went to the Manhattan Brewery. They sat at the same table and drank the same amount, win or lose. The only difference between the success or failure of the Yankees was their initial mood. O'Connell always left soon after one in the morning, alone and the worse for wear.

Hacker fingered the stiletto. It's needle-like blade glinted as it caught the light. It was his most favoured weapon for a close quarter hit. It was silent. The puncture it made in the skin was so small that virtually no blood seeped from it. The slender, narrow point would rupture the aorta and the demise of the target was almost immediate. He would watch O'Connell's eyes as the upwards thrust exploded his heart.

Chapter 23

Detective Inspector Boyd's mouth gaped at the revelations that he was hearing.

When Jarvis had telephoned him he had expected further information on the investigation into Penny Hacker's murder. His enquiries had reached a brick wall. It was obvious that the killing was the work of a professional hit man but he could find no one with a grudge major enough to kill for. Then Jarvis had rung him. Perhaps this would be the breakthrough he hoped for.

Jarvis had arrived with his solicitor in tow and another man who was introduced as Jennings. The name rang a bell but he knew not why at first. Then he remembered the explosion in the City a few months before. That had been in the office of a man called Jennings.

In the interview room Jarvis' solicitor had asked for the meeting to be recorded and for another officer to be present. Boyd called one of his sergeants down from upstairs.

"I wish to make it quite clear that my client has come here of his own free will to make a statement," Jarvis' solicitor had stated. "If criminal charges are forthcoming following this interview I would ask that it is made clear to the court that my client came forward voluntarily and gave his full co-operation to the authorities."

"That is understood," Boyd had replied, not knowing what was to come.

Jarvis had begun. Boyd had been investigating a contract killing and now found himself being presented with a massive money laundering operation with tentacles across the world.

"It was not until recently that I became aware that finances being moved were to pay for arms," Jarvis droned. His presentation gave the impression that it had been well practised.

331

"I thought that finance was being moved simply for fiscal purposes."

"You mean tax evasion?" Boyd interrupted.

"If that is what you wish to call it," Jarvis replied.

"What made you change your mind?" Boyd asked.

"It was an article in the *Irish Times* a few days ago relating to the missile equipment captured by the Irish authorities. In that the name Mutuelle Avionique was specifically mentioned. Several of the contracts I had an involvement in resulted in substantial amounts of money being paid to that company. I put two and two together."

"And did you make four?" asked Boyd.

"The more I thought about it the more I became convinced that the contracts which I placed were actually the financial consideration for the supply of missiles. It was then I decided to tell you all I know."

The questioning continued for another three hours. By then Boyd knew that he was dealing with an international fraud of colossal proportions. Some of the intricacies of how the deception operated were beyond him. He decided that help was required. He formally arrested Jarvis for various contraventions of the 1968 Theft Act and cautioned him. Jarvis was detained at West End Central and the fraud squad were brought in. They questioned Jarvis for a further six hours that night.

The following day things began to move rapidly. Three underwriters, Payne, O'Sullivan and Green, were arrested in Lloyds. The pubs and clubs in the City were awash with stories and rumours. These were exacerbated when it became known that Jimmy Wilkes, a Managing Director of Bannister Ellis, had also been arrested. Nobody knew why they had been apprehended but it did not stop multifarious tales being spread.

The Deputy Financial Editor of the *Daily Telegraph* often wandered into the City for a pint or two at lunchtime. He was in the Elephant that day when the rumours were flying around waiting for anyone to catch them. The most popular theory was that the underwriters had defrauded their members and consequently it was repeated with the most confidence. As the tale passed from mouth to mouth it was embellished.

The following day the *Telegraph* carried a banner headline.

332

'MASSIVE FRAUD IN LLOYDS – THREE
UNDERWRITERS ARRESTED'

On the Monday Lloyds members' agents were besieged by phone calls from worried members following the revelations in the *Telegraph* on Saturday.

The public relations office in Lloyds rushed out a statement saying that no names would lose money as a result of fraud by any underwriter. They stressed that all underwriters had to be insured against fraud. The statement was true in essence. It, of course, failed to mention that the insurances against fraud were also underwritten by other Lloyds underwriters.

Four days later the five conspirators were brought before the City Magistrates Court, each charged with one specimen count. The specimen used was the drugs importation arranged for Hubbard, as the complete evidence was available. The magistrates were told that substantial further investigation was needed. All five were remanded in custody.

10 DOWNING STREET – 14TH JUNE 1985

"This whole affair has turned into a disaster." The Prime Minister glared at the Foreign Secretary and his personal mandarin. "All we were supposed to do was turn a Nelsonian blind eye and the French and Americans would do a little reciprocal back-scratching for us. Now we have a bloody great scandal in our most prestigious financial operation and rumours that we have an involvement in supplying arms to terrorists."

"It may not be as bad as you portray, sir." The mandarin put on his most treacly tone to try to placate the PM's anger. "It may be temporarily embarrassing but I believe we may turn the situation to our advantage."

The Foreign Secretary nodded vigorously in agreement. He had not the least idea of what advantage could be gained, but hoped that his Civil Service minder did.

"And how are we supposed to gain an advantage from this debacle?" The PM asked scornfully.

"Both the French and the Americans are in a much more

invidious situation than ourselves," the mandarin oozed on. "They are the actual prime movers of the whole situation. I am sure that, using our best endeavours, we could run a damage limitation operation here for their benefit. That would, of course, then put them in our debt."

"How do you propose to do that?" asked the PM, hoping it was a light at the end of the tunnel, rather than the headlights of an oncoming express train.

"Thus far there has been one specimen charge brought against each of the accused. All these charges relate to the financing of an importation of drugs. I also believe that there are a number of other movements of drugs, which have been financed in the same way. In the public interest it is my belief that this is the area on which the authorities should concentrate." The mandarin stopped to pour himself more coffee. He looked at both politicians. Their eyes were practically pleading for him to show them the way out of their dilemma.

He sipped the coffee and continued. "I am sure that we can persuade our friends in the Directorate of Public Prosecutions that there will be ample charges relating to drugs and, in the public interest, these are the cases that should be brought to court. Any charges relating to other matters will, of course, simply remain on the file."

"Will they co-operate?" the Foreign Secretary asked.

"I have spoken to the Director and he concurs that charges relating to drugs are eminently preferable to a circus about international intrigue."

"Excellent," gasped the Foreign Secretary, his relief apparent. "I thought that was the route to go." He used the past tense to imply that the mandarin's proposal had originally been his conception.

"I believe there are some other points, Minister," the mandarin interrupted. "If we are to proceed as agreed, is it not fair that we should receive some consideration from both the French and American governments?"

"Consideration?" queried the PM.

"Yes, sir," was the reply. "The French, in particular, are in an extremely awkward position. They are actually the suppliers. I believe that a pledge from them to support our proposed changes to the funding of the European Community is the least we could expect for helping to hide their shame. In fact, I would also propose that they should be cajoled into supporting our proposals on the Agricultural Policy as well."

"I agree," commented the PM, who had perked up considerably. "What about the Americans?"

"They are waivering a little on the order for another two hundred Harrier jump jets. It would be nice if they firmed up that order, don't you think?"

"Good." The PM's relief was now apparent. "I think that has been sorted out very nicely. Thank you, gentlemen."

PRETORIA – 15TH JUNE 1985

Simon Zeltner was tired and irritable by the time he reached his hotel in Pretoria. He had first flown to London to try to ascertain how investigations were progressing. He had been confronted with a civil servant who spoke in paragraphs rather than words. It soon became apparent that the British authorities were concentrating on the importation of drugs rather than the supply of arms. He knew not why.

Direct questioning had proved fruitless, most of his queries being rebutted with, "As the matter is still under investigation that is sub judice."

Zeltner's own sources had thrown up two names, Mersonne and O'Connell, as the most likely organisers, but the British refused to confirm or deny these suspicions.

He was pouring himself a stiff scotch when the telephone rang.

"Simon, how was the journey?" Mathew Curren sounded buoyant. "Were the British helpful?"

"To themselves maybe," Zeltner replied. "The are covering more up than a fundamentalist during Ramadan."

"We had the same problem," Curren commented. "I do, however, have some good news. Are you free for dinner tonight?" They arranged to meet in the hotel bar.

Zeltner poured another whisky, pulled a file from his briefcase and sat down to study it yet again. Perhaps there was some small item he had missed.

The file contained reports from his operatives in America, France and the UK. All the information was circumstantial, but it all led directly to the conclusion that Mutuelle Avionique were the suppliers. The American connection was less clear, if Callard's report on his meeting with Jennings and his cohorts were ignored. Could or should it be ignored? Pinter's thesis carried an enormous weight of logic.

Finally he threw the file back inside the case and locked it. He had many theory but limited facts.

The telephone jangled again. He picked it up and listened. As the voice purveyed the latest to him his frustration grew. Two more Mirages had been brought down over Southern Lebanon. One pilot had been lost. The military were now seriously considering a halt to overflying the area. He knew that, if that happened, the border settlements would soon be attacked. He had two brothers and their families in that area. He slammed down the receiver.

Depression still sat on his shoulders when Curren bounced into the bar. He sat down, exchanged initial pleasantries and ordered a gin and tonic.

"It's nice to see someone so cheerful," Zeltner said wryly. "I hope you can implant some of it in me."

"I heard about the two planes you lost. I'm sorry." Curren's tone became serious. "However, I might have some good news for you."

Zeltner did not comment and waited for Curren to proceed.

"I decided that we had done enough ferreting about in the background, and that it was now time for some direct action." Curren continued. "As you know, Bob Callard is currently in Europe." Zeltner nodded. "For the last two days he and another of my people have been entertaining a guest in a farmhouse outside Le Havre."

"Mersonne?" Zeltner asked.

"That's his name," Curren responded. "He has been very tractable. Bob has asked him lots of questions and Monsieur Mersonne has answered them."

"Was Pinter's theory correct?"

"Virtually spot on," Curren smiled. "The missiles were given to the AAC as a test. Once their worth had been proved they were to be supplied to the PLO and the Contras in Nicaragua."

"What about the stuff seized in Ireland?" Zeltner queried.

"Mersonne says he knew nothing about that until it happened. He says he has been told that the Americans decided to give a little boost to the Irish vote at home. He did say he thought it may have been unofficial."

"So O'Connell is the man at the American end?" Zeltner mused.

Curren nodded. "And Dolan," he added. "We know that they are both tied in with NORAID."

"This is all very well," Zeltner sighed. "But it does not get around my immediate problem. There are units of the PLO in Lebanon shooting down our Mirages. We may have to stop overflying the area for a while until we can counteract the missiles."

"I think that puzzle may have already been solved." Curren smiled. "Our boffins have had these things for some time. We believe we have a way to neutralise the radar guidance system."

"You can't have." Zeltner knew that all their attempts to find countermeasures had, in the past, ended in failure. "We have been searching for a way to stop Exocets for years to no avail."

"Exocets, yes," Curren laughed. "But these are not Exocets. They may have the Exocet guidance system, but it is operating with the Yugoslavian launcher and warhead. Because the configuration had to be changed a weakness has appeared. We can jam the radar system. Once that is done the missile has to rely on the heat seeking equipment in the original missiles. We all know what a load of crap that is."

"Are you certain?" The monkey on Zeltner's back became lighter.

"I'm certain," Curren replied. "We have tested both in the lab and the field. Our people are sending all the technical data to yours now. The modification to your Mirages should take about two hours each plane."

Zeltner raised his glass. "I think I shall get pissed tonight. Perhaps tomorrow we can talk about admonition."

NEW YORK – 15TH JUNE 1985

"That French bastard is getting very twitchy," Dolan reported. "That fiasco in Ireland has put a burr down his trousers."

O'Connell did not respond. He continued to read through Dolan's report. "Are you still convinced that the leak is in France?" He looked questioningly at Dolan.

"I believe so," Dolan confirmed.

"Then you're a bigger idiot than I thought." He picked up a folder and threw it across the desk at Dolan.

Dolan opened the folder and Gerry Croft's face stared at him from the photograph. "What's this?" he stammered.

"It's a report from British Intelligence on the bastard who conned us. Gerry Croft is actually called John Hubbard. It's cost us twenty billion dollars to get it."

"It's what?" Dolan asked incredulously.

"That bastard was working for British Intelligence. The hooker he had in tow was genuine but he was a fucking plant."

"Where does twenty billion dollars come into it?" Dolan could not see the connection.

"Those bastards have got the whole story. They know we were involved. They were prepared to keep their mouths shut provided we confirm our government's order for two hundred of their fucking jump jets. We had no choice but to agree."

"How did they get on to it?" Dolan thought that security had been watertight.

"Luck," was O'Connell's reply. "One of Jim Cross' oldest friends is called Jennings. He runs one of the companies through which the finance was processed. That asshole Carter got sloppy on one of his other deals and this Jennings guy gets suspicious. He pokes his nose around and finds that things are not what they should be. He runs off to Cross and they set up a scam with this Hubbard as the front man. We weren't the targets, but got dragged in by accident."

"How much do they know?" Dolan hoped the answer would offer some alleviation. He was to be disappointed.

"Virtually everything," O'Connell snapped. "And who do you think is an old family friend of Jennings?" Dolan shook his head. "None other than George Pinter."

"Not the journalist?" Dolan asked.

"That's right," O'Connell spat, "George Pinter the journalist. He has been having his fun by feeding the story to that fucking scribbler at the *Irish Times*. If we don't act quickly this whole affair is going to blow both of us away."

"What do you mean?" Dolan guessed what the answer would be.

"I want those four out of circulation for good. Now!" The final word left no room for misunderstanding.

"Can the British help?" Dolan asked.

"Of course they won't," O'Connell snapped. "All they will do is turn a blind eye." He threw a file across the desk. "All the information is in there. I want you to do this personally. Any back up you use must be freelance. Use our friends in Belfast. I don't want any other people from the firm involved. I'm flying up to Washington tomorrow and will be in the office there next Monday. I'll be back for the Yankees game next Thursday. I want a full plan by then."

***

Danny Hacker was drinking his first coffee of the morning when the telephone trilled. Time was dragging. All the planning had been done, but the execution was five days hence.

"I've had a visitor." Jennifer's voice sounded chirpy. "He has a job for your particular expertise."

Hacker understood her meaning immediately. "What's he want done?" he asked.

"I don't know," she replied. "You are to telephone a man called Piers. It's a Manhattan number 212 6060. Apparently it is urgent."

Hacker noted the number. "I'll contact him, sis," he rejoined. "I should be finished with our Mr Smith by the end of next week."

"Good," was her response.

They chatted for a few more minutes. The content of the conversation was irrelevant. Whilst only siblings, the traumas of their lives had made them closer than twins.

Hacker replaced the telephone and poured himself a Wild Turkey bourbon. Jennifer was all that was left of his family. All their time together was precious to him and time apart barren.

He dialled the Manhattan number. The voice that answered, and identified itself as Piers, had an accent that was somewhere between the Bronx and Tel Aviv. 'Mossad' was Hacker's initial thought. They arranged to meet in a bar a block away from the World Trade Centre.

Hacker was on his second beer when the stranger approached. His nose served to confirm Hacker's conclusions as to his origin.

"Danny Hacker?" He proffered his hand. The handshake was firm and confident. As it was a Saturday the bar was quiet. This was a business area rather than residential. A few tourists, who had been to view the sights, were the only other customers. They took their drinks across to a table in the corner.

"You come highly recommended," Piers began. "Our friends in Pretoria could not speak of you well enough."

Hacker said nothing. He was now certain that he was dealing with Mossad. They had never used his services before so he waited to see how the conversation would progress.

"This is the problem that needs to be removed." Piers placed an A4 Manila envelope on the table.

'Direct and business-like', thought Hacker. He slid the contents from the pocket. He fought to keep his face muscles in place, but he could not stop his eyes from smiling. Staring back at him from the photograph was the face of Tom O'Connell.

He placed the likeness face down and scanned the two sheets of paper giving the details of his target. All the information was there, except for O'Connell's passion for the New York Yankees. He replaced all the documents in the envelope.

"He'll be expensive," he said simply, even though within a few days he had intended to kill O'Connell for nothing.

"How much?"

"To mess with the CIA, fifty thousand," Hacker replied. "Half now and the other half on completion."

"How do you want it paid?" Peirs replied. Hacker, for some reason, had expected the other to haggle. Perhaps all the jokes about the carefulness of the Jewish race were unfounded. Maybe Shakespeare was wrong and Shylock was a Gentile.

Hacker wrote Union Bank of Zurich and an account number in his notepad. He tore the sheet out and passed it to the other. "I want the first instalment in there by Monday night."

Piers took the paper and placed it in his wallet. "We would like the contract completed as soon as possible."

"Within the next seven days." Hacker raised his eyebrows.

"If you do, I will believe everything my South African friends have said about you," Piers responded. He shook hands formally and left.

As Piers left Hacker's face broke into the huge smile he had been suppressing. His plans for the demise of O'Connell were already finalised. Now he was to be paid for a labour of love.

STORMONT HOTEL, BELFAST – 17TH JUNE 1985

The first of Dolan's guests arrived soon after seven. He was a short, stocky man with a chin that was still blue despite having had the ministrations of a razor only an hour earlier. Dolan greeted him and a pint of stout appeared at the table. The three others followed soon after.

Several rounds of Guinness were consumed before the social niceties were completed. By nature the Irish are a gregarious race. Whenever they meet all incidents, meaningful or not, occurring between now and their last meeting must be explained and explored.

"Shall we get down to business?" Dolan interjected in a temporary lull in the exchanges. "These are the problem." He gave each a folder containing photographs of and information on Jennings, Hubbard, Pinter and Cross. He ordered more drinks as they studied the documents.

"I know two of the bastards." Mullen was the first to speak. "It's likely that they know my face as well."

"You mean these two," Kelly interjected, holding the notes for Pinter and Cross.

"They're the two. Cross is with the security people and Pinter is that nosey fucking journalist," Mullen responded. "I'd like to do the pair of them."

"Let's do one thing at a time," Dolan interrupted. "I want each of them followed. I need to know exactly what they do and

341

where they go. All four will have to be taken out, but I want them all."

"There's no way I can follow either Cross or Pinter." Mullen interpolated. "I am sure they know my face."

"The same applies to me," said Kelly.

"Then you take the other two between you." Dolan was becoming exasperated at the time being wasted. "I suggest that you sort it out among yourselves." He gave each another envelope. "These are your flights to Heathrow in the morning. Hotel arrangements and cash are in there as well. I will be stopping at the Tower Hotel. I want a verbal report every evening between nine and ten. I am booked in under the name of Martin Johnson."

The four reverted to exchanging anecdotes of past exploits and consuming Guinness until closing time.

HEATHROW AIRPORT – 18TH JUNE 1985

Boredom was already consuming Rostron's conscious mind, and he had only been on duty for two hours. As a young man the fact that he was blessed with a photographic memory had been a asset. Now it was an affliction. When he joined the security services he had imagined himself on a white charger smiting down the enemies of the state. The reality was he now sat endlessly peering at a video screen watching incoming passengers at Heathrow in the forlorn hope of identifying undesirables as they entered the country.

It was only ten in the morning and his upper eyelids were already losing a battle with the forces of gravitation. He switched his attention to another screen as the Belfast flight had recently arrived. A gaggle of passengers milled their way towards the exits. Suddenly the tiredness lifted from him. There was not one face but two. He picked up the telephone and dialled.

"I have two suspicious for you," he said to the voice that answered. "Seamus Mullen and Michael Kelly have both arrived on the flight from Belfast. Can you pick them up?" He moved the mouse across the pad and the arrow on the screen pointed to the two men.

"I have them," the voice replied.

Outside two officers sat in an unmarked Ford Granada. They were just finishing their daily breakfast of a Danish pastry and hot sweet coffee.

"Security three," the radio blared. "Two arrivals from Belfast. Seamus Mullen and Michael Kelly, follow and report."

One tapped the names into the console under the dashboard and photographs popped onto the small screen. He pressed 'Print' and two sheets popped out from under the screen.

"There they are," said his comrade. "It looks as though there are four of them."

Mullen and his cohorts ambled across and took their place in the taxi queue. As their taxi pulled out into the stream of traffic the Granada eased out behind them. It followed the taxi down the M4 and onto the Cromwell Road. It dropped its passengers at the Tara Hotel. The Granada pulled up across the road. The two watched as the four men entered.

"Report where we are." The second spoke as he alighted from the Granada. He strolled across to the hotel. The four had just completed checking in and were being ushered in the direction of their rooms. He went across to the receptionist and showed her his identification. "I want copies of the registrations of those last four who checked in," he whispered.

"I will have to check with the manager," she replied importantly.

"Do what you like," he retorted, "just get me those reservations copied."

She scuttled off towards a room marked 'Private'. She returned with a man in a well-cut pin-stripe suit. "Can I help you?" he enquired, giving the distinct impression that offering assistance was not his intention.

"You know what I want." Patience was now wearing thin. "Here's my identification." He held it under the manager's nose.

Suddenly subservience replaced pomposity. "Oh, I see," he blustered. "Please copy those for the gentleman, Mary."

She scampered off and returned with four photocopies. He looked at the forms. Smales, Plummer, Drakeford and Raggett were the four names. "Thank you," he muttered as he left.

The events at Heathrow had been transmitted to anti-terrorist headquarters. Within an hour measures were in place. Authorisation was obtained to monitor any telephonic communications to or from any of the four, and sixteen officers were designated to round the clock surveillance. The two unknown faces were identified as Tommy Blair and Kevin Murphy. All were known to be members of the Belfast Brigade of the Provisional IRA. Also Murphy was the brother of Sean who was now under guard at the Stoke Mandeville paraplegic centre following his abortive attempt on Jennings' life.

That evening the four played the role of tourists. They visited several Irish pubs in the West End and consumed much Guinness and Bushmills. Back at the hotel they continued drinking in the bar until the early hours.

***

Jennings first took notice of him as he came out of Lloyds just before lunch. Mullen had not arrived prepared to be invisible in the precincts of the City of London. Flaming June was an apt description. The sky was clear and bright and the sun blazed in the sky. The temperature soared to the high seventies. Brokers scampered up and down Lime Street, plying their wares, besuited and red faced. Mullen wore a polo shirt and slacks. Lone tourists were not a usual sight in the City.

He was standing opposite the entrance peering, apparently, at nothing. Something about the man was familiar to Jennings. As he went down the stairs to the Marine Club Jennings heard the cloakroom lady ask someone whether they were a member. The voice that replied had a Belfast accent.

"I'm not but how much is it to join?"

"I'm afraid you cannot, sir," the female voice replied. "This is a private club and members have to be proposed and seconded."

"Is this the only entrance?"

Jennings stopped and looked back at the tourist. Recognition sprang to him. The stranger would have been in his early twenties when Jennings had studied his photograph. The face was now plumper, but there could be no doubt that this was Seamus Mullen. He remembered the briefing at SAS

344

headquarters in Hereford before his first tour in Belfast.

"This one kills for the fun of it." The pointer had stabbed at the photograph of the young Seamus Mullen. "I am not telling you officially, but if you have this bastard in your sights, squeeze the fucking trigger." The briefing officer had been deadly serious.

Jennings continued down the stairs to where his luncheon host awaited. Over lunch he was not his usual ebullient self. Mullen was at the forefront of his thoughts. Why was he in the city and what was he doing?

Jennings saw Mullen several times during the afternoon. It was when he appeared on the same train at London Bridge that Jennings finally accepted that he was the target of Mullen's attention.

"What's the matter, Allan, is something worrying you?" Pansie had noticed that Jennings was quieter than usual.

"I am sure I have been followed all day," he replied, "and I don't know why."

He related how he had seen the same person everywhere he went. The only fact he omitted was his knowledge of who was tracking him.

"If you are sure you should tell the police about it," was Pansie's practical view.

"The trouble is," Jennings mused, "if he is just following me he's not doing anything wrong."

"If he's there tomorrow, why don't you just ask him why?" At times Pansie was even more pragmatic that Hubbard.

"I might do that."

Jennings poured himself a drink and wandered into the study. On impulse he telephoned Cross. He told him the full story including the identity of his attendant.

"If that bastard is in London someone should tell the authorities. He's certainly not here on holiday." Mullen had been one of Cross' prime targets at MI5. He had never been able to get enough evidence to nail him. "Do you want me to have a word with someone?"

Jennings concurred and rang off. He went back into the lounge. Pansie was busy in the kitchen.

Charlie was oblivious to his undercurrent of unease. He had

created his own version of Silverstone and was deep in the pretext of being Graham Hill. Jennings picked up the second tiny racer and said, "Come on then. I'll bet you can't beat me."

The two had just collided on Stowe Corner when the telephone burst into life.

"I don't know what is going on, but I think that we ought to get together." Cross sounded concerned.

"What's the problem?" Jennings asked.

"I have spoken to one of my old colleagues at the firm," Cross replied. "They knew Mullen was in the country and have had a tail on him since he got here. He's definitely been following you. The thing is there are three others with him. One seems to be on my tail, another George and, from the description given me, John's the other target. Just to add to the pot the other three are as nasty as Mullen. All four are Belfast Brigade members."

"Any idea on what they are after?" Jennings asked.

"Not at the moment. I've been promised that I'll be kept informed, off the record. I have spoken to John and George and arranged to meet tomorrow in El Vinos. Is that OK with you?"

***

Pinter was already settled at his usual table in El Vinos when Jennings arrived. A bottle of 1969 Puligny Montrachet nestled in the ice bucket.

"I presumed that you were buying, so I ordered a decent wine," was Pinter's greeting.

Cross and Hubbard arrived shortly after Jennings. Hubbard was a little fraught as Karen was in the course of packing and disappearing before the police enquiries dragged her into the morass. Hubbard had expected this but the refusal of sexual favours the previous night had come as both a surprise and a major disappointment.

Both Cross and Hubbard ignored the Montrachet and ordered fizzy German beer.

"I think that we have a full house," Cross remarked, looking through the window. Across the street Blair and Murphy peered intently into the window of a shop selling stationery. Along the

346

road two officers from the anti-terrorist squad admired a building of no significant architectural merit. Mullen was seated, on a stool, at the far end of the bar and Kelly impersonated the invisible man at the opposite end. Both had faced away realising that their faces were known by both Pinter and Cross. Neither knew that they had already been identified.

The drinks arrived. "I have a little more information," Cross whispered. "It seems that the four of us are being watched and our movements reported to a man called Johnson. He is stopping at the Tower Hotel."

"Fucking idiot!" Hubbard interjected. "He's still using the same name."

"What are you talking about?" Pinter enquired.

"O'Connell's sidekick used that alias. He struck me as an moron, so it's probably the same bloke."

"Why should he be connected with these bastards that are following us?" Pinter's nose smelled a story.

"I think that I can answer that," Cross interposed. "The real name of the link man is Martin Dolan. He's Tom O'Connell's protégé, but not very bright. MI5 have been told to turn a blind eye to his activities. I am told that surveillance is being lifted today. Those two," he indicated the anti-terrorist officers, "won't be there tomorrow. It looks to me as though O'Connell has set up a systematic removal of any evidence that could incriminate the CIA. I guess that we are the evidence that has to be removed."

"By those prats?" Hubbard took it as an affront that anyone so obvious could entrap him. It was also an assault to his self-esteem that the four were Irish. "I'll just pop across and tear the fucker's head off, if you like."

"Maybe later," Cross laughed. "For the present we operate as though everything is normal. If we can draw Dolan into the open then we can have O'Connell."

MANHATTAN BREWERY – 21ST JUNE 1985

The game had been about as boring as it could have been. The pitchers had controlled the contest. Both sides had been shut out until the penultimate innings, when the Yankees had sneaked a couple of bases. The only excitement had been when the last

Yankee batter in the innings had hit a home run. The two that were stuck on the second and third bases benefited. The Yankees pitcher had shut Boston out in the final innings and the match result had been three to zero.

It mattered little to O'Connell and his cronies that the match had been capable of boring a dullard extraordinaire. The Yankees had won. Money had been removed from the custody of bookmakers. Bourbon and pints of Light Amber flowed. Steaks, which had once been a major part of a cow, were produced. The Yankees were on their way.

Hacker watched with amused interest. Baseball had always seemed to be a particularly strange game. A man would stand on a pile of earth that resembled an elephant's burial mound, and launch a projectile at another who was armed with what appeared to be a gigantic juggling club. The receiver would be classified as an ace if he actually managed to hit the missile hurled at him once in every three times he attempted to do so. When someone actually connected with the ball it was invariably struck high in the air and another hero was made. Someone wearing ill fitting tights with a satellite dish on their hand would rush about and catch the projectile in the saucer. Massive applause would greet this totally expected event.

O'Connell and his party did not hold this view. They ate, drank and celebrated, for that night the Yankees were the greatest team the world had ever seen. They were on their way to the World Series. The fact that the rest of the world did not participate was an irrelevance.

The celebrations continued longer than usual. It was nearly two in the morning before O'Connell's brain became disassociated with the rest of his bodily functions.

The day had been good and tonight he could, at last, relax. He had that morning received confirmation that the equipment for the Contras would be at the rendezvous off the Bahamas on the following Saturday and at the time designated. Dolan had telephoned to tell him that the damage limitation operation in London was underway. A world, which had been about to collapse, would soon be as solid as a rock.

He stood and wished a fond farewell to his comrades in arms. The Yankees had done the job and now was the time to go.

He staggered as he progressed toward the stairs. The staircase was steep and winding. Sensibly he grasped the handrail and proceeded around the outside of the spiral. He took no cognisance of anyone. He did not notice the man that followed him.

The place and the circumstances were perfect for Hacker. He passed O'Connell on the stairs and turned to face him. "This is for my mother, bastard," he whispered. The upward curve of his arm drove the stiletto beneath O'Connell's jacket and under his ribs. The blade entered. The puncture in the skin was tiny. As the razor sharp point ruptured his heart, O'Connell looked into the eyes of his assassin. In that moment he recognised the features that Penny Hacker's genes had passed on to her son. Inside his chest a warhead detonated. He collapsed and bounced down the steps.

At first his plunge was ignored. At this time of night customers often fell in the stairwell. It was simply the combination of steep winding steps and too much alcohol. When he subsequently failed to move one of the staff decided to react.

There were no signs of violence. The stiletto had entered and been withdrawn with virtually no bleeding. An ambulance was called and resuscitation commenced. It was not until the post mortem that the cause of death emerged. By then Danny Hacker was drinking champagne aboard Concorde.

AMIENS – 22ND JUNE 1985

Callard shoved Mersonne into the driving seat of the Citroën. He opened the rear door and climbed in behind him. The Browning he held felt cumbersome with a silencer attached. His compatriot finished loading the boot, climbed in himself and pulled the lid closed.

"One false move and you are dead," Callard whispered to Mersonne. He squatted down in the well between the seats and pulled the blanket over him. He pressed the barrel of the gun into the back of the driver's seat to remind Mersonne of his role.

"Go!" he ordered.

It was past ten in the evening and the building was empty of people. The security guard at the gate was more interested in the

349

soft porn movie on the television than the comings and goings at the gate. He recognised Mersonne's as it approached and waved as he pressed the button to open the gates. The Citroën drove around to the back of the factory and stopped.

Callard dragged Mersonne from the car and opened the trunk to let his companion out.

"Security code?" he snapped at Mersonne. Mersonne replied with a six-digit number.

"Got everything?" His associate nodded and threw the heavy rucksack over one shoulder.

The three moved to the external door, the muzzle of the pistol bruising Mersonne's rib cage. The code was entered and the locking mechanism clicked open. Once inside the second man moved off alone.

"To your office!" Callard ordered. The office overlooked the main production floor. Through the window Callard's contemporary could be seen darting from machine to machine. He stopped at each for a few seconds, placing a small package and setting the timer. The whole process took only fifteen minutes.

Mersonne was propelled into his chair. As the tape was coiled around him, affixing him to the chair, it made a sound like a swarm of angry wasps. A strip was stuck across his mouth. Abject terror shone from his eyes. They pleaded for some sort of deliverance, knowing none would come.

Callard donned Mersonne's trilby and coat. "OK, lets go," he said.

As the Citroën drove through the gates the guard gave Monsieur Mersonne a cheery wave and returned to the titillation on the seventeen-inch screen.

The fire was short and intense. The gas main was breached, stoking the surrounding inferno. Fortunately, the papers reported, there was only one fatality, a director of the company called Thierry Mersonne.

Callard read about the fire as he breakfasted in Dover.

He arrived at the embassy in Trafalgar Square just before noon. The train journey through Kent, the garden of England, had been a delight. Orchards and farmland flanked the rail line for much of the journey. Every hue of green that was on display was complemented by the mass of colours from the blossom, which would make the fruit.

Inside the embassy Callard was shown to a private office. He dialled a Pretoria number. Curren answered.

"The matter has been closed," Callard said simply.

"Good," replied Curren. "Our friends in Tel Aviv tidied up the problem in New York the night before. I think we can now leave the rest to the politicians."

ATLANTIC OCEAN,
50 MILES OFF SAVANNAH – 22ND JUNE 1985

"Have we heard from *Warrior* yet?" the skipper asked.

"About half an hour ago, sir," the mate replied. "She will be at the rendezvous as agreed."

"Excellent." The Captain rubbed his hands. "Once we off-load this cargo we can make port in Charleston. I'll send off the confirmation to France that the cargo has been delivered and there's another two hundred thousand in the bank."

Neither the skipper nor the mate knew what their cargo was. They cared little as the payment to transport it from Le Havre and transfer it to the *Warrior*, off the Bahamas, was worth more than six months' normal freight.

"What's the latest on Myrtle?" the captain enquired.

"We might get the fringe of it, but nothing to worry about," the mate responded cheerily. "Miami are forecasting it will make landfall somewhere north of Wilmington in a couple of days."

Myrtle had started as a deep depression in the Atlantic. She had fed on the water vapour drawn from the ocean below. The water was like a steroid to her. She grew muscles and became stronger.

It was the Severe Storm Centre in Miami who had christened her Myrtle. In normal years the season for major storms begins in August. This year Mother Nature had decided to commence wreaking her havoc early. By the end of June thirteen major storms had been designated. Myrtle was unlucky thirteen. She trundled gently south, gathering more water into her as she went. It was not long before she had become a severe storm. She rolled south, driven by cool winds. Then the warm air stream confronted her. There was only one thing she could do.

The storm began to rotate. Myrtle had reached puberty and was now a hurricane. She was only a minor hurricane to begin with but the longer she stayed over water the more strength she drew from the vapours inhaled from the sea. It was not long before she had reached full adulthood.

"This motherfucker's going to be another Betsy." Myrtle was the biggest storm the Controller of the Severe Storm Centre had seen since Betsy. Hurricane Betsy decimated vast amounts of the eastern seaboard of the States in October 1965.

A hurricane's vigour is derived from the sea. It supplies the water to feed its intensity. When it makes landfall its strength torrents away as the vapour turns into droplets and falls on the earth below, like Sampson's golden locks dropping onto the hot sand. Betsy was different. She assaulted the coast, savaging the meagre constructions of man. But, instead of rushing headlong to her fate inland she turned and went out to sea to receive another life-giving transfusion from the ocean. She assaulted the coast again and retreated to her blue haven of rest. For ten days she wreaked her havoc from the Carolinas to Maine.

Myrtle had the same power. She had upgraded from a tropical storm to a grade five hurricane in just two days. She was also fickle. Even as the coastal residents in North Carolina battened down the hatches and prepared to evacuate from their homes she turned south. Her forward momentum suddenly accelerated. Now the Bahamas and Cuba were in her sights.

Her change in direction and momentum were both sudden and precipitate. The modest freighter was closing on it's meeting with the *Warrior* when Myrtle struck. The seas rolled onto the ship like the Manhattan skyline collapsing onto her bows. The ship was tiny when compared to the might of the storm. It fought a valorous battle, but to no avail. This was David confronting Goliath without a slingshot. The freighter fought a brief skirmish with this awesome element of nature before succumbing to her intensity. It sank, with all hands, to the peace and calm of the ocean below, its cargo never to become a tool of destruction.

WHITE HOUSE – 24TH JUNE 1985

"This whole affair makes the Bay of Pigs look like a triumphant success." The head of the CIA squirmed in his seat as the President lashed him with his tongue. "You assured me that there was nothing that could go wrong. Now I have the Israelis, the Limeys and South Africans sitting on my back. Christ knows how much we are going to have to plunder the national coffers to buy our way out of this fiasco."

"We could not have foreseen that the cargo would be lost in a hurricane." The CIA man was searching for any extenuating reason for the mire he now found himself in.

"Crap!" bellowed the President. "If it was just that we would not be in the shit we are now. I suppose it was just bad luck that two Israeli Mirages were shot down, and unfortunate that you were responsible for annihilating half the South African government and security forces." He slammed his fist onto the desk. "To top it all you have also managed to have your deputy knocked off in a bar in New York and a French munitions factory blown up. That's a lot of bad rolls of the dice."

The CIA controller did not reply. The President's switch to the definitive 'you' told him that his neck was firmly on the chopping block.

"Just tell me one thing," the President ranted on. "Is there any more crap in this particular pipeline that can fall on my head?"

The controller shook his head, desperately hoping that Dolan could tidy up the small problem presented by Jennings and his accomplices. Relief was his over-riding feeling when the President waved him away.

The President watched him leave and jabbed at the intercom. His personal aide scuttled into the room. When the boss was in this sort of mood it did not pay to be tardy.

"Has everything been tidied up?"

"It should all be completed by this afternoon," the minion replied.

"Just make sure that every document and every tape linking me with this fuck-up is cleaned up to show that I had no knowledge or involvement."

"Yes, sir," the aide responded and scurried from the room to continue re-writing recent history.

TOWER HOTEL – 27TH JUNE 1985

"I want all four taken out at the same time," Dolan instructed. "I'll leave it to the four of you to work out the details."

"What do we do them with?" Mullen asked. "We have no weapons available."

"I'll arrange that," Dolan replied. "You just work out your plans and let me know. I can supply the hardware you need. The only necessity is that I want to be out of the country before you do the bastards."

"And what about us?" Kelly interjected.

"For the moment the security services are turning a blind eye to your activities. You just do the job and go back to Belfast."

"Why do you need them taken out at the same time?" Murphy interjected.

"That's my business. Suffice it to say that they are all privy to certain facts. If one knew that we had hit the others those facts could become public."

"It won't be that easy," Mullen commented. "They all have different patterns. Jennings fits office-type hours, Pinter's timing runs with the newspaper and the other two have bugger all routine."

"That's your problem," Dolan retorted. "You're being well paid to do the job. I want a plan from you by Friday."

Chapter 24

Jennings could see Mullen from his office window. He had been sitting in the café opposite for the last two hours. He buzzed the intercom and his secretary replied.

"Can you organise a car for me in half an hour, Mary?" he said. "I want it to pick me up at the back of the building not the front."

"Yes, Allan," Mary Cantor replied. She thought it strange that he wanted the car at the back but made no comment. "Where is it to go to?"

"The Prospect of Whitby," was the reply.

George Pinter felt a little foolish huddled in the back of the van loaded with the first editions of the evening paper. The driver thought that Pinter's request for an incognito exit from the premises was something to do with a hush-hush spy story. He had happily obliged. The Prospect at Wapping was on his route.

Hubbard had taken Karen to Heathrow Airport. She had decided that the climate in the Carolinas would be more healthy.

Kelly had jumped into a taxi and followed them. He was more than relieved when Hubbard waved a farewell to Karen as she disappeared into the departure gate. Hubbard then did the unexpected. He boarded the bus for the long-term car parks. Kelly sat at the rear of the bus wondering what would happen next. When Hubbard produced the keys to a small Peugeot and drove off Kelly cussed profanely. He waved at, and was ignored by, several taxis before Hubbard's car disappeared from sight.

Blair only took a passing interest as Jane Cross' Vauxhall pulled out of the drive. She was alone in the car. Arriving customers at the Prospect of Whitby must have thought it strange to see Cross being released from the boot of the car.

"Any problems?" Jennings asked Cross, who was the last to arrive.

"Apart from spending half an hour in the foetal position in the boot of a car, no." Cross rubbed his back.

The four had decided that it was time to take the initiative. Cross' informant in MI5 had virtually confirmed that the four Irish visitors' intentions towards them were less that honourable. He also informed them that Dolan had said he would be leaving the country the following Monday. They still knew nothing of the plans that were being made for them. It was time they did.

"I think that we are agreed that either Mullen or Kelly is the leader of our band of mercenaries." Cross began. "One of them will have to be our target, but which?"

"If we go by the heirarchy in Belfast, Mullen is the senior of the two," Pinter commented.

"I agree with that," Cross stated simply. "How do we take him?"

"I think that Allan should go home early to see his lovely wife," Hubbard interpolated. "If he does, the mick will follow him. I'll be waiting."

Over lunch the air of expectancy grew. The hunted was about to become the hunter.

Jennings took a taxi back to his office, asking specifically to be dropped at the back entrance. He took the service lift to his office. Mary gave him several messages, most of which were not urgent. At first he could not see Mullen as he looked out of the window. After the first day Mullen had realised that a certain form of dress was required to remain inconspicuous. He had purchased a dark navy suit and now blended into the general melee. Jennings spotted his prey among a scrum of afternoon drinkers on the pavement outside the small pub opposite. His eyes continually darted around looking for his prey to emerge from the building opposite.

Jennings checked his watch. He had to leave Hubbard time to drive out to Surrey. Mary tripped in carrying a tray of tea.

"I think that I'll go home early and surprise Pansie," Jennings smiled. "I may be late tomorrow."

Mary made no reply. She was used to her boss' whims. It was not unusual, particularly when the office was quiet, for him to bunk off.

Jennings finished his tea, picked up his briefcase and wished

Mary farewell.

Outside he ambled along Fenchurch Street ensuring that Mullen was on his tail. The afternoon sun sparkled on the Thames as he sauntered across London Bridge. The river always looked its best with the summer sun glinting on its ripples. He had twenty minutes to wait for his train and wandered into the buffet for a pint. Mullen drifted about on the concourse, his eyes constantly monitoring Jennings.

Mullen knew the journey well having repeatedly followed Jennings. He joined the train two carriages behind that boarded by Jennings. At each stop he glanced out of the window knowing that his quarry would not disembark but checking just in case he did. The train pulled into Woldingham. Jennings, as usual, made for the telephone. His wife would appear in the Jaguar in about ten minutes and Mullen could return to London. He had followed Jennings to his home several times and gained nothing. The house was on a country road across the top of the Downs. Once home it seemed that Jennings stayed there.

The Jaguar arrived, Jennings jumped in, kissed his wife and they were gone. "Only two more days," Mullen thought. They had decided the previous evening that Sunday was the only time that the four could be hit simultaneously. On weekdays their movements were too erratic to make any plans and Jennings and Pinter, in particular, were invariably in crowded environs. Sunday seemed to be the day when all four relaxed. Dolan had produced the weapons and the Walther sat snugly under his arm.

His mind was meandering over getting the job out of the way and returning home as he turned the corner to the bridge that crossed the railway. Suddenly everything went blank.

He awoke in a cold dark room. He tried to move and realised that he was trussed like a capon ready for a banquet. What had happened?

"You had better get back, John," Jennings said after they had finished securing the unconscious Mullen to the chair. "Mr Kelly will be wondering where you have got to."

"Let us know when you have got something from the bastard," Hubbard muttered. "Use this if you have to." He gave the file of Pentathol and a syringe to Jennings.

Jennings went to the safe in his study and took out his

357

father's old Luger. The bluish metal of the barrel felt cold to the touch.

"What are you going to do?" Pansie's voice came from behind him.

"I'm going to find out exactly what is going on," Jennings replied grimly. He took the Walther from his pocket and gave it to his wife. "Keep this handy. He's a dangerous bastard."

She took the weapon and expertly checked the magazine and firing mechanism. Whilst she had been a wife and mother for many years the skills learned in the jungle with the freedom fighters were not forgotten. "Be careful," she said simply.

Jennings went out to the garage and took the kukri from the locked cabinet and slipped it into his belt.

A shaft of light leapt down into the basement. Mullen looked up and saw Jennings silhouetted in the doorway. He wrestled with his bonds without success. Jennings switched on the light and moved slowly down the stairs. The bowed blade of the kukri reflected the glare from the 150-watt bulb into Mullen's eyes. His attention drawn he could not remove his gaze from it.

"Well now, Mr Mullen, would you like to tell me what is going on?"

Mullen's eyes switched from the kukri to Jennings' eyes. How did he know his name?

"My name is Smales," he replied, trying to appear both indignant and defiant.

"Your name is Seamus Mullen," Jennings replied quietly. "You have been a member of the Belfast Brigade of the IRA since you were eighteen and on my first tour of duty there I was told to shoot you if I ever had you in my sights. I say again, what is going on?"

Mullen was the classic bully. Heroic when the odds were heavily in his favour but a poltroon at heart. The hint of a half-remembered tale gnawed at him. He made no reply.

"Knowing your background, Mr Mullen, I will not have any compunction in killing you. I've done it before." The voice was cold and unforgiving.

The half-remembered memory flooded into Mullen's consciousness. He remembered Jennings, not by face but reputation. Seventeen years before, the Armagh Brigade had been decimated in several actions with one section of SAS. Their commander was a former Gurkha and he always carried a kukri. Abject terror tore at his insides.

"I don't know what you are talking about." He tried to brazen it out.

"That's what Sean Murphy said, sitting in that very chair. Now he's in a wheelchair." The matter of fact delivery of the statement chilled Mullen's bones. He had planted bombs, hidden and watched the devastation he had caused. He and others had beaten individuals with baseball bats. He had hidden in dark places and shot people in the back, but never had he faced someone so inimical. This man would kill him as a fisherman would a salmon.

"I'm being paid to follow you and report." He tried one last bluff.

"Don't lie," Jennings snapped. "I want to know why you, Kelly, Blair and Murphy are following me and my friends."

"I don't know what you are talking about," Mullen croaked, fear beginning to paralyse his larynx. How did he know about the others?

Jennings took the kukri from his waistband. "You know the rule." His whisper could hardly be heard. "Now it is unsheathed it must taste blood."

Mullen did not feel pain as the razor sharp edge cut into his cheek. He only felt the gore running down his face and dripping onto his suit. A paralysing chill of fear engulfed his being. He would do anything, tell everything, just to escape from this cellar and this man.

***

"It seems that three of us are prone to habitual behaviour." It was the third time Jennings was repeating this conversation. Hubbard was the last of the three he telephoned. "It is all planned for Sunday. Jim and I won't arrive back from our golf clubs and George will not make it to his home from his lunch time pint at the pub."

"And me?" asked Hubbard.

"You were the problem. They reckoned to knock on your

front door and blow you away when you answered. You apparently spend all Sunday morning in your pit."

"Cheeky bastards," Hubbard laughed. "That's because Karen was giving me a seeing-to."

"It looks as though we are going to have to pre-empt them." Jennings continued. "Can you get hold of a closed transit van by tomorrow morning?"

TARA HOTEL – 30TH JUNE 1985

"Any sign of Seamus this morning?" Kelly shovelled more scrambled eggs into his mouth.

"I haven't seen him since yesterday morning," Murphy replied. "He's probably got himself some woman for the night. He was getting a bit restless."

"I know how he feels," Kelly commented, scooping bacon in to join the egg. "I just thank Christ that we finish this tomorrow."

They finished breakfast and made off, in different directions, for their day of terminal boredom.

Kelly was surprised when Hubbard appeared so early. On Saturday he seldom surfaced before eleven, and it was still before nine. He followed Hubbard's taxi along the Cromwell Road. It stopped outside a large garage and Hubbard alighted. Twenty minutes later he emerged, driving a white transit van.

"Shit!" Kelly muttered. Was the weak link in their plan to be tested? They were reliant on Hubbard adopting his usual indolence the following day. It was beginning to look as though this might not be so.

Hubbard pulled up outside the flat where he lived, but remained in the vehicle. Kelly alighted from the hire car and wandered along the pavement to have a closer look through the tiny rear windows.

"Move!" The voice ordered and hard metal jabbed into his back. The rear doors of the van crashed open and he was propelled inside. A massive fist met him from inside the van and there was nothing but blackness.

The mid-day news was reporting on a punishment beating in Belfast when Pinter emerged from his house. Murphy continued to listen as he followed Pinter's car towards Highgate. Murphy knew the recipient of the assault. He had previously been warned off and told that paramilitaries were the sole purveyors of drugs. He had taken no notice and the consequence was inevitable. 'Kneecaps and fingers' he thought to himself. Each perceived sin against the Provisionals had a specified retribution.

So engrossed was he with the news that it was not until he stopped that he realised that Pinter had drawn into Cross' drive. Parked immediately in front of him was Blair. He waited until Pinter entered the house and walked to Blair's car. Neither took any cognisance of the white van that pulled in beside them, nor the two occupants dressed in overalls that alighted. That was their fatal mistake.

***

Hubbard tossed Kelly, the last of the three, down the steps into the basement. As with the first two he tumbled down the stairs, his bonds stopping any attempts at remaining in the upright position. He regained his senses and looked around to try to assess his predicament. Mullen sat, white-faced, bound to a chair. The ugly gash on his cheek was only partially healed.

"Where the fuck are we?"

"This is Jennings' house," Mullen replied. "How did the bastards get you?"

"They just appeared." Kelly shook his head.

"Do you know who Jennings is?" Mullen's voice quavered, the sight of the kukri glinting in the light still fresh in his mind. "You remember the Gurkha in the SAS. That's him. He knew me."

"What are they going to do?" Blair asked, not really wanting to know the answer.

Upstairs Pinter was asking the same question. "We can't keep the bastards locked up in your cellar forever."

"Don't worry, George," Jennings replied soothingly. He had earlier contacted SAS headquarters at Hereford. "I have already spoken to an old army colleague. He now commands the second squadron. It was one of his officers that was tortured to death last year by the IRA. Both Mullen and Kelly were involved, but

361

it couldn't be proved. He's very interested in getting hold of those four downstairs."

Two hours later a plain green furniture van pulled into Jennings' drive. Six men alighted, all with cropped hair and icy eyes. The oldest greeted Jennings like a long-lost friend. Mullen, Kelly, Blair and Murphy disappeared into the back of the van. They would not reappear until six days later when they were all reported as killed in a fire fight with British forces in Armagh.

***

Dolan had checked out of the hotel and was waiting for the concierge to obtain him a taxi. He was flying back on Concorde. His business would be successfully completed later that morning and some very loose ends tied up. With the demise of O'Connell he felt that such an accomplishment would be well received by his masters. Enhancement within the firm was now most likely.

"Martin, how nice to see you." He felt both elbows being gripped and he was propelled towards a parked Jaguar. He turned and looked at the speaker. Cross smiled at him.

"Lovely to see you, Jim," Dolan needed time to think. "Are you giving me a lift to the airport?"

"Not quite," Cross replied. He stood back as Hubbard intimated that the choice facing Dolan was either to enter the car of have his arm broken. He elected the former.

As he tumbled inside he saw that the front seats were occupied by Jennings and Pinter. What had gone wrong?

Dolan tried to speak as the car pulled away. He was answered with silence. No one spoke until they were past Croydon.

"Your boys rather fucked up, Mr Dolan, or should I say Johnson?" Hubbard whispered.

"I don't know what you are talking about." Dolan knew that he had to buy time. British security knew of his operation.

Parry Bolan watched as the Jaguar eased away from the hotel entrance. He sauntered across to the bank of pay phones. Bolan was a first-class operative. Cross, as head of MI5, had seen this early and pushed Bolan's career rapidly forwards. He owed a debt to Cross. Bolan picked up a telephone and dialled.

"I'm afraid that I've lost him," was all he said.

"What the hell is going on here?" Dolan was now adopting his indignant pose. "I have a flight from Heathrow in an hour's time."

"You do have a flight, Martin," Cross replied grimly. "But it is not from Heathrow nor is it in an hour's time. You have to meet an old friend first."

Dolan's mind was now in turmoil. Who was the friend he would meet? It was crystal-clear from Cross' manner that whoever it was would not be best enamoured with Dolan.

The Jaguar pulled into Jennings' home and Dolan was bundled out of the car. A Volvo was parked on the drive. Two heavy-set men with deep tans and hard eyes sat in the front. Hubbard pushed the hapless captive through the door of the house.

"Martin, I have the families of two of my pilots who are dying to meet you." Zeltner's pale blue eyes were like frosty pools. Cross had spoken to him the previous day and told him of Dolan's involvement in the conspiracy. He had flown from Tel Aviv that morning. A Jetstream was waiting at Gatwick to return him to Israel with a passenger.

Epilogue

It would have been pleasing to climax this tale with the news that all the bad guys were incarcerated for many years, and the good lived happily ever after, but life, unfortunately, is not a fairytale.

Dolan remained incognito in Israel for two months, enough time for the spin doctors at home to ameliorate any political damage their masters may suffer. His release and return to his homeland coincided with the President announcing a new package of aid to Israel in excess of two billion dollars.

Dolan quietly retired to his home state of Idaho where, one month later, he was killed in a hit and run road accident. It was the first contract that Danny Hacker had acquired from the CIA.

The South African government, whilst saying nothing publicly, made it clear what they knew. Both the French and the American governments suddenly realised that the British were right to say that sanctions against the apartheid regime would only damage the black majority. Having never done so before, they suddenly elected to support the British opposition to sanctions in the UN council with unbounded enthusiasm.

The President asked for a congressional enquiry and opened up all the sanitised files in the White House for inspection. The enquiry concluded, inevitably, that O'Connell was acting alone and vilified the head of the CIA for allowing a subordinate to act without proper control. He resigned and increased his income and stature by joining the lecture tour circuit.

The French held their own enquiry and published the findings. The report would have liked to have placed Thierry Mersonne in the Bastille, then dragged him through the streets on an ox cart to the gentle attentions of Madame Guillotine. As this was not possible it simply vituperated him on every page, and bowdlerised everyone else involved.

The three Lloyds underwriters, Payne, O'Sullivan and Green, plus the brokers, Jarvis and Wilkes, were charged with ten specimen counts of fraud and tax evasion, none of which involved Mutuelle Avionique.

Jarvis, still tortured by the sight of Penny's mutilated body, hung himself in Brixton Prison whilst on remand. The others pleaded guilty, thus ensuring that little or no factual evidence entered the public domain. They all received identical sentences of six years, of which only two were actually served due to the kind intervention of the parole board. The two years were spent in a pleasant open prison, which allowed them plenty of time to manage their outside financial interests. Two now live in the Cayman Islands, one in the Turks and Caicos and the other in Jersey.

The FBI brought indictments against the godfathers and several others of all three Mafia families. Without the factual evidence of either Carter or Scorsi the prosecution failed in front of the Grand Jury. The families decided to revert to more traditional methods of transporting money, such as inside the spare tyre of a car, and continue to run their businesses very profitably.

The debacle of the attempt to indict the families discouraged the FBI from pursuing the matter any further. Carlos Pedrosa, Ted Hart and the other middle men retained their ill-gotten gains without suffering any sanctions.

Cross was offered reinstatement to his post in MI5 but declined and accepted an offer from Sutcliffe to manage his European operations. Hubbard joined him.

The international reinsurance market and Lloyds of London were virtually unscathed. Much merriment was exchanged in bars and restaurants at the demise of the three underwriters, all of who were in the category of being quite unpleasant human beings who felt they had to be shown deference, verging on subservience, because of the fiscal power of their operations. It was not long, however, before the general amnesia of the marketplace took over and consigned the matter to a distant, near forgotten, memory. The motto of all reinsurers kicked in: "Don't remember how you lost the last dollar, think how you are going to make the next one."